Also by Sean Williams

Twinmaker

CRASHLAND

A TWINMAKER NOVEL

SEAN WILLIAMS

BALZER + BRAY

An Imprint of HarperCollins*Publishers*

Balzer + Bray is an imprint of HarperCollins Publishers.

Crashland
Copyright © 2014 by Sean Williams
All rights reserved. Printed in the United States of America.
No part of this book may be used or reproduced in any manner
whatsoever without written permission except in the case of brief
quotations embodied in critical articles and reviews. For information
address HarperCollins Children's Books, a division of HarperCollins
Publishers,. 195 Broadway, New York, NY 10007.
www.epicreads.com

Library of Congress Cataloging-in-Publication Data
Williams, Sean, date.
    Crashland : a Twinmaker novel / Sean Williams. — First edition.
        pages cm
    Summary: "In this sequel to Twinmaker, the world's teleportation
network has crashed, armies of dupes are attacking—and Clair must
determine her allegiances, figure out how to find her mysterious online
friend called Q, and stay alive"— Provided by publisher.
    ISBN 978-0-06-220324-3 (trade bdg.)
    [1. Science fiction. 2. Space and time—Fiction. 3. Cloning—Fiction.
4. Friendship—Fiction.] I. Title.
PZ7.W6681739Cr 2014
[Fic]—dc23   2014002147
                                                                      CIP
                                                                       AC

Typography by Erin Fitzsimmons
14 15 16 17 18   CG/RRDH   10 9 8 7 6 5 4 3 2 1

First Edition

I saw a planet running out of days.
I saw a president with hands upraised.
I saw a clock that was very good at chess.
I saw a computer in a fine silken dress.
I saw a priest dancing a jig.
I saw a pop star with the heart of a pig.
I saw a surgeon choking on gas.
I saw a soldier in a tube made of glass.
I saw the infinite even though it was naught.
I saw the mind that thought this thought.

Folk Poem, c. 2036

[I]

THE DAY THE world ended, Clair Hill was sitting at a table in a tiny interview room opposite two uniformed peace-keepers, one of whom was the tallest woman she had ever met. With short blond hair and a friendly, open expression, PK Sargent's first order of business was to offer Clair a cup of coffee and summon a medic to look at her bruised elbow. The injury was minor but the memory of how she had gotten it was one of several running on rapid repeat through Clair's mind. There was nothing the medic could do about those.

The other peacekeeper, PK Forest, conducted the interrogation. In contrast to Sargent, who looked at most ten years older than Clair, Forest was a small man in his fifties, with narrow shoulders and thinning black hair. There was something wrong with his face. It jumped from expression to expression almost entirely without transition, one moment frowning, the next with eyebrows raised in disbelief. A second later he would tug his lips down as though profoundly saddened by something Clair had said.

She tried to look Forest in the eyes, not wanting to give the impression that she was hiding anything, but there was something wrong with them, too. They didn't track. They flicked from place to place with tiny, discrete movements. *Flick . . . flick . . . flick.* She forced herself to focus on the bridge of his nose instead, where his eyebrows almost met, and tried to concentrate.

His questions were relentless.

"I'm sorry you think I'm repeating myself"—*flick*—"but it's vital we know precisely what happened in the space station. You were a captive, yes?"

"Yes."

"A prisoner, you say, of this man?"

An image of Ant Wallace appeared in the default PK-blue wallpaper of her lenses. The man who had until recently been in charge of d-mat looked just as ordinary and trustworthy as he always had, but it was a mask that meant nothing now. Clair had seen the man behind it, the man who had drawn her into a trap and threatened to kill her friends and destroy her life if she didn't give him what he wanted. He had forced her to desperate ends that even now she could barely believe.

Apart from that image, her infield was empty, a blank window in her field of vision that would normally be filled with bumps, news feeds, and chat requests. She was still completely disconnected from the Air, and no one would tell her when that was going to change.

"Yes," she said, adding for the tenth time, "Ant Wallace took me prisoner."

"Was this person also present?"

The photo of Wallace was replaced by another image, this time of a woman Clair didn't know. Thick, black hair, Asian heritage like Forest.

"I don't think so," Clair said. "No, wait . . . is that Mallory Wei?"

"It is." *Flick.* "How did you know?"

"Something about the eyes." Mallory was Ant Wallace's wife, forced to cycle endlessly through the final stages of suicidal depression because Wallace couldn't bear to let her go. Her mask wasn't as complete as her husband's. Mallory's eyes held depths of empty despair.

"She was inside Libby's body. I never saw her real face."

"Liberty Zeist was also present?" Forest asked.

"No, just her body. I've told you a thousand times! Improvement put Mallory in Libby's head. It *killed* her, just like it killed everyone else who was Improved. Why aren't you doing something about that? Why are you asking me all these questions instead of trying to stop the dupes?"

Flick.

"We *are* trying to stop them, Clair," said Forest with an earnest expression she had seen before and didn't trust. There wasn't a single thing about him that didn't scream *fake* to her. "Every peacekeeper has been mobilized to deal with the situation. But what is the situation? It is not just the failure of d-mat. It is the failure of the

Virtual-transport Infrastructure Authority to oversee d-mat. And it is the failure of Ant Wallace to oversee VIA, in turn. He broke the most fundamental law he was obliged to uphold—that no one could ever be killed or injured by d-mat. How was this allowed to happen? We must understand what occurred, and you are at the center of this process, Clair. It is my job to ask the questions that will help me understand *you*."

"I'm just here to pretty the place up," said Sargent. A joke, but Clair didn't smile.

She looked down at her hands where they rested on the lap of her orange prison jumpsuit. She didn't know that it was actually a prison jumpsuit, but it was so baggy and characterless and tight around the wrists and ankles that she felt like a prisoner inside it. Her clothes and shoes had been taken away for forensic analysis when she had arrived at the peacekeepers' New York office, not far from Penn Plaza. Her skin and hair had been sampled for chemical and biological traces. Then Forest and Sargent had turned up and started on her. No one had threatened her; she wasn't in handcuffs. But it was clear that she couldn't leave. Not once had she been allowed to talk to anyone else, in person or via the Air. It was just her and them in a room that was effectively a cell, with plastic walls, floors, ceiling, and fixtures, like they hosed it down after every session. The air itself was sterile.

"I'm not at the center of this," she said.

"Who is, then, if not you?"

"You *know* who. It's Q."

Flick.

"Who is Q?"

She wanted to rip out her hair. "Qualia and Quiddity? The AIs who were supposed to keep d-mat safe? Wallace did something to them so he could make Improvement work, and that led to Q. I don't know how. But that's who she is. She thought she was real, and she *is* real, but she's not really . . ."

"Human?" Forest said.

"Define 'human,'" said Sargent.

"Not like us, whatever she is," Clair said. "I'm worried about her."

"Because of what happened in the station?"

"Yes." Clair dreaded the thought of the interrogation looping back on itself again. *You say you lied to Q. You said you'd always be her friend, and then you betrayed her, but she saved you anyway. She brought you back from the dead, breaking parity and the laws of d-mat to do it. Why?*

"Are you going to charge me with murder?" she asked, clearing her infield to wipe Mallory's real face from her mind. She and Turner Goldsmith, leader of the activist group WHOLE, had used grenades to blow up the station and everyone in it, including themselves.

"Why?" Forest asked her. "Do you think you are the same Clair Hill as the one who died in the station?"

"I *am* the same Clair Hill."

"Not exactly the same, and not legally the same. You are a copy made from the same pattern as that other version of you, taken the last time you went through d-mat."

"But I think I'm the same. Doesn't that mean I'm the same?"

"That's for the Consensus Court to decide," said Sargent. "Then there's the *other* Clair Hill we have in custody at the moment. Is she you as well?"

"Of course not! She's a dupe, not a copy—the person inside her isn't me."

"But how do we tell you apart if you're both claiming to be Clair Hill?"

"I don't know. Ask a lawmaker! Speaking of which, when are you going to let me talk to one?"

"Just as soon as someone makes the decision that you officially exist," said Forest. He leaned a fraction closer, his expression not threatening but not reassuring, either. His eyes held a challenge.

Clair put her head in her hands. It hurt, and not just because of the harsh white lights that had been glaring down at her for hours. Her thoughts kept coming back to the same problems, over and over again, and they were no less harrowing and exhausting than the interview. Wallace had stolen her best friend's mind. He had threatened her mother. He had to go. But there had been other people on the space station when it had blown up—his partners in crime, his minions—and she couldn't forget them. She couldn't forget what she had done. She couldn't stop accusing herself of being even worse things than Forest and Sargent were implying.

Murderer. Terrorist. Dupe.

The words made her feel sick inside.

Is that who I am now? Is Clair 3.0 some kind of monster?

"I just want to go home," she said through her fingers. "I want to talk to my parents. I want to see Jesse. I want . . ."

I want to know that Ant Wallace is dead and what I did wasn't for nothing.

"I just want d-mat to start working again," said Sargent. "The rest I can deal with, once that's fixed."

Clair raised her head. *Great,* she thought. Another thing on her conscience.

"If I don't exist," she said, "how can I possibly help you with anything?"

Flick.

Forest smiled.

"Good point, Clair. Excuse me. I will be back in a moment."

He stood briskly and walked to the door. It opened for him and he was gone without a backward glance.

[2]

THE DOOR CLICKED shut.

"Where did he go?"

"I don't know," Sargent said. "Maybe to stretch his legs.

He likes to walk when he thinks, and it's a bit cramped in here. You've probably noticed."

Clair sagged back into the plastic seat. It squeaked under her. She didn't realize how tense PK Forest made her until he left the room.

"His face bothers you, doesn't it?" PK Sargent put her hands on the table and folded them neatly in front of her. She was wearing a commitment ring on one finger, a simple white gold band. "Freaked me out too, when I first met him."

Clair leaned her head back and closed her eyes. She was tired and hungry and her elbow hurt.

"You're wasting your time, PK Sargent. You should be out there trying to find those dupes who got through before the crash, not in here trying to good-cop me into telling you whatever it is you think I'm not telling you."

"Is that what we're doing? Good cop/bad cop? You should know that the Inspector hasn't got a bad bone in his body. He's a very smart cop, and if you're lying about anything, he'll know. Do you want to know how?"

Clair sighed. "I'm not lying. Everything I've told you is true."

"It's because of his face," Sargent continued as though Clair hadn't spoken. "There's something wrong with his nerves. He needs muscle therapy to move anything above the neck, and even then he can't just let it happen like normal people do. He has to consciously make every twitch and glance, because people can't bear to be around him otherwise. Sometimes he uses that to put people off guard, and I suspect he's doing a bit of that to you now, just to see how you react. That's why the Inspector is so good at spotting liars. He knows things about people's faces that they never dreamed of."

Clair sat up again and opened her eyes. Sargent smiled, revealing white, even teeth. If she was trying to put Clair off guard in her own way, it was working, but only because Clair was too exhausted to fight back.

"Why do you call him that?"

"The Inspector? Because that's what he would have been, way back when, before we were all called PKs. Old names like that are partly why I joined up. My nickname as a kid was 'Sarge.' It's an old army rank. You know what the army was?"

"Of course."

"Sorry, don't mean to patronize you. And I know I'm babbling. I do that when I'm nervous." Sargent's long fingers wound and unwound around themselves. "This is big, Clair, perhaps the biggest thing ever, and it's taking longer to fix than anyone thought. The AIs that run VIA didn't boot up when the system restarted. There might have been deliberate sabotage; it might just be damage caused by what Q did; either way, VIA can't operate safely without them, not without producing even more dupes or killing more people. We're all worried about what's going to happen if we can't get d-mat working again soon. Do *you* know what's going to happen?"

Clair shook her head. "I . . . wasn't expecting to be here, remember?"

Sargent's mouth turned down at the corners. "That can't have been an easy thing to do. The hardest, probably. And the bravest under the circumstances."

Something broke inside Clair, something she had been holding in ever since she had arrived in the booth in Penn Plaza. She had been expecting to see Turner Goldsmith and a bag of grenades. In her heart and in her head, she'd been ready to die by her own hand to stop Wallace. Instead, she had been alive, and another Clair Hill had died, and there was Jesse, and the peacekeepers, and then the world had ended.

Her chest convulsed. It was like her body was trying to vomit, but all that came out was a single sob, startlingly loud in the cramped space.

She put her hand over her mouth and twisted her lips tightly together. Her eyes were hot and aching, but she promised herself that she wasn't going to cry. Not while so many people were worse off than her.

"Are you all right?" Sargent said.

Clair nodded. She didn't trust herself to speak.

"If I was playing good cop, I'd be patting you on the back right now and saying something stupid like 'There, there, it'll be all right.'"

Clair nodded again, heartily glad Sargent hadn't done that. She didn't know how she would have reacted. Screamed, maybe. Called her a liar at the very least.

"Here's how I think it's going to go down," Sargent said. "Lawmakers are struggling right now. If we don't want to, we won't have to charge you with anything. *You* didn't kill anyone; *you* didn't break parity. The Clair Hill who did that is dead. But we can't let you go, either. It's not safe outside, not until the dupes who got through before the system crashed are rounded up. We don't have an exact number, but there are thousands of them, and we have to act on the assumption that they're still trying to kill you. So you need protection. We can provide that. We can move you away from here without anyone knowing. We can hide you while things settle down. It's our job to keep the peace—and as the Inspector says, you are part of that process. We have a responsibility to you along with everyone else. Keeping you safe is *my job*. I want you to know that I'm good at it."

Clair took a deep breath and lowered her hands. She felt as though the immediate emotional crisis had passed, and if Sargent's little speech had something to do with that, no matter how small, then she was grateful. There was so much in her head, so much pressing her to act, to find Libby and Q, to finish whatever needed finishing, to do anything at all other than sit around talking. But she didn't feel like she would explode into a thousand pieces if she wasn't careful, not so much, not anymore.

"How many?" she asked.

"How many what?"

"People died . . . when d-mat crashed."

Sargent blinked but didn't look away. Her eyes, a clear jade green, seemed to cloud over. "There's no direct way to tell, with VIA still flatlined. But reports are coming in. It looks like hundreds, maybe a thousand."

Clair's shoulders slumped. "That's my fault."

"What? Don't be ridiculous. *We* shut it down. If we hadn't, the world would be up to here in dupes." Sargent raised a hand to the considerable height of her shoulder.

"But people will blame me. They know I was coming to talk to Wallace. They know I was with WHOLE. They're bound to think that WHOLE attacked VIA and I was part of what happened next."

"WHOLE *dreams* of taking out VIA. Turner Goldsmith was a tin-pot terrorist who never stood a chance of anything until you came along."

"He was more than that," Clair said, startled to find herself defending someone she had thought crazy just days ago. WHOLE might have been a bunch of hardline Abstainers yearning for a world without d-mat, but they weren't evil. "People don't know anything about what Turner was really like. They're afraid of WHOLE, and now they'll be afraid of me, too."

"There's no need to worry about that, Clair. Until

someone proves to us that you're a criminal it's our responsibility to keep you safe. If you'll let us . . . and under certain circumstances, even if you won't."

That made Clair sit up straighter. Her hands balled into fists on her thighs.

"So I could be innocent and you could keep me here anyway?"

"If your safety made a critical difference to an important investigation, yes. But not literally here. We'd take you somewhere much more comfortable, depending on how long you'd be with us." Sargent studied her sideways. "Don't look so worried. I'm not telling you this to threaten you. You asked, remember?"

"Yes, but I didn't expect you to be so honest."

"Why not? I'm an honest person." Sargent smiled quickly—another brief flash of her white teeth, and then they were gone. "You know what they say about civilization being just three meals away from savagery? Maybe it's the same with d-mat. What if this is the last conversation I ever have? I don't want it to be even partly bullshit."

Clair didn't want to smile, but she did. Not because Sargent had said anything funny. Quite the opposite. Clair needed to smile because otherwise she would have to cry. And once she started, she wasn't sure she would ever stop.

"Does my mom know where I am?"

"Yes."

The uncomplicated answer made her feel stronger. She tried another.

"Is Jesse okay?"

"Yes."

"Now I know you're lying," she said, although she wanted it to be true, very much. He had helped her; he had encouraged her; he had seen something in her. And she had seen something in him too. They had kissed. Then she had destroyed his world. "Everyone he knows is dead. His home was blown to bits. None of it was backed up. He has nothing to go back to."

Sargent shrugged and said, "That's not how he sees it."

Clair blushed. "When can I talk to him?"

"Soon, I hope. Your mother, too."

"She's *here*?"

"D-mat . . . broken . . . remember?" Sargent smiled. "No. I meant over the Air. That's working fine. When you get your privileges back we'll be able to put you through to her. She's in protective custody, in case the dupes try to take her hostage again."

Clair thought of her mother in a cell like this one, and Jesse in another cell, and she asked herself what *she* had to go back to, at that moment. She was the girl who'd taken on d-mat and won. The girl who'd sacrificed herself, *killed herself*, and lived. The girl who couldn't save her best friend, and had betrayed the new friend who'd tried to help her. What awful thing was she going to do next?

"If you want to make a difference," Sargent said, "tell me everything you know about what happened to Zep."

Clair came out of her thoughts with a sudden shock, as though she had been dropped naked into a bath of icy water.

[3]

"ZEP IS DEAD," Clair said, wondering how there could be any doubt about that even though she desperately wished it wasn't so. "He was shot."

"Yes, by a dupe outside the safe house in Sacramento Bay. We don't have a body but his blood was found at the scene, plus other evidence strongly suggesting that what you say is true."

"What kind of evidence?"

"Uh . . . brain matter. You really don't want to know."

She really didn't.

"Why are you asking me if you already know what happened?"

"Because it's not just about Sacramento Bay. It's about what happened on the station as well."

"Wallace brought him back and Mallory shot him again." More memories. Clair shuddered. "I told you all of that."

Sargent leaned forward, her eyes cloudy again.

"Zeppelin Barker came back from the dead," she said. "That's supposed to be impossible."

"Jesse's dad did too—"

"Yes, but Wallace had captured Dylan Linwood's pattern much earlier. He kidnapped Dylan specifically to dupe him, by forcing him into a booth so he could be scanned. Not Zep. Zep was just some random kid—sorry, but you know what I mean—just someone who got in the way. So where did the pattern come from? Wallace didn't know he'd need him later to blackmail you. There was no forcing him to be scanned, and any transit patterns should have been erased days earlier. How did Wallace get hold of it?"

"Zep was an earlier version of himself." Clair forced herself to recall his confusion and shock on finding himself where he hadn't expected to be. Exactly as Clair had felt on returning to New York, after the station had blown up. Zep had jumped from his dorm in Shanghai to meet her at school, and later a copy of him from that jump had been brought back, exactly as he had been but minus the memories of everything that had happened since that day. This version of him may not have experienced the events in the safe house, he might have been a few hours younger than the Zep who had first died, but he was completely real and alive in a way that still tore her up on the inside. "He didn't know what was going on."

"Keeping a pattern after transit is illegal," Sargent said.

"It leads to copying—and worse, editing copies to change what's inside, as we've seen in the last few days. No one's supposed to do it."

"Obviously Wallace did," said Clair.

"So what if the data's still out there? What if we could bring Zep back again? I think we'd be obligated to do it. Saving lives is what PKs do, right?"

"I guess." Clair didn't know where this was going, but she would take every small hope where she could get it. "You could save the lives of everyone who died in the crash."

"Exactly what I was thinking," Sargent said, leaning forward with sudden intensity. "I want to find those patterns. I want to convince the Consensus Court to let us bring them back."

The lock snicked and the door opened. Sargent leaned away from her. Clair realized only then how close their heads had been, like they were sharing a secret.

"The law specifically forbids the reactivation of the patterns of people who have been declared legally dead," said PK Forest as he circled the table and returned to his chair. He held something in his hands, a bundle wrapped in white paper. "Unless we find compelling evidence that Zeppelin Barker is still alive, he cannot be reactivated, pattern or no pattern. It would be profoundly inequitable. Here."

He offered Clair the bundle. She didn't move.

"You could at least sound sorry about it," she said.

Flick.

"I am not sorry. We call it 'reactivation,' but it would really be resurrection. Death is an essential part of human life. Society lacking that basic constraint would be . . . terrifying. Remember Mallory Wei."

Clair did. Her fate was a living hell. If Wallace had had his way, she might have repeated the cycle of resurrection and suicide forever.

A glance at Sargent told her that she was thinking something similar.

But did that mean it was wrong to bring back someone who died unnaturally young, too young to have really lived at all, who might actually *want* to come back? She wasn't just thinking of Zep, but Libby as well, and everyone else killed by Improvement. If their patterns could be found, they could be saved. . . . Wasn't what Sargent wanted to do the same thing *she* had been trying to do all along? Their means were different, but their ends were the same.

"Open it," Forest said, indicating the package. He was watching her closely.

Clair did as she was told. Inside was a sandwich, but not just any sandwich. She could tell instantly that it was an alfalfa-and-peanut-butter sandwich on *pain de mie* bread.

"How did you get this?" She stared at him in outrage. "It's from my private profile. You can't access this without telling me. That's not fair!"

Flick.

Forest raised his hands in appeasement and smiled almost charmingly. "This is me telling you that we are satisfied now that the other you is an illegal duplicate, and accordingly her ownership of your profile has been revoked. You will shortly gain full access, with new security provisions to ensure you aren't hacked again. We have no more reservations about your claims of selfhood. You are legally Clair Hill. Please eat."

Clair didn't pick up the sandwich. It was her favorite comfort food, but it didn't comfort her now. "What does that mean, exactly? That I'm not legally dead and never have been? Or are you making an exception for me?"

"*That* would be inequitable," said Sargent with a sharp look at Forest.

"It would indeed." Forest folded his hands in his lap. "Existing laws do not necessarily provide the best moral compass in these circumstances. What if they were to tell me that you could not legally remain alive? I can assure you that I would not feel compelled to shoot you where you sit."

"Well, that's a relief."

"Do not be too relieved. We have methods of dealing with inconvenient duplications that do not involve violence. It is not an uncommon crime."

Clair looked from Forest to Sargent and back again.

Forest's smile hadn't changed. It was a pretty good approximation, although it was beginning to look a little fixed. He clearly wasn't joking.

"We need you, Clair, and you need us. That is the simple truth of it." *Flick.* "Now, the sandwich. In a moment you will be too busy to eat, and I do not want you starving on my watch."

"The Inspector hates it when that happens," said Sargent.

That broke the smile. Forest shot Sargent a look of mild rebuke, perhaps for her use of the nickname, then settled back into a mask of blank impassivity.

"It was a test, wasn't it?" Clair said. "I recognized the sandwich."

"It wasn't that. You were upset about us accessing your profile," said Forest, "rather than what we might have found in it. That was what convinced me."

"I was already convinced." Sargent nodded encouragingly. "Eat up, and be glad the fabbers are still working. Remember, three meals . . ."

Clair ate the sandwich.

$$[4]$$

SHE HAD BARELY swallowed the last mouthful when her lenses flickered, startling her, and notifications began pouring in. Her infield immediately jammed. Bumps and caption updates from family and friends rose to the surface while everything else crowded in the background. It was a very dense background.

At first glance, all everyone was talking about was d-mat. Or, rather, the lack of d-mat. People were stuck in places both ordinary and weird. Most were at home, school, or work, but some were on the summit of mountains or on the bottom of oceans or in the middle of deserts, huge distances from anywhere civilized. Families had been torn apart. Friends were looking for friends. Public warnings flooded in from PKs and other branches of the OneEarth administration, telling people to stay out of booths for the time being. There were rumors of accidents and partially transmitted bodies and wild speculations as to what was going on. There were protests and petitions for action, and the occasional violent clash with the PKs. Clair could sense a global panic mounting.

She blanked her caption and searched for something from Q.

The only message in her inbox was the last Q had sent.

Friendship has to be earned.

Clair felt just as ashamed as she had the first time she read it.

"I know you can see what's happening," she sent in reply. "Please come back. I'm sorry I broke my promise. We need you. *I* need you."

She might have said more, but she didn't want to beg

while the peacekeepers were still watching her private profile. She could see a notification from them informing her of the fact. A quick glance at her public observers showed the PKs at the very top there too, followed by a large number of people, familiar and unfamiliar. Friends from school rubbed shoulders with celebrities and people she'd never heard of. One was a lawmaker called Kingdon who Clair assumed PK Forest had allocated her, now that Clair was legally recognized. The woman had sent her a brief message:

> Don't feel you're alone in this, Clair. Let me help you. I'm here if you need me.

Clair didn't pursue the offer then. She didn't know what she needed. The total number of people following her was hypnotic, in the hundreds of thousands already and growing before her eyes. So much for her dream of going back to an ordinary life once Improvement was dealt with.

In addition to the bump from LM Kingdon, there were dozens from her parents, swinging wildly across the spectrum of emotions. They were hard to read, and Clair sent a reply to the least crazy-sounding, telling them that she was okay and would call soon.

Before she did that, though, she had to know what her mother had been reading about her.

This was the most difficult thing of all.

For starters, the Abstainers thought she was a hero. Clair Hill was the girl who killed d-mat—never mind what she herself thought about that. She didn't want to be a hero, particularly not for a cause she didn't agree with. All she had wanted to do was stop Improvement and save Libby.

Then there were friends and acquaintances who felt betrayed by what they thought were her actions. Some called her a liar, others a dangerous fearmonger. To them she was the girl who killed d-mat for personal fame. Those who had supported her now felt that she had made them look foolish. It was going to take a lot to rebuild that trust.

Clair searched for word from her closest friends. Ronnie was home in Florida, anxiously surfing the Air through her augs, but Tash was in a jungle in South America, hacking her way through vines to get back to civilization. Tash had sent Clair a message that said simply, "You broke the world WTF!?!" Ronnie was ominously silent. Clair was too nervous to send them messages of her own, for fear of what her friends might say back.

The peacekeepers, at least, had issued a statement saying that the testimony offered earlier by someone claiming to be Clair Hill, effectively a confession that she had made up everything about Improvement, was false and that the real Clair Hill was now reinstated. That saved her the trouble of explaining about dupes and how she had become one—because that still sounded crazy, even in the world as it was now—and it made her numbers pop even more. But the dupes and Improvement and Ant Wallace and the station and anything that really mattered were all being swamped by the much more important crisis the world had to deal with, which was that it had effectively ground to a halt.

Hospitals were no longer just a jump away, and neither were peacekeepers or refuges for those under threat. And what about prisons, some of which had no doors at all, only d-mat booths: How were the guards going to get in and out? What about people working in space? What about the crashlanders trapped somewhere called the Cave of Crows over a mile below the surface of the Earth, where they had held their latest ball?

How was Clair going to fix *this*?

Someone took her hand. She blinked out of her infield and realized that the real world had changed around her. The seats formerly occupied by Sargent and Forest were now empty. Sitting next to Clair in the interview room's fourth chair was the one person who hadn't bombarded her for explanations via the Air.

Jesse.

Her throat felt so full and tight that she couldn't speak.

"Are you all right?" He was studying her face. She didn't know what it showed, but if it was anything like the emotional turmoil she felt inside, she was amazed he could bear to look at her. "I tried calling your name and you didn't seem to hear—oh, okay."

She had pulled him to her and wrapped her free hand

around his neck. It felt so good to be close to him, so safe and familiar. He had lost his world, and so in a very real way had she. But they still had each other. She wasn't alone, for all that LM Kingdon might think she was.

He returned the hug with both arms. His chin rested heavily on her shoulder and she closed her eyes, breathing into his hair. Again she found herself fighting back tears. They had been through so much. They had *survived* so much. It felt like it really meant something. And it did. They wouldn't have gotten this far without working well together.

She pulled back from him and looked down at their hands. It amazed her how tightly they were holding on to each other, and how right it felt that she could cling to him and he didn't mind.

"Sorry I didn't notice you," she said. "Lots to catch up on."

He nodded. "Too much. I've hardly looked at my augs. I'll never respond to everyone. Apparently we're famous now."

She had seen his name mentioned in the Air almost as often as hers.

"I know," she said, but without any sense of accomplishment. This kind of popularity was what Libby had wanted, not her. It wasn't something she had earned. She was under no illusions that the people talking about her knew or cared about who she actually was.

Also, being famous wasn't going to stop them from being killed this time.

"Are you going to make an announcement?" he said.

"Me?" Her heart sank at the thought. "Can't you do it?"

"People probably think I'm a joke. The last thing they saw me saying was . . . well, you know."

That you had a crush on me for years, Clair didn't say, *and I barely noticed you.* More fuel for the Clair-is-a-bitch crowd.

Jesse looked so anxious, so uncertain, that her heart ached. She kissed him to put that ache to rest, and because she wanted to. The world was ending. Zep might or might not be dead. Her friends hated her, and god only knew when she'd ever go home. But he was here, and he tasted like spearmint. She hoped her breath wasn't too awful—and then, for a wonderful moment, she wasn't thinking at all.

When they pulled apart, her heart was pounding. How had he learned to kiss like that?

"Uh, I'm not sure if we won or lost," she said, struggling to bring her thoughts back to the present.

"Won, definitely," he said, pulling at the collar of his orange jumpsuit. He looked as flushed as she felt. "Improvement is finito. Wallace, too."

She didn't know how much he knew about the space station and what had happened up there. It was a conversation she didn't want to have.

"And d-mat? Is that finished too?"

He looked uncertain again. "Abstainer, remember?"

"But you've used it now. It wasn't so bad, was it?"

"Only because I was forced to. Given a choice . . ."

"You're still you," she said. "I don't understand the problem."

"I'm still me," he said. "Maybe that's just it. It hasn't changed my feelings on this or anything."

There was an awkward silence.

"Let's not get stuck on this," he said.

He was right. There were more important things.

"I'm trying to figure out what happens next," she said, not wanting to raise bringing back Zep or Libby while Forest might be listening. "What have the PKs told you?"

"Well, *apparently* they're moving us," he said with his usual suspicion of authority. "They say they've got some kind of ultrasecure barracks in Washington, where they're taking everyone involved in the case. Hopefully not to vanish us into some bottomless pit, never to be seen again."

"Why take us anywhere at all? No, scratch that." She understood. The peacekeepers really were treating this seriously if they were packing up all their witnesses and getting them as far from VIA HQ as possible. "*How* are they moving us?"

"I don't know. They didn't say. By road, I guess."

She didn't like that thought. The memory of being

chased across the back roads of California was still vivid and painful.

"I'm not sure I want to," she said.

"Me either," he responded, and as he kept talking she realized that he misunderstood that she'd meant going by road versus going *at all*. "I think they should just cut us loose. We've done nothing wrong. We don't know who the dupes really are or what they want. We don't know who the psycho killer is who's pretending to be my dad—but at least they know now that he wasn't a murderer or a terrorist. Dad just wanted . . . just wanted me to be . . ."

Jesse looked down and his hair fell forward again.

"It's okay," she said, and immediately regretted it. Nothing about their situation was *okay*.

He shook his head but didn't look up.

"They've declared him dead, you know," he said. "They've given up on him. But I know what I saw . . . what *we* saw, on the station . . . and I don't know what to think. Would he let us bring him back if we could find him again? Would we be allowed to?"

Clair frowned, wondering what he was doing even thinking along those lines. Maybe someone had put the possibility of resurrection into Jesse's head just like Sargent had with her. Were they being tested, somehow? If they said the wrong thing, would they be dropped into that bottomless pit in Washington and never let out? The door opened behind them, and Sargent herself leaned in.

"We're leaving. Did Jesse tell you? I'll give you a minute if you like and then I'll come back and get you."

"Do we have to go?" Jesse asked.

"It's the safest option," Sargent said. "There have been several attempts to enter HQ already. Personally, I don't want to sit around waiting for them to succeed. Do you two?"

Clair hadn't thought about it like that. Moving was probably her best option. Somewhere else she might be able to find a way to do all the things she had to do. If the PKs couldn't fix d-mat on their own, they would need her help convincing Q. Perhaps she could trade that help for leniency when it came to reactivating her friends—in which case that lawmaker, LM Kingdon, might come in handy.

"Okay," she said, "I'm ready."

Jesse grunted, but with some grace. "I guess I am too, then."

He stood up and left his hair where it fell, covering his eyes. Her knees were stiff from sitting for too long, and her back ached. Moving would be good for that, too.

"I'll be with you every step of the way," said Sargent as Clair walked out the doorway for only the second time in three hours. The first had been to go to the toilet. The hallway outside was boxy and nondescript. "We're not going by road, by the way, Jesse."

So they had been listening. "How, then?"

"I can't say."

"Helicopter?" asked Jesse, trailing behind them. "Subway?"

"I *really* can't say. It's the biggest secret on the planet at the moment," said Sargent, guiding them ahead of her. "I wouldn't want to ruin the surprise."

———————————————————— [5]

AT THE END of the hallway was a large, windowless meeting room that contained twenty office chairs on wheels, scattered apparently at random, half of them occupied by people in orange jumpsuits like Jesse's and Clair's. Most of those people were handcuffed at their wrists and ankles. Clair's lenses supplied names. She recognized Ant Wallace's assistant, Catherine Lupoi, who in the flesh was a striking brunette with a defiant expression. There was a peacekeeper Clair remembered from her return to New York, a man called PK Drader, who had previously been assigned to Jesse but was now watching over the people in orange. Behind them in a corner on his own was a slender teen with wispy red hair, wearing a black Nehru suit done up to the neck. In a chair opposite him was a young woman in orange who Clair instantly recognized, although the text hovering above her head wasn't a name she knew. She was blond, willowy, and folded into herself like a trap, or a building on the verge of collapse.

Clair's lenses said "Xia Somerset."

The face belonged to Tilly Kozlova.

The only way they could be different was if the wrong person was inside Tilly's body.

Clair stopped dead in the entranceway for an instant, then numbly let herself be led through the others to a chair next to Jesse. She was sitting in the same room as her childhood hero, and there was no avoiding the fact now that Tilly Kozlova had been an imposter all along. She was one of the Improved, a beautiful young shell that had been given to a dying musician—an old woman who wanted to live another life. She wasn't a dupe: a dupe was a temporary copy with someone else's mind jammed in, an arrangement that lasted only a few days. Dupes could be created over and over again, whereas the Improved stole lives singly and permanently. By a slow and methodical process, the original Tilly Kozlova had been scooped out of her own skull and thrown away like so many pumpkin seeds. Clair felt unclean, as though her love for the music Xia Somerset had made in Tilly Kozlova's body had tarnished her, made her somehow complicit in Wallace's dreadful scheme. She rubbed her hands together as if to wipe them clean.

Seeing this familiar face was a reminder of just how much mess was left in Wallace's wake.

"She turned herself in, you know. The first of the Improved to do so, right before the crash."

The bump appeared at the top of her infield. She didn't

recognize the name of the sender: Devin Bartelme. According to the profile that came with it, Devin Bartelme was ambiguous regarding his gender but preferred the male pronoun. He had no fixed address, which was a bit unusual but not entirely so. Some people didn't live anywhere permanently; they wandered from place to place as the mood took them, fabbing everything they needed on the other side of their latest d-mat jump. His profile contained no photo.

Another bump came, hard on the tail of the first.

"Five others also surrendered. The rest of the Improved are lying low, except for four who committed suicide. I'd like to credit them with guilty consciences, but maybe they're just afraid of what you'd do if you caught them."

Clair raised her head slightly. She felt like she was being watched, but the clump of prisoners was staring anywhere but at her.

"Keep looking up," said a third bump. Then: "Now, to your right. Hello. I'm Devin."

The ginger teen near Tilly Kozlova lifted an eyebrow in greeting. He was so fine-featured she could easily have mistaken him for a girl, if not for his Adam's apple, which protruded prominently like the keel of a ship. The name supplied by her lenses matched the one that came with the bump.

"Who are you?" she bumped back, opening a chat.

"RADICAL."

She rolled her eyes.

"That's a noun, not an adjective," he said. "Strictly speaking, it's an acronym, like WHOLE and VIA. You've never heard of us?"

"No."

The corners of his lips turned up slightly. "That's the answer I was hoping for. We like to hide in the noise."

Clair searched the Air for anything called RADICAL. If there was a hit, it was deeply buried and she didn't see it.

"You just searched for us, didn't you?"

"Yes," she admitted. "What are you doing here? You're not one of them or else you'd be cuffed."

"Voluntary attaché. The PKs don't really want me here, but we have transparency laws for a reason, and RADICAL knows how to insist. It's our job to protect the interests of future humans."

He had to be joking, surely. No one could really be that pompous.

"RADICAL used to stand for 'Radical Assembly of Digitalists, Ideators, Cyborgs, And Longlifers'," he explained without prompting. "Note the way it contains its own name: that's supposed to be clever. Woo."

"What does it stand for now?"

"Well, it became the 'Radical Association for the Diligent and Intelligent Creation of Artificial Life', but it's still a moveable feast. Sometimes we're radicalized instead of just radical, depending on our mood. And sometimes it's control rather than just creation, depending on the circumstances."

"What are the circumstances now?"

"Control, definitely," he said. "The life of every human is at risk. We could all be dead within a year, and not because of killer duplicates and mind-rape and the crash and all that stuff you're worried about. We're seeing a much bigger picture. The entity's the problem. I'm here to figure out what it's doing and what needs to be done about it."

"What entity?"

"You know: Q."

She felt herself gape at him. She couldn't believe they were back here again. "Q is not the problem."

"Isn't she? I'd like to talk to you about that."

Clair was about to suggest that any discussion they had should be conducted in public so it didn't seem like they were sharing an illicit secret, when the door opened and PK Forest walked in, his face a businesslike mask.

Behind him, cuffed at the wrists and ankles, shuffled Clair's dupe.

Clair stood up. The dupe's sweeping gaze locked on her. They stared at each other for a long moment during which Clair didn't think at all. It was like looking into a mirror—but at the same time not *like* a mirror at all. This was no reflection, nor was it a recording in her infield. This was *her*, right down to the pores. A replica that would bleed blood identical to hers if she pricked it.

A wave of dizziness swept through her. She balled her fists and held her breath. No way was she going to throw up. Not with so many people watching. Not with *her* watching.

"Get. Out." Jesse was on his feet too. "*She's* coming with us?"

Sargent nodded. "Is that a problem?"

"Are you kidding?"

Clair touched him on the shoulder, to reassure him but also to take reassurance from him.

"She's evidence," Sargent said. "She has to come with us before she breaks down or dies or whatever dupes like her do. The more evidence the Consensus Court has, the quicker it can come to the decisions we need."

Clair understood the necessity of that, but she couldn't bring herself to feel okay about it.

"I don't understand how you can even look at her . . . it . . . whatever she is," said Jesse.

PK Forest pressed the dupe into a seat while Clair asked herself the same question. If the real Clair had died on the station as Wallace had intended, this other Clair would have gone back to her home and lived her remaining days in her place, a human cuckoo in her parents' nest. When she expired, her grieving parents would never have known the truth—that the real Clair had died much earlier without ever seeing them again.

Seeing the flesh-and-blood proof of that plan made Clair's pulse pound in her ears.

"Why do you do this?" she asked her other self, taking two cautious steps closer. "Why would you possibly *want* to?"

The dupe just stared up at her with her own eyes, her own hands curled in her lap, restraints fastened tightly around her own wrists. Clair couldn't see any evidence of a tremor, from nerves or anything else.

"Are they threatening you? Threatening your family? Do you do it *for fun*?"

Clair studied her own face, marveling at how different it looked from the one she imagined every day.

"No, it can't be fun, living like this. In and out of people's bodies all the time . . . Do you ever actually leave? Do you stay until you're discovered or the body breaks down? Do you know how many times this has happened to you?"

The dupe shook her thick brown curls. *I need a haircut,* Clair thought in a moment of dizzying displacement. And since when had she had that frown line between her eyes?

"I am nobody," the dupe said, "but I remember Charlie."

The dupe Clair had confronted in California had said *I am nobody* too, but that wasn't what struck her now. Charlie was the toy clown she had lost as a child, the day she realized d-mat wasn't magic after all. This dupe didn't just have her body. *The dupe had her memories, too.*

She fought a sudden urge to smash her own face against the wall.

"Keep her away," she said to Forest.

"Of course," he said.

"And don't let her say another word to me."

"I would like to talk," said the dupe.

"Shut up," she said. "While we're in the same room, you don't say *anything*. You don't even look at me. You make one wrong move and . . . I don't know what I'll do. Is that clear?"

The dupe nodded and, after a moment, lowered her eyes.

Clair realized she was shaking, and she carefully returned to her seat on legs that felt like straws, aware of everyone watching. Not just Devin Bartelme, but Tilly Kozlova as well.

We have methods of dealing with inconvenient duplications, Forest had said. He hadn't elaborated, and now Clair wished he had.

"It's unbelievable," said Jesse, sitting next to her and staring at the dupe with a look of disgust. "I can't believe they got away with it for so long."

"Neither can I," said Sargent. "And it won't be over until the last of the dupes is dealt with and all their patterns are erased."

"How do we do that?"

"We have to find the source. We know it wasn't Wallace's

secret station. That was destroyed, but the dupes kept coming. There's somewhere else, a cache we haven't found yet. The Improved don't know where it is and our dupe friend here says she doesn't know either."

"As if," said Jesse.

"It's possible—who can say where the patterns fabbers use are stored in the Air? Not me: you just ask and out they pop, although I'm sure someone knows, somewhere. Maybe it's the same with the dupes."

"If they hack into the network and get d-mat working again, we'll really be in trouble. . . ."

"Oh yeah. We'll be swamped. But while they keep coming we'll know that cache exists, and there's hope for everyone they killed, directly or indirectly."

While Jesse and Sargent talked, Clair concentrated on breathing in through her nose and out through her mouth. She thought about Libby and Zep. Chances were their patterns were stored in the same place as the dupes. There was hope.

Finally her hands steadied.

"Do you think the PKs staged that little pantomime to see what you would do? Or what the dupe might say?"

She ignored Devin's bump and concentrated on breathing.

"Okay, we are ready," said PK Forest, shutting the door.

Clair's lenses went blank. She looked around, startled. She had thought they were waiting for a train or a truck or something, but Forest had said nothing about moving. Ready for what?

Suddenly—

chug

—the room shook as though gripped by a powerful fist, there was a double thump like a massive mechanical heartbeat, and a wave of yellow light swept from one end of the room to the other—

chug

—and then everything was exactly as it had been, except somehow, even though her lenses were still dark, Clair knew that they had moved.

The whole room must be a booth like Wallace's office.

D-mat wasn't supposed to be working. But this hadn't felt like d-mat. There had been no thinning of the air, no flash of white light or popping ears.

There was another way of getting around that wasn't d-mat.

[6]

A RISING CLAMOR from everyone in the room indicated that she wasn't the only one startled by this development.

"Ah," said a high-pitched voice that wasn't surprised at all. "The shadow road. I wondered."

She looked around. It was Devin who had spoken, aloud for the first time.

"OneEarth has its own network," PK Forest explained. "We call it Net One, but it is referred to as 'the shadow road' by conspiracy theorists." *Flick.* The merest glance, acknowledging Devin. "For emergencies only, completely isolated from the main trunks and with its own independently serviced control software."

"So you can be reasonably sure Wallace never touched it." Devin nodded knowingly.

"Exactly," said Sargent. "It's not as extensive or as fast as anything VIA had, or as reliable, and it's already running well above its usual carrying capacity, so don't expect any miracles."

"'Needs must when the devil drives,'" Forest said. "This is the first stop of two, intended to throw off anyone who might be watching. We will be here for a minute or so until the next transit window opens. You will be reconnected to the Air at the other end, but all geographical data will be scrambled. The safe operation of Net One is something we are keeping secret for now. The barracks is in Crystal City, not far from the center of Washington, and sudden jumps in location would be a giveaway."

In Washington, Clair promised herself, she would renew her efforts to find Q. If she could help bring d-mat back to everyone, maybe that would restore the world's faith in her.

Jesse suddenly pounded the arms of his chair.

"Don't you people ever *ask*? Fuck!"

Everyone stared at him, and he retreated back into the seat a little.

"I'm sorry, but not everyone thinks this a *good* thing. Maybe taking d-mat offline for a while is a positive step, giving people time to think about what it really means, how it's being used, without taking it for granted like they usually do. . . ."

He sounded like his father—a heretic in the church of d-mat—and for a second Jesse even looked like him. There was a defiant jut to his jaw, and a fire in his eyes that Clair had never seen before. She stared awkwardly elsewhere, not wanting to look at him like the others did. They clearly thought he was crazy for having objections to something they all thought was normal.

There was one other person who wasn't watching him, though, and that was PK Sargent. She was staring at Clair with an intense expression, as though she had just realized something important. Clair was about to ask what it was when her dupe broke the awkward silence.

"Charlie says hello," she said, kicking backward with both feet against the floor and sending her chair rolling headlong toward Clair. She ducked under PK Drader's widespread arms and kicked again, accelerating.

Clair barely had time to raise her hands when she and the dupe collided, spilling them both onto the floor. She landed on her bad elbow and hissed in pain. Clutching her arm to her chest, she tried to roll away from the dupe, but how could she possibly outrun *herself*? The chain of the cuffs caught Clair around the neck and for an instant she was being strangled.

Booted feet surrounded them. Drader and Forest pulled the dupe up and away from Clair, one on each arm. Clair wrenched free and scrabbled backward across the floor, clutching her throat. The dupe's face was like nothing she had ever seen—her own features twisted in a snarl that looked barely human. Clair couldn't tell if the dupe was angry or in pain. The sound she made was incoherent, a forceful groan through grinding teeth.

Then, with a loud bang, the front of the dupe's orange jumpsuit exploded.

Someone screamed. People scattered to all corners of the booth. Clair was hit on the side of her face by something hot and wet, and the air was suddenly full of stinking yellow smoke, through which it was hard to make out anything or anyone. She reached out for something to hang on to, then found Jesse. He was on his feet already and helped her to hers, blinking and gaping with shock.

The dupe lay flat on her back in the center of the booth with one arm bent awkwardly underneath her. The midriff of her jumpsuit was a gaping hole, and judging by what Clair could barely glance at, so was the midriff of the dupe.

"Did someone shoot her?" Jesse said over the sound of coughing. "It looks like she blew up."

Clair cautiously approached the body, covering her mouth with one hand. A tiny voice whispered in her ears, a voice saying words she couldn't quite make out. She tilted her head and blocked her ear with one finger. It seemed to be coming from her augs. Something about *didn't see that coming.*

Was it issuing from the body?

The corpse twitched, and Clair jumped backward, bumping into Devin. Blood dripped from his hair.

"She did blow up," he said. "Can't have been a real bomb or the shadow road would've picked it up. Chemical and fat stores, probably, triggered by the body's natural electricity. Didn't know dupes could do that."

Clair stared at him in disbelief. He sounded *fascinated.* That was almost as horrible as what lay on the floor in front of her.

Around them, the other occupants of the booth were regaining their feet. Incredibly no one was hurt. Covered in gore, and Tilly/Xia had thrown up, but not actually hurt.

"Didn't someone once say the dupes were booby-trapped?" Jesse wiped his hands on his jumpsuit, succeeding only in smearing blood everywhere. "Guess that's one way of getting rid of the evidence."

"There are no secrets anymore," said Devin. "It doesn't make sense."

Clair felt sick to the core at the sight of her own dead body, but she couldn't look away. It was almost too horrible. The dupe's face was locked in a terrible grimace that looked *pained* the longer Clair stared at it.

"She went for me," Clair said. "She tried to hurt me, maybe kill me."

"Again, why not earlier?" asked Devin, scratching his head and looking even paler than usual when his fingers came away red. "Unless something triggered the booby trap, and she decided to use it to her advantage. But what was the trigger . . . ?"

Shock and awe. Never gets old, just keeps changing faces. . . .

"Can anybody else hear that?" asked Clair. The whispering was still there, one voice talking in a constant stream at the edge of her hearing, the words just beyond understanding.

The dupe's body twitched again, making everyone jump backward. Devin returned to his corner, well away from the corpse.

A droplet of sweat trickled down Clair's back between the orange fabric of her prison jumpsuit and her skin.

"This is vile," said Jesse. "Can't we just get out of here?"

"There is nowhere to go except by Net One," said PK Forest, his blank expression seeming even more out of place in the context of such chaos. "We are in a relay station one mile underground. We will be on our way any second now, though, straight to Crystal City this time. We have priority, under the circumstances."

"No," said Sargent, speaking for the first time since they

had left New York. "Wait, we shouldn't—"

chug

The room quaked again.

chug

Sargent put herself in front of Clair as the dupe made a sound that could have been a cough and then exploded a second time.

Clair screamed in a mixture of anger and horror. There was more blood, more smoke, and if possible she felt even more of a shock that such a thing could possibly keep happening *to her own body*. Several sharp pinpricks pierced her exposed skin, and she heard cries of pain as well as fright from her fellow travelers.

"What the *hell*?" PK Drader cried out.

"Secondary detonation," Sargent said, pressing Clair as far from the body as she could. "Common terror tactic. Triggered by d-mat, I think."

Clair peered past her, even though she didn't really want to see. The body was now on its side, and this time it had burst open down its chest and face, putting splintered ribs and skull on display. Clair glanced hastily down at her jumpsuit and saw a tiny thornlike protrusion sticking out of the orange fabric. Bone, she realized with disgust. She hastily brushed it off, grateful to Sargent for protecting her from the worst of it. All around her, people were making sounds of discomfort as they removed the ghastly splinters. Tilly/Xia retched again.

"Your eye, PK Sargent," Devin called out from his corner. "You might want to do something about that."

Sargent touched her face in puzzlement, and Clair saw a bone fragment sticking out of Sargent's tear duct like a malignant eyelash.

"Doesn't that hurt?" asked Jesse.

Sargent just stared at him. *Shock,* Clair thought. She had been all business before; maybe it was catching up with her now. Clair sympathized.

"Here, let me," Clair said, tugging Sargent's shoulder gently downward. "You're no good to anyone half-blind."

Sargent resisted for an instant, then gave in. She looked up and away as Clair opened the lids of the injured eye with one hand and with the other reached for the splinter.

"I'll try to be gentle." That was what her mother would have told her.

Sargent didn't even wince when the splinter came out.

"There."

"Thank you," said Sargent stiffly. She blinked and a single red tear trickled down her cheek.

"How did you know that the shadow road was going to make it explode again?" Clair asked her, carefully not thinking of the dupe as *her* anymore.

"It made sense. Any unexpected transit would mean the living dupe had been discovered, triggering the explosive response. I should have thought of it sooner."

"That explains why Libby's body didn't blow up in the train or submarine," said Jesse, flicking away the last of his bony splinters. His jumpsuit looked like he had been wrestling with a cactus. "I wondered about that."

"The second blast did more than frighten," said Devin. Everyone else was hugging the walls, staying as far from the body as possible in case it blew up a third time. He alone approached it, extending the toe of one delicate shoe and shifting the body slightly. The floor beneath the dead dupe was a bloody mess. Through the hole where carpet had been Clair saw a cracked mirror surface. The booth was damaged.

"If this had happened before the last jump," Devin said, echoing Clair's own worried thought, "and you had stopped us jumping, PK Sargent, we could've been stuck a mile underground."

Sargent's ears turned a shocked red. "I didn't know. I was afraid of what a second jump would trigger."

"Not an unreasonable fear," said PK Forest. *Flick.* The doors were opening. "Of no consequence now. We have arrived."

Through the door came a peacekeeper dressed in body armor, followed by the sound of alarms.

[7]

"I THOUGHT YOU said these barracks were secure," said Jesse to PK Drader.

Drader was a solidly built man of average height, with

crooked shoulders, one higher than the other, a round face, and slightly protruding ears. His chin was dark with stubble and his uniform had seen better days. Under the fresh blood spatter there were smears of building dust and soot from the action in New York.

"They were supposed to be secure," he said with a questioning look at the PK who'd just come in.

"We came under guerrilla attack on our northern fence line the moment your patterns were processed," explained the PK. "We've identified six known dupes and spotted another three unknowns. Crystal City is on full lockdown." She saw the mess in the center of the room. "Shit. This is one of only three operational cages. Get these kids out of here and I'll call the techs in to see if they can fix it."

Clair bristled at "kids," but PK Forest was already hustling her and Jesse out of the room ahead of him. PK Sargent followed, looking around her at the blank, gray walls as though expecting to be somewhere else, with Devin tagging along behind her. Clair looked over her shoulder. The prisoners in orange suits looked pale and lost, stuck in the booth with the body and PK Drader. The peacekeeper nodded at Jesse and raised a hand in farewell. Jesse didn't respond.

Clair refused to feel sorry for Tilly or Xia or however she thought of herself now. So what if she had turned herself in? She shouldn't have done what she did in the first place. Who knew what the real Tilly might have grown up to become but now wouldn't? Unless somehow Clair could find her pattern and reactivate her, too . . .

Was that her mission now, Clair wondered—to hunt down all the lost girls and boys and bring them back? At what point did she draw the line?

"This way." PK Forest hurried them along a series of corridors that looked identical to the ones in New York. Only the alarm was different, a piercing, repetitive siren that made her want to cover her ears. At least the air was fresh, a welcome change from the foulness they'd left behind.

"Where are we going?" Clair asked, filled with the same anger that had fueled her on the station. The dupes had attacked her in a secret d-mat booth in peacekeeper HQ, and now they had come after her in Crystal City. They weren't going to let her escape easily. Doing nothing in response was only going to get her killed. "What are we going to do?"

She had originally planned to look for Q. Now the dupes were the bigger problem. But how was she going to stop them? She was just a sixteen-year-old girl with a sore elbow, a bruised throat, and a boy she liked but was still getting to know, a long way from anywhere familiar.

"Someone? Anyone?" She wasn't going to be ignored.

"Through here," said Forest.

They turned left into an atrium that afforded them a glimpse of gray skies outside and passed from there into a series of changing rooms, complete with uniform fabbers down one wall. The Air returned, filling Clair's infield with a new flood of notifications, and five fabbers started whirring industriously.

"Shower and change," said Sargent, indicating three cubicles in a row. "Undersuits and light body armor will be outside the curtains when you're done."

Armor sounded like a step in the right direction.

"Uh, I'm not volunteering to defend your little fort," said Devin, trying and failing to brush the dried blood off his Nehru jacket. "I'm an observer only."

"You can observe all you like," said Forest. "That was the agreement."

"Well, we're not going to just sit here while someone attacks us," said Jesse.

Clair agreed. "Otherwise, you might as well send us home."

"That would never be authorized," said Forest. "Net One is strictly limited to priority transits. You are no longer a priority now that we are out of danger."

"You can hear that siren, can't you?" said Jesse, pointing at the ceiling. "I'm not imagining it?"

"No one's going anywhere," said Sargent, raising her hands for calm. "Including the dupes, unfortunately. In order to stop them we need to understand them, and in order to understand them we need data. We have drones, but they can't watch everywhere at once. That's where you guys come in. Crystal City is short of monitors, thanks to the d-mat shutdown and lags in the Air, and we need all the eyes we can get. If we can track the dupes, we can pin them down, maybe even capture another one of them, see if we can get it to talk. Are you in?"

"Observation I can do," said Devin.

"When do we start?" Clair said. The sooner she got the immediate problem of the dupes off her back, the sooner she could get back to working on the rest.

"Showers first," said Sargent, pointing firmly at the cubicles. "Don't think we're doing this just to make you smell nice. Another common terror tactic is combining chemical or biological agents with light shrapnel, to ensure the agent gets in. I'm talking about poisoned blood and bone darts. Scrub yourself completely clean and report any odd reactions around puncture wounds. We'll be doing the same, so don't think you're being singled out."

Clair looked with new concern at the red line stretching down Sargent's face from where the sliver of bone had stuck into her. Standing there arguing was giving those "agents" a chance to spread through the peacekeeper's body.

"All right." Clair stepped into the cubicle and tugged the curtain closed behind her. She would do as she was told as long as in return she wasn't going to be brushed off like some inconvenient kid. She had seen and done too much to be pushed to the sidelines, by the dupes or by anyone else.

SHE TUGGED OFF the jumpsuit and threw it into one corner of the stall. Then she turned on the shower, producing a powerful stream of hot water. There was soap, shampoo, and conditioner, even a pick for her hair. She used the soap thoroughly, checking every part of her for cuts or puncture wounds that might have come from the exploding dupe. Her elbow was loosening up under the patch the medic had given her, and her throat hadn't even bruised. She felt surprisingly okay, physically, considering she had killed herself and watched her own dupe die in the last few hours.

As she applied conditioner and worked steadfastly through the numerous tangles in her hair, she checked her infield for a message from Q. Still nothing. Using the same address, she bumped Q again, while she had the chance.

"I feel awful about what I did, and I'm really sorry. Can you see why I had to do it? Wallace would've won if I hadn't. Maybe more people died this way—I don't know. But it's better, isn't it, to fix something than to leave it broken?"

She sent the bump, too late realizing that she had inadvertently reiterated the argument behind Improvement. *You can be Improved.* Except having a big nose wasn't the same thing as being broken, not by a long shot. Or living in a broken world.

Clair's mother, Allison, was in a PK station in Windham, their hometown. She answered practically the nanosecond Clair requested a chat.

"You're safe! Thank everyone and everything. Where are you? When are you coming home?"

Clair explained as best she could, hoping the shower would cover the sound of the siren. It was difficult to admit how little she knew about current events without sounding completely irresponsible. Allison wanted to know if her plan to enlist VIA had worked and if everything was going to be all right now, but what could Clair say?

For the moment she tried to focus on the small and personal, rather than the whole world.

"Where's Oz? Is he with you?"

Allison shook her head. "He went back to the apartment to get some rest. The PKs have been deputizing volunteers in the old town hall. Everyone's doing their best to band together, but no one really knows anyone else. He's worried about riots if this goes on much longer."

"Riots in Windham?" Clair couldn't imagine it. Windham barely qualified as anywhere. "Tell him to be careful, Mom."

"I have. He might be more inclined to if it comes from you. He's worried about you too."

"I'm sorry." Clair hesitated, caught on the tipping point of saying nothing and saying everything. "I love you, Mom."

"And I love you, dearest child of mine. Please be safe."

"I'm doing my best."

"Promise me."

"I promise. And, hey, ditto."

"Ditto." Clair could hear the smile in her mother's voice, but it was on the surface only. Underneath was all worry.

Devin bumped her as soon as she closed the chat. "Don't be under any illusions that the PKs are acting out of the goodness of their hearts. They want something from you. That's why you're here."

"Are you spying on me?" she sent back.

"Perfectly legally. I saw you call your mother. I guessed what you would talk about. It wasn't hard."

Clair checked the list of people following her profile, and sure enough, there he was, along with LM Kingdon and all the others. He couldn't see the content of private conversations at his level of privilege, but he was probably telling the truth about the rest.

She thought briefly again about taking up the lawmaker's offer, but decided that she should only get legal advice once she actually had something concrete to talk about on the matter of reactivation. No use tipping her hand too early, in case PK Forest was paying attention.

Applying a second layer of conditioner to her hair and

tying it up in a temporary knot, she ignored the embarrassment of talking in the shower to a boy she hardly
knew and opened a chat.

"So what if the PKs want something from me?" she said.
"So do you."

"At least I'm being honest about it."

"How do you know they haven't been?"

"Because I know them. Prove me wrong."

She had to admit that he wasn't. But she didn't see the
harm in what he was suggesting. She wasn't being entirely
honest with the PKs, either. They made her feel safer, but
if they stood between her and what she needed to do, she
would escape without a moment's hesitation and get on
with it her way.

"They're after the same thing as you, aren't they?" she
went on. "It's all about finding Q, even though they're
pretending it isn't. That's what Wallace wanted. That's
what you want."

"I don't *want* her," he said. "I want to know what she *is*,
with a view to containing her. And I know you don't want
to hear that, but . . . Look, do you know why we don't have
smart AIs running the world?"

"Sure, Turner Goldsmith told me. Because—"

"Because AIs are either too big and spread too thin or
too small to be good at more than one thing. Yes? Well,
your friend in WHOLE was lying. Real AIs can be anything they want, which is why they're so dangerous.

They're not impossible at all. We don't have them because they're *banned*."

Clair mulled this over for a moment.

"Q isn't dangerous," she said. "She's just a kid . . . a kid version of an AI, whatever that's called. She helped me, and she helped everyone harmed by Improvement."

"Sure, but how did she do it? By hacking into systems that were supposed to be utterly secure and destroying the oversight capacity of the entire VIA network. She almost wiped VIA HQ right off the surface of the Earth just to get you back. Imagine what she could do when she grows up! Creating something like her and losing control of it was Wallace's real crime, Clair. You have to understand the gravity of the situation."

"Well, she's not talking to me any longer, so if you think I'm going to betray her or talk her into turning herself in, you can forget it. I couldn't do it even if I wanted to."

"We'll see," he said. "She's not talking to us, either, and we've tried hard to get her attention. Maybe you can help us find her, wherever she's gone to ground."

"Is that what you think she's done?"

"Either that or she's done us all a favor and erased herself for good."

Clair gasped. Q had followed her lead on more than one occasion. What if she had done so in the worst possible way?

Distantly, she heard the sound of Devin's shower

clicking off two cubicles along. The chat stayed open.

"What was that you said earlier?" he asked. "You could hear something, back in the booth?"

"Yeah, did you hear it too? Like a private chat bleeding into my feed. Whispering."

"No, nothing like that," he said. "You sure you didn't get any of that poisoned shrapnel in you?"

"Whether I did or not, Devin, I was hearing things before that happened."

"Ah. Well, then it's just ordinary everyday hallucinations. Watch out for those. Reality can be such a letdown when it kicks back in."

She ended the chat, not liking being made fun of and figuring it was time she got out of the shower too.

She finished rinsing out the conditioner, wrapped her hair in a towel and reached through the curtain for her new clothes. They were the perfect size, made to the measurements in her profile, and consisted of a sleek black undersuit that looked whisper-thin but was supportive in all the right places, plus a set of shoes, pants, and a hooded top made of blue and white segments that slipped neatly over each other. It was only marginally bulkier than jeans and a sweatshirt, and felt considerably lighter.

There was a mirror. When she checked herself out, she looked like a young peacekeeper, apart from her hair, which, released from the towel, was already bushing up as it always did. If they'd given her a helmet, she might have worn it just to keep the frizz under control.

She remembered what Jesse had said about her having potential in this line of work. The figure in the mirror was a glimpse of her possible future, if she wanted it. A zit on her chin emphasized that this future should have been much further away than it seemed right now.

Her stomach was full of butterflies. There were dupes nearby and they were trying to get to her. As she stepped out of the stall, she bumped her stepfather. Oz was asleep, but her message would be there for him later.

───────────────────────────[9]

FOREST AND SARGENT showed them how to use the hoods of their uniforms. They were soft and pliable when inactive, but turned rigid and skull hugging at a simple command. The PKs wore similar outfits but with pouches and packs—the complete kit, Clair assumed, unlike their stripped-down versions.

"We should give our squad a name," said Devin. "Clair's Bears, perhaps."

Clair winced, thinking of Zep's nickname for her: Clair-bear.

"This isn't a game," said Jesse. He was standing with his wet hair slicked back, looking stern and nervous at the same time. Devin shrugged.

Forest's gaze flicked across each of them, as though testing them.

"All right," he said. "This way."

The Crystal City barracks network connected with her lenses as she walked through its echoing gray corridors and stairwells, offering menus and links to Forest and Sargent and a number of other PKs, several of whom appeared to be actively monitoring drones already. She had access to more than two dozen audiovisual feeds showing the barracks and its surroundings. Some had detailed commentaries. The rest were blank. She guessed that was where she and the others came in. A couple of hours of scoping out the dupes, she hoped, and she would be free to get back to finding Q.

"Well, so far Washington is a huge disappointment," said Jesse with a half smile. "Where are the monuments? The museums? The trees?"

Clair realized only then that, unless his father had physically taken him cross-country from the West Coast and back again, Jesse would never have been to the former U.S. capital before. She had visited twice on school trips and once with her family, all via d-mat. It had been as close to her as any other place in the world, before the crash.

"Overrated," she said, matching his attempt at lightheartedness with one of her own. "And we're a ways off from the interesting bits."

She tried not to think about all the school kids and tourists out there, stuck in Washington until d-mat could get them home.

"Through here."

Forest waved them into a darkened suite containing six sleek reclining chairs arranged in a circle, feet-inward.

"There's a fabber if you're hungry or thirsty," Sargent said. "Order what you want and I'll bring it to you when it's ready."

Clair chose the chair opposite the door. As she sank back into the black leather, she opened the fabber menu via the barracks network. It wasn't as if she was hungry—the image of her exploded dupe was still horribly fresh in her mind—but she couldn't remember the last time she had eaten. Thinking of what her mother would say, she ordered coffee, chocolate, and beef jerky, plus a hair band to bring her thick curls into line.

Devin waited until Jesse had sat next to Clair and then chose the seat farthest from them, on the opposite side of the circle. Maybe he just didn't like people, she thought.

"PK Beck will guide you to your drones," said Forest.

Clair made herself physically comfortable and concentrated on navigating the new windows opening in her lenses. There was a quick tutorial, a practice simulator, some FAQs . . .

"They're going to a lot of trouble to look after a couple of kids, don't you think?" bumped Devin.

"*Three* kids," she shot back. "You forgot to count your-self."

"I'm here voluntarily. Besides, my relationship with them isn't in question."

"Not with them, maybe. I still don't understand why they're letting you tag along."

"I'm the closest thing to a specialist anyone has when it comes to Improvement and the dupes. Apart from you, I guess. You blew everyone else up."

Clair supposed his explanation made sense, and maybe they thought that she was more likely to trust him because they were roughly the same age. Boy, had they gotten *that* wrong.

Sargent folded out a tray from the arm of Clair's seat and placed her snack next to her. Clair glanced up and said thanks, wondering if Devin had a point. Was Sargent being weirdly servile or just practical? Clair couldn't decide.

"You should eat," said Forest to Jesse. "How long since your last meal?"

"Uh . . . it's fine." Jesse looked up from fiddling with the hood of his armor, which he had flipped forward to provide a HUD to make up for his lack of modern lenses. "I'm not hungry."

"You ate nothing in New York." Forest came around the chairs to stand over him. "I know, you are an Abstainer. I understand. But we have only fabbed food here. If you do not eat that, you will starve."

"Then I'll starve, okay—or are you going to force-feed me?" he snapped. His anger quickly evaporated. "Sorry. I just don't want anything now, really. Some water. That would be good."

Forest nodded.

Clair reached between their couches to touch the back of Jesse's hand. He looked down and flipped his hand over. Their fingers tangled in soothing knots.

"You must think I'm stupid," he said.

She shook her head. Not stupid, just different, and stubborn. That was something they had in common. He might have inherited his beliefs from his father, but it was his right to defend them, and no one could take that right away from him. She actually felt proud of him, although worried at the same time.

"Please don't starve to death," she said.

"That chocolate smells amazing."

"Yeah, sorry. I'm totally going to eat it."

He smiled. "I would in your shoes."

PK Beck issued the virtual equivalent of an "ahem" and began assigning drones. The principle was the same as any eye-in-the-sky drone: they were autonomous but could be overridden by human control at any moment. Anyone in the network could examine the world around the drone through its many senses—in the regular world "anyone" meant literally anyone over eighteen, but around

Crystal City it meant only those authorized by PK Beck—in order to guide the drone toward any sites of interest. Oz put in a few hours a week in random places around the world, and Clair had watched over his shoulder a few times. Once they had seen an actual crime, and the way the community of observers had converged on the scene had amazed her. Until backup drones and PKs arrived, there had just been the one drone, "controlled" by Oz and more than a hundred other people in a rapidly evolving consensus that was made possible by the same participatory algorithms that lay behind OneEarth itself. There were no leaders and no followers: everyone found the way together.

Chewing on a stick of jerky, Clair picked one unsupervised drone at random and accessed its feed. Drone 484117B was cruising at a steady speed over one of Crystal City's many aboveground buildings, a boxy structure containing offices and data storage, according to the map her visual overlay provided. Visible were several other PK buildings, the old airport site, now a nature reserve, greater Washington and the Potomac River, and to the south a long, gray wall that was the Great Alexandria Barrage, one of the more awesome attempts to keep the ocean in place after the Water Wars. Fifty yards high and more than two miles long, it looked like storm clouds stuck on the horizon, never coming closer and never going away.

The drone was intuitively easy to direct. Clair

experimented with various commands, pitching, yawing, and diving until she was sure she had it all worked out. Then she put the drone back under its own control and concentrated on the feed. There were dupes out there somewhere, trying to get to her. Her job was to stop them, and if she learned more about them into the bargain, all the better.

"Where are they?" she asked, studying her windows in vain.

"Stick to the assigned flight path," said Sargent. "If you notice anything out of order, let us know."

"Don't get your hopes up," bumped Devin. "They won't be giving us any real work."

"Stop it," she said. "I'm trying to concentrate."

But there was a chance he was right. The task was simple and soon became routine. Her mood soured. Every five minutes she was automatically assigned a new drone, to stop her from getting complacent about the view, she assumed. The drones flew over empty rooftops, empty lawns, and empty physical training grounds.

When not absorbed with this menial task, Clair explored the network of Crystal City and the small insight she had to the wider world of the peacekeepers. It reminded her of the vast complexity of Wallace's secret network, into which Q had briefly plugged her in the station. That had been epic in scale, spanning the entire world, and this was much the same. There were literally millions of PKs and their new deputies active at that moment, all over the world. She couldn't tell what they were doing, but she could see their names and where they were. Some came online while she watched and others dropped off. She hoped the latter weren't dying. Maybe they were using the shadow road to move around.

Reports about dupes were coming in from all over. That was good, if slightly unnerving, to know.

A flicker on her drone's feed brought her out of her observations. The view was alternating between bright white and blackness as though the camera lens was blinking at the sun. She was puzzled for a second until the drone identified it as a laser attack. The drone wasn't damaged, but its vision was being deliberately obscured.

Finally, Clair thought, although not without a twinge of nervousness.

"I think I've got something," she said to PK Beck.

He slipped smoothly into the drone's control systems.

"Great. Let's give her a touch of rotation . . . like this."

The drone—Clair refused to refer to it as a "she"—turned on its gyroscopes and fans, blinking all the way. At a certain point the vision in one camera cleared.

"The source of the laser is now blocked by the body of the drone, see?" PK Beck explained. "That gives us a set of possible angles. All we need is another and we can triangulate, get some countermeasures in place. Let's take her over here and see what happens."

The drone jetted off along a new trajectory, tilting and swaying to define the laser's path. Clair watched the view through the cameras closely, trying to tease out useful information from the interference. Image-processing algorithms did the same. She saw notifications appear in the corner of the field telling her that Jesse and Devin had joined her feed as well.

Glimpses of Crystal City's urban landscape came and went. Clare locked on to one particular frame and zoomed in as far as she could, sweeping her point of view across a stand of bushes next to a park named after the last president of the United States, Caroline J. Oswald.

"Could that be someone's arm?" she said, highlighting a particular patch of shadow.

"Maybe," said PK Beck. "We'll check it out. Good work."

"That's not an arm," Devin bumped her. "Hypervigilance and false positives. The PKs are nervous. I wonder what they're not showing us."

"I thought you said they were doing this just to keep us occupied."

"I can't have it both ways?"

"That siren is too annoying to be a fake."

"True."

A flash cut across the PK lens interface, distracting Clair from her task. She blinked and focused on the new notification. It had to be important to rise up out of the morass of other messages.

When she saw what it was, everything else ceased to matter. A chat request had come through her most private channel. It was from Libby.

[10]

SEVERAL THOUGHTS COLLIDED in Clair's mind at once. But Libby was dead! No, she might not be—not if her pattern had been saved in the same place Zep had come from. Should she mention it to someone? There wasn't time— if she didn't take the request now it might go away and never come back!

She opened the chat and peered into a new window that opened in her infield.

There was Libby, seen through someone's lenses, looking exactly as Clair remembered, skinny and vibrant in sweatpants and halter, birthmark and all, standing on a bed and singing something—a jitter-punk song that had been big a few months back, "Pinch Me" by the Ponies. Seeing Libby again was like a physical shock to her entire system: not jealous Libby or Libby the dupe, but Libby, her best friend, who was generous with rice broth when needed, constantly late, and compulsively fashionable, and whose favorite aromatic oil was vanilla. Clair could smell that perfume now, as though Libby were in the room with her. It made the muscles around her eyes tighten as though she might cry. Her mouth opened, but no sound came out of it.

Libby was dancing with great enthusiasm to her own singing, mocking the lead Pony's distinctive hip roll, while in the background someone laughed hugely and without restraint. Clair knew that laugh. It was Zep. When he came into view to sing the chorus, Clair's pulse knocked hard in her throat. His voice was terrible, which only made it funnier, and sadder, and more heartbreaking.

A second laugh joined in. It was Clair's own.

And suddenly she remembered this moment, from before everything had gone wrong. It had been after school a month ago, while they were supposed to be studying. The room was Libby's bedroom, and the recording had been taken from Clair's augs. She didn't remember saving it, but she must have. She didn't remember that shirt Zep was wearing either.

The recording must have been lifted from her profile by the dupe.

But why send it to Clair now? Why use Libby's profile to do it?

Clair considered closing the chat, but she couldn't tear her eyes away. Those had been happier times in every way, hanging out at each other's places or jumping all over the world, watching as Zep competed in various contests, crashing Libby's cliques, strolling through Clair's favorite art galleries and making fun of the old-fashioned hair-styles. Clair had gotten along well with both Libby and Zep, and the trio had become duos at various times without jealousy or competitiveness, at least until the whole having-a-crush-on-Zep problem had surfaced. The reason it had taken her by surprise was precisely because of how content they had been. It was like a bomb had fallen out of a clear sky and blown her happy world to smithereens.

She wondered if she was kidding herself. Perhaps even then the cracks had been forming, too slowly and too subtly for her to notice but there nonetheless. People didn't contemplate cheating with their best friend's boyfriend if the friendship was healthy.

Or was that too harsh a way of looking at it? Being attracted to people was normal. Handling it badly, that was the problem.

Whichever way she looked at it, she felt awful.

In the recording, Zep and Libby finished their duet with a theatrical *ta-da!* and collapsed laughing onto the bed. The Clair taking the recording looked away, and caught sight of herself in Libby's bedroom mirror. She wasn't smiling. Staring at her reflection, she took one step closer to the mirror, then another.

Clair couldn't take her eyes away from this image of herself. There was something off about it. Her hair had been shorter than that back then, she was sure. Her stare was too intense, her isolation from the others too keenly felt. Surely, they would have noticed and said something?

The giggling stopped when she was so close to the mirror that her image filled the entire window.

The Clair in the recording turned around. Her friends were standing right behind her.

"You know what we want," said Zep.

"Don't wait too long," said Libby.

The recording flipped to black, and she gaped in shock at the void where her friends had been.

"Clair? Clair?"

Someone was calling her. She shook her head and the drone interface came back into focus. The voice belonged to PK Beck.

"Yes, what?" There was a tremor in her voice, and no wonder. One of her private memories had just been turned against her, leaving her shaken and upset.

"I asked you to take control of 462441A and check out that arm. Can you do that?"

"Yes, yes," she said, even as she wondered why the dupes had come after her this way. Would they really have gone to the trouble of staging a reenactment? It could have been the original recording, edited.

But there was Zep's shirt. Why would they edit that too?

"Clair, are you all right?

She forced herself to concentrate. There were dupes in Crystal City, alive and dangerous and looking for her. That trumped dupes somewhere else, messing with her head. Both might be different prongs of the same attack, but she couldn't deal with everything at once. And she couldn't curl into a ball, no matter how much she wanted to. She owed it to the real Zep and Libby to keep going.

"I'm here—462441A, got it."

Her drone was flying a close circle over Oswald Park, every sensor pointing straight down, rotating so lasers only blinded half at a time. She brought it out of its holding pattern and into a broad loop that would take it over the stand of bushes. Devin was wrong and Jesse was right. This was much more than a game.

As the drone passed over the bushes, something moved. The drone dipped to zoom in more closely. The leaves parted, giving Clair a brief glimpse of a face. It was one of the members of WHOLE she had met on the Skylifter, which meant that it was a dupe. Before she could say anything, there was a piercing flash of light and heat. The drone twisted away too late. It died with a sharp, cracking sound. Clair felt a secondhand shock as she was wrenched out of its feed and thrust back into her body. She clutched the armrests of her chair for balance.

"I'd say *that* was something," Devin conceded.

"Okay, we have an active engagement." PK Beck's voice took on a sharper edge. Clair saw new tags joining their corner of the network. "One asset down. Location Oswald North-East. Moving new eyes into position."

Clair sought another drone and found it already

controlled by Jesse. He was bringing it fast between the buildings, sparing no battery life. As the park came into view, she saw two figures detach themselves from the bushes and run across the open grass, heading for the trees. They were hard to see—green textures rippled across active camouflage suits that covered them from head to toe—but infrared made them out clearly. One of them was a child.

Clair thought of Cashile, the young boy she had met the night Zep died in Manteca. Cashile had been with his mother, Theo, in the camouflaged vehicle that had swept Clair away from the dupes. He had talked to her, distracted her from her loss. Then the dupes had caught both him and Theo, and Clair was sure now that it was Theo's face she had seen through the leaves a moment ago. Her mouth went dry.

"We have targets," said PK Beck without hesitation. "Returning fire."

"Wait," she said. "Shouldn't we try to talk to them?"

"Let's give them an incentive first."

Gunfire stitched the earth in a curved line closing in on the running dupes.

The small one fell.

Clair flinched. Jesse took the drone upward a split second before she could, instinctively recoiling from the violence. As they gained altitude, several camouflaged figures broke from cover on the other side of Oswald

Park and strafed their drone and the others converging on the scene. One drone went down, spinning wildly and shooting sparks, but Jesse's escaped unscathed thanks to giddy-making swoops he made as it ascended. The sound of popping guns grew fainter.

An altitude alarm sounded. They had hit some kind of airspace restriction, a jurisdiction relic, she assumed, since there weren't any planes anymore. Jesse took the drone in a circle, scoping out the fringes of the park, looking for more dupes and providing valuable intel for the gun emplacements.

The PKs returned fire. This time Clair saw where it came from: an emplacement on a nearby building. Another dupe went down, then another. She wanted to look away, but she had to face it if she could. She was part of this. This was what it meant to fight the dupes the PK way.

The remaining dupes kept firing, now at the PK emplacements. More lasers flashed from a different location in Crystal City. PK Beck called for more reinforcements.

"How many of them are there, do you think?" asked Jesse over the interface.

Her chest felt hollow. "I don't know. Maybe no one knows."

"How many do we have to kill before they stop coming for you?"

Clair took another deep breath. She seemed to be having trouble getting air, as though she were with the drone in rarefied atmosphere, rather than in the barracks.

"They'll stop if I give them Q," she said aloud. "They just sent me a message telling me that."

In the real world, Jesse turned in his seat to look at her. His hair, now mostly dry, flopped back in front of his eyes. "Seriously?"

"How?" asked Forest. "What exactly did they say?"

She explained the gist of the message.

"Did you save the video?" asked Sargent.

"No," she said. "I was so surprised, and then all this started. . . ."

Drones and dupes were still duking it out in Oswald Park.

"So they want Q too," said Devin. "Not surprising, given Wallace and everything. But it's interesting that they're using psychological warfare on top of the terror tactics we've already seen. Maybe we're underestimating them."

"Are you going to do as they ask?" asked Sargent, leaning over Clair's couch like a watchful giant, not smiling now.

"I *can't*," said Clair. "I have no idea where Q is, and if I did I wouldn't give her to *them*. I didn't last time. Why would I now?"

"What I don't understand," said Jesse, "is why your dupe tried to kill you before. When she blew up, I mean. Why do that if they want you to tell them where Q is?"

"Maybe they changed their minds," said Devin. "They're

leaderless, making this up as they go along. Wallace did try to kill Clair before he realized about Q. Maybe some of the dupes didn't get the new orders and are stuck in their old missions."

Clair nodded. That made sense to her, although it wouldn't make the dupes any easier to stop if there were now two batches of them. What if their goals differed on more fronts than just her?

"Keep that channel open," said Forest, his expression one of studied severity. "Record anything else that arrives. If you allow us, we will try to trace the source."

"Okay." She was sure that Q could have done it in a flash.

"One of our techs will send through a permission request."

"Meanwhile," said Devin, "round one goes to Clair's Bears."

Clair only noticed then that the siren had fallen silent. She turned her attention back to the PK interface. The grounds below Jesse's drone were littered with corpses.

"We tried to capture one," said PK Beck. "He took himself out before we could get anywhere near him."

Clair's eyes were drawn to the small body splayed out far below the drone. Her gut knotted. She forced herself to look somewhere else. It didn't seem as though the PKs had tried very hard to capture a dupe, but she knew firsthand the lengths the dupes would go to rather than be interrogated. Mallory had shot herself in the head, her own dupe had exploded . . .

She turned the drone's sensors to the horizon and rotated it in a slow circle, reminding herself of what was good and right in the world. The dupes in Crystal City were gone, so now she could focus on Q. The sky was blue. The beltways where roads had once been were green. Washington's monuments and memorials, much grander than she had made out to Jesse, had been perfectly preserved from the seas and stood in marble defiance against the elements. The Great Alexandria Barrage—

If she'd looked an instant later she would've missed it. Light flashed on the top of the distant wall, and at first she thought it was another laser. But the drone's vision was unimpaired. A string of rippling flashes stretched silently from the center of the barrage outward in both directions, throwing up clouds of what looked like smoke into the air. Fireworks? On a day like this? Clair knew that couldn't be the case, but her mind resisted the alternative.

With a grace that spoke of scale and distance combined, the barrage burst in the middle and began to peel apart, setting free the ocean's pent-up deluge. Foamy white water spilled over the crumbling wall, still in perfect silence. The catastrophe was so far away that the sound had yet to reach her.

"Oh crap," she said through the interface and aloud at

the same time. "I think we're in trouble."

There was silence for a second as the sight sank in. Then a new siren began to wail.

"We have to get to higher ground," said Jesse, sitting upright in his couch and pulling back his hood-HUD in one swift movement.

"No arguments here," said Devin, practically leaping to his feet. His expression was shocked.

Monuments, thought Clair. Kids on excursions. The hairs stood up on the back of her arms.

When the sound hit, it was a deep-throated thunder that didn't end.

"I'm checking the Net One cages," said Sargent. "It's going to be close."

"How close?" asked Clair, itching to flee from what was bearing down on them. Every cell in her body was screaming at her to run.

"We will need to move quickly," said Forest, his lenses dancing with data. An understatement, Clair assumed, since he wasn't actually answering the question.

One by one, they hurried ahead of him out of the telepresence room.

"Five minutes before the water hits," Devin finally said, jogging alongside Clair, "depending on the lay of the land. The top of the building might be safer in the short term."

"We'll be sitting ducks up there," said Clair.

"That could be why the dupes did this, to flush us out,"

said Sargent, urging them rapidly through the corridors. Her stride was so long it was hard to keep up. Jesse, who was almost as tall, took Clair's hand and hurried her along. Devin fell behind.

Clair said, "I saw explosions just before the barrage collapsed, right after their attack failed. It was like they were waiting for me to look."

"You think this could be specifically directed at you?" Sargent said.

"I guess," she said, hoping that somewhere nearby evacuation plans were being put into rapid effect, not just for them but for everyone else in the flood's path.

"How does anyone know we're here at all?" asked Jesse. "That's the thing that gets me."

"The shadow road obviously isn't as secure as you thought." Devin glanced at Forest as though for a reaction, then added, "Or you've got a leak. A spy."

"He won't give anything away." Clair bumped him, making several typos as she ran and not bothering to correct them. "His face doesn't work."

"His *fate* . . . ? Oh, face, right. Damn. I wondered why I wasn't getting anything off him. Do you think Sarge could run any faster?"

Devin wasn't much taller than Clair, and he didn't have the benefit of someone to pull him along. The only person slower than him was Forest himself, who ran like a man long used to d-mat.

They rounded a corner and arrived at the cage they had

taken to the barracks. There a tech was abandoning her work on the peeled-back silver floor.

"No good," she said, downing tools and looking worriedly at the arrivals. "One and Three are still cycling. They'll be at least six minutes."

"The water will be here in four," said Devin.

"We're going to have to find another way out," said Clair.

"Thank you, Captain Obvious, but there isn't one."

"I say we go up top anyway," said Jesse. "Maybe we can hold them off long enough for rescue to arrive."

"What kind of rescue are you expecting, exactly?" asked Devin with naked scorn. "Emergency services normally use d-mat. The big rigs they use to get people off buildings come in pieces or through industrial booths. Unless there's something nearby, we're stuck indefinitely."

"You're the one who suggested going up to the roof," snapped Jesse.

"Yes, but that idea was shot down, as surely as we would be."

"Well, I'd rather be shot than drowned."

"Take it easy, you two," said Sargent. That did the opposite of calming anyone.

"There must be another way," said the tech, kicking helplessly at the ruined floor.

"It seems insane," said Clair in frustration, "to be stuck in a building full of d-mat booths and we can't go anywhere."

Devin snapped his fingers.

"That's it," he said. His lenses flashed. "Yes, being an observer sucks if it means you die. Three minutes left. We might just make it. Best to be on the safe side and start heading upward. Now. Quickly, quickly. Up we go."

He ushered them back along the hallway, to the nearest stairwell, where they began a hurried ascent.

"The roof after all?" said Jesse.

"No, but don't ask me to explain. I don't want to get your hopes up. Besides, you won't like it." Devin hauled himself around another flight of steps. "Is there any particular reason you people don't use elevators?" He wheezed.

"Most people d-mat in and out," said Forest, red-faced. "Official policy is we need the exercise."

"Yeah, yeah," Devin panted. "The same as everyone else."

———————————————————— [||]

CLAIR GLANCED AT the drone interface as she ran. Water was foaming along the path of the Potomac, bursting its banks and spreading through the suburbs of Washington with frightening speed, demolishing everything in its path. Already it was halfway to the barracks. She didn't want to think about the possibility that once again she had brought death to people simply by existing.

She switched off the feed from outside the barracks.

That was cowardly, she knew, but she was more afraid of being paralyzed than of what she would see. She would face that reality later, if there *was* a later.

"Two minutes," said Devin as they reached the end of that particular stairwell. "Left here."

"But the roof is this way," said Forest, pointing to the right.

"We're not going to the roof. Along here, right to the end."

Clair checked the map. There was nothing on the top floor in that wing but executive offices, and above them only an air-conditioning unit. They would have magnificent views of the flood as it rose up to engulf them, but what good would that do anyone?

From the next level came a clattering of footsteps. Forest and Sargent produced pistols from inside their armored uniforms and pointed them up the stairwell.

"Identify yourself!" called Forest. Clair tugged Jesse behind her and took cover farther along the corridor.

The PKs suddenly relaxed their stances. PK Drader stepped into view, closely followed by a young woman in an orange prison jumpsuit: Tilly Kozlova.

No, Xia, Clair told herself firmly. There was no Tilly Kozlova left.

"Hail, fellows, well met," said PK Drader, looking surprised to see them. There was fresh blood on his armor. "Going up?"

"No!" said Devin, fairly bouncing from foot to foot in

his desire to keep moving.

"Good. Too dangerous. Lost two prisoners to snipers before we could get back down the stairs."

"They're shooting their own?" asked Sargent.

"Getting rid of the evidence, I guess. I would in their shoes."

Xia burst into tears and backed away from Drader. He gripped her tightly by the arm and pulled her back in, which only made her wail all the louder.

Clair bit back a reprimand. Being scared was natural, but panicking wasn't going to save anyone.

"Come *on*," said Devin. "We're running out of time."

"We are right behind you," said Forest. To PK Drader he added, "Come with us."

"Here's hoping we'll all fit," Clair heard Devin mutter as they ran up the hallway.

Then she knew. She didn't know how it was possible, but she understood what he was hoping to do.

"I need to open this door," Devin said to Forest when they reached the last executive office on the right. "Now, please."

It slid smoothly open, revealing a corner suite. The view was one of autumn treescapes and devastation. The flood had reached Crystal City, carrying with it a foam of mangled debris. Clair could feel its passage as a vibration through her feet. She imagined water smashing through windows and pouring into the lower floors of the buildings around her, including the one she was in. To the south loomed a much higher surge, one that looked like it would sweep the entire barracks away.

In a matter of minutes, Crystal City would be an island in the middle of a much wider river, if it survived.

Within the office was a desk and two couches, a fabber, and a second door.

The door led to a d-mat booth.

"Okay," Devin said, leaning on the corner of the desk to catch his breath. "Here's what's going to happen . . ."

"Your friends in RADICAL are going to take over that booth somehow and get us out of here that way," said Clair.

"Exactly. And thanks for stealing my thunder, by the way." He looked genuinely peeved, which gave her some small satisfaction under the circumstances. He deserved it for needling her. "But yes, that's essentially what I had in mind. The VIA network is still in place, after all. The booths are still receiving power from orbit, and the capacity is there to carry data. It's just not operating. So why not *make* it operate?"

"You make it sound easy," said the tech. "There are multiple firewalls, and no operating oversight—"

"I know, but you wouldn't believe the resources RADICAL has at its disposal. If the best hackers on the planet can't hijack one little booth, they should hang up their hats and go home."

"Will it be safe without the AIs?" said PK Drader. "Only . . . isn't that why we had them?"

"Sure, but there's only a few of us, and the system is empty right now. Most important, it'll be safe from the dupes, too, since they won't be expecting anything like this."

"I don't like it," said Jesse.

The building shook beneath them as the next wave of water struck.

"I told you you wouldn't," said Devin. "Got an alternative?"

"Swim?" Jesse said.

"No," said Clair, taking Jesse's hand and squeezing it. "There are no alternatives."

He swallowed but didn't say anything. She hoped that meant the matter was resolved.

"Right, then," said Devin. "Give me a second."

Devin's gaze turned inward, and he drifted into a corner to do whatever he was doing over the Air. His eyes moved, following information sparkling across his lenses.

The booth door slid open. Clair peered inside. The mirrored interior was small, as befit a private executive suite, large enough for two or three people. It didn't seem possible that they would all squeeze in there.

"Can you activate another one?" Sargent asked. Her businesslike facade cracked for a moment, revealing something that might have been anxiety, and with good reason. She was as big as Clair and Forest combined. She would be taking up more than her fair share of space.

"Maybe," Devin said, glancing at her. "But my pals in RADICAL have been working on this particular line since we left the cage downstairs. It'll take them a while to hack into another."

"We don't have a while," Clair said.

The building shook again. The roar of water was echoing up the stairwells now, not just from the outside. The air was getting colder.

Xia looked anxiously at PK Drader, then the others.

"I could stay behind," she said.

"That *would* give us more space," said Drader, earning a sharp glance from Forest.

"She would drown."

"I don't mind," Xia said. "I've had more time than I deserved, I know—"

"No. You are too valuable to this investigation."

"And she's a person, too," said Clair. She couldn't believe she was sticking up for a murderer. "She's coming with us even if we have to squeeze in there like sardines."

"What if she blows up?" asked Jesse. "The last dupe did."

"We know she won't because she didn't before," said Devin. "Right?"

Clair nodded. She hoped that was correct. Xia was designed to be a permanent dupe, not a temporary swap to be erased if discovered.

Sargent, watching her, nodded too.

"So . . . is anyone claustrophobic?" asked PK Drader, performing a nervous warm-up.

"Not for long," said Devin. "Who's getting in first?"

Sargent stepped through the sliding door and into the corner.

"You next," Clair said to Xia so the woman wouldn't try to escape.

PK Drader went in after her, then Devin, then the tech. It was already a squeeze before Forest wormed himself into the middle. Jesse, the second tallest after Sargent, and the skinniest overall, went to slide into one of the front corners, but the fit was too tight.

"Don't be afraid to push," said Devin. "We really have to go now."

Clair could hear water gurgling in the hallway outside. She shut the office door in the vain hope that it would slow the flood down.

Jesse balked.

"I can't," he said, taking one step back from the booth. "I don't want to."

"You have to," Clair said. "Don't argue."

"But it isn't fair!"

"So what? Get in or you'll die!"

She pushed him angrily inside, using all her body weight against his. It was an uneven contest, and he fought her for an instant, trying to wriggle out of her grasp. She wouldn't let him. No way was she leaving him to drown or be shot by dupes, not when something as simple as going through a booth could save him.

Finally, he tucked his arms into his sides and closed his eyes in resignation. Clair pushed harder. Various groans ensued as the others did their best to make space for him. Sargent raised her arms above her, and Xia squeezed her head into one of PK Drader's armpits. He put his arm around her and pulled her even closer, until she complained about being unable to breathe.

Digging her feet in as firmly as she could on the soggy carpet, Clair used all her weight to get Jesse in. And then he *was* in, and Devin laughed and said in a muffled voice, "Cozy, isn't it?"

It was Clair's turn.

She bit her lip. Water had entered the room and was rising rapidly up her ankles. She splashed back a step, ignoring the creep of cold water up her calves, and rubbed her hands together. The booth was full. There was no doubt about that. No one else was getting in there, and as the water reached her knees Clair knew she didn't have time to wait for the booth to cycle through.

"Is this water a problem?" she said.

"Not unless the shield is breached," the tech said. "We'll be okay."

You have to go without me, Clair wanted to say, but she knew Jesse wasn't going to stand for that, and she couldn't let both of them drown. There had to be another way.

Looking at the mass of arms and legs and bodies squished together, though, she simply couldn't see it.

"Clair?" said Sargent. "What are you going to do?"

Water was up to her thighs. She went up on tiptoe, feeling light on her feet.

And then she knew. There was space in the booth, if she just looked at it a different way.

"Jesse, hold out your hands. You're going to have to take my weight. Everyone else . . . get ready."

He did as she told him, bracing himself against the side of the booth and the people behind him.

She stepped one foot into his hands, pressed down, and lifted herself up out of the water. Placing her hand on his shoulder, she launched herself over everyone else's heads, into the booth, and brought her dripping legs in after her. People shifted, taking her weight as best they could. She tried her hardest not to kick, hoping she wasn't elbowing anyone in the face. There were more groans. She ignored them.

"Right," said Devin. "Let's do this."

The door hissed shut, stopping and starting twice so people could pull errant limbs inside.

Clair's face was pressed uncomfortably against the mirrored wall at the back of the cage. All she could see was her own reflection. But at least she was out of the water. A fleeting thought of how awful it would be to drown inside the booth came and went. She closed her eyes tightly and hoped the doors held.

"Are you sure it's going to scan us correctly?" asked Jesse. "We're not going to end up all mixed up together or anything?"

She could hear the same edge of panic in his voice that she was holding barely at bay.

"No chance," said Devin. "Hold on. Just powering up the necessaries."

What a Neanderthal, whispered a voice in Clair's ear. *Like that kind of thing ever happens anymore.*

He's got a right to be worried, T. His mother died in one of these things. I'm just amazed no one's mentioned the possibility of electrocution yet. I don't want to think about the current that'll be running through this thing when it switches on.

You heard what the tech said. It'll be fine.

You're not the one in a glass coffin that may or may not be leaking.

Stop being so wet.

Very funny, T.

Clam it now. I'm concentrating.

Clair hadn't noticed the absence of the whispering until it returned. It was faint but undeniably present, and clearer than it ever had been before, although it was hard to make out anything specific about the voices involved. It sounded like a conversation, but the speakers were so similar as to be identical.

Could it be two dupes? It sounded like one of them was inside the booth. Perhaps Xia was less wretched than she pretended to be.

Here we go, said the whisper, *in five . . . four . . .*

Something important occurred to Clair then.

"Where *are* we going?" she asked.

. . . three . . .

"Somewhere safe," said Devin.

. . . two . . .

"I've heard that before."

. . . one . . .

"Not from us."

Blinding light flared from the corner close to her face, dazzling Clair even through her eyelids. She drew in a sharp breath and felt everyone else in the booth do the same.

—————————————————— [12]

THE RHYTHM WAS the same as ordinary d-mat, but the sound was different.

phhhhhh-click

Suddenly Clair was dropping. Not through empty air— she was still on top of everyone else in the booth, but *they* were moving. The walls around them had vanished, and they were falling apart like bowling pins. Clair came down in the midst of them, unable to find anything reliable to hang on to.

There was a loud splash.

Clair landed on Sargent's knees, the tech's outflung arm, and Xia's head. Her elbow twanged under her, and she rolled over, seeking solid ground and finding it, finally, on her back, staring up at a featureless white ceiling. Around her, everyone else recovered their own way, gratefully spreading out across the damp surface beneath them, making guttural noises of discomfort and relief as they went. Whatever booth they had jumped into, it was considerably bigger than the one they had just left.

"You're totally insane," Clair heard Jesse say. "You brought us *here*?"

Clair lifted her head, took in the desk and chairs, the double doors, the arched entranceway, and the shutters on the windows. She breathed in and smelled it all coming back to her—the fear, the desperation, the despair.

Wallace's office in VIA HQ.

"We can't stay here." She was shocked by the shrillness of her voice. She backed up against a wall, away from where Mallory had pressed her to the ground with a boot, where Zep had been shot again, where Wallace had threatened to destroy her life and the lives of everyone she loved. Where she had made the decision to kill herself to save the world. There was no visible blood on the damp carpet or walls. It had all been cleaned away when the contents of the room-shaped booth had reset. But she knew.

"Last place they'd expect," Devin said, standing up and brushing himself down. The hood of his armor had activated during the fall and took a moment to retract. "Wallace's private network was broken when the station went up. The PKs annexed it, leaving it open to hacking, but the Faraday shield sealing off this room from electromagnetic radiation is still intact. It seemed a suitable middle ground before we decide where to go next."

Clair wondered what the whispers in her ears would have to say about that, but they had ceased. And she had bigger things to worry about, like trying to think straight when every reflex was telling her to run around in circles, throw up, or scream.

"Are you all right?" Jesse squatted next to her and put one hand on her shoulder.

She shook her head. "Are you?"

"I will be when we get out of here."

"I don't get it," said the tech. "Where are we?"

Drader explained. Clair leaned into Jesse and he ran his fingers up her neck and into her hair. That felt good. She closed her eyes, wishing the images she saw behind her eyelids weren't of death and destruction all the time.

"This is where it started."

Clair opened her eyes. Xia was standing in front of her and Jesse, looking at them with wide eyes. "This is where he told me what he could do. And this is where I came back . . . *after.*"

Xia wrapped her arms around herself, clutching her waist with the slender fingers that had performed such beautiful music. Clair shuddered. She would never be able to listen to Poulenc's double piano concerto again, or Satie's "Je te veux," one of the most joyful pieces of music ever written. It was all ruined.

"I was afraid of what it would be like—living a lie, losing everyone I ever loved, being . . . what I am now." Xia looked down at her body, and Clair was surprised to see loathing in her eyes. "This is not my body. It's stolen. It's *wrong* . . . but the temptation was too great. It wasn't anything to do with the music, although I tried to convince myself it was. I was simply afraid that dying would hurt. I was a coward." She was weeping now, slow, silent tears that had none of the hysteria she had displayed earlier. Why she felt the need to confess, Clair didn't know. Maybe because of Libby.

"I feel her inside me, you know," Xia said.

"Who?" asked Clair, sudden hope blooming. "Tilly?"

Xia nodded. "No thoughts or feelings . . . just the shape of her, the negative space where she used to be. It's like an echo I can only hear when I'm startled or distracted. Of all the things he did, that's the worst. I'm constantly reminded of what he did to her. If I could bring her back, I would. That's why I turned myself in. I hoped someone would know how to do that. But without *him* . . . if he's dead . . ."

There was such wretchedness in her expression that Clair almost felt sorry for her. Not as sorry as she did for Tilly, though. Or Libby.

"Are you sure you killed him?" Xia asked her, a faint flicker of hope visible in her eyes.

She understood now that *this* was why Xia was talking to her. Not to unburden herself, or to explain, but to confront the very possibility that Clair had been trying her utmost to ignore.

Are you sure you killed him?

"I mean, he could be behind all this," Xia went on. "The dupes, the barrage . . . He could have made a copy of himself and stored it somewhere, a backup."

"He could've done it in his sleep," said Jesse, staring at the spot where his father had appeared briefly.

A black pit seemed to open in Clair's chest.

"Are you telling me it was all for nothing?" she said, her voice raw. "Everything I did?"

"Don't say that," said Sargent. Clair hadn't realized she was listening. "You exposed Wallace for what he was. You stopped Improvement. You discovered Q. That's all something."

The PK's expression was earnest. Clair wondered if she was thinking about reactivation, too.

"Maybe it is," Clair said, fighting an urge to weep. "I

don't know. But the dupes just won't stop. And now it looks like Wallace is still alive. What can we do about any of that?"

Forest and PK Drader had been silent until then, perhaps communicating via their suits' private networks. Her question interrupted the PKs' private conversation.

"We are doing everything in our power," Forest said, "to find the source of the dupes."

"That's just dandy," said Devin, "but is it enough? You're stretched too thin. Without ready access to d-mat, and faced with an enemy who uses your own technology to its full potential, you're practically helpless. What's your plan if your best effort fails? Who's going to save the day if you can't?"

"Are you going to suggest RADICAL?" said Sargent.

"Well, we've already saved you once," he said.

"If you'd all just listened to *us*," said Jesse, "we wouldn't be in this mess at all."

"I suppose that's true," said Devin. "And I really would rather be starving to death in a sewer, if we had never used d-mat to stop the Water Wars."

"Easy, you two," said Forest. "What did you have in mind, Devin?"

He shrugged. "Nothing, really. I have no idea where the dupes are coming from or where Wallace might be hiding, assuming he actually is still alive. But I know who would."

Clair groaned. "I keep telling you. *I don't know where Q is!*"

"You can help us draw her out."

"So you can use her and then erase her? I don't think so."

"Who said anything about erasing her? We just want to make sure she's safe."

"On your terms," she said. "Does she get a say in what those are?"

"You're looking at this situation all wrong, Clair. It's not about making new friends. It's survival of the fittest. She's an entirely new kind of being, as alien to us as bird flu virus or a god. If it comes down to her against us, who are you really going to choose?"

"Q isn't like that."

"I'll never know unless you show me."

"Let's just get out of here," said Jesse. "We can argue later."

"Agreed," said the tech. "If the dupes are tracing our jumps, they could be here soon."

"We should look outside before deciding anything," said Sargent. "I don't want to walk out into anything dangerous."

"If we open the Faraday shield, they'll definitely know where we are," said Clair.

"So will we, in a strategic sense," said Forest. "I too think it would be wise."

There was a moment's silence as everyone looked at

everyone else. The only person who hadn't offered an opinion was Xia, who had wandered away to sit listlessly in one of the chairs. She had nothing to gain either way, Clair supposed, with another guilty twinge of sympathy. If she stayed with the PKs, she would go to jail. If the dupes got her, there was no guarantee they would let her live. They had killed the other Improved in Crystal City, after all.

Clair had bigger problems, she told herself. And no one was making a decision, which made her blood boil. She didn't want to be cooped up in Wallace's cage any longer than she had to be.

"Just open it," she told Devin. "At the first sign of trouble, we close up again and jump out of here, if we can."

"We can. And you won't have to tell me twice."

Something clunked in the walls. The shutters began to slide up the windows, letting in the golden light of sunset. From above, the devastation wrought by Q on the streets below was even more impressive. There were craters in the plaza and smoke still billowing from a nearby office building. Swathes of the lower, broader section of the VIA building had been stripped of its windows, exposing the metal beams and framework within. It looked like a giant dog had picked the building up and shaken it before dropping it back down again.

The only movement came from drones circling the VIA building, monitoring every approach. Presumably the route up from the flooded subway was also being watched, and Clair took some comfort from the thought that the building wasn't under attack. Yet.

Her lenses reconnected, flooding her infield with a rush of news grabs and bumps. There were images of the devastation in Washington, with estimates of fatalities in the thousands. Speculation on who was to blame was running wild. Some thought it was an accident exacerbated by the absence of structural engineers, thanks to the crash. Others thought it was terrorists, perhaps WHOLE, taking advantage of the situation. No one mentioned the dupes—but they were mentioning Clair Hill.

Her name appeared in a series of short pieces being forwarded widely through the Air. The main source was a gallery called "Clairwatch" that had sprung up in the last few hours. Its mission was simple. "She lied to you and now she's trying to hide from you," said the information page. "We're not going to let her."

Every page contained data relating to Clair's recent movements, activities, and communications, including blurry pictures captured from drones and PK feeds. From the climactic conclusion of her race to New York to the present, everything was covered. There was her removal from the plaza and parts of her interrogation by the PKs, lifted from the public record. There were details of Forest's and Sargent's careers, plus histories of Devin and RADICAL. There was her sudden appearance in Washington and the terrible flooding that had happened there. There was even a page on her current location, appearing within moments of the Faraday shield lifting. *She's back in the Big Apple!* was the caption. *What does she know that we don't?*

"What *do* you know?" Ronnie asked Clair in a terse bump. She must have been watching Clair surf the Air, thanks to her close-friend privileges.

"Nothing," Clair bumped back. "I'm as lost as everyone else is, I swear."

"But you're part of it somehow. You're moving around like no one else can. What's going on? Are the PKs lying to us about d-mat?"

Clair didn't know how much she should say. She could see Ronnie sprawled on her bed, surrounded by empty chocolate bar wrappers she hadn't bothered to recycle. Both her parents had been on the other side of the world when d-mat failed. They were in constant contact with one another through the Air, and there were no fires or other disasters in the area. But still, Ronnie was trapped and alone. She didn't know her neighbors, her best friends were either missing, potential criminals, or currently stuck in a jungle valley picking off giant leeches. The photos Tash was posting to her infield were terrifying.

"Look up something called the shadow road," Clair said. "That'll explain part of it."

"What about Washington?" Ronnie reached for another

chocolate bar. Anxiety eating had always been her great-est weakness. "And that space station? Are you a terrorist now?"

"No. If anyone tells you I am, they're lying through their teeth."

"How can I believe you?"

"I don't know," said Clair. She wanted to say that she was exactly the same person she ever was—even though she was a duplicate of the Clair who had killed herself in this very room—but how to explain that without sound-ing even crazier than people already claimed she was? If she could only go to Ronnie, she was sure she could convince her in person, but she doubted the PKs would let her do something so frivolous, in their eyes. In Clair's, it was of utmost importance. If her friends didn't trust her, why would Q?

"D-mat will start working again soon, you'll see," Clair said, because it had to be true. "Everything will be fine."

"Why should I listen to you? I don't know who you are anymore, Clair."

Clair's eyes filled with unwanted tears.

"I'm doing my best," she said, even though all she seemed to be doing at the moment was struggling to stay alive.

Right on cue Sargent said, "Movement." Clair came out of her lens interfaces to join the others at the window. There didn't seem to be anything else she could do.

[13]

"WHAT?" JESSE ASKED, looking around as though coming out of a daze. "Where?"

Sargent pointed down West Thirty-Third Street. A metal canister skittered along the road and exploded in a puff of thick brown smoke. Through the smoke Clair could make out indistinct figures in flickering urban-camouflage suits, moving fast from cover to cover, but she couldn't see their faces or tell exactly how many of them there were.

"Dupes?" Clair asked, wiping her eyes.

"One assumes so," said Devin, keeping well back from the glass, even though it was undoubtedly bulletproof. Wallace had spared no expense in his inner sanctum.

"Definitely dupes," said Jesse, still looking slightly dumbfounded. "I got a message, too."

"Share it with us," said Forest.

"No," he said with a quick shake of his head. "Just Clair."

"What's wrong?" she asked him. "Show me."

Jesse didn't look at her as his fingertips danced against his leg, tapping out commands via his ancient augs. A moment later, a new window opened in Clair's lenses. It contained a video.

"What you see in the street below is one of two things," said Dylan Linwood's dupe in the video, his left eye filled with bright-red blood from the original pattern. He was shown against a yellow desert backdrop that could have been anywhere. "An escort or a death squad, depending on how long it takes for you to hand her over."

The image cut to another recording, this one taken in low light. Clair recognized Zep's room on the Isle of Shanghai. The camera was pointing at the bed. Audio hadn't been included. The images conveyed everything.

Clair closed the window as quickly as she could and deleted the message from her infield.

"That wasn't me," she said to Jesse, cheeks burning. "I never . . . Honestly, we never. . . . I swear."

He nodded, but still didn't look at her. "It's dupes. I figured. They're just messing with me now, so I've deleted it." To the others he said, "They want us to hand over Clair or they're going to kill us all."

"We're not doing that," said Devin.

"Of course we're not," said Sargent. "But at least they're talking to us before they bring the building down around our ears."

"We should get out of here," said Clair, feeling a flicker of panic. The dupes just wouldn't let up.

"Wait," said Forest. "Reinforcements."

He indicated the window. A squad of peacekeepers was deploying at the base of the building. As a pair of canisters rolled across the plaza, gunfire broke out between the two parties, faintly audible from the ground below.

Clair hoped the PKs showed no mercy. How long until

that video of her and Zep turned up on Clairwatch for the entire world to see?

"That's all well and good," said Devin, "but the dupes are theoretically unlimited in number, while you guys are not."

"More are on their way from New York HQ," said Forest.

"The fact remains. Unless you start duping your officers—"

"That is illegal," said Forest with an irritated frown.

"You could change the law—"

"If we were allowed to do it, they would be too," said PK Drader. "I can't see the lawmakers agreeing to that. LM Kingdon made it very clear in a ruling this morning—"

"Look," said Jesse, pointing at something above street level. "There's another show in town."

On the building opposite the old post office, a trio of masked figures had appeared. They weren't wearing uniforms or armor. They had backpacks, which, when they reached the edge of the roof garden, they took off and opened. Carrying what looked like glass bottles in each hand, the masked figures leaned over the edge, directly above the thick brown cloud created by the dupes.

One by one, they threw the bottles at the points from where gunfire appeared to be issuing. Each bottle exploded on impact, sending tendrils of fiery liquid in all directions.

"Your friends, I assume," said Devin to Jesse.

"No one I know personally," said Jesse. He bumped Clair a statement from WHOLE listing all the people killed by dupes in recent days, followed by a call to arms. These three had responded. "They're local Abstainers."

"How did they get up there so quickly?" she asked.

"They know their way around because they don't use d-mat."

Clair remembered the people who had flocked to see her on her train journey to New York. At the time she had felt sorry for them, but now she saw that their lifestyle actually gave them an advantage during the crash. As Turner Goldsmith had said, they were in every town, everywhere, and they didn't treat their homes like temporary rest stops, with their real lives happening somewhere else entirely.

A bottle bomb exploded in the middle of a clump of dupes, sending bodies flying.

"If a terrorist helps you, PK Forest," said Devin, "are they still terrorists?"

"They're not helping us," said Sargent. "They're helping Jesse."

"And Clair," Jesse said. "She's the girl who killed d-mat."

"I wish people would stop saying that," Clair said.

"I'll go down and tell them now, if you like," said Devin. "Then they can go back to whatever hole they crawled out of and leave us to die in peace."

Clair shot him a sharp look that had no effect whatsoever.

"We can't stay here," she said, just as horrified by what was going on outside the room as what lay within. How long until someone innocent was killed by one of those bombs? "*I* can't stay here."

"We don't have to leave just yet," said Sargent. "We're in no immediate danger."

"Can you watch this? I can't," she said, balling her fists and rubbing them into her eyes. It didn't help: she saw the images just as clearly in her mind. "I don't want anyone else to die because of me."

"It's about more than you," said Devin. "There's an ideological war taking place down there, one that's been brewing for a while . . . but I take your point. You're the flashpoint, the trigger. If you go away, most likely the dupes will too. But go where? That's the question."

"Let's join the guys fighting out there," said Jesse eagerly. "Go underground, travel quiet. They'll know where to hide. They can keep us safe."

"It could work," said PK Drader, scratching his ear.

"We'll be spotted the moment we set foot outside the building," said Sargent, her expression betraying her alarm at the scheme, alarm Clair shared. "If we're cornered, there'll be no way to escape."

"You don't have to come with us," said Jesse. "In fact, the fewer there are, the easier it will be to stay out of sight."

"We cannot allow that," said PK Forest.

"Why not?" Jesse asked. "Are we your prisoners?"

"No, but you are critical to our investigation." *Flick.* "Not to mention vulnerable. It would be irresponsible of me to allow you to leave our care at this time."

"You can't make us stay." Jesse glanced at PK Sargent, the biggest person in the room. "Can you?"

"They're the ones with the guns," said Devin. "That gives them a certain bargaining power."

"Yes, but—"

"He's right, Jesse." Clair put a hand on his arm. Sargent was right too: it was a crazy idea. Besides, she was exhausted. She couldn't remember the last time she'd slept. On the train, perhaps, near Chicago. It felt like a lifetime ago—and was, in a sense, exactly that.

"We can't go back out into the real world," she said. "It's not safe for us *or* for anyone near us. We have to go somewhere else, somewhere the dupes won't find us, somewhere preferably without any people at all. That's the only way we can be sure we've shaken them. . . ."

"How about Antarctica?" asked Devin. "RADICAL conducts some pretty extreme research, and we don't like prying eyes. Valkyrie Station is on Dome Fuji, thousands of miles from anyone. You can't get any farther from people without actually leaving the planet . . . which I assume you don't want to do?"

Clair shook her head. She wasn't going back into space for anything. The one and only time she had done so, Wallace had threatened to blow her out an airlock.

"I don't like it," said Jesse. "We'll be completely isolated down there."

"That's the point, isn't it?" said Devin.

Clair waved him silent. "Give us a moment."

She pulled Jesse by the arm into the privacy cubicle, trying with every step to ignore the memories that short walk prompted. Her heart danced a shuffle, uncertain of the tempo.

Jesse pulled away the moment they were alone.

"What are you doing, Clair?" he asked in a tense whisper. "Are you signing up with those guys?"

"No," she said, "but I'm not signing up with WHOLE, either. I'm somewhere in the middle. You understand that, right? We need to get the dupes off our back, and if RADICAL can do that, great. If not, we try our own thing."

Jesse hesitated, then nodded.

"What if I said I was going to stay behind this time?" he asked.

Her heart shuffled again. Would he really leave her over some small difference of opinion? Did she mean that little to him?

"I'd talk you out of it," she bluffed. "Can we just take that for granted?"

He bit his lip and didn't say anything.

"I understand," she said, and she did understand, or at least was trying to. "The first few times you had no say in when you had to use d-mat, and that last one wasn't really your decision either. It was either do it or drown. No contest, from where I was standing."

Clair took his right hand in both of hers.

"This time it's your choice," she said, "and I'm *asking* you to trust me. Nicely. I promise you it'll be okay."

"How can you promise that?"

She reached up on tiptoes and kissed him long enough to make her point. Out of the corner of her eye she caught a reflection of the two of them in the glass: short and tall, both with so much hair. It worked. *That* was the only thing she could promise.

"I guess it's only fair," he said in a resigned tone. "You crossed the country the Abstainer way, so now it's my turn. Besides, the damage has been done. If d-mat does turn you into a zombie, that's what I am now."

Clair hated that word. It reminded her again of his father, who had been unpleasant enough even before being turned into a dupe.

"Does that mean you'll do it?"

He hugged her. "Yes," he said, and she breathed a sigh of relief into his neck. It was all well and good to stick to one's principles—admirable, even, and one of the things she liked about him—but being reasonable would keep them together. And staying together was more important than anything else, short of saving the world.

[14]

BEFORE THE SHUTTERS came down and she was cut off from the Air again, Clair posted a caption. It was a picture of her own face accompanied by the words "Watch this space." She couldn't think of anything cleverer than that, and it was the basic message she wanted to convey. The dupes were telling lies about her, and she didn't know how to stop that at the moment. She could only hope that people wouldn't make up their minds too firmly, too quickly, and that when she, the real Clair Hill, was able to reappear later they would recognize the person she had always been.

But was she really that same person anymore? She didn't know. It wasn't just the things she had seen and done, and the small matter of being a copy—it was the weirdness of seeing herself do things that she definitely hadn't done. Her dupes took liberties with her body that no one should ever be able to; their very existence cast her own sense of self into question. When the rest of the world was so easily confused about who she was, even her closest friends, it was hard not to feel that way herself.

"Ready?" Devin asked when the view of the fighting outside was cut off.

"Actually," said PK Drader, raising a hand, "I'm wondering if some of us should peel off. Me and Xia here, for instance: I really should take her into permanent custody. You can come with us to HQ, if you want," he added for the benefit of the tech. "Cold weather doesn't agree with me."

He winked at Jesse, who didn't respond. Clair assumed the odd, one-sided camaraderie harked back to when Jesse had been in his custody, while Clair had been interrogated. If it was another good cop/bad cop scenario, then it was doomed to fail with Jesse because he had been raised to think that there weren't any good cops at all.

"Very well," said Forest with a nod. "That is what we will do. If you can arrange it, Devin . . . ?"

"Easy," said Devin, pointing at PK Drader, Xia, and the tech. "You three stand to one side. It'll be simpler to split the pattern that way."

Once those words would have sent a shudder of dread through Clair. Altering a pattern was supposed to be dangerous, and it was definitely illegal, but it had happened to her so many times now that she barely thought about it anymore.

PK Drader and the two women stepped to one side. There was no blood on the floor, but Xia was standing exactly where Zep had fallen dead for the second time.

"Au revoir," said PK Drader. "And bon voyage to us all."

Clair took Jesse's hand again and squeezed it tightly. He brought the back of hers up to his lips and kissed it.

mmmmm-click

Then her hand was empty, awkwardly upraised, and she was alone with Devin in a cylindrical space approximately ten yards across, with no visible doors or windows. Contorted reflections of her danced in curved mirrors as she twisted to look behind her.

"What is this?" she asked, alarmed by Jesse's sudden disappearance. "What went wrong?"

"Nothing. You're exactly where I said I'd take you. Look."

The mirrored walls turned transparent, revealing a flat, snowy expanse dotted with a dozen black silos mounted on thick struts that speared down into the ice. The sky above was bright blue, dusted with long streaks of white. Streamers of wind swept back and forth across the fields and drifts of snow. It looked like nowhere on Earth.

She reached instinctively to the Air to orient herself. She had basic access only—no bumps, no chats. Taking neither Devin nor RADICAL at their word, Clair confirmed for herself that she was deep in Queen Maud Land, on the East Antarctica ice sheet, the largest remaining ice sheet on the planet. The temperature outside was forty degrees below zero. She shivered at the thought of it.

"Is this some kind of trick?" she asked, sweeping the Air aside and rounding on Devin. There was no sign of anyone else but the two of them. They were alone at the bottom of the world. If he thought that made her his prisoner . . .

He backed away from her with his hands upraised, as though she were about to attack him. "No trick, honest. I just want to talk to you alone."

"About what? About why I should trust you?"

She proffered the hand that had until seconds ago been holding Jesse's. She could still feel the faint pressure of his lips against her skin.

"This is so not helping," she said.

"Just hear me out, will you?"

"You've got one minute." What she would do at the end of that minute she didn't know, but it was important for him to know that she wasn't a pushover.

"There's another ideological war going on," he said, "and you need to be clear about who's on the winning side."

"I'm not going to join WHOLE," she said. "I thought that was obvious."

"It is, but I'll be honest and say that it'd be easier if you did. WHOLE and its goons are predictable, within certain parameters. You know, I was surprised today, when they came out lobbing bombs at the dupes. They're usually so self-limiting, too busy looking backward to see what lies ahead. Most people are, so don't take offense when I say that you're no different. You're not looking back quite as far, that's all."

"Again," she said, "if you're trying to win me over, great job."

"This isn't about talking you into something you don't want to do, Clair. I'm just trying to put RADICAL in perspective. We may not agree on everything, but we're unquestionably your allies. You just haven't realized that yet. Look in your right hip holster."

"I don't have . . ."

A holster, she was about to say. But she looked down and discovered that she did, one containing a sleek automatic pistol.

"Did the PKs arm you?" he asked. "Of course they didn't. They want you dependent on them. We want you to make up your own mind. We . . ."

He stopped and looked around in puzzlement and alarm. The booth was humming around them like a giant metal beehive.

mmmmm—

"This shouldn't be—"

—click

"—happening. How did you get in here?"

PK Sargent put herself between Devin and Clair.

"I'm a PK," she said. "We're not completely useless. Are you all right, Clair? Has he tried to hurt you?"

"No," she said, surprised but glad to see her. "Where's Jesse?"

Sargent pointed out into the Antarctic at one of the twelve silos. "See that tank there, third along? He and the Inspector are okay, if a little confused as to where you disappeared to."

"What's wrong with wanting to talk in private?" Devin asked, from the side of the tank he'd edged into, away from both Clair and Sargent.

Sargent turned on him again, her expression severe.

"Privacy is a privilege, not a right," she said. "You can earn that privilege now by doing less talking, more communicating."

He exhaled as though the world wearied him. "Fine. You and your Inspector friend are bad influences on Clair. That's what this is about. You encourage the perception that someone's going to wave a magic wand and d-mat will be fixed so everyone can go back to school, work, whatever. Clair needs to know that this is unlikely ever to happen, and that it would be a bad thing if it did."

"I'm right here," she said. She was quite capable of making up her own mind, if people gave her the right information. "What are you talking about?"

"The cat is out of the bag," he said, "and this time I don't mean Q. D-mat is the second most powerful technology on the planet. But unlike AI, unregulated d-mat is unquestionably a *good* thing. The collapse of VIA is not the disaster everyone thinks it is. It's an opportunity."

"Not if you use it for something illegal," said Sargent.

"Like duping?" said Clair.

Devin looked wounded. "Absolutely not. I'm as morally opposed to everything Wallace did and may still be doing as you are. I want him and his army stopped, and soon— before people get the wrong idea about what d-mat is and what it can do for us."

"I come into this . . . where?" asked Clair.

"Isn't that obvious? You have the ear of someone very powerful—if not now, then maybe again in the future. With her in our camp, we'd carry the day for sure."

Clair sighed in frustration. It always came back to this. "You sound pretty confident that you could convince her when you can't even find her."

"I think it's connected. There's no current legal framework in which she's allowed to exist. Only RADICAL offers any chance of providing that framework, so it's in her best interests to talk to us. All she has to do is prove that we can trust her. You'll tell her that, won't you? You won't tell her we definitely want to get rid of her or anything? Because that would be wrong."

"She's way too useful for that. Sure."

"Hey, Sarcasm Queen, you want to use her too—only you want to do it to restore the status quo."

"You say that as though it's a bad thing," said Sargent. "Why?"

Devin smacked his forehead with one hand. "So conservative . . . and so predictable! From you of all people. That's how we got into this mess in the first place. Wallace ran rings around the PKs for years because you never thought anyone in his position would be so audacious. And he knew that. Absolute power, PK Sargent, lies not always in kings and presidents. Don't think we're safe just because we don't have them anymore."

"What do you mean 'from me of all people'?" Sargent asked, a dangerous look in her eyes.

"Billie" was all he said. "You know what I'm talking about."

Clair didn't, and the way Sargent and Devin were glaring at each other suggested that she wasn't going to be told anytime soon.

"Stop arguing," she said. "You've had your say, Devin. I'll think about it. All right?"

Devin's expression didn't change. Clearly he didn't feel like he had had his say at all.

"All right," he said, rubbing his right cheek with slender, well-manicured fingers. "I'll take you to Jesse, if that's what you want."

She nodded. "And leave us alone for a while, both of you."

"Is that okay with you, Sarge?"

The peacekeeper nodded. To Clair she said, "I'm close by if you need help. We'll bump you with any major developments but won't disturb you unless something dramatic happens."

"This far south," Devin said, "you don't even see penguins."

———————————————————————— [15]

THE TANK HUMMED and clicked, and Clair was suddenly in Tank Six, where she found Jesse looking flustered and unhappy. He too had been d-matted to their new location, and he wasn't pleased about it.

"You asked me to trust you," he said, pacing the room, banging the curved wall with his knuckles. It rang like a gong, but the icy view was unchanged. "There's no reason to keep *doing* this. Why can't we just walk?"

"It's cold outside," Clair said, reminded of a creepy old song Oz liked to sing after a couple of drinks, about some guy trying to pressure a girl into staying over because of the weather. It drove her mom crazy.

"So why build down here at all?" Jesse's question was a good one. "What happens if we want something to eat—do we have to go through all that again?"

"I don't know. Maybe." She was beginning to get annoyed herself. "And so what if we do? Isn't it worth it to get Libby back? And your dad?"

"That's never going to happen," he snapped.

"Don't say that."

"You really think the PKs will let us bring them back, even if we find their patterns?"

"If we can prove they're still alive. We saw them in the station, after all—*you* saw them—"

"I'm not testifying to bring them back. They're dead, Clair. Get over it."

She thought of Zep's shattered face. *"Don't say that."*

With a soft sound, a rectangle appeared in the Antarctic plain and a head poked through a door that hadn't been there before. Clair swung around at the intrusion, ready to tell the person who had interrupted them to get the hell out. She and Jesse had never argued before. Like they needed an audience.

The head belonged to a girl of around nine years old, with long, sun-bleached hair in braids. She was wearing white jeans and a pink flowered top. Clair was startled. The last thing she had expected to see in a research station at the South Pole was a child.

"Mom says we're ready for you to come on down now," she said. "Are you hungry?"

Clair stared at her in confusion, unable for a moment to speak.

"No," said Jesse.

"Come down anyway," the girl said. "It's nicer in the garden."

Garden?

The girl retreated through the hatch, which stayed open so they could follow. There was a short metal landing on the other side, with a ladder leading downward, presumably through one of the tank's thick legs into the ice cap.

The girl was already several yards down the ladder. Clair hurried to keep up. Warm yellow light rose up to meet her. The ladder emerged from the roof of a large chamber that had been hacked out of the ice and insulated from the cold. Vines tangled along the rungs of the ladder as Clair passed between spreading tree branches and palm fronds. The air was thick and warm, and smelled of *green*. Sunlight shone from the ceiling, either a convincing replica or piped down from the outside. Somewhere, water was trickling. There were bees.

At the bottom of the ladder Clair stepped onto a thick, mossy mat that had the springiness of soil. The undergrowth was thick and dark, and something mouse-sized rustled to her left, as though reacting to her appearance.

The girl was waiting for her at the bend in a path that led deeper into the underground forest, waving for her to follow. Clair looked up, considered waiting, but decided not to stick around for Jesse. He wasn't far behind. He would find them.

The girl led Clair to a clearing in the heart of the cave, where a woman who looked like an older version of the girl was waiting for them. Same hair, same oval face, same quartz-gray eyes, same smile. Clearly her mother.

"Welcome," said the woman. "My name is Hassannah. Devin asked us to meet you here. We hope you'll be comfortable."

In the center of the clearing was a thick camping rug. Rolled up nearby, two sleeping bags.

"Thanks," said Clair, remembering to be polite. "That's very kind of you. What *is* here, exactly?"

"If you get hungry," said the girl, ignoring her question or just not interested in it, "you can help yourself to anything in here." She waved one arm theatrically, taking in the entire cave. "The fruit and vegetables are all edible, and so are the mushrooms, and most of the leaves, too. There are nuts, but you need to cook them. I can do that for you, if you want."

She looked so eager, Clair didn't have the heart to say no, but Hassannah intervened.

"Not right now, Akili," she said. "Maybe later. Our guests are tired."

"Thanks, Akili," said Jesse from behind Clair. She hadn't heard him arrive. "This is amazing."

He was looking around with a delighted expression, and the girl practically danced on the spot.

"There's a spring over there for drinking," she said, pointing. "You use your hands."

"Facilities past the old oak," said Hassannah helpfully. "We'll leave you to rest now."

"Why?" asked Clair before they could go. "I mean, why is all this here?"

Hassannah smiled. "We believe in making contingency plans."

"Contingent against what?" asked Jesse.

"Humanity almost destroyed the world once. It could easily do so again."

"Do you live here?"

"We take turns tending the gardens," said the girl, shaking her head. "Today is our turn. If you'd come tomorrow, you would've met Sam and Kanathia."

"So this place is a kind of ark?"

"A refuge," said Hassannah. "One of many."

When Clair had first met Devin, he had said something grandiose about protecting the interests of future humans. Maybe he had meant it exactly as it sounded. Maybe there were similar enclaves under each of the twelve silos visible at the surface. Maybe each was a different kind of environment—jungle, plains, desert, farm . . .

Just in case Q goes crazy and kills us all, Clair wanted to say sourly, but she didn't want to scare the girl.

"We'll leave you now," said the woman. "Questions can wait until the morning."

Tugging her daughter by the hand, Hassannah continued along the path and vanished into the foliage. Clair heard Akili say something about Jesse's hair, but any reply was cut off by the sighing of another door.

Clair and Jesse were alone, exactly as she had requested. But it wasn't how she had expected it to be. The argument had merely been paused, not finished. Some questions couldn't wait.

"What about Zep?" he asked abruptly.

"What about him?" His tone was difficult to read, although it was clear that his delight at seeing the garden had been superficial.

"Do you want to bring him back too?"

"Of course I do," she said, wondering why it felt like a confession. "Why wouldn't I?"

"Because he's really dead. You saw what happened to him."

"But it shouldn't have happened, and if we can find that pattern Wallace dug up—"

"This isn't like Libby or Dad, Clair. Zep wasn't duped or Improved. He was shot twice, and you can't bring him back just because you want to."

She folded her arms and glared at him. "You don't get to tell me what I can or can't do, just because we made out a couple of times."

"This isn't about that—"

"Are you sure? It's because of that stupid clip. You're jealous, admit it. You're glad he's out of the picture and you want him to stay that way. That's why you're practically putting a gun to his head and shooting him all over again."

That shocked him, and Clair was shocked in turn by how much that pleased her. A fierce bubble of vindication rose up in her, so hot and powerful she wanted to shout, *Ha!* in his face, just to rub it in.

"Maybe this is too hard," Jesse said. "You and me, right now, on top of everything else."

The hot feeling turned to ash. She instantly regretted what she had said. Her anger wasn't really directed at him, but at PKs like Forest who would stop her saving her friends. Attacking to make a point was what Libby would have done, at her worst. Clair hadn't known she was capable of that.

"Don't," she said. The last thing she wanted to do was scare Jesse away. "You don't mean that. I'm just tired, and I know I was out of line. I'm sorry."

He looked cautiously relieved. "I'm sorry too. And you're right. I am jealous of Zep, always have been. I shouldn't let myself get confused . . . about the wrong things."

Clair wondered if her feelings were completely clear-cut on that front too, when it came to the thought of bringing Zep and Libby back so they could continue their relationship in front of her.

"Let's just eat," she said, too exhausted to talk anymore.

They foraged in the sub-Antarctic garden, reaching up to take fruit from branches and digging through the undergrowth for vegetables and fungus. Clair had never eaten part of a living thing before, and at first it made her feel queasy. Then she realized that whenever she dialed uncooked fruit and vegetables through a fabber, they were undoubtedly this fresh, taken from the tree and put straight into the scanner, so the only difference was that this time she was seeing the rest of the plant.

"Thank you, fruit factory," she said, pulling a peach from a low-hanging branch.

"You're welcome, meat machine," Jesse replied in a pretend voice on behalf of the plants.

It was a weird way of looking at the world. She wasn't sure she liked it, but she could live with it if it meant they both got to eat.

THEY WASHED THEIR hands and faces in the spring, which was clear and cold, probably melted snow from the surface, and took turns with the refreshingly modern "facilities." Then they unfolded their sleeping bags and helped each other from their outer layers of armor. They lay on top of the sleeping bags and peeled up the sleeves and legs of their undersuits to compare bruises. Clair's elbow hardly hurt at all now, so she took off the patch and put it down by her shoes, for recycling later. She felt self-conscious of her body in the undersuit, but Jesse didn't seem embarrassed about his, and she was content to take his lead. He was skinny but not as bony as she had imagined he would be, with long muscles in all the right places. From gardening, she assumed, not sports. Competing with other schools required using d-mat, so he had never been on any of Manteca New Campus's teams.

"You gave me a beauty on the shoulder when we all fell out of that booth," Jesse said, flexing his right arm.

"Sorry. But I'm not giving you a massage."

"Rats." He frowned in mock disappointment. "Worth a try."

Clair liked that he wasn't holding a grudge after their argument. She felt like she could be herself around him, even if that meant occasionally disagreeing. Or maybe they were both less irritable with food in their bellies.

"Where were you?" he asked. "Before, when we arrived."

"Talking to Devin in one of the other tanks," she said. "He can't make up his mind whether Q's good or bad, so he's taking it out on me."

"Really? That's a bit rough. It's not your fault."

Maybe it is, she wanted to say, but didn't. She hadn't told him about her broken promise to Q. She still felt too ashamed of that, on top of the collapse of d-mat and everything.

"PK Sargent shut him down in the end, thank goodness. I'm glad she hacked her way in."

"Is that what happened? One moment Sarge was with us, the next she cycled out. Guess she and Forest drew straws. I think Devin's a bit frightened of her."

"Good," said Clair firmly. "What did you and PK Forest talk about?"

He didn't answer immediately.

"About Zep, actually," he said. "That's why he was on my mind. Because of the, uh, video and who was in it, Forest wanted to know exactly what I'd seen in the station and the safe house. He had me go over it twice—and I'd already told PK Drader twice before."

"Did you talk about anyone else?" she asked, wanting to keep the topic well away from the fake sex tape.

"Dad too, but not so much. He was never really himself

any of the times his dupe died. Forest didn't seem as interested in him."

Building a case, Clair thought. Deciding who was going to be allowed to live and who wasn't. Lawmakers and the Consensus Court would decide, but PK Forest was sure to make his opinion known. Hopefully Sargent was building a case of her own, although she hadn't mentioned it for a while.

Sore shoulder or no sore shoulder, Jesse folded his hands behind his head and closed his eyes.

"How many days has it been," he asked wearily, "since you bumped me to ask about Improvement?"

She checked her lenses. "Five. Bet you wish you hadn't answered."

"Never." He opened an eye. "Does that make me an idiot?"

"Completely and utterly. It's your most attractive quality."

He smiled. "This idiot needs to sleep, unfortunately. But have I told you how fantastic you look in that outfit?"

She blushed and grinned at the same time.

Jesse crawled into the sleeping bag and rolled onto his side with his back to her. The forest's sunlight didn't dim, but that didn't hold him back. Within moments, his breathing was deep and regular.

Clair was too restless to sleep, torn between concern about the outside world, about the future, and feelings for Jesse that were neither simple nor open to exploration at the moment. Perhaps in a real forest, miles away from any cameras and under completely different circumstances . . . Under ordinary circumstances they might have dated like people usually did—but awkwardly, given how much of that kind of thing required d-mat. Clubs and cafes, for instance: were there any nice ones near where he lived? She'd never had reason to find out, despite going to school just around the corner. Likewise, there would be no jumping off to a romantic sunset or show anytime they felt like it; they'd have to check the Air beforehand to get the timing right. Dating a Stainer would kill any kind of spontaneity.

But it wasn't as if her previous dating experiences had amounted to much, up to and including Zep. She had lived vicariously through Libby, not confident enough to pursue anything serious with any of the boys who had asked her out. Now, after Zep, she liked the thought of being still for a change. She wished that everything apart from Jesse would go away for a while, but of course that was a fantasy she couldn't afford to indulge, except in her mind. At least her mom wasn't around to scold her for spending the night alone with a boy.

While she had basic access to the Air, she surfed it for random news grabs and gossip. D-mat still wasn't working, but people weren't taking that lying down. Telepresence services were going through the roof. Ad hoc organizations like those in Windham under the guidance of local peacekeepers and their new deputies were ensuring that essential services didn't stall. There was no sign of the three-meals-to-savagery problem that Sargent was worried about, and Clair supposed there wouldn't be while fabbers still worked.

Ronnie was sound asleep, several more empty wrappers added to the pile at her feet. Her caption showed a child's face covered in chocolate, with the line *Overeating my way to oblivion.* In the last hour, Tash had killed a python with her machete and posted a picture of its headless body. *Didn't expect to do this today,* Tash said in the post. *Guess I have Clair Hill to thank for that.*

Clair didn't read anything else to do with her former life. It hurt too much.

The investigation into VIA was producing more reports and opinions than Clair could possibly read in one sitting. Test transmissions of inanimate objects with complex geometric properties proved that the network had the capacity to function normally, if only it could be trusted with precious human traffic. There were rumors that one of Q's parent AIs, Quiddity, had survived the crash and, if brought back online, could be sufficient to run the network on its own. OneEarth, however, insisted that no one but PKs would use the network until its integrity was completely assured. Claims of elitism were inflamed by deaths that might have been averted had patients been able to get to the hospital the usual way. In the midst of all this, the Abstainer movement—and, Clair assumed, WHOLE, too—was campaigning vigorously, seeking new recruits among those feeling disempowered and frightened by the system's collapse.

Then there was Clairwatch. It was amazing to think that, with everything else going on, there were still people who had time to monitor her activities and the fallout resulting from them. Rumors continued to circulate about Clair's role in the crisis and the accusations that her dupe had retracted. Events in New York and flooded Washington were closely analyzed, with numerous competing theories arising to explain them. Some were completely fantastical; others were canny and insightful. Drone footage from both locations had been used to identify several dupes. That they used to be members of WHOLE only muddied the waters even further.

At least no one knew where she was now. Or, if they did, they weren't talking about it. She was sure that Q would know, if she was still out there, but her inbox contained no replies to the many messages she had sent. Feeling both snubbed and desperate, she tried yet again.

"A lot of people want to talk to you, Q. They all want something from you, or they're afraid of you, or they don't understand you. RADICAL wants me to tell you that they don't *necessarily* want to erase you, which I think they expect you to find totally encouraging! I want you to know that I'm not on anyone's side. I'm just worried about you. Tell me you're okay. Will you at least do that?"

After an hour of waiting for a reply that might never come, Clair dialed down her lenses and got up to walk around. Moving silently through the forest so as not to disturb Jesse, she found and ate a handful of sweet red strawberries and examined with some interest the vein-like irrigation channels threading through the cave. There were several species of bugs making homes in the roots and canopy above. Without birds or wind, it was eerily quiet.

By the door to the facilities, her toe caught on a patch of turf and lifted it up off a harder substrate below. Squatting to pat it back down, she grew still.

The turf was barely an inch thick. Below that was nothing but mirror. The "cave" was another big d-mat booth, which meant the forest might be completely unnatural. She had assumed it was maintained hydroponically, but for all she knew it could have been built from scratch moments before she and Jesse had climbed down into it. Maybe that was what Akili had meant by "tending" the gardens—editing the patterns, not actual weeding. By doing that, the resource could be re-created fresh at any time in the future.

A wave of weariness rolled through her. Too many lies. Tomorrow she would try to pin down RADICAL and the PKs on exactly what they knew about Wallace and the dupes. For now, it was a case of *sleep or die*, as snake-killing Tash used to say. Clair went back to her sleeping bag and curled up inside it, covering her eyes with the soft fabric so the light wouldn't disturb her. The fake forest stirred around her, full of fake life. Jesse probably deserved to know the truth, she thought, but she wasn't going to be the one to tell him.

[17]

CLAIR DREAMED SHE was being drawn deeper and deeper into a vast virtual map much larger than the one of Crystal City. It was a tangle of connections in brilliant colors, almost fractal in its detail. Every time she thought she had reached the end of a particular line, new connections appeared before her, tugging her onward.

"Getting colder," said Q in her little-girl voice.

"Why can't I find you?" Clair asked. She was hopelessly lost, but she kept looking and looking. There was no going back now.

"You never lose at hide-and-seek when you don't have a body."

Clair could have kicked herself. Why hadn't she thought of that before? "No fair! Play by the rules!"

A thunderous boom shook the floor beneath her, and Clair jerked awake in a panic, thinking it was the Great

Alexandria Barrage exploding again . . . no, the space station . . . and then realizing that it was neither. She was in a fake forest deep in the Antarctic ice, and she had no idea what the sound was.

She sat up at the same time as Jesse. His hair was a mess and his eyes were wide.

"Wait—what?" he said, shaking his head as he slowly regained consciousness. "Have they found us?"

"Yes," said Devin. His voice came over an intercom somewhere in the forest rather than via their augs, his tone brisk and urgent. "I don't know how, but I suggest we get moving."

Clair and Jesse crawled out of the sleeping bags and pulled their armor into place, taking hasty turns in the facilities as required. There was no sign as they ascended the ladder of the mother or daughter who had welcomed them. Clair thought about grabbing some fruit on the way, but there wasn't time.

The icy waste outside was now marred by a plume of black smoke rising out of a crater a mile or so to the east. Black lines starred out from the crater, stark against the snow. Two white drones not dissimilar to PK models circled the site, streaming information back to the tanks. What the drones saw appeared in a window to one side, with technical data trickling in red text across it.

"Impact," said Devin, "not explosion. They dropped something from orbit."

"Why?" asked Clair, not hiding her bad mood.

"To show us they could, I guess. The next one could come down right on top of us. *You have been warned*, that kind of thing."

"I haven't had any more messages," said Clair. "Maybe they mean business this time."

"It's possible that the next one is already coming right at us," said Devin. "Depending on the orbit, it could have left hours ago."

"Why not take out the powersat so we're all stuck here freezing to death?" asked Jesse.

"Valkyrie Station has its own power supply," Devin said.

Contingencies, Clair thought.

"I wish they'd make up their mind," she said, kicking the floor with the toe of her boot in frustration. "Are they trying to kill me or not? If Wallace is alive, you'd think the dupes would have sorted themselves out by now."

"I definitely think Wallace is still alive," Jesse said. "And we're dealing with two factions of dupes."

"Interesting, but not very helpful," said Devin, "given that neither is remotely on our side and they both might be working with Wallace. I don't think we can afford to take the chance that at least one of them has decided to wipe us off the board once and for all."

"So where are we going this time?" asked Jesse.

Clair could tell by looking at him that he wasn't stepping

into another d-mat booth without good reason. He had a point.

"I'm sick of running," she said. "It's time we pushed back."

"You have my wholehearted agreement," said Devin. He sounded surprised, but not in a bad way. "RADICAL can help with that, too. We just need a little time to get ready. To gain that time we're going to have to try something really tricky."

"Such as?" Clair wanted to know exactly what the wunderkind from RADICAL considered "really tricky."

"Hang on." The view through the tank walls changed again. Devin appeared in front of the crater, still dressed in his PK light armor, and Forest and Sargent popped into view nearby.

"Here's my thought," Devin said. "Naturally, we have our own private version of the shadow road—"

"Naturally," said Forest.

"Yes, no surprises there. Just like yours, it's stretched way beyond capacity right now and it lacks AI oversight. And just as with Net One, the problem is how to stop someone from finding us when we arrive. This is a scenario we've struggled with, and like good scouts we've figured out a means of working around it. You might not know *this*, Inspector, but our network is designed to keep someone moving constantly and randomly so they can't be tracked or intercepted. The relay stations are small, low power, and can only handle four or five people at a time, total, but they have an advantage in sheer numbers: they're all over the world. We call this network the Maze. Once we're in there, we can stay mobile as long as we want, constantly jumping, while we prepare to push back against the dupes elsewhere. Hopefully they'll be so busy looking for us that they won't notice."

"Push back how?" asked Sargent.

"I'm not sure we should settle on that now. Let's get through this part first, and then discuss the possibilities. As I say, it's going to be tricky. And, Jesse . . . you're really going to hate it. It'll involve dozens of jumps, maybe hundreds. So I think we should split up again." Clair went to protest, but Devin kept talking right over her. "Jesse, you and Forest can either stay here or go directly to the rendezvous point, taking your chances either way. The rendezvous point is a seastead, one we built and run ourselves, stationed in the Arctic Ocean. You should be safe there, since it's Clair they're after, not you. When she comes out of the Maze, we'll all be together again, I promise, and then the fun will really begin."

Clair and Jesse looked at each other. She could tell from his expression that he was torn, and so was she. She was sure he would agree to leave the Antarctic via d-mat—after all, what were the alternatives?—but multiple jumps all over the world . . . she couldn't ask him to do that.

"What happens if you get lost in the Maze?" she asked,

looking for weaknesses in Devin's plan.

"It's not that kind of scenario," said Devin. "Not really. Blame lazy nomenclature. It's more like Whac-A-Mole, but with thousands of holes and only one mole."

"Whac-a-what?" asked Clair.

"An old game," said Jesse. "Not a very good one."

"If Clair goes, I go too," said Sargent.

"Yes, I presumed you'd want to," said Devin. "Does that mean we're decided?"

"I want to know more about the seastead," said Jesse.

"You will when you get there. Can I just remind everyone that time is of the essence? We're keeping an eye out for more falling rocks, but they're small and fast and could be coming from any direction except down. You wouldn't want to be cycling in a booth when one of them hit you."

"All right." Clair turned to Jesse. "Will you be okay with this?"

"There's not much I'm okay with at the moment," he said, making a face. "But if it really does get the dupes off your back for a while, I'm all for it."

Clair likewise didn't see that she had an alternative. No one else had put any other suggestions on the table. She certainly didn't have one.

"All right, I'm in your hands, again," she told Devin. "When do we begin?"

"Now, if you're ready."

"Not quite."

Acutely conscious of everyone watching, Clair stepped close to Jesse and reached up to kiss him. His right hand wrapped around her and touched the small of her back, sending a shiver up her spine. Another promise. To hell with the dupes, she thought, and RADICAL and everyone else who wouldn't let her get on with her life.

They parted. Clair took one last look around and shivered again. A swirl of icy spray was rising up from the crater, white against the cold blue sky. She was glad she wasn't going out into the actual weather.

"All done?" asked Devin. "Good. This'll be soaking up a lot of our bandwidth, so be patient if things go slightly weird along the way. I guarantee it'll all work out okay in the end . . . for most upbeat definitions of 'work out,' 'okay,' and 'end.'"

"O-kay," said Jesse. "Thanks heaps for that."

mmmmm

Clair didn't know what to expect, but she braced herself as the booth hummed around her.

mMMMm

The humming peaked for a second, and then Jesse and Forest were gone. They vanished in midbreath as though they had never existed.

mMMMm

Now Devin and Sargent were standing in the tank with her. Or Clair was standing with them. There had been no sense of movement to a new location, or at least not of arriving. The booth was still working hard around them, analyzing and building, analyzing and building—

Destroying and re-creating, she tried not to think. That was the Stainer line: every time someone went through a booth they were killed and a copy of them emerged somewhere else, identical but soulless. Who was to say that copy was really identical? Who was to say that the Clair in this booth wasn't just a pale shade of a girl who died years earlier, and hadn't realized it yet?

She was to say, she told herself. She knew who she was, and no one had the right to tell her otherwise. She'd never entertained any doubts on that score before meeting Jesse and the dupes.

mMMMm

Suddenly the view was gone. The tank walls had contracted around the three of them without any sense of motion at all. She, Devin, and Sargent were standing in a smaller version of the Valkyrie Station tank, constructed to the same scale but barely higher than Sargent's head. Clair felt a mirrored surface directly at her back, and saw nothing but reflections to infinity.

Nothing, that was, except a single number: *418*, painted in red against the reflections. Her lenses said *Albuquerque.*

mMMMm

The number clicked to *588*, her lenses to *Qarshi.*

They were moving. They were in the Maze.

———————————————

"**SO HOW DOES** this work, exactly?" asked Clair. Her skin tingled and there was a light feeling in her stomach, as though she was falling. Apart from that, there was no sensation at all.

mMMMm

"Promise me you won't freak out," Devin said.

"Uh, no, I can't promise you anything like that."

"All right. Just remember, then: it's something that happens to you anyway, so you've got no reason to be worried."

mMMMm

The number said *274*, her lenses *Port Lincoln*.

"The first d-mat booths needed days to cycle a single lab rat, which obviously wasn't practical," Devin explained. "It took lots of very clever engineers to shave the time down to anything remotely sensible, using a number of very clever shortcuts. One of the algorithms they use is called . . ."

mMMMm

". . . well, what it's called isn't important. What it *does* is get 'you' up and running slightly ahead of the physical version of you."

"I have no idea what that means," Clair said.

"It means you think you've arrived before you actually have. Or, to put it another way . . ."

mMMMm

". . . consciousness lags behind sensory input—like hitting a tennis ball, when your arm starts to move before you consciously tell it to. This is normal. The algorithm we're using right now just takes it further. It models the parts of you that haven't arrived yet, and puts it all together while the data catches up so everything *appears* to function normally."

Clair found this hard to imagine. "I think I'm alive, but I'm not really."

"Not entirely, no. Part of you is simulated. The messiest, most complicated part . . ."

mMMMm

". . . the brain, mainly."

That did freak Clair out a little, the thought that she could be present and not present at the same time, like some weird physics experiment. Ronnie had tried to educate her once about a cat that was both alive and dead, and she was getting a similar tense feeling at the back of her neck trying to swallow this thought too.

"So how does all this relate to the Maze?" asked Sargent.

mMMMm

"In here, everything overlaps," said Devin. "Departure, transmission, arrival . . . all of it. We're not data ghosts or anything weird like that, but we do spend about half our time being simulated in transit rather than as physical beings. If we're not physical, how can someone track us?"

"Or *attack* us." Sargent nodded approvingly.

"Unless they hack us," said Clair. Their conversation was beginning to sound like a sinister Dr. Seuss book.

mMMMm

994 read the number in the mirror. Clair's lenses told her *Surabaya*.

The constant humming and throbbing was making her feel dizzy. Clair couldn't help but wonder how much of her was real at that moment. Or *this* moment, she thought, as the humming peaked again.

mMMMm

It seemed to her that the reflections were shimmering, particularly the ones farthest away, at the very edges of visibility. Or maybe her eyes were blurry from staring too much. Despite the infinities they revealed, the mirrors seemed very close, almost claustrophobically so. The air inside the miniature tank was dry and smelled of static electricity.

"How long do we stay in here?" she asked.

"Until they're ready at the other end," said Devin. "Don't forget, time is passing much faster on the outside."

That was something Clair hadn't considered. Each jump in an ordinary booth seemed to last a second or two, but came at a cost to the traveler of a couple of minutes in the outside world, the time it took the machines to work. How much lag had they accrued so far?

mMMMm

Clair blinked. Devin and Sargent were flickering, and their reflections danced too as though in a heat haze. The booth quivered. Clair put a hand to her forehead, wondering if it was just her.

mMMMm

This time something weird had definitely happened. Sargent's reflections still stretched to infinity, but she herself, the real Sargent, was gone.

Devin had done it again.

"We don't have much time," he said, turning to Clair. "I need to ask you if you trust the others."

"What are you talking about?"

"Someone gave away our location in Crystal City, New York, and Valkyrie Station. It's the only way the dupes could have found us. I trust my people—what about yours?"

mMMMm

Sargent flickered back into view, then out again.

"Quick. We can explain this away as a glitch, but not if it goes on too long. Tell me about Jesse and the PKs. Would they betray you?"

She didn't think about the question at all. Peacekeepers were peacekeepers. They didn't side with dupes. And Jesse betraying her was unimaginable. "Of course not!"

"Just because they're PKs? Just because he's your boyfriend? *Someone did this,* Clair. We have to know who or you'll never be safe."

"It can't be one of them . . . can it?"

mMMMm

Sargent was back, alarmed at first but clearly relieved when she saw Clair.

"Are you all right?"

"Phasing error," said Devin. "Happens sometimes. Hope you guys didn't experience any discomfort."

"I'm okay," said Clair, wondering now if there was indeed a chance that either of the PKs was secretly working for the dupes. Or, more significantly, *was* a dupe. Forest was secretive by nature, thanks to his disability: that either ruled him out or made him a more likely suspect; Clair couldn't decide. And Sargent . . . had she been nice to Clair in New York simply to make Clair less suspicious? The PK had seemed more distant and edgy since then, but perhaps that was to be expected under the circumstances. Babysitting someone being endlessly hunted by dupes might do that to a person.

mMMMm

What if Devin was raising these suspicions simply to deflect them from himself?

853. La Plata.

Her hands were shaking. She tried to keep them still, but they quivered in time with the reflections in the mirrors, as though reality itself was being shaken apart. She wondered what would happen if they stayed in the Maze much longer, but was afraid to ask. Was there a risk that their patterns would merge, like Jesse had been afraid of in New York? She'd heard an urban myth once about lovers who had sworn never to be separated, and had only ever gone into booths together. One trip, the machines made their wish come true, turning them into a single person with—depending on which version of the myth was being told—various numbers of arms and legs, but always two mouths, both of them screaming.

mMMMm

Clair didn't want to be blended with Sargent or Devin—a fear that took on a new edge when she realized that she could hear the whispers again. She squinted her eyes and tried to concentrate on the sound.

Are you sure it's not just random drift?

Definitely interference.

Well, do something about it, T. Don't just sit there fishing!

Clair was about to ask the others if they could hear the whispers too when the rise and fall of the humming suddenly changed.

mMmMm

The pulses came faster, and the numbers in the mirror ticked over so quickly they seemed to blur. Or was that her eyes again? *276, 474, 317, 655.* Clair put a hand to her forehead, disoriented.

One of her own reflections turned to look at her.

mMmMm

Devin and Sargent were flickering in and out of her vision again. *427, 517, 118, 853.* She was moving through the Maze too quickly to tell where she was in the real world. The Air was draggy, with patches frozen and metadata skewing wildly.

Still the reflection was looking at her, even when Clair deliberately glanced away.

mMmMm

The reflection's lips moved, but Clair wasn't speaking. It wasn't her. It had to be—

A dupe.

Clair reached out to take Devin's arm. She had to warn him. She opened her mouth to speak, but no voice came out. Her lips moved as soundlessly as those of her reflection.

The Maze had been hacked.

This is bad, said the whisper, as though it could read her mind. *This is very, very bad.*

MMMMM

The hum was deafening The numbers said *658, 274, 857, 658, 658, 481, 658, 658, 658, 658, 658, 658.* Clair put her hands over her ears, but nothing could keep the noise out. Her eyelids had no substance. Her hands were light as air, as though if she pressed too hard they might pass through each other and she would dissolve into nothing.

[19] ————————————————————

MMmmm—

Suddenly it all stopped. Silence fell and the reflections steadied and went back to normal. Clair's hand felt solid again. The number said *432.* Clair's lenses told her that she was on a tiny island called Ons, near Spain. Sargent leaned against one wall, the fingers of her right hand touching her temple. The reflection of Clair's dupe was gone, if dupe it had been. She started to mention it to Devin, but he was already talking.

"That was close," said Devin. He looked a little too relieved for Clair's liking, as though "close" might be a massive understatement. "They caught us in a loop of some kind, but we managed to—"

Watch out!

The whispered shout came a split second before an enormous bang sent Clair reeling. With tremendous force, one side of the miniature tank tore right off, shredding the mirrored surface into a million tiny shards that stung Clair in a dozen places. Bright light streamed into the shattered tank, temporarily blinding her.

Someone fell heavily against her, collapsing to the ground at her feet. It was Sargent, blood pouring out of her in a crimson flood. Clair dropped down beside her and tried to find the source, but there were too many of them, penetrating deeply into every weak point in the PK body armor.

Sargent's jade-green eyes stared up at Clair as she tried helplessly to stem the flow, pressing at random spots in the hope of doing something positive. Words gulped from the PK's throat, none of them audible. One hand reached up to Clair's face, but it fell away before touching her.

"No," Clair hissed. This couldn't be happening. "Don't . . . you can't—!"

"She's finished," said Devin in a higher pitch than usual. "For the record, I do care about that . . . but we need to move. Now."

He was peering anxiously at the hole in the side of the ruined tank. There was no sound apart from the ringing in Clair's ears and the glassy fragments crunching under her knees.

"We can't just leave her," Clair said, hating him a little for suggesting it.

"You know we have to. And we can't carry her. The booth was sabotaged. There could be dozens, hundreds, thousands of dupes converging on our location right now."

He was right, but that didn't make her feel better about it at all. Besides, he had his own problems. He was bleeding from wounds to his face and right arm, and maybe more she couldn't see under his armor. For the first time since she had known him, he looked young and scared.

Shaped charge, said a whisper. *Only one was meant to survive.*

No one's perfect, T. There's still time.

Whatever the whispers were, they were telling the truth. Sargent had been standing between Clair and the epicenter of the blast and taken the larger force of it. If she hadn't been so big, Devin might have caught even more than he had. The dupes couldn't get one of their own into the Maze, but they could do the next best thing: sabotage the booth and kill the people with her, leaving Clair unharmed, but isolated and immobile. This time, at least, they wanted her alive.

"We need a plan," she told Devin even as she still tried futilely to help Sargent. "We can't just run away at random. Is there another booth on this island?"

He nodded. "The nearest is in the lighthouse on the other side. It's about six hundred yards northwest. It's currently . . . not in our hands."

"Which means?"

"The dupes are hacking into the system, just like we did in Crystal City. It there aren't already some here now, there will be very soon."

Two on their way, said the whisper.

"Just two of them, though," said Devin with forced cheerfulness. "We can handle two, right?"

"Wait—that voice is talking to you?" she said, staring at him in surprise. The revelation put all thought of dupes taking over d-mat from her mind. "I've been assuming it was the dupes."

"It's not the dupes." He shook his head. "Later."

"Promise?"

"Yes."

Clair still had the pistol Devin had given her in its holster. His hands were empty.

"Take this," she said, offering it to him.

He waved it away. "Never use them. Too dangerous."

"Isn't that the idea?"

"Well, you should feel free. Just don't shoot me in the process."

"Don't give me a reason to," she said, wishing he didn't have to be so patronizing, "and I'll try to resist."

"Let's just get moving," Devin said. "Please."

She nodded, but he didn't go anywhere.

Impulsively, she bent down to hug Sargent, not caring about blood, worried only that she didn't hurt the injured peacekeeper in the process.

"Sarge," she said. "Can you hear me? Sarge, I'll stay if you want me to."

The peacekeeper shook her head. She was very pale, and her eyes seemed to be sinking back into their sockets. Her hand twitched in a gesture that might have been *Get the hell out of here.* Or equally *Take my pistol before you go.*

Clair had to assume it was probably both, even if the thought of shooting someone still made her squeamish. But the thought of dying made her feel worse.

Sargent didn't move after that. She looked peaceful, but that didn't make Clair feel any better. Leaving her was a betrayal of their brief camaraderie, whether Devin's suspicions were warranted or not. *I'm sorry,* Clair thought, promising to come back when she could. *If* she could.

CLAIR GOT TO her feet, wiping her hands on her armor so
her grip on the gun wouldn't slip. Her breath shuddered
in and out of her, sounding almost like weeping, but there
were no tears. Not yet. There wasn't time.

They eased through the hole in the tank, shards of mirror turning to white dust with every step. The machine
was situated in the center of an ancient deconsecrated
chapel. All the religious trappings had been removed,
along with the pews and the carpets. Someone had taken
a stab at turning it into a home but given up midway, leaving dark-stained wooden beams to gather cobwebs and
dust. The tank—a blocky, angular thing on the outside,
now featuring a substantial hole in its side, with thick
cables snaking to a nearby drain—looked no more out of
place there than it would have anywhere else. A closed
wooden door with a modern lock led to the exterior world
on the other side of what would once have been the nave.

They crossed to the door, where Devin fiddled with the
lock. It clunked and swung open, revealing a hilly, green
landscape with gray sea visible nearby. The air smelled
of salt and fish. A path led north, inland. Clair couldn't
see the lighthouse, but the Air showed her where it was.
She had full access now that she was outside the chapel.
A flurry of patches and bumps clamored for her attention,

including several from Jesse, sent hours before, while they were still in the Maze. She swept them all aside to concentrate on the landscape and what threats it might contain.

"See anyone?" Devin asked her.

"No. No drones, either." She wished Q was around to tell her if anyone was nearby. "Not much in the way of cover."

"Don't sound so disgruntled. It's better than the alternative: six five eight—the number that kept repeating in the Maze?—that was Beijing. We'd be up to our ears in dupes if we'd gone there, like they wanted us to."

She wasn't listening to him. Their best bet, she figured, was to follow the path. "How long do we have?"

"A minute or so before those two dupes arrive. If we hurry, we might get to the lighthouse before them."

"I can tell you've never run six hundred yards before."

"Not wounded," he said in a hurt tone, then corrected himself. "No, you're right. Never."

She pulled up her hood and broke cover, pulling Devin after her. Clair set a steady pace, trying to watch every direction at once. The hills were gentle; in theory it would be easy to spot anyone coming toward them. The memory of dupes in active camouflage in Crystal City was still strong, however. She wasn't going to take anything for granted.

Halfway there, Devin panted, "Okay, they're here. The two dupes. We've got to be careful now."

She agreed, and she didn't like the way his breathing was coming. He was pale and he clutched his right arm tightly to his chest. Blood dripped from the elbow, leaving a thin trail along the path. He seemed to be getting heavier to pull along with every step.

"We need to split up," she said. The map showed a low valley nearby. She could follow it almost all the way to the lighthouse, and maybe she wouldn't be seen along the way. "I'm going in that direction," she said, pointing. "You . . ."

"Keep going along the path to draw their fire? You must think I'm— Wait, yeah, they'll be looking for you. So there's a chance they'll let me walk on by. Or they'll kill me just to get me out of the picture. How do you figure my odds?"

"Zero if you stick with me," she said.

All you have to do is survive, she told herself. *Get to the booth and get away, live to fight another day.* Jesse would be waiting for her at the other end.

And there, she promised herself, she would stop running and start retaliating for real. Somehow.

Devin shrugged. "Okay. You take the high road, I'll take the low. Wish me luck, will you?"

"Good luck," she said, sincerely hoping he wouldn't need it. "See you at the other end."

"If I don't see you first."

"Put up your hood!" she hissed, darting to her right off

the path and heading for the valley, pausing only to make sure that he had obeyed her instruction, which he did with a shrug.

She checked the map one more time then clicked off the Air entirely, to reduce the chances of her being tracked. Her green-tinged lenses went dark. She was on her own.

Clair stayed low, hoping a tangle of thorny bushes that hugged a narrow creek at the bottom of the valley might provide some cover. The space between her shoulder blades burned, even though she knew the dupes were ahead of her, not behind. Sargent's pistol felt unnatural, clutched tightly in her hand. She hoped it would act as a deterrent and she wouldn't need to use it. That would depend, she supposed, on whether these particular dupes were coming to capture her or kill her.

Two small birds shot out of a nearby bush, and Clair's heart almost stopped. Her eyes tracked the birds as they skated away from the interloper, seeking shelter over the nearest hill. When she looked forward again, Cashile was standing five yards in front of her.

Her heart was already pounding from the last fright. The only move she made was to raise the pistol, held tightly in both hands.

"Get out of my way," she said.

He shook his head, a small boy of maybe ten with corn-rows and skin the same color as hers, staring at her with adult eyes. She had last seen him dead in Crystal City, but that hadn't really been him either. Clair's final memory of the real Cashile was of him waving as he roared off with his mother on an electrobike. She wished she had an electrobike now, even though she didn't know how to drive it. Anything to put some distance between her and the doppelgänger standing patiently in front of her.

"You're done," dupe-Cashile said in an adult voice. "Give it up."

"Not a chance," she said. "Get out of my way."

"If I don't? Are you going to shoot me?"

"I don't want to."

"I know you don't. You're not a killer. You're just a kid who's out of her depth, like Cashile was. If you're not careful, you'll drown too."

The mismatch between the boyish face and the all-too-knowing voice was stripping Clair of her resolve. She had to get past the dupe, but she couldn't shoot him, even if he only *looked* like a child.

"Who are you really?" she asked.

"We don't have names anymore," he said. "We're the hollow men."

"Like the poem."

"I don't know anything about a poem. That's just what we call ourselves."

His ignorance shouldn't have surprised her. He was a killer, not an English major.

"Where's the other one?" she asked.

"Behind you," said a voice.

She spun around and saw another Cashile coming down the same hill over which the birds had flown.

[21]

HER MIND BALKED at the sight. Even though she knew what the dupes were and what they were capable of, this was the first time she had seen indisputable evidence that someone other than herself had been duplicated. Here she was talking to two identical people, except for their minds. If she'd entertained any doubts that VIA was truly broken, they were now completely dispelled.

"You're probably wondering why we've come to you like this," said the second Cashile. He had a slightly different accent from the first. "It's not to fight you. We're unarmed." He held out his arms and wiggled his child's fingers. "We just want to talk, that's all."

"About Q," she said, swinging the pistol between the two of them, not believing for a second that they meant her no harm.

"Yes. Tell us where she is or there'll be no more talking."

She imagined them clamming up like kids having a tantrum. "What makes you think I know?"

"If anyone does, it's you," said Cashile-1. "If you don't,

then we don't need you."

"Your only chance of surviving is to tell us."

Clair fired once at Cashile-2. He was coming too close. The bullet sprayed the dirt a yard in front him. The recoil kicked the gun up in her hand with surprising force, and he stopped dead. She was glad she hadn't missed and accidentally shot him, even if he was a dupe. Birds scattered in all directions, abandoning the tiny valley that probably had been theirs alone for years.

"If I don't tell you, I'm dead," she said. "If I do tell you, I'm probably dead too. It's kind of lose-lose for me."

"Wallace's offer still stands. Help us and you get your friends back. We'll even throw in Jesse's dad, if you like." Cashile-1's smile perfectly matched the other's. "We're not unreasonable."

"You're murderers and liars"—noting as she said it the implied confirmation that Jesse's father's original pattern still existed, somewhere, along with the patterns of her friends. "I'd be insane to trust you."

"You trust Devin Bartelme, don't you? The difference between us is not as great as he would like you to think."

Clair raised her eyebrows. "What do you mean?"

"Come with us and we'll tell you." The Cashiles were closing in again. "Let's get off this rock and go somewhere civilized."

"No." She backed away.

"Devin has already left, you know. He's abandoned you

to save his own skin."

That was entirely possible. He'd had time to get to the lighthouse by now.

"That means the booth is tied up," she said. "It's just you two and me now."

"There are other booths. The next dupes you meet won't be so reasonable."

Clair couldn't afford to doubt that. What had happened to PK Sargent was proof. Maybe the Cashiles genuinely wanted to make her see reason, but their dual purpose could be to delay her until the killers arrived. The distinction between *tell us or die* and *tell us and die* was a thin one. Which faction did these dupes belong to?

"I'm going to the lighthouse," she said. "You can either try to stop me or let me go. Or come with me, I guess."

With a reasonableness that made Clair feel like she'd slipped into some kind of dream, Cashile-1 said, "We'll come with you, of course. Can't have you wandering around on your own. You never know what could happen."

Warily, she set off along the valley again, with one Cashile on either side of her. At first she tried to stay ahead of them, but that way she couldn't see both at once, which only made her more nervous. They settled into an easy lope, the three of them side by side, as though going out for an afternoon stroll through the countryside.

"Hollow men," she said, finding the silence as

uncomfortable as the veiled threats. "Don't you have any hollow women?"

"It's a convenient phrase," said Cashile-2, with a glance at Cashile-1. "And it is from T. S. Eliot, since you asked. Some of us are better read than others."

"How many different, uh, hollow people are there?"

"A surprising number. You might think it'd be simpler to be all the same, but it's not. Different people have different strengths and weaknesses. You don't want an army of soldiers who all share an identical blind spot, physically or mentally."

"Is that what you are, then, an army?"

"We could be," said Cashile-1. "We're prepared to fight, anyway."

"And you don't mind the thought of dying after a few days in someone else's body?"

"We'll always come back. That's the deal. We do this, and we don't ever die."

"But you don't live in your own body. Or is that still out there, somewhere?"

Cashile-2 shrugged. "What does it matter? A body is just a body. It's what's inside that counts."

Once again Clair struggled with the absurdity of the situation. Here she was arguing philosophy with dupes on an island in the middle of nowhere while people all over the world were stranded and dying because of the crash. Why were the dupes being so frank all of a sudden?

It made a welcome change from being shot at or blown up or hassled about Q, but it didn't make any sense.

Then she realized with a jolt: they were trying to make her *understand*.

Clair almost laughed—did they really think she would ever accept them or what they did?—and stopped herself in time. The lighthouse was in view, a stubby finger protruding from a brick fist relatively high up on a headland. This unexpected chance to learn more about the dupes wasn't going to last much longer.

"You're not like the others I've met," she said. "There's one I've seen a couple of times. . . ."

"He calls himself 'Nobody,'" said Cashile-2.

"Yes," she said, surprised. That was exactly who she had been thinking of. He had been in her dupe, and before that in Dylan Linwood's body in California. He had tried to kill her both times.

"We know all about him," said Cashile-1 with a roll of his eyes.

"He's one of the first," said Cashile-2. "The boss asked him to retire once, but he wouldn't. Which wasn't a problem while he was . . . useful . . . which I suppose he still is, in his own way."

"He wants me dead," Clair said. "Is that what 'the boss' wants?"

Another exchanged glance. "Nobody's way off program. You can't tell us what we need to know if you're dead."

Clair nodded, not taking that as definite confirmation that there were two factions among the dupes, one of which wanted her dead. Maybe the Nobody dupe was under separate orders to terrorize her into capitulating.

"Are you officially telling me that Ant Wallace survived?" she asked, trying to maintain the chatty tone. "He must have if that deal he offered is still on the table."

"We're not officially telling you anything," said Cashile-1, with bright coyness. "But if you want to trade information, now's the time. . . ."

They had reached the path leading to the lighthouse. Another figure was walking in the same direction as them, along the weathered tarmac, so their paths crossed. Clair froze. It was Dylan Linwood, dressed exactly as Clair had last seen him, in scruffy shirt and shorts, left eye filled with blood. She stopped short of actually running, but only just, as she remembered all the times he had threatened her and chased her in the past. In her mind the worst of the dupes were synonymous with his ominous, craggy face. She took this as a sign that the warm and fuzzy get-together was over now.

"See reason, Clair," said the Linwood dupe. He put himself on the path in front of her, forcing her to stop. The Cashiles stood behind her so she couldn't run. "You don't have any options left."

He didn't sound like Nobody, but he was right regardless. The Linwood dupe had a pistol in his hand, pointed at her just as hers was at him. The question was: if it came down to it, who could fire first?

Clair took a deep breath and looked down at the path, trying to prepare herself for what surely had to come. There was no trail of blood from Devin's injury, which was worrying. Maybe the Cashiles had been lying about him reaching the lighthouse, and he had collapsed after she had left him. Maybe the dupe of Jesse's father had killed him. There was her motivation to shoot dupe-Dylan, she told herself, if she needed one. Killing a wounded, unarmed teenager in cold blood warranted *some* kind of retaliation.

"I can't tell you anything about Q," she said. Why did no one ever believe her about this? If she'd said it once, she'd said it a hundred times. "I don't *know* anything about Q. No more than you do, honestly. So if you're going to kill me, you might as well do it now." She gripped the pistol tightly and braced herself. "Or try to."

The dupe of Dylan Linwood moved with fluid speed, wrenching the pistol from her grasp before she could pull the trigger. He tossed it to Cashile-2 while Cashile-1 whipped Clair's other pistol out of her holster. Suddenly she was standing unarmed in the center of a ring of dupes, all of them pointing deadly weapons at her. Her eyes filled with acid tears of embarrassment. *Shit.*

"We're not going to kill you, Clair," said Cashile-1, "even if you really don't know anything about Q's whereabouts.

You still have some value as a hostage."

"And while you might be prepared to throw it all away to spite us," said Cashile-2, "we know Q wouldn't let you. That's how the crash happened in the first place, right?"

Don't be so sure about that, Clair wanted to say. *She might not do it a second time.* But convincing them of that point could mean a death sentence, so she stayed silent. No more frank exchanges with the enemy, not when they had the upper hand.

"This way," said the third dupe, indicating the path up to the lighthouse.

As they walked her up the hill a fourth figure stepped into view at the entrance to the lighthouse, and her heart sank. How many dupes did Wallace need to bring her in?

But this dupe had red hair and was holding a boxy contraption in both arms, wires draped behind him.

"Clair, watch out!" Devin cried.

The box flashed, and Cashile-2 flew backward in a pink mist.

[22]

CLAIR RECOILED. CASHILE-2 had been struck with sufficient force to tear his body to rags scattered a surprising distance down the path.

The box flashed again. This time the incredible force

struck the ground to Clair's left, missing both of the remaining dupes and gouging a crater a foot deep and several yards long. Cashile-1 ran away. The third dupe raised his pistol. He fired at Devin the same instant the box flashed a third time.

Clair was moving by then too. She felt rather than saw the third dupe go down much like Cashile-2 had, but less definitively, with half his body still intact. She was running in a long arc for the lighthouse steps, avoiding a direct line between her and whatever it was that Devin was using to blow the dupes away. She glanced once over her shoulder and saw only the two bodies on the path below. Cashile-1 was nowhere to be seen.

Devin staggered and fell as she came up the steps. The box he was holding—an ordinary fabber, with its mirrored door removed and gleaming power cable leading into the lighthouse—fell with a thud to the ground. She ran to him, saw a gaping wound under his armpit that hadn't been there before.

"Got me before I could get him," he said. "Damned dirty dupe."

She slipped her arms under his armpits and dragged him inside, leaving a red path behind them.

"The fabber!" He flapped an arm at the fallen box.

She returned for it, keeping low in case Cashile-1 had already returned with sharpshooting friends.

"Jerry-rigged d-mat gun," he panted when she returned.

"Can make atoms with any velocity. Just a matter—get it?—of giving them all the same velocity, in the same direction. *Boom.*"

He looked bright-eyed and feverish, and there was far too much blood, much more than before, but at least he was still talking.

"You won't use guns but you'll use this?"

"I like a challenge," he said. "Anyway, guns didn't help you. Watch the windows. See who gets here first. Help's on its way."

Clair propped him up in one corner of the room so he could cover some of the view while she ran to check the rest. The building was too large for just two people to defend it. Maybe if they went up into the lighthouse itself . . . that way they could see for miles around without obstruction. But they could also *be* seen and would therefore be vulnerable. Barricading the doors behind her was the only option.

There were two tables in the room, plus a cupboard and heavy chest of drawers, which she slid hastily into place as best she could.

The lighthouse's single d-mat booth, a small affair, barely large enough for two, was a burned-out ruin two rooms down. It looked as though it had imploded.

"What happened back there?" she asked when she returned.

"Was cycling someone," Devin said. "Couldn't tell who.

Didn't want to take any chances."

"You cut off our escape route."

"Seemed sensible at the time. Tried to bump you, but you were off the Air. Very antisocial."

She nodded. "Seemed sensible at the time."

He smiled. There was blood on his teeth.

"They ignored me . . . at their peril."

"Don't try to talk."

She saw movement on the hillside below, and she reached for the modified fabber to shoot anything that looked remotely threatening.

"How does this work?"

"Point and click. Power switch on the back. Suggest opening window first. Glass dust . . . very nasty."

"You've done this before?'

"Vivid imagination."

She waited, fabber at the ready, but the movement wasn't repeated.

"Nothing?" Devin asked.

"Just a rabbit," she said.

"Sure?"

"No."

"Why are you still off the Air?"

She shifted to another window, glad it wasn't nighttime. A thousand dupes could have crept up on them unseen if it were.

"Too distracting," she said in answer to his question,

which was honest enough, as far as it went, but wasn't the whole story. It was simpler this way. One problem, one solution. She wished everything was like that.

"Jesse and Forest are okay," he said. "They're being looked after."

She nodded. That was welcome news, but it wasn't what she needed to concentrate on right now.

There was a long silence during which she watched intently for any sign of the dupes, until she realized that silence from Devin probably wasn't a good thing.

His head had slumped forward so his chin pressed hard on his chest. His eyes were shut. She hurried back to his side and checked his pulse. He was alive, but he didn't look well at all. He was sitting in a deep puddle of his own blood and his breathing was ragged.

I saw a planet running out of days, said the whispers as soon as she was next to him. It sounded like an old trick poem she'd read once, but with different words.

"Is that you?" His eyelids fluttered and half opened. "It's not you. What do you want, Mother?"

"I'm Clair," she said. "Don't go to sleep. You need to stay awake."

. . . I saw a computer in a fine silken dress. . . .

"It *is* you," he said, batting at her with a limp hand. "You inherited her bedside manner. She always loved you best."

"Tell me all about it, Devin," she said, going along with him even as she tried to keep an eye out for dupes. "Or tell me about the whispers. Tell me anything. Just don't you die on me as well."

   . . . I saw a pop star with the heart of a pig. . . .

"That old poem," he said. "She never let us forget, did she? Never take anything for granted, never ever *ever*. How could we do that when she was always changing things? Nothing was good enough for her. *I* never was, anyway."

Distantly, through Devin's angsty raving, Clair heard gunfire. She jerked around to peer anxiously through the windows on the other side of the room but couldn't see clearly. Was it the help Devin had promised her or more dupes closing in? Without leaving his side to check properly, she could only imagine what was going on out there.

   . . . I saw a soldier in a tube made of glass. . . .

Devin shivered and his eyes drooped closed. She shook him as violently as she dared.

"Hey, wake up. Just a little longer. Help's on its way, remember?"

"She never wanted children," Devin said in a warbling voice. "Guinea pigs, that's what we were to her."

   . . . I saw the mind that thought this thought.

"She loved you best . . . ," he said, eyelids shutting again, ". . . but she was most proud of me."

Clair stood up at a noise from the ground floor of the lighthouse building. It sounded like a door being kicked in. Stepping sideways so her back wasn't facing the window, she clutched the fabber in both hands and waited, debating whether to fire first or ask questions of anyone who tried to enter. She didn't want to shoot someone coming to help them, but she didn't want to give the dupes a chance to overpower her either.

Heavy footsteps, growing nearer.

"Stay out there." Clair was sure now that someone was outside the one door she hadn't been able to barricade. She placed herself protectively between that door and Devin. "Don't try to come in until you tell me who you are, or you'll regret it."

"It's okay, Clair," came an unexpected voice. "Don't panic. It's me. I found you."

Clair knew that voice, even though it was impossible.

"No," she said.

"I'm going to open the door. Don't do to me whatever it was you did to the dupes out there."

"Wait."

"I'm coming inside now."

"Don't!"

The door opened, and PK Sargent stepped through.

———————————————— [23]

SARGENT WAS BLOODY but very much alive.

"It can't be," said Clair. "I *saw* you."

"Did you really think I'd leave you like that?"

"But you died . . . didn't you?"

"Does it look like it? I'm not going anywhere in a hurry."

Clair didn't know what to believe. It looked like this Sargent was a copy made to replace the one who had died, a copy that had fought her way to Clair from another booth, bloodying herself in the process. But Clair didn't understand how this fit with what Forest had said about reactivation, and how keenly Sargent had interrogated her about the possibility that Zep might have come back from the dead. If the PKs could already break the law, why Sargent's anxiety? Or was this a new thing?

Besides, it wasn't impossible that Sargent was still alive. Clair hadn't checked for a pulse, after all. Sargent could have woken up, removed the glassy shards, and got moving again. It just didn't seem very likely . . . or, as more gunshots sounded, the most important thing in the world at that moment.

They both turned to look out the window.

"The island is thick with dupes," Sargent said. "Took me forever to get through them. I'm sorry."

"Why are you apologizing?" said Clair. "Devin and I left you for dead."

Sargent seemed to notice Clair's companion for the first time. Her eyebrows came together in concern. "He looks terrible."

Clair checked his pulse. Still there, but only weakly. The whispers were silent. "We have to get him to a hospital."

"We just need to hold out a few more minutes, if we can."

Clair was still holding the souped-up fabber. "Devin made this."

Sargent examined it. "Did he? He's a smart boy, and a very dangerous one. Be glad he's on your side, for now."

The slight young man slumped over on the couch didn't look especially threatening at that moment.

"On my side for now, or be glad for now?" Clair asked.

A window shattered to their right, followed a split second later by the sound of the gunshot. Plaster puffed on the other side of the room. They ducked.

"I'm not sure what I meant," said Sargent, which was a strange thing to say, but not half as disturbing as what she said next. "If we left him here, we'd increase our chances . . ."

"We're not leaving him," Clair said. She felt as though she was being tested. This time she wasn't leaving anyone behind, not while she was sure they were still alive. She had barely known Devin a day and already he had saved her life more times than she could count. None of the ominous things the dupes and PKs said to her would change that.

"All right," said Sargent, accepting her reservations without rancor. "You take that way. I'll watch over here."

From the shattered window Clair could see two dupes creeping up the hill. One was in Cashile's mother's body;

the other was someone Clair had never seen before, a man with broad shoulders and a lumpy bald head, like a potato. She raised herself, took aim quickly, and fired the fabber.

There was no recoil and very little sound. Just a burst of heat and light—and suddenly the dupes were scattering from a smoking gash in the hillside. Clair fired after the one she didn't know. She wasn't trying to hit him, just discourage him from coming any closer. He ducked and complied.

Behind Clair, Sargent fired twice in quick succession, prompting a bark of pain from someone Clair couldn't see. A flurry of shots peppered the lighthouse, smashing glass but hitting no one. More gunfire answered from outside the building, then three figures in dark-gray armor ran into Clair's line of sight.

"Don't shoot at them," said Sargent. "They're our way out of here."

Indeed, the new arrivals were firing at the two dupes Clair had scared away earlier. More of them were coming from across the hill and hurrying up the path. So many of them, Clair thought. Where had they all come from?

Boots stamped on wooden floorboards. Sargent dismantled one of Clair's barricades to allow the new arrivals into the room.

There were three of them, two big and bulky, one small and slight, not wearing full armor like the other two. All three faces were obscured by helmets. They looked like peacekeepers, but with more attitude. Clair was reminded of soldiers in old movies.

"We have the perimeter secured," said one of the big ones. "Anyone else here?"

Sargent was equally brisk in response. "Just us. We're ready to move out."

The skinniest and smallest of the new arrivals was already bending over Devin. "Give me a moment."

When the helmet came off, Clair saw bright-red hair and a familiar face.

"You've got to be kidding," she said, backing warily away. Was *everyone* copying themselves now?

"What?" said the second Devin.

"The dupes told me you were like them. I should've listened. What happened to being morally opposed to duping?"

"I'm not a copy," he said.

"Come on. I have eyes."

"Don't be stupid. He and I are completely different. I'm Devin's twin, Trevin."

The teen stooped over Devin's still form, measuring his vital signs and administering patches and fluid-replacement blisters.

Twin, thought Clair. He certainly looked like Devin, with the same gender ambiguity and taste in pretentious Nehru collars. It was entirely possible that they were twins, but she had seen so many dupes lately that that was the obvious assumption.

"Prove it," she said.

"How?"

"No time for chatter," said one of Trevin's two burly companions. "Hurry up, sir."

Trevin waved him silent. "I'm not having him die en route."

"We should move while we still have *une route*."

More gunfire came from outside, followed by a distant explosion caused by something that might have been a grenade.

"How many are there?" asked Sargent.

"Thirty, and that number is growing exponentially. The south booth is open and they have control."

"An army of dupes," said Clair, remembering what the Cashiles had told her.

"Why not?" said Trevin. "This is war. A real war, not an ideological one."

She stared at him for an instant, shocked. There hadn't been a major conflict since the Water Wars and the creation of the peacekeepers. There weren't even countries anymore. It was supposed to be impossible.

"Seriously?"

"You're not on the school playground, Clair, not now that the dupes are in the VIA network."

Clair bristled at his tone but was cut off by Sargent.

"We'll have to fight them for the booth," said the PK.

"We came in from the north. The booth up there is still ours."

"But that could change if they get the drop on you." Sargent turned to Trevin. "Is there anything I can do to help?"

"No. Almost done." Another patch to Devin's shoulder, another patch to his throat. "There." Trevin stepped back and wiped his bloody hands on his armor.

The two burly soldiers or whatever they were eased Devin from his slumped position and gently lifted him into the cradle of their linked arms. Trevin put his helmet back on as they led the way from the room.

Clair hesitated, then put the fabber down on the floor. The cable barely reached as far as the steps. Without power it was just a box.

"If this is war," she asked Sargent, "what does that make me?"

"That's up to you. What do you want to be?"

There was that question again.

"I'll decide when I'm out of here," she said.

"We'd better get moving, then," Sargent said, indicating the door through which the RADICAL soldiers had vanished. "This island is getting more crowded by the minute."

Sargent went after Clair, scanning the terrain ahead. Trevin wasn't waiting around. He and the two soldiers carrying his twin were already vanishing over the nearest hill, moving northward at a steady clip.

Briefly, Clair considered suggesting a detour to see what lay in the chapel, but decided in the end that that was one sleeping dog she should let lie. *For now.*

[24]

AT AN ABANDONED cottage pockmarked with weapons fire and climbing roses, they found a squadron of RADICAL soldiers guarding a series of booths that folded out of each other like *matryoshka* dolls. Each was busy bringing more soldiers to the island, or more booths, or a combination of the two. Presumably in the south of the island, the dupes were doing the same.

"You, with Devin," said Trevin to Sargent. To Clair he said, "With me."

She instinctively rebelled against his bossy tone. He was even worse than Devin. "Where are we going?"

"To the seastead. You'll be—"

"What, *safe*?"

"No. I was going to say 'brought up to speed.' You'll never be safe anywhere until this threat is dealt with."

"So what's the point of going anywhere with you?"

"If you're going to fight a war, you need an army. We're volunteering."

"Why?"

"Does it matter? Beggars can't be choosers."

"If you think I'll tell you anything about Q—"

"I'm certain you don't know anything about Q," he said with a dismissive flick of one hand.

Surprised, Clair grabbed his shoulder as he went to step into a booth. "So why has Devin been asking me all this time?"

"I'm not the optimist my brother is. We gave the entity many opportunities to help you and it took none of them. This leaves us with just two conclusions: one, it was destroyed in the crash, or two, it no longer feels any kinship with you. The latter makes me nervous, frankly: until it emerges again, we have no way of knowing what it wants now. But it's okay if you can't help with that. We require you for other qualities you possess."

Q is a she, not an it, she wanted to say, *a person, not an entity,* but she figured it would make no difference to anyone in RADICAL.

"What qualities?"

"Let's discuss this in safer environs," he said, indicating the booth. "PK Forest and your friend are waiting for you there."

Clair considered his offer. Seasteads were floating cities that plied the open ocean, never making landfall. They had been another solution to the problem of rising sea levels, but even before that, long before OneEarth, they had also been miniature city-states, where people with weird ideas had formed their own private empires so no one could bother them. Clair and Libby had once visited the *Serbia*, a famous wreck on the equator where tens of thousands of people had died of an incurable and highly contagious disease. The massive vessel had foundered and been left that way for decades, rising and falling with the water levels, until declared safe by peacekeepers and opened to tourists. Perhaps RADICAL used one like that as a headquarters, as WHOLE used to with its antiquated Skylifter. Perhaps they found it a suitable home for their weird ideas.

Sargent and Devin were already gone. She had no reason to stay on the island any longer. If Trevin was as good as his word, Jesse would be at the other end. Perhaps some answers, too.

"All right," she said. "After you. Jesse had better be there, or I'm leaving."

"You're free to leave any time you like. But where would you go?"

She had no answer to that.

Trevin hitched up against the back wall of the booth so there would be room inside for her, too. He smelled faintly, and rather incongruously, of rose water. *Hang in there, hang in there,* said the faintest of whispers in her ears, and then the light flashed and they were gone.

mmmmm-click

The sound brought back recent memories of the Maze,

and her gut roiled anxiously. It felt like days since she'd last eaten or drunk anything, but it had only been since the Antarctic forest. Her throat was parched from all the running and the tension.

The doors opened on a wide staging area containing more than fifty booths and twice as many people in gray armor running back and forth. The air smelled of oil, electricity, and salt, and was full of urgent voices. Before they left the booth, Trevin touched the corner of his right eye, the universal sign for *check your lenses*. She switched them back on and found among the endless flurry of bumps and grabs a series of patches requesting interfaces and shared data, all dressed in hard metallic colors. She put the patches on hold until she learned more about her location. All she could determine at that moment, thanks to her limited access to the Air, was that they were not far from the coast of Greenland. Outside it would be dark, the exact opposite of how it was on the other side of the world, in Valkyrie Station. There was no immediate sign of Jesse.

Trevin guided her through the throng to a side area, where Devin was being loaded into what looked like a steel coffin. Mirrors on the inside confirmed that it was a medical booth, designed to transport the gravely injured to a hospital. She had seen such things before, at her mother's workplace as well as in dramas.

Hold on, D, said a solitary whisper.

D *for Devin,* thought Clair.

"You're T," she said, staring at Trevin, then back to Devin as the medical booth closed over his brother. "The two of you are the whisperers!"

"Of course," said Trevin. "We're linked by an entangled neural network—twin telepathy made real by technology, if you like. It was something our mother gave us when we were young."

Clair was tempted to pursue the Bartelme family history but instead opted for a more practical question: "So why can I hear it?"

"The Air doesn't like the unusual traffic we generate. Too radical, you might say. Get close to us and augs interfere. Some people can't take the hint."

He looked haughtily at Clair, who was standing next to him by the medical booth.

She wasn't backing away. "Why didn't he tell me?"

"It's not something we advertise."

"So you can talk about people without them knowing?"

"So we can pool our knowledge in every situation. Devin's the mobile one. I prefer to stay at home, watching his back. Between the two of us, there's not much we can't handle . . . and we don't like being apart, particularly when one of us might be dying."

She glimpsed a closeness then, behind the bravado, and realized that he was more worried about Devin than he was willing to admit, either here or on Ons Island. The poem he had whispered to Devin while Devin raved about their mother might have been something shared from their childhood. Clair had never had a sister or a brother, but she knew the power of childhood memories. She thought again of Charlie, and squirmed inside at the thought that a dupe called Nobody had shared this memory with her.

"Is he going to be all right?" asked Clair, indicating the sealed booth.

"Oh yes, D will be fine now."

"Do you have surgeons on the seastead or have you sent him somewhere else?"

"No surgeons," he said. "We grew out of that medieval practice years ago."

"Then how . . . ?" she started to ask, but was distracted by the arrival of Jesse and PK Forest. Forest was wearing the same armor as before, and Sargent acknowledged her fellow peacekeeper with a nod. Forest's expression didn't change, but he did raise a hand in something that might have been welcome, or even gladness. It was hard to tell.

Jesse had changed into nondescript gray overalls that looked like a dressed-down version of the armor worn by the soldiers around them. The outfit suited him much better than the PK gear. They grinned as they approached each other, then hugged. They didn't hold on for long, but he squeezed her tightly, and she took strength from the embrace, glad for the opportunity, however brief it was, to let Jesse support her.

"You made it," he said.

"I'm glad you're safe."

"Safe as houses. You know what that means?"

She smiled at this shared memory of marching across California badlands and sniping at each other in the dark.

"I get the idea," she said.

Jesse explained that he and Forest had gone straight from Valkyrie Station to the seastead, where they had been following her progress via Devin's lenses as best they could, anxiously awaiting her return. She had been in the Maze for six hours, and contact with Devin during that time had been sporadic. Only moments ago, the news of the sabotage and the ambush on Ons Island had filtered through.

"Is it all like this?" she asked, stepping away from him to take in the cavernous space around them.

"This is the busiest part," he said. "There are places where nothing is happening at all. Living areas, that kind of thing. They made me explore while we waited for you."

"*Made* you?" she said with a smile. "They twisted your rubber arm?"

"No, really. I was getting in their way, and I was . . . well, I was worried about you. They said it could be a long time and eventually it was simpler just to believe them. I'd love to show you the engines of this thing . . . or the anchor . . . ?"

He gave her the chance to indicate that she did indeed

want nothing more than to admire stupendous machines and mountains of metal, and he capitulated graciously when she did not.

Clair stood hand in hand with him for a moment, reflecting on everything that had just happened. The VIA network was compromised. Dupes were openly attacking anyone in their way. The world was falling apart around her, and only worse lay ahead.

War. The very idea of it was so strange and overwhelming. But if the dupes weren't going to let up, she couldn't see what she could do but fight them back. The Cashiles hadn't denied that Wallace was still alive, so she felt comfortable running with the assumption that he was. Someone had to stop him. *Properly* stop him, this time, hopefully more successfully than Clair had been, the first time.

"So what happens next?" asked Clair. "Who decides?"

"We do," said Trevin. "You, Jesse, Forest and Sargent, Devin—everyone involved from the beginning. If we can reach consensus, RADICAL will follow."

Before Clair could express her doubts about that ever happening, the medical booth slid open and Devin sat up, looking disoriented but otherwise perfectly healthy.

"Hello, everyone," he said, rubbing his shoulder where he had been shot. There was no sign of the wound. His armor was gone. Now he was wearing a simple blue tunic, like a hospital gown, and looked perfectly healthy.

"What happened? Did I die?"

[25]

"NOT QUITE," SAID Trevin, brows bunching in annoyance that Clair was sure hid relief. "Please don't do that again."

"I'll endeavor not to."

"How did you get well so quickly?" asked Jesse, his eyes so wide the whites showed around the edges. "It's not possible."

"It is with d-mat," said Trevin, glancing at Sargent and Forest. "You might want to avert your eyes, peacekeepers."

"Why's that?" asked Sargent.

"We don't hold to your exacting standards regarding what's acceptable and what's not," Trevin said.

"I was scanned into data," explained Devin, swinging his legs out of the booth and dropping down to the floor beside them. "My healthy form is on record, and medical algorithms compared the injured me to that record. My injuries were erased, without surgery, drugs, transfusions, anything primitive like that. I was made whole, then returned as you see me now."

Sargent said nothing, and neither did Forest. Clair couldn't tell what Jesse was thinking, but he didn't look happy about it, and his hand was squeezing hers just a little too tightly. She wasn't sure what she thought. This was Improvement as it was supposed to work, not tampering with a birthmark or a nose, but fixing someone's injuries, saving a life. In theory this was a good thing, or could have been, but it was on a long list of d-mat misuses that Clair had broadcast from the train as they'd passed Philadelphia, a list of unsettling things in a world where d-mat was unchained.

"Imagine that world," she had told her viewers. "If Improvement isn't stopped, that's exactly what's coming."

Had she already been living in that world without knowing it?

"*This* is what the dupes meant," she said, "when they said you weren't so different from them. RADICAL and the dupes are both using d-mat illegally."

"That's absolutely true," said Trevin, "but there's a world of difference between us and them, still. We don't copy or mind-rape people. We believe in free and informed experimentation with the forms we have. It's your body; you should be able to do whatever you want with it."

"No need to preach, T," said Devin. "The best way to convince people is to show them what we can do. And *this* is what we can do. This is what everyone can do given the ability to change their patterns."

"The Consensus Court has ruled human pattern editing to be unacceptable," said Forest.

"The Consensus Court is wrong." Devin shrugged. "I know that's a big claim, but we're not forcing it down anyone's throats. We're just getting on with our own thing, keeping our heads down—and not letting anyone tell us what we can and can't do. No offense, but don't think you can walk in here and tell us to stop."

Flick. Forest's expression became one of apparently sincere regret. "I assure you that this is not my intention. I merely wish to clarify the position I am required to take in future negotiations . . . and to indicate that, moving forward, there are certain details that perhaps it would be best I did not know."

Devin and Trevin nodded identically.

"Right," said Trevin. "Got it. Which brings us to the question I have for you, PK Forest. Do you actually have any plans for moving forward? Because I see precious little evidence of you and your kind doing much of anything so far."

"Easy, tiger," said Devin before either Forest or Sargent could respond. "I, for one, would like a set of proper clothes before we start flinging accusations around. Does that sound reasonable?"

It did to Clair, who felt like she had been wearing her filthy armor for days on end. For the sake of consensus, too. Arguing now would just make things difficult later.

"All right," said Trevin. "We'll meet again when everyone's ready. No one is to release any planning or policy statements before then. Understood?"

He looked at Clair when he said that, which surprised her. She wasn't about to declare war on the dupes without discussing it first.

"So we're just ignoring this?" said Jesse, indicating the

booth with a scowl. "People are editing their patterns whenever they want and suddenly this is *okay*?"

He had a point. It was just the wrong time to explore it.

"Why don't you show me around?" Clair said, taking his hand. "You, me, and that anchor makes three."

—— [26]

HE KNEW SHE was trying to distract him, but he didn't fight it.

"All right," he said, guiding her around the booths, from which people in gray RADICAL uniforms still came and went at a steady pace. He walked quickly and without talking, pulling her through two huge metal doors and onto a ramp wide enough for a dozen people. It spiraled up the inside of a chimney, at the top of which Clair saw only darkness. Possibly the night sky, because the air was sufficiently chilly to suggest that the chimney was open to the elements. They wound twice around the chimney, each loop granting Clair glimpses of several other staging areas, each identical to the first.

"What is the point of this place?" she said. "They didn't build it just for today, did they?"

"It think it's a contingency," he said. "That's what Hassannah called Valkyrie Station, remember? Maybe this is another one of those. There's enough space here for thousands and thousands of people. I get the impression it's kept ready for times like this."

Preparations for global disaster would explain the energy levels of everyone she saw, Clair thought. Not just focused industry, but a bit of panic as well, hidden behind bluff and bluster in Trevin's case.

RADICAL was taking this *very* seriously, she realized then. Seriously enough to risk friction with the PKs. RADICAL wasn't a terrorist organization like WHOLE, but clearly it shared a similar disregard of the law when the law got in the way of what RADICAL thought was right.

Clair glanced over her shoulder and saw a large, armored figure trailing behind them. PK-blue armor, not RADICAL gray. It was Sargent, keeping an eye on them. Perhaps she was afraid Clair might run off with RADICAL given the chance.

"Devin said something about new clothes," she said. "And I'm dying for a drink of water."

"I'll take you there, if I can find the way. They gave us a double berth. I know that's a bit presumptuous, but I don't think we'll be here that long, and if we are we can always ask for something else. There's a fabber. One of the guys here showed me how to use it."

Clair hid a smile at his awkwardness about the bed arrangement. It was sweet. "You won't eat the food but you'll wear the clothes?"

"As long as it's not going *in* me, I can live with it."

She supposed that was progress.

"Uh . . . this way," he said, peering across a metal antechamber that could have accommodated a small circus. "I read once how they sent the first permanent moonbase in one piece seven times, recycling it over and over until they got all the leaks out. But this is way bigger than that. Look."

They had reached a railed landing where she could lean out and see forward and back along the side of the seastead. The massive vessel was lit with strings of navigation lights and bulged around the middle. She guessed it was a mile or two from end to end and maybe a quarter of a mile across. She had never seen anything so huge, and she could hardly believe it floated on water: no doubt Jesse could tell her how, if she asked. The dedicated powersat beam that kept the lights and mighty engines going was visible as a faint yellow stream, flickering through the atmosphere in a perfectly straight line from the south, touching down somewhere on the giant vessel's stern.

From far below she imagined she could hear the whisper of waves, but underfoot she felt not the slightest hint of motion, either forward or side to side. Perhaps she would be safe from the dupes here, for a while.

"Does it have a name?" she asked.

"Athene," Jesse said. "Doesn't seem big enough, does it?"

She agreed. Small dogs had bigger names, which perhaps said more about the people who named such things than the things themselves.

"I used to call my bike Trigger," Jesse said. "I wonder if it's still where I left it. . . ."

Clair had to think for a second to remember what he was talking about. Jesse had chained his bike up at school the day his father had confronted Gordon the Gorgon. It felt like that had happened a thousand years ago to an entirely different Clair. In several senses the latter was probably quite true. What Clair was she up to now—4.0?

The memory of school was equally distant. What would be happening if none of this had taken place? She would be hanging out with her friends, agonizing over Zep and other romantic entanglements, dodging homework and the Mean Girls a year above them—the same girls Libby had defended Clair from in the earliest days of their friendship.

Clair wondered if Q thought of *her* as the equivalent of a Mean Girl, for what she had done. That was a depressing thought. Equally depressing was the thought of where her other friends were now, thanks to her. Libby was almost certainly gone forever, unless Clair could find a way to bring her back. Ronnie and Tash didn't seem to notice her, perhaps because of some kind of filtering the seastead put on her access to the Air. Ronnie was pacing from one end of her house to another like a caged lion: she could have left anytime, but what was out there for her? Without d-mat she was cut off from everything she knew and cared about. Tash, meanwhile, was climbing up a steep massif, glimpsed only in snatches by the lenses of her fellow climbers. She wasn't talking or posting. She was just moving forward the only way possible for her.

Clair had to do the same.

"That bike's the last thing you have left," she said, feeling a tug of sympathy for Jesse. "It had better still be there or . . ."

He laughed. "You can't fix *everything*, Clair. That way lies insanity."

She blushed. "Sorry."

"Besides, I'm not completely penniless. I own the patterns Dad created. It's not like I'm going to starve or anything."

"No one starves anymore," she said. "Except for you, when you're sticking to your principles. Or are you being metaphorical?"

"Abstainers do sometimes starve, if the weather turns bad, if crops fail, if there's no one nearby to help out. . . . It probably sounds utterly barbaric to you, but it does happen."

"Please tell me you don't want to live like that," she said.

"No . . . but I really don't want to put that fake stuff inside me either," he said, looking at her in a way that made it very clear that his feelings about Devin's injuries hadn't been erased. "If I had to choose . . . I mean, if what Devin just did is . . . ah, hell. Just don't make me choose. That's all I ask."

"Are you having second thoughts again?" she asked. It

took more courage than expected. She didn't want this to be something they kept coming back to, even though they always seemed to.

"Hell no."

His face came out from under his bangs, and she took the opportunity to kiss it, enjoying the increasingly familiar taste of his lips and the feel of his long body against hers. They were on a giant metal ship in the middle of an icy ocean, vast forces were gathering around them, but there was still time for this. For *them*. If she didn't have Jesse, she wondered how she would cope.

"Clair," said a voice.

They pulled apart. It was Sargent, hurrying across the landing toward them. "Something's come up, Clair. Something important."

It must have been important to make Sargent abandon the pretense of following her unnoticed.

"What is it?" Clair asked, feeling more than a twinge of alarm. "What's going on?"

"It's your mother," said the PK, coming to a grim-faced halt in front of her. "She's been kidnapped."

[27]

FIVE MINUTES LATER, in a glass bubble Devin called the crow's nest at the top of the giant vessel, Clair barely managed to sit through the official debrief. It was hard to listen without interrupting constantly. She was angry at the PKs for letting it happen. She was angry at her mother, too, for putting herself in danger. She was most angry at herself, although it was hard to see what she could have done. Maybe if she hadn't given the dupes a chance to act, if she hadn't relaxed . . .

"Your mother was contacted by this person at five p.m. yesterday," said Forest, sending her an image of a woman Clair had never seen before. The woman was dressed in a PK uniform. "She was advised that you would meet her outside the safe house at six p.m. and accompany her to a more secure location. At five forty-five p.m. your mother's escort was relieved and replaced by these people." Two more images, also unfamiliar. "At five fifty p.m. your mother was removed from protective custody and taken to the rendezvous two blocks away." Clair saw an image of an ordinary house. There was PK tape across the door, which chilled her. "By the time reinforcements arrived on the scene, she was gone. The people she went with have disappeared. All attempts to trace them have failed."

Clair imagined PKs running from the other side of town, unable to d-mat like they normally would, and the image was almost comical—except it wasn't funny at all. Her mother was gone.

Jesse was watching her with white lips. At least he understood how she must be feeling.

"They must have been dupes," she said in a voice that

sounded horribly even and sensible—nothing like how she felt inside. Just when she thought she had escaped the dupes for a little while, back they came with something even more horrible. "Mom had no reason to think they weren't real, so she did everything they said."

"She must have realized in the house, when they forced her into the booth, right?" Jesse looked worse than she felt, no doubt thinking of what had happened to his father. "Why didn't she call for help?"

"It's likely no one forced her to do anything," said Sargent. "If her daughter was there . . . or someone who looked exactly like her daughter, at least . . . why *wouldn't* she go with them?"

Clair wanted to fold forward across the table and wrap her head in her hands. Only the thought of how it would look stopped her. Devin and Trevin were there, leaning against the glass wall on either side of the door like protective statues. She didn't want them to think her weak. But she *was* weak, wasn't she, if she had let her mother down this badly?

"We have heard nothing, no demands or threats," said Forest, and for once she was grateful for his blank face. He wasn't patronizing her with something fake, something intended to be sympathetic or soothing. "I feel confident assuming that their demands haven't changed. If you tell them where Q is, your mother will be returned. Meanwhile, your mother's biometric data has been added to the list of known or suspected dupes. We have no recorded sightings yet."

Clair nodded, not wanting to think too hard about *that*. Her mother the dupe. What if the next time Clair saw Allison Hill she was really an assassin?

Part of her was momentarily glad Q was still missing. She didn't like to wonder which way she would have chosen, had she been asked to choose between her mother and her friend. . . .

"Facial recognition," Trevin said to Forest with a sneer. "Surely you can come up with something better than that to find the dupes."

"What else do you suggest?" said Sargent. "It's very difficult to trace the dupes back to their source because they come and go at random. Drones are therefore our first line of defense. Once dupes are visually identified, deputies deal with them on the ground."

"*Posses*, you mean," said Devin. "How many innocent lives have been lost due to mistakes or vendettas?"

"Casualties are unavoidable," said Forest. "While the vast majority of our forces remain immobilized—"

"As they seem likely to be forever." Trevin's sneer was unwavering. Clair wished he would stop picking at the PKs and concentrate on finding a way to get her mother back, or at least finding Q so they would have more options. She was sure Q could find Allison in a second. "Are you ever going to get d-mat working again?"

"We've isolated the reason why the system won't reboot," said Sargent. "The AI called Quiddity isn't alive after all. It's not functioning, not viable—*dead*, in other words. We're vetting former VIA technicians to jerry-rig a new overseer algorithm. We're also looking at ways to keep unauthorized users permanently out of the system—dupes and the general public alike." She glared back at Trevin. "Be warned: this includes RADICAL. If we have to pull the power on you, we will."

That surprised both twins.

"Shut off the powersats?" said Devin. "Are you serious? You know what that will do."

"Yes," she said in a tone that shocked Clair with its ferocity. "Everything will *really* stop then. No fabbers, no Air—all of it grinding to a dead halt. Next time you feel like complaining that life is tough, think about that first."

Three meals, Clair thought, staring at Sargent in disbelief. Turning off the powersats would be the end—not just of her mother but of everyone. That possibility jolted her out of her anxious self-recriminations. The dupes were striking at the very heart of her, yes, and it was time she struck back. But not like this. There had to be another way to destroy the dupes that didn't mean destroying the world with them. . . .

Forest's face *flicked* from one expression to another, as though trying out several to see which fit best. When it settled, it was one Clair had seen before, in New York:

stern, with a hint of warning.

"Our imaginations are running away with us," he said. "Let us instead ask what the dupes hope to achieve by kidnapping Clair's mother. What is it they want?"

"They might be trying to flush Clair back out into the open," said Sargent. "The videos they sent obviously didn't coerce her and their approach on the island didn't convince her, so maybe now they're trying to force her."

"Because of Q?" asked Jesse. "Do we really think she's still out there?"

"We've searched every byte of the Air," said Devin, "every server, every line of code in existence. There's no sign of her."

"We have searched too," said Forest. "If she still lives, she is well hidden."

"*Very* well hidden," said Sargent.

"That doesn't mean she's dead, though," said Clair.

"That's true," said Devin, "in which case you're our only hope. And the dupes' only hope too."

"I'm amazed," said Trevin, "that anyone's still laboring under the illusion that Clair knows anything about anything."

"I know *this*," said Clair, stung by the sharpness of his dismissal. "I know we don't know where Mom is, or Wallace, or what the dupes really want. Maybe it is all about Q, but what will they do with her if they get her? Put Wallace back in power by making more and more of them until they take over the world? We have to find a way to stop them. If you want to sit here and argue about who knows what, that's just fine, but don't single me out, all right? You're just as much in the dark as I am."

Trevin retreated with the corners of his lips pulled down. Devin was smiling, as though he liked seeing his older brother put in his place.

"You're right, Clair," Devin said. "We have to stop the dupes, but what do they even want? Mayhem and murder is about as high as they're reaching at the moment. They're not storming castles or plastering manifestos. Sometimes it seems more like an infection than a coordinated attack."

"A disease," said Sargent. "That's a good analogy."

"I'd describe the potential collapse of civilization as something slightly more serious than a head cold," said Trevin.

"The collapse of *your* civilization, you mean," said Jesse. "The idea that someone can copy you and move into your head . . . Who in their right mind would use d-mat after that gets out?"

"You don't seriously think the Abstainers are going to emerge on top of this, do you?" said Trevin, eyebrows almost comically high.

"They were fighting back long before you."

"Nobody's going to be on top of anything if we keep snapping at each other," said Clair, sticking her fingers into her curls and gripping her skull. She was sick of the endless *arguing*. "It's not helping Mom. . . . It's not helping anyone."

———————————————————— [28]

JESSE PUT A hand on her shoulder, to comfort her, Clair presumed, but it would take more than that.

"Sterling work, peacekeepers," said Trevin. "If you can't save one woman, how do you expect to save the world?"

Clair stared out of the crow's nest's glassy sphere along the broad, hulking mass of the seastead. The words she had just said still rang in her ears.

Nobody's coming out on top of anything if we keep arguing.

Nobody's coming out on top. . . .

"Whatever the dupes are doing," she said, "they're doing it while we stand around fighting each other."

Sargent tilted her head to one side. "You think the kidnapping of your mother is a diversion?"

"Maybe," she said, even though it felt like a betrayal to suggest that her mother wasn't important. Allison Hill was very important indeed, to Clair, but to the rest of the world she was just one more person in trouble. "Maybe not. Either way, we have to do something to stop them."

"Like what?" asked Jesse.

Clair didn't have an immediate answer, although the need for one burned inside her. Was all-out war really the best option? In all likelihood it had started already. She might not want to accept it, but the dupes would keep chipping away at her life until they destroyed everything she loved. When that failed, they would destroy her, too. She couldn't just stand around and let that happen. She *wouldn't*.

Clair would kill them all, every last dupe, every single hollow man and hollow woman, if that was what it took to bring her mother home. Behind cold anxiety, fury had begun to blaze, flaming hot and building fast.

Jesse was still talking. "We can't fight them because they're everywhere. We can't track them because we can't predict when they'll appear. We can't cut them off at the head because we're not sure if they even have a head. We can't ask them what they want because they're not talking."

"I for one am not surrendering to a dupe," said Devin. "Better dead than someone else in your head."

"What if it was your mother at stake?" Sargent asked.

"Leave our mother out of it," said Devin, tight-lipped. "She has nothing to do with this."

The debate raged among those tasked with coming to a strategic consensus. What on earth could bring peacekeepers, Abstainers, and RADICAL to any kind of agreement? Clair despaired of ever finding a solution . . . but there was something in her mind, some thought she needed to extract. She could feel it wriggling and gnawing at her, like a worm in an apple.

That metaphor made her think of Mallory gnawing her way into Libby's mind . . . and all the other Improved . . . and how uselessly she had marched into VIA HQ expecting to save them, handing herself and Turner to Wallace practically on a platter in the process. . . .

The worm swallowed itself and morphed into a light-bulb.

She had an idea.

"I know how we can fight them," she said, not caring who she cut off.

"Do tell," said Trevin.

"Well, we can't take on a whole world of dupes, not now that they've hacked into the VIA network. No one's crazy enough to think that, I hope. So what we do instead is lead them into a trap."

"How?"

"I'll send them a message, telling them we want to talk. That'll imply I know something. They'll be suspicious, of course, but the only way for them to find out is to make contact. And if we cut ourselves off from the Air, the only way to do that is to come here."

"Here?" said Trevin.

"Why not? It's away from cities, full of soldiers with guns, easily defended. That's why you're out here, isn't it?

So we use that to our advantage." Clair folded her arms. "Unless you're afraid."

Trevin bristled. "We're not afraid of a few dupes. But to what end? What do we gain from it?"

"We flush them out. Not just them, but their source, where they come from. Somewhere there has to be a server containing their original patterns, the ones they keep copying over and over again. If we can trick them into duping themselves here, we can track them—track their data right back to its source. And when we have that source, we erase it. Then we can get on with finding Mom, finding Q. Once the dupes are dead and their source is gone, they'll never come back, ever."

The angry flame in her heart burned brighter at that thought, which shocked her at the same time as it energized her. These weren't people, she told herself, but dupes, greedy ghosts stealing bodies in exchange for immortality. *Hollow* indeed, empty of all conscience and morals.

And they had attacked her and the people she loved. If Clair could threaten them in return, maybe they would give Allison back.

"Hang on," said Devin. "You've missed something. How are you going to lead them here? It's all hypothetical until you figure out a way to do that."

Here some of her confidence crumbled slightly, not because she wasn't sure of her plan, but because of what it might mean to her. "I'll have to offer something personal, so they can be sure it's not you guys talking. I'll have to wrap the bait in something completely honest, like telling the world my side of what's been going on, as I did before. If I do it just the right way, all everyone here has to do is be ready for them. Will you be?"

Devin and Trevin looked at Forest and Sargent.

"How about it, peacekeepers?" asked Trevin. "Are you going to commit?"

"We need to confer," said Forest. "This course of action will undoubtedly put lives at risk. It is not simply a matter of agreeing or disagreeing with something we personally feel is right."

"But you won't stop us, will you?" said Clair, suddenly afraid of what might happen if the PKs decided that it was in the world's best interest to halt the war between the dupes and RADICAL before it had even begun. . . .

Sargent shifted awkwardly on her seat.

"We will confer," was all Forest said again.

"Yes, you do that," said Devin. "Sooner rather than later, so we'll know exactly who we can rely on."

"Perhaps we should take a break," said Clair. "I'll start on my thing while everyone else does theirs."

"Do I have a thing?" asked Jesse.

That stumped her for a second.

"Talk to WHOLE," she said. "Find out who's in charge now that Turner is gone. You never know when that will come in handy. Maybe they can work with the PKs, tracking down the dupes like they did in New York. Okay?"

No one looked excited by that idea, but it was all she had. Maybe if terrorists and peacekeepers could get over their differences, there was hope for her and Jesse in the long run.

"Okay," Jesse said with a shrug. "Let's get this war on the road."

The group disbanded, Clair and Jesse heading back to their cabin to commence work on their particular tasks, she already dreading the lie she was going to have to tell.

[29]

I AM THE real Clair Hill, she wrote, *and I am telling you the truth.*

From there it got harder. In the hours following the meeting, she went backward and forward through the text of her announcement, trying to find exactly the right words for what she needed to say. She felt like she was going in circles, making no progress at all in defining either of the things in the opening sentence—the truth or Clair Hill.

We saved the world from Improvement, she wrote, *but that was only the beginning.*

And perhaps that was why she was having so much trouble. Her victory had come at a cost she was sure some people thought was too high. So what if a few listless kids were killed in order to give actual geniuses a second chance at life? Was it worth breaking d-mat to fix that relatively small problem? Was it worth switching off the powersats, if it came to that?

Dupes walk among us. . . .

If you see someone behaving strangely . . .

Not everyone is who they seem. . . .

Clair opened her eyes and stared up at the ceiling. The room she was sharing with Jesse was small, possibly the smallest bedroom Clair had ever seen—and it was meant for two! At least it had separate bunks, narrow though they were. Clair hoped she wouldn't be asked to sleep in them. They were about as comfortable as planks of wood.

Her lenses were confused. Sometimes her menus were the blue of ocean and arctic skies, sometimes they were the hard blue of steel and machines, courtesy of the seastead's internal networks. As she lay back on her narrow bunk and tried to concentrate, she could hear Jesse's fingers working hard on the bunk opposite, tapping out messages via his augs. His legs, crossed at the ankles, reached vertically up the wall because the mattress wasn't long enough for him to stretch out flat. Every now and again he reached out to touch her hand in wordless reassurance. She appreciated it, except for when it interrupted her train of thought. Overall, it was a good thing.

"Any luck with WHOLE?" she asked.

"Some," he said. "People know I've used d-mat now, so I have to win their trust back. It's tricky. But I've found out who took over from Turner Goldsmith. She's in Russia. Her name is Agnessa Adaksin. She's a hardliner, not one of the public Abstainers. People are blaming WHOLE for the collapse of d-mat, so she's abandoning the old cell structure and calling WHOLE to muster to her—and they're coming, every way they can."

Clair understood the instinctive need to find safety in numbers.

"Will she help?"

"I don't know. She won't take orders from me or the PKs, but I don't think she'll have any objection to fighting the dupes in a bigger way. Maybe we can just leak her the info she needs . . . make it look like she's in charge of any joint operations, not anyone else . . ."

"That's a good idea." And it was. In his own way Jesse was making more progress than she was.

I have been imprisoned, impersonated, threatened, and attacked. My mother has been kidnapped, my friends have been killed—and I'm not the only one who has been targeted this way. Some of the people who committed these crimes have been brought to justice, but others remain at large. Using everything we have, we're tracking them down and stopping them.

At least she hoped they were. But who were "we," exactly? Clair still didn't know.

Locating Sargent through the seastead interface, she sent a bump to see if there was any movement on that front. She felt more comfortable talking to Sargent than to Forest. They agreed on at least one important thing: giving people the right to return if their deaths were premature.

"We're still conferring," came the immediate reply. "It's complicated."

"How is it complicated? The dupes are the bad guys. They have my mother and they have to be stopped."

"Read this."

With Sargent's brisk reply came the results of a preliminary survey handed down by the Consensus Court. Clair had never been particularly interested in the workings of OneEarth, beyond watching her parents participate in the Consensus Court on matters that moved them. But she knew in principle how it worked. Everyone over eighteen could contribute if they wanted to, guided and informed by lawmakers. Lawmakers took their lead from random samples of people, creating a feedback loop that provided governance without needing any one person or group of people to be in charge.

Since the crash, lawmakers had been busy, along with peacekeepers and everyone else. Testimonies offered up by Jesse, Clair, and others, such as the Improved, had been processed. The results were just starting to come in.

People were to be judged, the preliminary survey said,

by their appearance. So if someone *looked like* Dylan Linwood, that was how he would legally be treated. In the case of disputed identities, where two people looked the same, everyone was to be kept in custody until some kind of consensus was reached as to who was who.

In other words, no one was ordering the peacekeepers to kill the dupes at this point, just to capture them and lock them away. And as for the Improved, they would be allowed to remain inside their new bodies indefinitely.

"What about parents who've lost their kids to Improvement?" Clair shot back, annoyed and frustrated by the ruling. "What about the families of the dupes? What about *me*?"

"I know, it's crazy," said Sargent. "And look, here's another one."

This survey concerned the legal status of people who had died in the process of being duped or Improved. It all came down to how they had last been *witnessed*. If the victims were last seen alive, then they were considered still alive and retrieval from a data cache was allowed. If they were last seen dead, then retrieval of an earlier pattern was not allowed. They had to stay dead.

By that ruling, Zep, Libby, and Dylan Linwood had all suffered verifiable deaths, either witnessed directly or recorded from afar, as in the case of Wallace's secret space station, and therefore they had to stay dead. That Ant Wallace and Mallory Wei were considered dead too was only a small consolation.

"This is wrong," said Clair, kicking one leg restlessly against the stiff mattress, barely able to contain her agitation.

"I know, but what can I do about it?" asked Sargent. "A peacekeeper's job is not to define the peace or how to keep it. That's what the Consensus Court is for."

"So if the Court told you to kill every firstborn . . . ?"

"That wouldn't happen. OneEarth is self-monitoring, self-correcting."

"Isn't that what they used to say about VIA?"

Sargent didn't respond to that, which only made Clair more anxious.

At least the decision hadn't been unanimous. One of the loudest dissenting voices belonged to LM Kingdon, the lawmaker who had offered her legal advice after the PKs had taken her in for questioning. She was a gray-eyed, middle-aged woman from London who believed that all dupes should be wiped out immediately, whatever the cost. Clair skimmed a speech Kingdon made to the Consensus Court and found herself agreeing with every word.

As Clair watched that speech, a bump came from Kingdon herself.

"Is now a good time?"

Surprised, because she'd thought she was invisible to anyone looking at the seastead, Clair hesitated, then answered, "It so isn't."

"I mean, to chat."

A request followed. Clair hesitated again. She had understood what Kingdon meant, but she didn't understand why the lawmaker was contacting her. Clair was far from a model citizen at that moment, given the company she was keeping. Besides, it wasn't long ago that she herself had had ambiguous legal status, existence-wise. Bringing Kingdon into the mix might only make her situation more precarious.

Turning Kingdon down, though, could be even worse, depending on what the lawmaker wanted. Everyone seemed to want something.

"Okay," she said, accepting the request.

"It's good to talk at last." Kingdon's voice was warm and British in Clair's ears. It came with a live image. The lawmaker was in a wood-paneled office, leaning back into her seat and crossing her legs in front of her. She wore a dark-blue suit with a white shirt and open collar. There was a silk tie lying on the desk in front of her, pink with blue spots. Her smile was relaxed and natural. Kingdon's voice had the same kind of easy authority that Clair associated with the least annoying school counselors.

"You're a tough girl to get hold of," Kingdon said. "It's taken me a long time to get through. But I've been following you with interest: Libby and Improvement, your friend Zep's death, that terrible situation with Ant Wallace in New York . . ." Here Kingdon paused, and Clair wondered if she was considering adding *your brave and pointless sacrifice*. "Now there's your mother. . . . My dear, if anyone has reason to hate the dupes, it's you."

Me and a million other people, Clair thought, but she wasn't so cynical that she was unmoved by the woman's concern.

"Thanks for your messages," she said, clearing her throat.

"My offer of legal advice was sincere," Kingdon said. "It remains on the table."

"Thanks, but—"

"You don't need to decide now. I'll never turn you down. We have to look out for each other, Clair. We have much in common."

"We do?"

"I like to think so. We're both determined to put an end to the injustice of this situation. I don't know what exactly you're doing right now, but I'm sure you're not sitting idly by—as I am not. You can see what my efforts have been, and I want you to know that I won't give up until the natural sovereignty of ordinary people over their bodies is fully restored. That's something you agree with, isn't it?"

"I guess so."

"Of course it is. People are people, and they have all the proper rights accorded to them by law. Illegal duplicates are not people and as such have no rights—and we, lawmakers and peacekeepers and citizens of OneEarth alike, must be clear on this. Ambiguity is unacceptable. Tolerance is unacceptable. We must use every measure available to permanently eradicate this threat to our lives and liberty."

Kingdon had left her seat and was roaming around her study, pausing to adjust the placement of service awards, to straighten a framed OneEarth flag, and to brush the dust off a bust of Martin Luther King, Jr. Clair felt as though she was being lectured at—and it was then she wondered what the lawmaker was really doing. She had called Clair when Clair was alone, presumably so they wouldn't be interrupted, but at the same time the chat was public from Kingdon's end. People could hear everything Kingdon was saying to her. Was Kingdon using Clair as a means of getting her message across to a larger audience?

That was okay, to a point, Clair thought. They did agree with each other when it came to the dupes and the laws required to bring back people like Libby and Zep. It just stung that Kingdon didn't care about *her*. The sympathy was fake, and maybe the offers to help were too.

Still, Clair told herself to be relieved. As long as she didn't say the wrong thing, as long as she played the game, she wouldn't draw the full attention of the Consensus Court and find herself under investigation again. As long as she was useful to Sara Kingdon, Clair Hill would be fine. And if Clair Hill was fine, a chance remained for Allison Hill.

So she nodded and tried not to look bored until LM Kingdon had finished her spiel. They exchanged pleasantries.

"Let's talk again when all this is over," said Kingdon with another broad smile. "I can even help you with your vocational choices, if you like. The world always needs bright new lawmakers."

Clair made polite noises even though the last thing she wanted to be was a lawmaker. Of that she was certain.

One sentence of Kingdon's speech remained with her when the chat was over.

We must use every measure available to permanently eradicate this threat to life and liberty.

It sounded so black and white, and in principle Clair agreed, but how was she to know when she had done enough? Was it possible to do *too much*?

Clair considered waking Jesse to talk through the slightly surreal experience, but decided to let him sleep. Instead, she wrote and erased several sharp messages to Sargent, without whom she couldn't really do anything, eventually settling on the simple but testy, "Seriously, how long does it take to *confer*?"

"Just finished," Sargent immediately sent back. "We're sending official observers to the seastead, so we'll have PKs on the ground when this goes down. They're authorized to respond if provoked. When the dupes attack us, in other words, we will fight back."

"Even if there's no official position on the dupes? Even if they send dupes in bodies that are still legally recognized as people?"

"Doesn't matter who or what's breaking the peace. Human or otherwise, we're obliged to stop it."

"Okay," Clair said, forcing herself to accept what concessions she could get. "I can live with that."

Clair returned to her draft, somewhat reassured. With RADICAL and the PKs on her side, and the backup of leading lawmakers like Kingdon, how could the dupes possibly beat her?

All she had to do was write the right message.

There's so much I want to say, but there's so much I still haven't worked out. Maybe it is partly my fault that d-mat isn't working at the moment—but wasn't it really Ant Wallace's fault in the first place for using d-mat to kill people? Someone had to stop him. I wish it had been someone other than me, because then Libby would still be alive. I wish that every day. You can believe that.

Oh, but if you see any videos of me doing crazy stuff? It's probably the dupes trying to make me look bad again. Follow me, follow what I'm doing, because actions speak louder than words. Let's kick out the dupes, get this world working again. For my mother, and for everyone else in danger.

Until they're all safe . . .

Clair hesitated. Even in a rough draft, a long way from

reaching its audience, she found the final sentence hard to write. She didn't know why. It wasn't as though the words had magic powers and a dupe would suddenly appear in the cabin with her and Jesse. His eyes were closed, lashes surprisingly long and delicate now that she took a second to notice them. She wanted to sit still and study him, marveling in him while she had the chance. All those years they had been at school together and she had barely noticed him. Now she couldn't get enough of him. It amazed her how quickly things had changed. She didn't want to think about how quickly things could change again. It made her heart race to imagine where they might be in a few hours, either way.

There was no time for stillness. She had to move forward, her eyes on the destination and everything she would need to do to get there.

Until they're all safe, she wrote, *I talk to Nobody.*

—————————————— [30]

"YOU'VE STOPPED WRITING," Devin bumped her fifteen minutes later. "Does that mean you're finished?"

She didn't reply. He was monitoring her lenses again, thanks presumably to the seastead's interface. Just because she had finished the message didn't mean she was ready to send it. One Rubicon at a time. How would the dupes respond? What if the dupes took her message as the challenge it was and raised the stakes even higher? What if they killed her mother—or worse? What if they ignored the message completely?

Sitting around watching Jesse sleep wasn't helping Clair work up the courage to commit to this crucial component of her plan, so she put on a shirt she had fabbed and slipped out of the room. The fabric of the shirt felt stiff and starchy against her skin, reminding her of the uniforms soldiers used to wear. If anyone expected her to shave her head they'd find themselves in a whole world of hurt.

The seastead hummed and buzzed around her as she wandered its empty metal corridors, meandering through mysterious chambers and marveling at the extravagant weirdness that was in essence a mobile city. Only before the Water Wars could something like this have seemed a sensible idea. In every other period of history that she was aware of, especially her own, it was the city that stayed put and the people who moved. But here she was, sailing the high seas on the back of a machine big enough to move an entire population. It did have a certain grandeur, she supposed, but so did a lot of other crazy things from the past, like atomic bombs and emperors.

She wondered what her mother was thinking right then, if there was anything magnificent in *her* circumstances, or just misery and fear.

She hoped the dupes understood that she would never, ever stop if they harmed a single hair on her mother's head.

Clair bit her lip to stop herself from crying like a baby.

"Going anywhere in particular?" Devin bumped her.

"The place with all the booths," she said, regaining her composure and picking a destination at random. "Where we arrived."

"You're way off course," he said. "Left up here."

She followed his directions and saw nothing but more corridors.

"You wandering around lost, me giving you directions. No matter how many friends in high places you get, we'll always have this."

Clair sighed and opened a chat, knowing she'd never be able to restrict a conversation with him to merely a few lines.

"What do you want? To tell me off for talking to LM Kingdon?"

"No, the call was scrambled at her end. If anyone traced you from there to here, they've got Q-level skills. I'm just after your draft letter."

"Who says it's finished?"

"You're not fooling anyone. What's the problem? Cat got your tongue for once?"

She recoiled at the thought of handing it over, even though it was more or less complete. It was her plan, and she was the one with the *reasons*. What would her mother want her to do? That was what really mattered to Clair. Was she taking every available measure, or one too many?

"I don't see that there's any great hurry. Why don't you look for Q while you're waiting? I'm sure Trevin's not right about her refusing to help."

"The PKs are sending their troops in an hour. We don't want them to get bored."

"That's . . . really soon," she said.

"War waits for no one. Or should that be waits for Nobody?"

"Don't joke about this."

"Not joking, Clair. I'm in no hurry to die. But that's the trouble with world-changing events. Individual opinions don't matter. When it comes to war, we're lemmings. One lemming always has to go over the cliff first."

"Are you threatening me or cracking a joke?"

"Neither. T's the funny one."

"Your brother is even more of a dick than you are."

"Listening right now," came Trevin's voice over the chat. She was learning to differentiate them. "Parapsychic twin-link, remember? Always on."

Clair didn't care. She had reached an empty weapons hold and stood there for a moment, thinking of the plan as they'd left it. Perhaps there was some way to make it less risky.

"We should shut down the booths," she said. "All of

them. Physically disconnect them, if possible. That way the dupes won't sneak up on us."

"Not even one?" asked Devin. "How will they get here, then?"

"They'll find a way." She was sure of that. The dupes had shown themselves to be endlessly resourceful. "Let's make them earn it."

"All right," he said. Via the chat she could see him nodding in approval. "I like that."

She did too. Maybe it would limit the fighting to just a handful of dupes. On the flip side, without the seastead's booths in operation, there would be no escape until it was over. They would be stuck for good or ill while the gambit played out, after which she and her mother and the rest of the world would be safe, or they wouldn't.

The message was the only plan she had. There was no point delaying. Still, she gave herself one more minute in case inspiration struck, then when it didn't sent Devin the draft.

Two minutes later he responded, "Nice. That'll do the trick."

"Do you think he'll get it?"

"Nobody? He'll get it for sure. He wanted to talk to you in New York, before he tried to kill you, and how many times has he come after you since? He'll know it's a trap, but he'll come anyway. He thinks he can afford to. He is legion."

She shivered.

"Don't worry," Devin said. "You have powerful enemies, and powerful friends, too. I'm not talking about LM Kingdon. If anyone's going to beat these guys, it'll be us."

She still wasn't entirely sure what RADICAL was getting out of this. The chance to take the credit for putting the dupes out of action, perhaps.

"With the PKs," she reminded him.

"I remain uncertain that they're entirely our friends. They haven't been eager to line up and be counted, that's for sure."

"It's their job to stop wars, not fight them," she said.

"Particularly wars that aren't in their best interest."

"Do you mean what happened to Sargent on the island? According to PK Forest, any kind of reactivation is completely impossible."

"And I bet he's killer at poker. What I mean is that Sargent has personal reasons for resurrection to become the norm."

"What reasons?"

"Her girlfriend's pattern was lost in the crash. Did you not know about that?"

Clair forced herself not to react to his tone. That particular piece of information would explain why Sargent had grilled Clair so passionately about Zep during her interrogation in New York. But why had she never mentioned it? There had been lots of opportunities.

"So we're all the same," she said, feeling a new kind of weariness. "No one apart from Forest cares about the consensus. Why are we even bothering to fight this war? Why don't we just all shake hands and get on with copying whoever we want?"

"No one wants there to be no laws at all," Devin said. "It may not matter if Sargent was resurrected and everyone pretends nothing happened, but it does matter if we erase death from the equation entirely. That changes humanity as a whole in ways we're probably not ready for. RADICAL stands for giving individuals the right to choose what happens to them—and in that sense we're like WHOLE, rather than the dupes. We don't want dupes bossing us around any more than we want AIs. Which is why I feel sorriest for Jesse in all this. He's made it clear he doesn't want to use d-mat, but we keep dragging him through anyway. I'd be a lot angrier about that if I were him."

Clair was surprised to hear Devin express sympathy for Jesse, and it made her like him a little, and RADICAL, too, although she felt slightly unnerved by their willingness to go to war over matters of principle. Who thought that way? Who lived their life always looking ahead, planning for things that could go wrong? Who would fight for the right to ask questions?

Perhaps that was the most important battle to fight of all, she thought, remembering Devin's comment about lemmings. She might be a lemming, teetering on the edge of the proverbial cliff, but did that mean she was a soldier lemming, or a terrorist lemming, or something else entirely?

"So when the PKs are ready," she said, "we send the message. Then what?"

"The PKs are coming through now," Trevin said. "We'll leak your location when the message goes out, so the dupes will know exactly where you are and who you're with."

She nodded, although the imminence of conflict made her quail.

"Keep me out of your twin thing," she said. "Am I almost there yet?"

"Not far," Devin promised her. "Wait, you mean the staging area?"

"Yes."

"In that case, you've still got a ways to go. Turn right up here and I'll show you the rest of the way."

[31] ————————————————————

IN THE STAGING area, numerous blue-and-white-armored PKs were already stepping from the booths and assembling in rows. Clair stood in the middle of the space for a moment, feeling not unpleasantly lost in the hustle and bustle. Much easier, she reflected, to be a cog in a giant machine than the person with her finger on the GO button.

"Hey, Clair," said a voice, making her jump.

PK Drader was standing behind her with his helmet resting on his hip.

"What're you doing here?" she asked.

"Got sick of doing prisoner transport and came to see some real action," he said. He hadn't shaved since New York, and his face looked swarthy with the beginnings of a beard. "Before I joined the PKs I studied economics. I know, right? No wonder I never managed to keep a girl-friend. Eventually I realized that my true calling was to stamp out bad guys—but it's kinda hard to do that when all the action's taking place on the other side of the world. So here I am, ready for anything."

"You volunteered to come here?"

"Of course." He grinned. "All it takes for evil to win is good people doing nothing. Is that how the saying goes? You feel that way too, I imagine. You're obviously not standing around watching as the bad guys ruin every-thing for everyone else."

Clair supposed that was true. She *was* a volunteer, in that she could have been doing any number of other things, hiding in protective custody being one of them. This felt better, looking at what she was doing this way, rather than as an attempt to fix the mistakes she had made in the past.

All the same, Clair found PK Drader's eagerness unset-tling. It was almost as though he was trying too hard to prove his readiness for battle.

"What happened to Tilly? I mean, Xia?"

"They got to her. I don't know how." He looked down at his feet. "I put her and the others safely into custody in HQ, but last night someone hacked the system and put poison in their food. Gone, every one of them. But it's okay," he said, watching her face fall and misunderstanding why. "When we find the person responsible, they're going to be up against the wall for sure."

Clair wasn't worried about who had done it. She was just sickened by more pointless deaths. The Improved had done terrible things, but they remained people. And it was even worse than that: by law Tilly Kozlova was now officially dead. She had joined the ranks of Libby and all the others, more victims no one seemed to be fighting for, except her.

"On the bright side," Drader said, his grin returning, "we're making progress tracking the dupes. Here, take a look."

A patch popped up in her infield, requesting permission to install a new interface. She allowed it, and the familiar PK colors unfolded in a new window.

"See? We've been fabbing drones in record numbers and updating algorithms as fast as we can. Now we can track anyone, duplicate or dead, all across the globe—and the crash has actually helped us by freeing up data channels we couldn't access before. It's a gold rush on dupes, and we're cashing in."

The interface was a sea of colors that confused Clair

until she zoomed in close on a random location. The sea resolved into dozens of individual points, some yellow, some blue, some red, all across the rainbow except for green. Selecting one of the dots told her the name of the pattern—Jamila Murray, in this case—and its exact location. A sentence or two outlined its activities and the steps taken to deal with it.

She zoomed back out. The globe was crawling with dupes, like ants invading a termite colony.

Clair wondered if her mother was with one of those multicolored dots, or if she had *become* one of them, but was afraid to ask.

There was also a button that changed the view to show only green dots, which represented peacekeepers. It was hard to tell which group outnumbered which, green or multicolored. They looked about evenly matched.

A bright cluster of green was forming near Greenland, and Clair told herself to take comfort in that.

"Get something to eat, Clair. You look done in. Promise me?"

She assured him she would.

"See you in the trenches," PK Drader said before returning to his preparations.

Clair felt a strong urge to salute. She resisted.

Retracing her steps to a mess hall she had passed earlier, Clair sat at a table on her own, making some final tweaks to the message. She had until all the PKs were aboard before it needed to be sent. She planned to use every moment she had to perfect it.

Sargent came into the mess, dressed in heavy armor with a helmet clipped to her side. She went straight to the fabbers, muttered impatiently until the machine accepted her instructions. Only when she reached in and took out the tray did she see Clair. Without asking, she walked over to the table and sat opposite her.

"You look terrible," Clair said, and Sargent did: pale and stressed, with heavy bags under her eyes. "Are you all right?"

"Just hungry and tired. It caught up with me."

"I can see that. Don't talk. Just eat."

Sargent nodded and did as PK Drader had told Clair to do, tackling the array of food on her tray as though it was a challenge and damned if she was going to quit. Most of the vegetables were raw, as was the egg in a glass to one side. There was some sushi, a sliver of rare steak in black bean sauce, and a bowl of blackberries topped with a dollop of yogurt. Sargent worked through it in no particular order, wielding her spoon in her left hand while Clair watched, warily fascinated. Who ate like this? PKs, maybe. She had never seen one eat before.

"You should go into RADICAL's machine," Clair half joked. "The one that fixes you up without your having to see a surgeon. I'm sure that would make you feel better."

"Not allowed," Sargent said around a mouthful of steak and blackberries. "The Inspector wouldn't approve."

"I know. That's what I thought, but . . . even in a war?" Clair wanted to ask her outright about being reactivated, but couldn't bring herself to.

"Never," Sargent said. "Why? Do you want to do it? I could look the other way. . . ."

"No," said Clair. "I'm just . . . that is . . . I don't know. Devin told me about your girlfriend, and I guess I understand what that feels like . . . sort of."

When you come back from the dead but someone you care about can't.

Sargent stared at Clair with her spoon hovering unmoving over her plate, a bean sprout protruding from the corner of her mouth. Clair couldn't read her expression.

"Billie was a good person," Sargent said slowly, staring at the ring on her wedding finger as though seeing it afresh. "She shouldn't have died."

Clair nodded.

"That's why you disagree with the Inspector."

"*Yes,*" said Sargent. Her eyes grew very full, as though they were made of glass.

Then she seemed to collect herself. Clearing her throat and tucking the bean into her mouth with her right hand, she said, "But the Inspector could be right. Even if we did make reactivation legal, who gets to make a decision like that—to bring someone back from the dead or not? You?

Me? The Consensus Court? I'm not sure we're grown up enough to make that call. Do you?"

"I don't know." Sargent was looking at her now, and Clair felt bad for intruding on the woman's grief. It had made Sargent babble, "I'm sorry. It's okay if you don't want to talk about it. . . ."

Sargent shook her head firmly.

"Some things are more important than the people we love." The spoon swooped in for another load. "That's what I try to tell myself."

Clair hoped she never had to choose between her job and her mother, or Libby, or anyone else she was trying to save. It was an unbearable thought.

She was almost glad when a bump came from Devin.

"Everything's ready. We want to send the message now."

"Wait," she sent back. "Here's the latest version."

She had added a section asking people for help finding Ant Wallace. If he was still alive, as Xia suggested, and if he could be tracked down and stopped a second time, then maybe the dupes could be turned back. Maybe he could even be reasoned with. Maybe the Improved who remained could be un-Improved, as Xia had hoped.

No one is entirely evil, she had written. *Not me, not Ant Wallace. I sacrificed myself to try to stop him, and my friend Q brought me back. I'm not saying that was the right thing to do, but it has given me a chance to understand that what I did was wrong. Everyone deserves a second chance. Wallace tried to give me one, in his own way, but I took that possibility away from him. For that, and for many other things, I am sorry.*

She didn't think her confession would make Wallace turn himself in. She just hoped Q would be listening and that she would understand that Clair was talking to her as well as the rest of the world. At the same time, Clair dreaded what her mother would think upon reading it, if she was able to. Clair was publicly discussing being dead by her own hand, and a murderer to boot.

"All good," said Devin. "Come up to the crow's nest and we'll send the message off together."

Something similar must have reached Sargent at the same time, because she grunted, nodded, shoveled one last spoonful into her mouth, and said to Clair, "Right. Are you ready?"

"Are you?"

"Too bad if I'm not," Sargent said, pushing back with both hands on the table. "There's no getting out of it now."

She flashed a nervous smile that Clair returned. At least someone else wasn't looking forward to the fight.

————————————————— [32]

THEY PICKED UP Jesse on the way. He was bleary-eyed and startled, having been woken only moments before by PK

Drader. She and Sargent found the two of them scrabbling around behind the mattress in search of the audio component of Jesse's augs, which had slipped out while he slept.

"Chill," said PK Drader in response to her anxiety that they might be late. "They won't start without you. You're the star of the show."

Clair didn't respond. If he was trying to make her feel better, he was going about it completely the wrong way.

Forest was pacing back and forth in full armor in the crow's nest with Devin and Trevin.

"RADICAL is ready," said Trevin. If it had ever seemed odd to Clair that an adolescent spoke for the entire crew of the massive seastead, his confident tone dispelled any remaining shreds of doubt. RADICAL trusted the twins, so she supposed she should too. "Post the message now, Clair. We'll lift our firewalls long enough to give you access to your profile."

"Any news on Mom?"

"None," said Forest. "I will advise you the very moment—"

"Yeah, I know." She couldn't help hoping, though. Inhaling deeply, she held the decision in her mind a moment longer. "All right. Let's go."

The view through her lenses shifted, taking on her usual wallpaper shapes and textures, and suddenly her infield was flooded with all the bumps and grabs she had been avoiding since coming to the seastead.

"Where are you now? Come home! Your fault! Fix this!

Who is this? Is it true? Tell me everything! Don't lie!"

The anxieties of the entire world were pouring through her lenses in one tangled flood, mirroring and adding to her own. When she had concocted her original plan in the Farmhouse, days before the crash, she had dreamed of a few thousand followers. Now they numbered in the tens of millions and "Clair Hill" was a meme, not a person. The thought of it terrified her just as much as the dupes. If the behemoth turned on her, she could be in more danger from her fans than from anyone else. And what about the PKs? Would they continue to protect her if her meme became a threat to peace?

"Clair? Are you going to post?" That was Devin, one voice among millions. "You're visible now. The seastead is vulnerable. We have to close the firewalls."

She wished they would. Her news grabs contained a thousand calamities in a thousand places, some natural, some not. There were fires and other catastrophes that Rescue and Repair couldn't get to. There were criminals in makeshift jails and empty hospitals far from scenes of accidents. Small enclaves were forming where PKs couldn't reach, ruled over by opportunistic tyrants who declared this the End of Days. Pitched battles were being waged between communities where long-held differences had bubbled over into conflict. The stats for rapes, murders, and other violent crimes were way up. Healthy communities banded together, but even in those places it was becoming difficult. A lot of people hadn't left their homes since the crash, like Ronnie. While they had fabbers, what reason did they have to leave?

Xandra Nantakarn and the rest of the crashlanders were still stuck at the bottom of their cave. One of them had broken a leg in a fall and bled to death, while two others had been forcibly restrained after an argument had escalate into physical conflict.

Tash was lying on her back and staring at the sky, exhausted. Both she and Ronnie had noticed her reappearance through the Air and were already writing messages that Clair was sure she didn't want to read.

"If you don't post it now, Clair," said Trevin, this time, "we'll do it for you."

He was right. She had to.

With a feeling of stepping off the cliff and into free fall, Clair posted the message to her profile.

At first it was just one slab of text among many others, but it attracted attention instantly. Even as the firewalls remade the barriers around her, she saw people starting to notice. People were sharing. Her friends stopped messaging to read. Dupes were doing the same, she hoped.

Then the shutters came down, the real world disappeared, and her lenses were restored to their former steel-gray appearance. She mentally returned to the crow's nest and the view of the illuminated seastead below. There was an electrical storm on the western horizon. Her mouth felt dry.

"Every booth on the seastead is offline, as you

suggested," said Trevin. "Nothing comes in or out until we put the plug back in. And I mean *nothing*. If the dupes can find a way in here via d-mat, I'll eat Devin."

"I think I'm safe," said Devin, "although I would be quite tasty. How are you PKs doing?"

"Ready, here and around the world," said Forest. "As soon as the dupes appear, the routes their patterns took through the Air will be traced."

"And the source erased," said Drader. "All you've got to do," he said to the twins, "is stop them from destroying the seastead first."

"We should get you armored up," said Sargent to Clair.

She nodded. *Hope for the best, prepare for the worst.* If they *did* find the source, she would need to be on the ball. She didn't want any cache erased until she was sure none of her friends were in there too. "How long do we have?"

"Hours, most likely," said Forest. "The dupes need to find a way to cross the distance here. We will probably get bored waiting."

That might have been a joke. It was hard to tell with his face.

Trevin turned his head to the left, as though something had startled him out of the corner of his eye. An instant later Devin did the same thing, and Clair guessed that they were sharing something via their parapsychic twin thing.

"We've detected a launch from the Atlantic," Trevin

said. "Suborbital, by the look of it: a Quicklaunch space-gun, like a big tube lying mostly underwater so there's no exhaust or heat spike to give it away. We saw it any-way and we're tracking the projectile now. Its trajectory looks . . . worrying."

"Already?" said Jesse, with alarm.

"Definitely coming this way," said Trevin. "Doesn't have to have a payload to cause us trouble. A direct hit would be bad enough."

"ETA seventeen minutes," said Devin. "It's going to come in hot."

"We underestimated them," said Clair. "Again."

"Get everyone in position," said Forest.

"Drag will make it hard to project its course," said Trevin, but Sargent wasn't letting Clair stick around to hear the rest. She pulled her by the arm out of the room and down the ramp to get suited up.

[33]————————————————

JESSE SENT CLAIR a patch so she could track the projec-tile as more data became available. There wasn't much to see, but she kept it up front on her lenses so she wouldn't miss anything. In another window was the dupe-tracking interface that PK Drader had given her. Nothing appeared to be changing on that front. The multicolored dots were still everywhere.

Sargent kept Clair up-to-date on other fronts as they hurried.

"The dupes' launch site is under attack. Hypersonic drones, with payloads. We can fab them faster than they can fab spaceguns, so it's likely there'll be just the one missile."

Clair wasn't sure about *anything* to do with the dupes now. The speed with which they had responded was frightening.

"Does this count as breaking the peace?" she asked. "Are you committed now?"

"Depends what the missile does. If it's a warning shot, as in Antarctica, no."

"But this time we're not going to run."

"I guess it depends on what they do when we don't, then."

Sargent hurried her into a medical suite and told her to strip. There wasn't time to be embarrassed. Clair slipped out of the uniform and stood hugging herself until the fabber pinged. Sargent handed her a new undersuit and she slipped into it as the next cycle started. It was made of a stiffer material than the one she'd worn before, with metallic threads forming an extra weave across her torso and throat. There was a cowl that came up over her head, with an oval barely large enough for her face to poke through. She left that dangling down her back, thinking it was a mistake. She was expecting a suit similar to Jesse's, with the hoodie they had had before. It didn't seem possible to fit her hair into this one.

What emerged from the fabber in several stages was heavy blue-and-white armor identical to Sargent's, lacking only the insignia. Sargent helped her put each segment in place, making sure every joint and seal was correct. There was a lot of overlap, but her movement was almost entirely unimpeded. The armor as a whole was amazingly light for something that felt so comprehensively *safe*.

A lens interface lit up as her chest plate went on, providing instant updates on her own respiration, heartbeat, temperature, blood sugar levels . . . Last to come out of the fabber were a helmet, a pistol, and a jagged knife.

"Uh, I don't think I'll need that," Clair said as the last was clipped firmly to her side.

"Take it," Sargent insisted. "Better to have it and not need it than the alternative."

Clair couldn't imagine any circumstance under which she might willingly stick a sharp object inside another person, but she took it anyway. Two weeks ago she couldn't have imagined shooting at someone either.

"Looks like it's coming down about a mile from here," Jesse bumped her as she made her way back up to the crow's nest, feeling like someone in fancy dress. Her hair, with Sargent's help, had been smoothed back into the cowl. She felt naked without it in her peripheral vision, despite everything she was wearing.

A mile seemed a long distance, but she supposed that in terms of a missile launched a quarter of the world away, it wasn't really.

"We'll be able to see it?" she asked.

"Depending on the weather, probably."

Clair and Sargent returned in the middle of a conversation about deploying PK attack drones in advance of the missile's arrival. PK Drader was elsewhere, checking up on the disposition of the peacekeeper observers.

"We will provide you with drones," Forest was saying, "on the condition they are not used to initiate conflict."

"Okay, so send us the patterns," Devin said, "and we'll fab them. There's enough time before touchdown to get them in the air."

"Give me control of the drones," said Jesse. "I can pilot them if someone else does any shooting."

"We'll hitch you up with a gunner, no problem," said Trevin before Clair could volunteer.

Data exchanged hands. Ports opened on the seastead's upper reaches. Energy swirled within the ports, and drones began to emerge in a steady stream. It seemed like magic until Clair realized what the ports actually were: they were weaponized fabbers, like the d-mat gun Devin had jerry-rigged on Ons Island. Fabbing drones en masse was probably the most peaceful of their intended uses.

Jesse backed up and closed his eyes. His fingers danced. Clair still had the drone interface she had used in Crystal City, and on opening it she could see him taking command of the flock of drones and sweeping them off to the likely impact site.

A timer was counting down. One minute to go.

"We're seeing no increased activity in the Air," said Sargent. "No spikes in data flow indicating a surge of duping."

"So it hasn't started yet," said Clair.

"Let's be ready for anything," said Devin.

"We have an orbital asset changing attitude," said Trevin. "Powersat. Beam coming our way."

Clair looked around the glass bubble at the night outside. "Should we move somewhere less exposed?"

"No need," Trevin said.

The view outside the crow's nest went black as the glass turned to mirror. An instant later, an identical view took its place, projected onto the interior of the bubble. Clair saw a new beam of hazy light stabbing toward them from the south, sweeping the ocean like a searchlight.

Seconds later, a fiery, red line flashed across the view. Steam rose up from the eastern horizon. The missile had struck the ocean.

"No sign of a chemical or nuclear explosion," said Trevin.

Clair hadn't even considered the latter. In the normal world, making dangerously radioactive elements in a d-mat booth was utterly forbidden. She waited for movement as the shockwave struck, or even a sound, but there was nothing.

The powersat beam adjusted its trajectory slightly and began burning away the steam.

"I see something in there," said Jesse, shifting everyone's attention to the drone interface. His flying eyes had been widely scattered by the arrival of the missile, but several had penetrated deep into the steam and were sending back data unimpeded. It was very hard to tell what was going on in there. Occasionally a drone would hit the fringe of the powersat beam and fizz out in a wash of static.

"Where?" said Clair.

"Here." He wrapped a frame around one corner of a view from one of the drones, the image caught in midswoop. "It's a structure of some kind."

If she squinted she could see something black sticking out of the choppy water below the drone. Slowly more images arrived, giving her a sense of what it might be. It resembled a giant raft from which three tall, angled chimney stacks protruded.

"Doesn't look like a ship," said Jesse.

"They're mad if they think we're going to let them sail right up to us," Trevin said.

"No communications?" asked Clair. "No public response to my post?"

"Only this," said Forest.

The powersat beam hit the ship or whatever it was and locked on. At the touch of the energetic beam the construct came to vigorous life, sucking energy and turning it into new shapes, new mass, new functions. The chimneys extended, and flared slightly at the open end.

Devin said, "Does anyone else think they look like . . ."

"Cannons, yes," said Trevin. "Built to fire big shells."

"For taking out a big boat?" said Sargent. "I guess that makes sense."

"We'll increase our armor on that side, just in case, and pull our head in."

Clair could already feel a grinding vibration through her feet as the seastead fabbed new layers of protection. That was added to a sinking sensation as the crow's nest retreated into the body of the vessel.

"We could totally take it out right now, before anything happens," said Devin with an eager look in his eye.

"Yes, and that would make you the aggressor," said Forest.

"Even pacifists must dream of casting the first stone *sometimes*. . . ."

[34]

"WE'RE GETTING SOME serious activity now," said Sargent, eyes dancing across data Clair couldn't see. "Something's building out there. Literally."

With a flash of yellow light, the middle cannon fired, unleashing a sphere that arced across the ocean in a flat parabola toward the seastead.

A harsh, electronic siren blatted once. The chat opened wider, indicating that the RADICAL twins now were talking to more than just those in the crow's nest. A rustle of distant voices made Clair feel like she was standing in a crowd.

"Here it comes!" called Trevin. "Can't tell if that cannonball is hot or not."

Clair stood closer to Jesse. Both of them put their helmets on, just in case, but left the visors open. Everyone's attention was on the data as it streamed in from the outside. Every sensor on the seastead followed the sphere closely, measuring it in every possible way. It was four yards across and dark gray, and it cast soft reflections in radar.

"Could be explosive," said Devin. "Could contain acid to corrode the hull. Could be anything. Can we fire now?"

Forest nodded, and Clair let out a sigh of relief.

Defensive fire from the seastead raked the dark surface of the sphere, but it kept on coming, absorbing the impacts like pebbles thrown down a well.

"Brace yourselves," said Devin.

Clair had just enough time to take Jesse's gloved hand before the missile hit. There was no movement through the hull, and no explosion, either. Drone cameras zoomed in on the impact site to see what had happened.

The missile had splatted flat against the hull without exploding or breaking open. Instead, it rebounded into a squat hemisphere, like a giant raindrop on a giant wall.

"Is that it?" asked Jesse.

"We're picking up vibrations," said Trevin.

"Drilling?" said Forest.

"We'll get crews down there to seal off the area, just in case."

"Data is spiking," said Sargent. "We are seeking the source of the dupes."

Finally, thought Clair.

"Two more of those things on the way," said Devin.

She glanced at the second and third spheres, already well across the gap between the structure in the water and the seastead.

"Can we take out the cannons now?" asked Devin.

"As a precaution," said Forest, "I do think that would be sensible."

"Jesse, are you on it?"

He nodded and let go of Clair's hand. The view through the drones shifted. Weapons systems activated at someone else's command as he sent half of his flock into vertical dives, aiming for different sections of the construct.

Before the cannon emplacement could respond, it was in flames, blown apart by detonating drones.

"We've got another one," said Trevin, indicating a patch

of sea much closer than the one Jesse had just set on fire. A second construct had appeared, this one with seven chimneys. They were already firing, sending a series of black balls arcing to all points of the seastead, which responded with a cloud of drones thick enough to blot out the stars.

War, Clair thought. There was no mistaking this situation for posturing or bluster. It was happening, and it was happening in earnest.

A third construct appeared while Jesse took out the second. Underwater microphones picked up the sounds of heavy industry all around the seastead.

"Torpedoes away," said Devin. The sea became a foam of spray and bright bubbles bursting from below. *Now* Clair could feel the seastead move, a slow sway from left to right as though the Earth was shifting uncomfortably beneath them.

"What have you got?" Clair asked Sargent.

"Still no source, but information flows are higher than ever."

Outside, on the hull, the first bubble had swollen to double its initial size. An external crew was approaching from three sides, while on the inside of the seastead Trevin reported that there was no sign of anything cutting through the hull. There were now seventeen such bubbles scattered across the seastead.

"This is weird," said Devin. "Why aren't they doing anything?"

"Maybe they tricked us into firing first," Clair asked, tugging off her helmet. It was making her feel claustrophobic. "Could that be what this is about?"

"Wouldn't hold up in the Court," said Sargent. "This is an attack, even if it doesn't seem to be actually harming us in any way."

"It's given us zits," said Trevin. "I don't like it. We're going to section off those areas and send them to the bottom of the ocean."

External fabbers began unfurling huge sheets of curved metal designed to enclose the still-growing spheres, while crews supervised the carving of the thick hull around them. Within moments the now grotesquely swollen first sphere was half-covered in metal restraints. When it was completely contained, it would be cut free and allowed to fall into the water.

Jesse's drones circled the seastead. Schools of sleek torpedoes were finding fewer targets in the swollen seas. It felt like the crisis was over, or soon would be, once the mysterious spheres were gone.

Clair didn't understand it. What had she missed? Why would the dupes go to so much trouble if the spheres didn't actually do anything?

"Feels like a stunt," said Trevin.

"Maybe it was a distraction," Clair said.

"Either way, a complete waste of our time." He sounded annoyed, as though it was a personal slight.

The deck kicked sharply beneath her. She caught Jesse as he stumbled into her, his senses swept up in his augs. The rustle of voices in her ears became a roar.

"That came from inside," said Trevin, looking alarmed.

"An explosion?" asked Devin.

"More than one. Hang on. Here."

Maps of the seastead flickered across Clair's lenses. Two bright-red patches flared in a lower section of the starboard bow, showing the sites of the explosions. Damage reports flooded in.

"How did they get inside?" she asked.

"They can't have," said Devin. "The booths have no power. There's no possible way—"

The seastead kicked again. More red patches flared.

"This can't be happening," said Devin.

"What are those areas?" asked Forest.

"Nothing special," said Trevin. "Accommodation, mess—"

"They're near the hull," said Sargent. "That's what's special about them."

"They can't sink us, if that's what they're thinking," said Devin.

"Are the explosions close to those things stuck on the outside?" Clair asked.

Barely had the words left her lips when the first of the black spheres burst open like a boil, spilling a swarm of dark shapes radiating outward across the seastead's exterior.

"What *is* that?" asked Trevin.

A drone swooped in closer. The swarm was composed of things that looked like bugs, but that was only because of the scale. Each "bug" was the same size as one of the members of the RADICAL crew, which was quickly overwhelmed. The "bugs" had arms and legs and heads. More important, the same head over and over, with Dylan Linwood's face.

Dupes.

[35]

"REPAIR CREWS TO the damaged areas! Shore up our defenses!"

Trevin was shouting and so was Devin. Under pressure, it was hard to tell their voices apart.

"Jesse, get those drones back here! Forest, Sargent—time to act now if you're ever going to!"

The peacekeepers were already directing their contingent across the seastead. Clair could see the Linwoods attacking a weak spot in the hull, leaping through armor buckled by the explosions to gain access to the spaces within. Even as drones and external crews picked them off, more emerged from the burst sphere—which appeared to be some kind of mobile d-mat booth, one capable of surviving the impact with the seastead and delivering an inexhaustible army. Drones and gun emplacement turned their attention to it even as the swarm of dupes attacked the weak spot nearby. Jesse flew with precision and speed, like someone well used to operating via telepresence. Clair supposed he was, given the Abstainer thing. Maybe it was a welcome distraction, too, from the blatant misuse of his father's face.

"They're boarding!"

The deck shivered as more explosions rippled through the seastead.

"How are they *doing* that? Are you tracing them, PK Sargent?"

"Trying," she said, looking harried. "Look at the rest of them."

In the PK interface, multicolored dots were coming and going at a furious rate.

"There's too much data, too many secondary sources," Sargent said. "As fast as we delete one, two more pop up somewhere else. It's overwhelming us."

"They knew what we were up to," said Clair. "How?"

"A lucky guess?" said Jesse, although it was clear he didn't think that was the case. But what was the alternative? That the dupes had out-thought them on every front?

Drones were issuing from external fabbers in droves. RADICAL soldiers had engaged the dupes pouring into the lower decks, peppering them with real bullets and confinement foam capsules. A second black sphere popped open, then a third. The clamor of voices over the open line was deafening.

However they had known, the dupes had to have some kind of access to the interior of the seastead. Clair remembered the dupes' trick in the Farmhouse, of penetrating defenses bit by bit until they were able to fab a transmitter to complete the job. Q had turned the tables on them in New York. What if the tables had been turned on RADICAL once more?

Or . . .

Here Clair's worldview quavered.

What if Q was working with the dupes?

That terrible possibility made a dark kind of sense. If that was the case—if Q had been inspired by Clair's betrayal—it could be how the dupes had seen through their plan so quickly, and also explain Q's determined silence and why she was so hard to find: because she was hiding in the same place as the dupes. But could Q really be so vindictive? It didn't seem like her—but as Devin kept trying to say, how well did Clair know Q, really? Who knew what conclusions a mind like hers could come to, particularly one that was still growing, still changing, still *learning*? What if Clair had accidentally taught her how to be a Mean Girl?

This was a horrible possibility that Clair had to rule out, if she could.

"Look for strange transmissions from within the

seastead," she told the open chat.

"We've tried," said Devin. "It's a big ship with lots of transmitters. The frequencies are saturated."

"If you could narrow down a location, that would help," said Trevin.

"The transmitters will be small," Clair said, not wanting to be more specific for fear of how RADICAL might react, "which means they'll need to be close to the bombs. They'll be on the inside, near the spheres."

"Good thought," said Forest. "We will send a team to investigate."

"I'll go," Clair said. "You don't need me up here."

And, she didn't add, *if I find the transmitter first and recognize the design, I'll know that Q is behind it.*

Sargent didn't look happy about the prospect.

"Let me come with you," she started to say.

"I'll keep an eye on her," said PK Drader over the chat. "Clair, meet me on Deck Five below the crow's nest, at the base of Ramp H."

"Okay," she said, giving in and checking the map in her lenses. "Let's take the section under the last sphere. That'll give us the most time, if the last to arrive is the last to burst."

"In theory," said Jesse.

"You concentrate on keeping the rest of the ship safe," she said, tucking the drone interface out of sight so it wouldn't distract her. "And I promise I'll wear my helmet."

"Deal." He gripped her gloved hand for an instant, then let her go.

[36]

"ON MY WAY," said PK Drader as the crow's nest opened to let her out, revealing a corridor that hadn't been there before. The glassy sphere had sunk deep into the heart of the seastead, protected by dozens of bulkheads from the outside world. That didn't seem as reassuring to Clair now that the dupes were inside.

The square-toed boots of her armor thudded on the metal floor as she hurried to Ramp H to begin looking for the transmitter. She was as good as her word, with her helmet securely on, but she kept the visor open. The air tasted faintly of smoke, or perhaps that was her imagination. The parts of the seastead currently burning were fortunately nowhere near her.

She ran down one of the big, spiraling ramps that looked as though they had been designed for an army, feeling alone for the first time since before she had used Improvement. Her suit had cameras providing a view all around her, but that only accentuated her isolation. She couldn't watch every angle at once. It would only take a second's distraction for someone to sneak up on her.

She wondered if wars were like that—being alone at the center of great chaos. She wondered if that was what someone who had no idea what war was *really* like might think.

On Deck 5, she clomped slowly to a halt, looking around for PK Drader. He wasn't there. No one was. Her sense of isolation increased, as did her sense of vulnerability. Had something happened to him? Was this an ambush?

"I see you," he said over a new chat connecting the two of them.

Something moved to her right, matching a green dot on the seastead map. Another armored figure, carrying a stocky rifle across his chest. She raised her hand in greeting, hoping he couldn't see her slight tremor.

"Sorry," he said as he came up beside her. "Got held up. You ready to do this?"

"Sure."

"Okay. Follow me."

I can read a map, she wanted to say, but she was content to let him take charge for the moment. It was good to have company, and she was still getting used to the armor. Only after she had reached the bottom of the ramp did she realize that the armor was assisting her movements: it wasn't a full-on power suit, but each step was slightly easier than it would have been on her own. It threw her off-balance while at the same time not letting her fall.

They went down two more levels and along Deck 3. Here the corridors were deserted, evacuated due to their proximity to the last of the spheres. Clair kept all her senses alert for any sign that an attack was imminent, and tried to ignore the fact that there were several pitched battles taking place elsewhere already. The floor lurched underfoot on more than one occasion. Sirens broadcast staccato warnings from far away, echoing through the empty spaces around her.

They jogged for ten minutes until PK Drader brought her to a halt.

"This is it," he said in a hushed voice. "The sphere is right through that bulkhead."

He pointed with one gloved hand upward and to his left, and Clair followed the gesture with her gaze, seeking but not finding anything in the metal wall to make it stand out from all the others surrounding her.

Clair doubted the transmitter would just be sitting in the corridor, exposed for all to see. It would be hidden, though not so well that it was impossible to find. It had to be powerful enough to punch through the bulkheads and reach the dupes outside. It was also likely to have its own internal power supply, otherwise RADICAL would notice an unexpected drain. It might just be tucked unnoticed in a darkened corner somewhere, ignored by everyone.

There were a few such corners near her, but they were empty.

"Let's look around," she said. "See if we can find anything suspicious."

"If we split up, we'll cover more ground."

"Sure," she said. That way if she did find anything that looked like it came from Q, she would have a chance to decide what to do about it without someone looking over her shoulder.

"Don't go too far, though," he said. "Check in regularly."

"All right. You too."

He touched the tips of his gloved fingers to his helmet, telling her to close her visor, and kept heading along the corridor, looking through doorways as he went.

Clair turned and retraced their steps, doing the same. She kept her visor up, unwilling to shut herself off completely from the outside.

Each doorway led to stylish but empty apartments, all of them identical in dimensions, all of them unfurnished. If things got really bad, she assumed, there would be somewhere for members of RADICAL to live permanently, far away from the rest of the world. It was a depressing realization on two levels. The first was that people smart enough to have built such a thing might actually think it necessary one day. The second was that, having built themselves a safety net, the members of RADICAL were presumably prepared to use it, and to hell with everyone else.

She added that to the list of things she had to do: stop the RADICAL twins from abandoning the world to whatever fate they deemed too horrible for themselves.

Apartment after apartment, equally sleek and empty.

No transmitters, and no explosives, either. Clair didn't know what the latter would look like—probably not a cartoon bomb with a hissing fuse sticking out of it. She kept an eye out for anything out of place.

"Why don't they have fabbers here?" she asked PK Drader over the chat connecting them.

"They do," he said.

"Where? I don't see them anywhere."

He slaved his senses to her suit's. "In the main room, left-hand corner opposite the door. There's a panel above the shelf. See it?"

She did.

"Push in and slide the panel back into the bulkhead."

An exploratory nudge produced a click, and the panel moved under her fingertips. It slid aside, revealing a standard fabber door.

"Why hide them?"

"Don't fit with the aesthetics, I guess."

She experimentally poked the fabber door. It looked like it opened the same way. "Have you found anything?"

"Nothing."

"How long until . . ."

She stopped in midsentence. The fabber wasn't empty. But it didn't contain anything that looked like a transmitter, either. It was full of a white, gel-like substance wrapped tightly in plastic.

"Clair? What . . . oh no." PK Drader's voice took on an

anxious edge. "Clair, step away from the fabber. Don't touch a thing. Don't even close the door. Just get out of there now—and lower your damn faceplate."

"What is it?" she said, backing away with both hands upraised. The suit sealed itself tight at her command, shutting out the room's lifeless air.

"One of the explosives we're looking for. You're lucky it wasn't booby-trapped."

Adrenaline made her heart race. That was an explosive? How on earth did it get in there?

The answer, when it came to her, was so obvious she was not just angry at herself for not thinking of it earlier, but angry at everyone else on the seastead too.

"They didn't use d-mat to get the explosives onto the seastead," she said, easing through the door. "They *fabbed* them."

"We're getting this," said Devin over the open chat. "Shutting power to all fabbers immediately."

"But how did the data get in?" she asked. "There still has to be a transmitter somewhere."

"Clair, heads up," said Jesse. An image came from outside of a long, tapering snout poking out of the waves and a new kind of missile being fired toward the seastead. It looked like a dart, with a pointed tip and a cylindrical body that flared at the tail. "Coming your way."

She was out in the hallway now, looking for PK Drader.

"Where are you?"

"Go on ahead," he said. "I'll catch up."

"What are you doing?"

"Checking fabbers. I've found three more explosive stashes. We need a disposal crew down here immediately."

"On their way," said Sargent. "Clair, you really need to move."

Clair forced herself to do as she was told. She had achieved one of her goals and found the source of the explosions; there was no shame in beating a retreat now. It was PK Drader's choice to stay behind, surrounded by explosives and facing this new kind of attack—and typical of him to do so, she thought with grudging admiration. Presumably the dart had something to do with the discovery they had made. Could it pierce the hull even if the bombs had been defused? Were the dupes already changing their tactics?

As she ran, part of her wondered why the bombs hadn't gone off. That was what she would do in the dupes' shoes. The explosives had been found. Why waste them? And if killing Clair was one of their objectives . . .

"Missile changing course to follow you," said Devin. "Clair, turn left —*now*."

She did so, heading deeper into the seastead and exercising all the power of her armor to put as much distance between her and the outside as possible.

Red patches flared in her vision as all the explosives

hidden in the seastead went off at once. The floor bucked beneath her, and she stumbled.

Walls and ceiling collapsed with the sound of metal screaming as the missile forced its way into the seastead, sending her flying. Clair felt a moment of terrifying weightlessness, heard Jesse calling her name, and then, for a long time, nothing.

──────────────────────── [37]

SOMEONE WAS COUGHING. It was Clair. Her lungs were full of smoke, making it impossible for her to hold a breath longer than a split second.

"Clair? Clair, you're back. Good. Can you hear me?"

A small face peered at her through the helmet's smashed visor. Her lenses were scrambled. She blinked and the face came into focus.

Cashile.

Her head spun. Was she imagining this, or was it real?

"Clair, listen to me," the Cashile said. "We don't have long."

"What . . ." Her voice was too loud, made her pulse thud thickly in her ears. "Can't . . ."

"We need you to call him off."

Her first thought was of the drones. "Who? Jesse?"

"I'm talking about Nobody. You know—the dupe we

talked about on Ons Island?"

She wanted to touch her face. It felt like blood was running down her temple, into her eyebrows. But she couldn't move her hands. Her suit was immobile, like a statue.

"Let me go," she croaked. "Please."

"We will. Soon. We don't mean you any harm."

"Is that why you kidnapped my mom?"

"We didn't do that."

She laughed with a bitterness that surprised her. "Pull the other leg."

"I'm serious," the Cashile said. "We don't know who did that, just like we don't know who blew the barrage in Washington and fired on Valkyrie Station."

"Wallace said . . ." She paused to swallow, tasting blood. "He said he would destroy my family."

"We know. That was Wallace. Forget about him. He's not your problem now. It's Nobody. He's threatening to ruin everything. He won't listen to us anymore."

She squinted up into the face of the child the dupes had killed in California. Did the dupes think she would believe them just because their lies came dressed as Cashile?

"Good cop, bad cop," she said.

"This isn't a game, Clair. Don't misunderstand me. Nobody is *both* our problems now. Once he's killed you, we think he'll turn on us and then all bets are off. You think this skirmish is big? He's only warming up. In a week's time, he could be everywhere."

"The Linwoods . . ."

"On the seastead? All him. And all for you. Does that make you feel special?"

It made her feel faintly ill. Every gruesome copy of Jesse's father contained the same disturbed mind, duplicated hundreds of times over. Could it really just be to intimidate her?

Did the Cashiles choose their form to have the exact opposite effect? If so, it wasn't working. The whole dupe thing was too weird, almost surreal, the way it began to strip all sense of recognition from faces she had come to know well. They became masks that hid unknowable things.

"How did you get in here?"

"There's always a back door. We don't need anything as crude as missiles and rockets. If we wanted to kill you, we would've done it already."

The Cashile retreated and her suit came alive. She could move again.

"We're not the threat here, Clair. We're the messengers. If you don't believe me, watch what happens next. I told you we didn't have long, remember?"

Clair sat up suddenly, banging her helmet on a crumpled bulkhead that might once have been the ceiling. She was in a twisted space barely larger than a booth. The air was full of smoke. She could hear gunfire in the distance, coming closer.

The Cashile stood with four others by her feet, all dressed in sleek child-sized flak suits. They offered their hands and she let them pull her out of the tangle, into an area where she could stand. Her suit's plates ground against each other with a horrible sound. Her interfaces were still down.

Factions, she thought. Dupes fighting dupes. Some trying to kill her, some not. Some loyal to Wallace, some pursuing their own agenda. Or were they all loyal to their creator, ultimately?

"We're supposed to tell you that this is your last chance," said one of the Cashiles. "But let's be realistic. Come to us at any time, and we won't turn you away. A new age is coming no matter what. We're not the threat you think we are. In fact, we're your allies, if you'll let us be. Take a long, hard look at Nobody, and you'll see that compared to him we're actually on the same side."

"How are we on the same side?"

"We both think the Consensus Court is wrong, for starters."

He was talking about Zep and Libby. He had to be. Could she learn to live with dupes if it meant her friends could come back? She didn't even need to think about the answer.

"I'll never be on the same side as Ant Wallace—"

"Forget Wallace," said another Cashile. "This isn't about him."

"Of course it's about him. He's making this happen!"

"Don't give the man more credit than he deserves, Clair. He's a pawn—just like you were until you broke out of the box he tried to put you in."

"So who does Wallace work for?" asked Clair. "You're just trying to confuse me."

"If you're confused, Clair, it's only because you don't realize what a unique position you're in now," said a third Cashile with a wide-eyed look that might have been admiration. "If you could only know what you know . . ."

The gunfire intensified, and all the Cashiles looked around with an eerily similar motion.

"This ends badly for us," said the first one, "as it seems to every time we meet. But it's only a temporary setback. We'll see you again."

"I strongly advise you to go that way," said one of the others, pointing along a narrow seam that might once have been a corridor. "We'll hold him off as long as we can."

Dozens of childlike figures crowded the seam in the opposite direction. Torchlight rippled along the walls, such as they were. Wild shadows danced.

"Go!"

Small hands pushed her away. She let the momentum carry her onward, picking up speed, not wanting to look back as the gunfire sounded again, horribly close, and she could hear the Cashiles falling silently, without the slightest cry.

[38]

CLAIR RAN AS best she could, fighting the grinding friction in her knee and hip joints, climbing over wreckage whenever it got in her way. There was very little room and very little light, too. Once she got snared in a web of cables and had to cut herself free. She sent silent thanks to Sargent for insisting she take the knife.

Her interfaces were still scrambled. There was no sign of anyone in the tangled mess. It was just her and whoever or whatever was on her tail.

Because there was definitely something on her tail. She sensed it in the same way she had sensed the dupes following her in California. Her spine was screaming at her, louder and louder with each step: *Behind you!* She didn't turn around even once for fear of what she might see. All she could hear was her own heavy breathing in the confines of the helmet, and a deep creaking that came from the seastead. It sounded like a wounded beast, groaning in its death throes. The gunfire had stopped a while back.

She spilled out of a particularly narrow crack and found herself facing a heavily scored wall that didn't match the others around her. It was black, and there was a cylindrical curve to it, suggesting that she had happened across the dart-missile that had stabbed deep into the body of the seastead. She could see where the bulkheads had been torn away from it, warped and twisted by the impact.

She couldn't go any farther forward, so she began looking for a way along it. There was space to her left, but that way led outside. She wanted to go deeper, away from the ocean and away from the dupes . . . unless they had taken over the seastead completely while she was out, and there was nowhere left to run. With her suit out of action and her augs scrambled, there was no way she could call anyone to find out.

Metal squeaked and clattered behind her. Clair spun around, pistol in hand, and saw Dylan Linwood easing through the crack she had just crawled out of. He was bruised and red-eyed, grinning widely. She fired instinctively, closing her eyes for an instant as she pulled the trigger.

The bullet threw him back. Then he came toward her again, pushed by the dupe behind him, another Dylan Linwood. The body flopped at her feet.

She fired again, and kept firing until the crack was full of bodies and her right elbow was singing with pain. The gun never seemed to run out of bullets. She suspected it was a miniature version of a fabber, designed solely to make the same bullet over and over. But wouldn't it run out of power eventually? And what would happen then? The dupe called Nobody would force his way through the corpses and catch her.

She had to keep moving.

Trying not to hyperventilate, feeling like she was caught

in a nightmare, she backed up along the side of the metal needle, testing her footing carefully behind her before putting her weight down. She held the gun outstretched in both hands, ready to fire at anyone who came after her.

The pile of bodies shifted as dupes on the other side of the bulkhead fought their way through. Red eyes gaped accusingly at her.

"What do you want?" she shouted. Echoes flew back at her. The air smelled of blood and the ocean. She was glad Jesse wasn't there to witness this horror. "Leave me alone!"

The crack widened out slightly at her back, and she turned around, ready to run.

Dylan Linwood was standing there with his arms outstretched.

She screamed and shoved away from him, tripping over a sharp lip of curved metal and landing heavily on her side. The pistol slipped from her hand, but she snatched it back up before he was on her and lifted herself onto her good elbow, and fired once, twice. He fell forward, dead, pushing her back down. Grunting in revulsion, she shouldered him aside in time to shoot the next one. And the next.

They kept coming and she kept firing, even when the bodies rose up over her like a tidal wave, crushing her back down into the deck. There was no light or air. She closed her eyes and sobbed in revulsion and fear. It was almost impossible to breathe. Was this how it was going to end, with her buried alive under a mountain of dead dupes?

Then a hand clutched at her shoulder, slick with blood. A bubbling voice whispered, "Want to talk to you . . ."

It was one of the dupes. Injured, but not dead.

She struggled to pull away but found it impossible to move.

A voice on the other side echoed, "Want to be with you . . ."

A third said, "Want to *be* you . . ."

And that was when she knew.

This was the nightmare.

[39]

A MACHINE GUN rang out in the tangled metallic space. She heard bullets striking flesh and closed her eyes even though doing so would make no difference at all to what happened to her. If the bullets hit her, they hit her. There was no way she could dodge anything, trapped as she was under the weight of the dupes. At least the gunfire drowned out their ghastly whispers.

But who was firing?

Only then did she realize that none of the Linwoods had fired at her. She wasn't even sure they were armed. That made it worse—the thought that she had mowed them down in cold blood, even as Nobody tried to . . . what? *Become* her to death?

The bodies shifted, and she squeezed her eyes even tighter. The mass of flesh lifted up off her and then fell away. Bright light swept over her, followed by a rush of cool air. She sucked in a lungful and sat up.

A chevron-shaped drone hovered over her on roaring fans, stubby gun barrels thrusting at her under the single white eye of a spotlight. It bobbed in greeting.

"*Q?*"

But the voice that issued from a grill next to the spotlight didn't belong to her missing friend.

"It's me." *Jesse.* "Oh god, I'm sorry it took so long to find you. We knew you had to be alive somewhere. Looks like we found you just in time. Are you all right? Did he—did *they* hurt you?"

She looked down at herself. Her armor was covered in gore, but she was barely injured. Her throat felt raw and her hands were shaking. She pulled herself out of the crater of bodies, and the drone bobbed away to make space for her. Her gorge rose, and she bent over with her hands on her knees, fighting the urge to be violently ill.

"We've been looking everywhere for you," said Jesse through the drone, his relief unstoppable although she would have killed for silence. "There was a massive electromagnetic pulse when that dart thing hit the hull. It must have shorted out your armor, so we couldn't track you or even tell for sure if you were alive."

She took long, slow breaths, telling herself to be glad that Jesse had found her. Jesse had saved her. What's more, he had done it in the cleverest possible way. He had thrown the rope in the form of a drone, rather than come after her himself.

"How *did* you find me?"

"You were screaming," he said. "I followed the sound."

Screaming? She hadn't realized. But that explained the soreness in her throat.

A sob bubbled up, but she swallowed that down too.

"We have to get you out of here," said Jesse. "We're going to evacuate."

She nodded. The deck was swaying under her in a highly disconcerting fashion.

"What happened to PK Drader?"

"He was looking for you in the wrong place. I've told him you're safe. He feels awful about putting you in danger."

"Is he coming here?"

"No. I can guide you to safety, although it means going back to the hull for a short stretch. . . ."

That didn't worry her.

"How much weight can this thing lift?" She pointed at the drone.

"More than you think. The standard payload is seventy kilos, and it can redline another ten on top of that. Why?"

"Ditch the payload. We're not going back empty-handed."

Only then did she allow herself to look at the bodies surrounding her. Some were still moving, slithering along the floor in an attempt to reach her. Their injuries looked serious, but she was sure Devin's magic d-mat booth could fix them up. Not that Clair wanted to heal them completely—just make one of them well enough to talk . . .

"All right," said Jesse. He sounded faintly ill, and no wonder: how many times had he seen his father killed now? "But I'll need your help getting him onto the drone's back. . . . Are you up to it?"

She would have to be. Nodding, she put all her qualms in a box and locked them deep inside, and set about sorting through the bodies to find a suitable candidate.

"Can anyone else hear us?" Clair asked Jesse as he guided her through the wreckage, a dupe strapped tightly to the drone's back. Her lenses were still scrambled, perhaps by the pulse he had mentioned.

"In theory, not if I don't want them to," he said. "But it is a RADICAL drone."

Clair didn't mind so much if anyone from RADICAL listened in. She just needed him to talk so she wouldn't have to . . . and for the PKs to stay out of it, for now.

"Tell me what's been going on. Is everyone safe? Did the plan work? Why are we evacuating?"

Jesse's account was long on technical details and

refreshingly clinical because of it, which she was grateful for. The black spheres had popped as expected, one by one, and an army of Nobodies in Dylan Linwood bodies had entered the seastead by the hundreds, identical in mind and body, united by a single purpose. While the defense of the mighty vessel had concentrated on certain key areas—keeping the fabbers and d-mat booths switched off, rooting out any more explosive caches, protecting the powersat beam receivers—the dupes had seemed intent on just one thing: finding Clair.

"How can they be the same person?" asked Jesse. "I get how they can copy bodies over and over, but minds as well?"

"I guess it's all in the brain," said Clair. "If you copy that, you copy the person as well."

"Some people don't deserve *one* life, let alone as many as this guy has had. . . ."

Jesse fumed, and she let him. His anger at the ongoing abuse of his father's face was completely justified. They had seen no other dupes thus far on their journey through the wreckage. Perhaps, Clair thought, Jesse had killed every one of them in the area, getting to her.

When he calmed down he told her that, now that she was safe, relatively speaking, RADICAL was abandoning the ship. The Nobodies could have it, or go down with it into the freezing water for all anyone cared.

"What about casualties on our side?" she said. "Any

signs of people coming back from the dead?"

"None—and the PKs have lost a lot of people," Jesse said. "Here's something weird: the only explosives that didn't go off were the ones around you. Why do you think that is?"

"No idea."

"PK Drader didn't know either. He said it might be because they didn't want to blow up the transmitter you were looking for, but he didn't find it."

"It must be somewhere. How else did the Cashiles get in?"

"Maybe *he'll* tell us," Jesse said, rocking the dupe from side to side.

They traveled without speaking for a minute, the only sound the straining of the drone's fans. The dupe's eyes were open. Clair had gagged him so he couldn't speak and tied his wrists and ankles carefully with wire stripped from the drone's normal payload. She considered blind-folding him as well so she wouldn't have to endure that hot, red-eyed stare.

Let him see, she thought. *I'm not beaten. He'll never beat me . . . and he'll never be me, ever again.*

The thought of his mind inside her body, as it had been in the dupe that had exploded, made her skin crawl as though it didn't belong to her.

Don't think that way, she told herself. *I'm Clair Hill. I may not know what I'm doing, but I do know that.*

THE AIR GREW colder and wetter the closer they got to the tear in the hull. Clair walked more carefully, feeling her tread slip underfoot several times. When she reached the outside and contemplated a long climb across warped, slick metal, she was relieved to see the lights of an external crew coming toward them.

"They'll help you up," said Jesse.

The two-person crew consisted of a pair of soldiers in giant mechanical combat suits.

"Step on," the first one said via external speakers. His face was visible through the hard shell visor, partially obscured by a ropy yellow mustache. "We'll get you inside before you know it."

"Thanks." She climbed onto his back, toes and fingers slipping into holds designed for passengers.

The other soldier took the dupe and tucked it over one shoulder while Jesse's drone backed off.

"Dupes coming this way," Jesse said.

"Okay, we're moving on up," said Clair's ride, raising one enormous gripper to begin climbing up the hull. Clair hung on for dear life, glad she didn't have to think of anything more complicated than that. Her face was wet with spray coming in her open faceplate—or was it tears? She couldn't tell. She still felt oddly disconnected from her own body, overwhelmed by events, and not unreasonably so. She was a sixteen-year-old girl, not a soldier. This wasn't the way her life was supposed to go.

Over her shoulder the sea grasped and hungered, just dying to suck down the crippled seastead into its pitch-black depths. Flickering beams crisscrossed the night sky, delivering power to the machines the dupes had built, enabling still more dupes to be created. Twinkling clouds of metallic flecks trailed in the wake of drones, attempting to scatter the beams. They flashed all the colors of the rainbow, creating fleeting auroras that would have been beautiful under other circumstances. The electrical storm Clair had seen earlier had reached the battle zone, adding sheets of rain and erratic lightning flashes to the catastrophic mix. Thunder rumbled.

They reached a hangar door without being attacked by anyone, and stepped back into relative calm and quiet. These corridors were undamaged, their right angles seeming impossibly clean and neat. When the soldier carrying her said that she could get down if she wanted to, Clair said no. She was happy to ride, and would only slow them down if she didn't. The idea of being held was very appealing, although it made her think of her mother and the possible failure of Clair's plan to save her.

With heavy, wide-spaced footfalls, the soldiers ran deeper into the seastead, followed closely by the drone. Jesse wasn't letting her out of his sight, but she resisted all attempts at conversation. She was physically and emotionally exhausted, and might actually have fallen asleep but for the occasional trumpeting of a siren dragging her back to full alertness.

Nevertheless, she was taken by surprise when the soldier carrying her slowed to a lope, then a walk, and then stopped at the entrance to the crow's nest.

The door slid open and Jesse himself emerged, closely followed by PK Sargent. She let them help her down, flexing her fingers and ankles as she came. And when they didn't say anything, just began taking off her armor, she let them do that, too. She was glad to shed the weight of it, light though it had seemed when she had put it on. As each piece came off, she saw just how much blood she had been soaked in, and she felt faint. Mechanical grippers caught her before her sway could become a fall, and then held her under the armpits as her leg plates and boots came away. When she put her feet back down, she left bloody footprints.

"None of that is yours?" was the first question Sargent asked her.

Clair shook her head. That was true, apart from some minor scrapes. She pointed at the dupe, still trussed up on the other soldier like a grisly backpack. "All *theirs*."

"You want to interrogate him?" Sargent asked.

"Yes."

"Why?"

Take a long, hard look at Nobody, the Cashiles had said. Besides, he might be able to tell her where her mother was.

"He could know where Wallace is hiding" was what she said. That excuse would fly better with the PKs.

"All right. You'll have to be quick, though."

Clair's lenses had returned to normal the moment her helmet had come off. A request from Sargent appeared in her infield.

She opened the chat.

"We were going to leave as soon as you got here," the peacekeeper said, so the dupe wouldn't hear her, "but if we take the dupe with us he'll just explode like the other one."

"We're evacuating via d-mat?"

"Yes, and we don't want the dupes to know that we have that capacity."

"Did you find out where the dupes are coming from? Or the transmitter?"

"No."

"That's another reason to talk to him, then," she said, even as her heart sank. She had come out of the battle with no transmitter and nothing to use as a lever against the dupes—but nothing to connect the explosions to Q, either, and she wasn't unhappy about that last detail. This was her last chance to salvage something from this mess.

"Where do you want to do this?" asked Sargent, looking

up at the dupe on the soldier's back.

"The crow's nest is as good as anywhere."

"All right. Do you want to get changed first?"

Desperately. Jesse was hovering like the now superfluous drone, and his expression made her anxious. She pulled up a view from the drone's forward camera in order to see exactly what she looked like. She barely recognized herself. Her hair was still tucked into the black undersuit, and her face and hands were black with dried blood. She looked wild and desperate.

Fine with her. They needed to evacuate soon so she could get as far away from the dupes as possible. Perhaps the way she looked would encourage her captive to talk quickly.

————————————— [41]

THE ONLY PERSON in the crow's nest was PK Forest, who they interrupted in midpace. He acknowledged Clair with a nod but no welcoming expression. They all had more important things to worry about than what their faces were showing.

Clair's lenses went completely blank, indicating that the room was now Faraday shielded.

"Set him down over here," she told the soldiers. They did so and stayed nearby to intervene if needed. Sargent kept a pistol at the ready as Clair stepped in and squatted in front of the dupe, forcing herself to get close to him even though every instinct screamed at her to go in exactly the opposite direction. His was the face of terror and despair. It had chased her to the ends of the Earth. It haunted her waking dreams.

"Be careful," said Jesse. He was staying well away from the man who had stolen the body of his father, staring at it with undisguised loathing.

She reached out and tugged the gag away.

"You wanted to talk to me," she said to Nobody.

"The feeling is mutual, I know," he said, and again she detected a faint hint of an accent she had heard before. Like the others, he was neither armed nor armored. His skin was pale and there were feverish circles around his eyes. He slumped to one side as though barely able to sit upright.

He had a bullet wound to the shoulder. Clair considered RADICAL's rejuvenator, but dismissed it. There might not be time, and he didn't need to talk for long. Just long enough.

"So let's trade," she said. "What did you do with my mother?"

He didn't look up. "I had nothing to do with that."

"That's what the other dupes said."

"Do you believe them over me?"

"Why shouldn't I?"

"Because my interest is in you, not your mother. Can't you tell?"

He raised his head and stared at her with one blue eye, one red eye.

She held his gaze, matching his stubbornness with some of her own.

"Do you always try to kill the people who interest you?"

"You're the one who got away."

"Give me a real answer."

"How about the same one a different way? Death is a gift that can be given but never stolen. It belongs to the dying, and is lost with them."

"What is that?" asked Jesse. "A riddle?"

Nobody turned his cryptic gaze on him. "I will only talk to Clair."

Jesse didn't looked away. "So talk properly. We haven't got all day."

Nobody sighed and turned back to Clair.

"Everyone asks me who I *am*. That annoying boy of yours did; they all do—except you. You asked me who I *was*. And I realized that I was unhappy with the answer. I am a hollow man, condemned to repeat the same experiences over and over again. Different bodies, but the same mind—different circumstances, but the same fate. We're plucked from the void and return to the void no wiser, communicating with each other from mouth to ear, repeating the same words, sharing the same archives, believing we have the same memories but knowing that each of us is slightly different, growing further apart from each other the moment we step out into the world until the moment we leave it. . . ." He raised his bound hands to touch his bloody eye, his bruised temple, injuries that had belonged to the original Dylan Linwood when he had been forcibly scanned. "You showed me that life with neither endings nor beginnings isn't life at all. It's just . . . persistence."

This she could accept, although how he got from there to trying to kill her remained impenetrable. "And you're punishing me for that?"

He shook his head. She didn't think it was a negative, and his next words confirmed that.

"*Trade.* Tell me why you asked who I was. What makes you different from everyone else?"

She rocked back on her heels, clutching her knees tightly to her chest.

"I don't want to be different."

"But you are."

"I bet there are plenty of other people who would ask the same question if you gave them the chance."

He shrugged. "No one did until now. You're either different from everyone else, or you had a reason. Which is it?"

She had avoided thinking back to that terrible moment in California, when she had thought she was about to die. The truth was, though, that so many terrible things had happened to her since then that it didn't seem so bad anymore.

"At first I was trying to distract you," she said. "You hesitated when I asked you how long you live in each body. I thought I was getting to you. And I was, wasn't I? That was when you told me you were Nobody."

"Not me," he said. "The one who died. I have only the record of his words."

Clair understood what he was saying. The dupe in California had been killed. This dupe was another one, created just hours ago to attack the seastead. But he knew what had happened to that earlier version of himself, and he clearly suffered from the same psychological angst.

"He took *his* death with him," she said.

"Yes. He is the lucky one."

"And you're trying to give *me* a death in return? Is that it?"

"Yes."

"Why?" They were back to this question.

"Because you deserve it."

"What have I done to deserve dying?"

"You've lived," he said in a voice that was almost a hiss, "and you have so much life ahead of you. You are *new*, Clair. You can be anyone. I . . . I am no one, Nobody, persisting through a series of brief and violent lives that I experience only secondhand. I would like to be like you, but the best I can do is make myself in your image—or you in my image, metaphorically. You don't deserve that. Kinder, I think, to give you that which I crave most of all and be done with it. You would understand, were you me."

Clair tried to fathom what lay at the heart of this grim, accusatory confession.

"You're killing me because *you* want to die?"

"Yes."

"Why don't you just kill yourself instead, like Mallory?"

"Because unlike her I know it will make no difference."

"Is that because Wallace keeps bringing you both back or—"

"Let's talk about Charlie," he interrupted her, slapping one blood-slick hand against his thigh. "Who is he and how is he important?"

"He's not important," she said.

"Tell me who he is."

"Just my old toy clown. Why?"

He looked downcast. His hand slid to rest on the floor.

"I-who-was-you asked you about him. I didn't know why. Now I understand. Charlie was a host memory. Toys mean nothing to *this* me."

Clair had to cast her mind back to New York to know what he was talking about. Her dupe, the one who had exploded, was the one who had brought up Charlie. She had almost lost Charlie as a child, but what did it matter now?

The lesson that young Clair Hill had learned that day was that the world wasn't permanent. Anything could be fabbed and re-created at any moment, without mattering in the slightest. That was what happened to people, after all, when they moved from place to place via d-mat. There were gaps between *here* and *there*, *lost* and *found*, that were intriguing to contemplate, in the same way it was intriguing to wonder what happened to *Clair Hill* when she fell asleep every night. Was she the same person when she woke up, even though she had stopped *being* for a while? No one in their right mind thought so, and no one worried about d-mat gaps either.

Charlie says hello, the dupe had told her in New York. The impermanent, replaceable Charlie, whose loss she had ultimately borne by accepting the world she lived in, gaps and all. Was Nobody implying that he lived in the gaps, with Charlie and every other impermanent thing?

There were more important questions.

"My turn," she said. "Where are you coming from? Every hour there are more of you. How do I make you stop?"

"I don't know," he said.

"I don't believe you."

"It's true. I know how to call more of myself into being—there are code words, easily spoken, and many bodies to choose from—but no one ever told me how to stop it from happening. Until you work out how to do that, my fate lies in this world with you."

She couldn't decide if his expression was now beatific or spiteful, or another complex mixture.

"Tell me where Wallace is, then. Who's 'the Boss' if it's not him?"

"I don't know where he is. That was two questions, by the way. Why do you want to find him so badly?"

"To stop him, of course. To stop all of you."

"What makes you think stopping him will stop me? I'm bigger than him now. Bigger than all the other dupes put together. That's why they're afraid of me. Nothing can stop me, unless I want to be stopped."

"I thought you said you wanted to die."

"I did," he said. "You know that phrase, being of two minds about something? That's exactly how how I feel, multiplied by . . . however many there are of me at this point."

Perhaps he smiled at that, but his lips were so thin and white that Clair couldn't tell. His eyelids were drooping. Clair could tell just by looking at him that there wasn't long left.

"What do the other dupes want?" she asked.

"The same thing they've always wanted. What do *you* want?"

"For everything to go back the way it was, of course."

"Is that even possible now, Clair?"

Devin had raised that point on the way to Antarctica. If she wasn't fighting for the world she had known, why was she fighting at all?

"My turn," she said. "Why do the other dupes think I know something important?"

"Because you do."

"Is it about Q?"

He tut-tutted. "Why haven't you asked me what it'll take to make me stop fighting you?"

"I don't know. *Will* you do that?"

"Maybe. If you answer one question honestly."

"I've answered all of them honestly so far."

"Really? Sometimes I forget how young you are." He exhaled sharply. "Only the very young . . . and the dying . . . have no time to lie."

"Answer my question, then. Will you stop fighting me?"

"Perhaps . . . if you tell me my real name."

"What? I don't know what that is." She looked up at Forest and Sargent. They shook their heads. "None of us do."

"Nonetheless . . . that's what it will take. I'll stop fighting you, and you can work out how to kill me. If I have to go, I'll go as the person I was, and not before."

"All right," she said, figuring she had nothing to lose. "I'll find your name, and the rest. I promise you."

"Don't promise *me*," he said irritably. "Promise the me you're going to tell, who you haven't met yet. He probably doesn't even exist right now. He'll come out of a fabber sooner or later, not knowing that he's the one who will change everything. . . ."

His eyes were slipping shut. His slump had become even more pronounced.

"Hey," she said, poking his uninjured shoulder. "You're not going anywhere just yet, not without telling me what you dupes think I know."

"It's *my* question, Clair," he said, his voice little more than a mumble. "And it is this: what did you see?"

"Where? When?"

"What did you see, Clair, in the stars . . . what did you see?"

[42]

NOBODY SLIPPED OVER and Clair caught him, propping him gently upright even as she resisted the urge to shake him to get the answers she needed.

"I don't understand," she said. "Tell me more."

He didn't respond.

"No riddles, remember?"

Sargent was at her side, reaching past her to check the dupe's vital signs. Only then did Clair realize that he wasn't breathing.

She sagged back into a sitting position as Sargent did what she could. Jesse came to stand behind her, hands on her shoulders, not seeming to mind the crusted blood there. His father's blood.

"Well, that told us nothing," he said, "except that Nobody is one fucked-up dude."

She shook her head, not disagreeing with his diagnosis but suspecting that Nobody had actually told her a great deal. The Cashiles, too, in their elliptical way. She just had to work out what it was.

"He's dead," said Sargent, stepping away and wiping her hands on the thighs of her armor. "Let's get rid of the corpse before it springs any nasty surprises on us."

One of the soldiers stepped forward, scooping up the body as though it were a doll, and the other followed him out of the crow's nest. When they and the body were gone, Clair's lenses came back to life. She felt like closing her eyes and sinking into blackness, but she couldn't do that yet. Not until she was sure they were safe. Those who were left.

I'm so sorry, Mom, she thought with a heavy heart. If both factions of dupes were telling the truth, that meant there was a third group acting against her—and she had no idea who they could be.

"I'm out of ideas," she said, leaning back into Jesse's ready embrace, his chest pressed solidly against her back. "I guess we can evacuate now."

"Yes." The answer came over a chat she hadn't even known was open. Devin and Trevin were part of the conversation from elsewhere in the seastead. "Preparing for breakup."

"Breakup?" Clair echoed.

Sargent helped her to her feet. "The seastead is compartmentalized. Seal the bulkheads, and whole sections act as giant booths. RADICAL can take what's inside of them and then remake all the bulkheads and everything so it won't look like anything's gone anywhere. It'll be like the *Marie Celeste*, only bigger. It'll delay the dupes while they work out what happened."

"How is the data going to get out? I thought we were cut off."

"From the Air, yes," said Devin. "But we are connected to the powersat grid. The beam powering the seastead is intense enough to cover any transmissions going up to orbit. We'll come back to ground using the same trick. No one will be able to track us."

"We'll only get away with it once, though," said Sargent.

"And it sets a dangerous precedent," said Forest. "The powersat grid is not protected against this kind of exploitation. It will need to be."

"Yes, well, you can look into that on the other side." Devin sounded unrepentant. "Unless you have a better plan to get out of this mess?"

"I do not."

"Where will we go?" Clair asked.

"That's the question," said Trevin. "Anywhere that has a powersat receiver, heavy cargo booths, and a d-mat network that we can hack into—i.e., pretty much any city anywhere. But the dupes will track the signal eventually, so it has to be somewhere defensible, or somewhere that can be abandoned at a moment's notice. Our best suggestion is now sunk, or might well be soon, so over to you guys."

There was silence. Sargent glanced at Forest, and Clair knew that they were communicating silently, perhaps considering options. OneEarth was bound to have all sorts of strongholds, but would they let RADICAL in? And were they secure enough to keep the dupes out? OneEarth was required by law to be transparent when it came to things like this, so every weakness of every redoubt could be easily exploited by the dupes, as in Crystal City.

Clair's mind was blank, still reeling from everything that had happened in the previous hours. If that had been war, she wanted no more of it. Time for yet another strategy, but what? Her primary goals hadn't changed: if it felt like they had receded even further into the distance, it was only because she was tired and nothing she had tried so far had worked. That didn't mean she was never going to succeed. There had to be a way to ensure that all the death and destruction on the seastead hadn't been a complete waste.

Her mother liked to say, *The only thing separating success from failure is giving up.* Allison had lots of sayings like that, some of them helpful, some of them not so much. Some, like this one, were true, but didn't help solve anything, really. Not in a concrete here's-how-to-rescue-me kind of way. That, Clair would have to figure out for herself, when she had time and energy to try again.

Then she remembered something Jesse had said earlier, before the fighting had started.

"Russia," she said in a voice she could barely hear. The audacity of what she was thinking startled even her. "That's where we should go."

"Why?" asked Devin. "What's there?"

Jesse stared at her in surprise; then a cautiously delighted smile spread across his face. "Agnessa Adaksin. The muster."

"The what?" asked Trevin. "Whose master?"

"Muster," Clair corrected him. "WHOLE has a new leader and she's gathering everyone together in one place."

"So?"

"There's only one other group that hasn't underestimated what d-mat can do," Jesse said. "Who else has as good reason to hate the dupes as much as us?"

"That may be true," said Devin, "but they've got good reason to hate us as well."

"And us," said Sargent.

Clair nodded, not unaware of the hurdles ahead of them. But Jesse was beaming, and she felt an instinctive *rightness* about the idea. Every high-tech attempt to evade the dupes had failed. Maybe it was time for something simple.

And she could be sure of one thing: there would be no Cashiles or Dylan Linwoods in a community guaranteed to have no d-mat booths or fabbers.

"We'll deal with everyone getting on with everyone else when we get there," she said. "Where exactly *is* there, Jesse?"

"New Petersburg," he said. "On the Neva Straits."

"Send me the exact location," said Devin, sounding resigned. "I am painfully aware that we are running again."

"You're not the only one," said Clair. "But let's just do it, if we're going to. I bet the dupes aren't wasting any time working out what to do next."

"I have no objections," said Forest.

Sargent nodded. "It's not as if the other peacekeepers can't keep looking for the dupes while we're off doing this."

"And for Q, too?" said Devin. When neither peacekeeper responded, he shrugged. "Fair enough. RADICAL will be doing the same without us, while working on the next contingency. It looks like we might need it."

"That's settled, then," said Trevin. "Hold on to your hats, people. We're on our way."

eeeeeee—

Clair felt rather than heard a rising whine that tickled the backs of her eardrums. When it reached its peak, it threatened to tear her head apart.

—EEEEEEE—

"Is this the way it's supposed to go?" she bumped Devin.

"Beats me," he bumped back. "We've never actually ridden a powersat beam before."

"Are you for real?"

"Never been realer."

Clair clutched her head as the screech blasted her from all sides. It felt as though every cell inside her body had burst and her blood had flashed instantly to steam. Her body exploded into countless tiny fragments—and yet, when she opened her eyes to see what had happened, she found herself standing exactly where she had been.

"Welcome to Russia," said a shaky-sounding Devin.

Except for that part, she thought.

[43]

THE SECTION OF the seastead containing them had arrived in a cargo booth the size of a small building. When the crow's nest doors slid apart, the corridor outside ended in a vertical mirror several yards along. They had to go down a ramp two floors, onto another mirror, this one horizontal, where Devin joined them.

"Well, that was fun."

"Which part?" asked Jesse.

"None of it, to be honest." He looked around as though

getting his bearings. "I'll come with you for the next leg and have all this shipped elsewhere. If we step outside, I'll cycle the booth and get us some transport."

"What about Trevin?" asked Clair, following Devin to the hangar-sized doors.

"He's got things to attend to." Devin tapped his forehead. "We'll still be in touch."

"Speaking of which," said Sargent, "we're not keeping this a secret, are we?"

"No point," said Devin. "And probably impossible. Better to be up front about something we can't hide."

Clair nodded, agreeing with the sentiment, although nervous about what awaited her in the Air. She was more worried about that than she was about walking practically unarmed into the WHOLE stronghold. Unarmed and completely exhausted. She ached from head to toe.

"We're about four miles from the muster," Devin said. "As far as getting there goes, I thought we'd try something a little different."

The wall of the giant booth cracked open, creating a horizontal aperture through which poured icy-cold air.

Devin guided them outside into a deep, winter night lit only by blue streetlights. The enormous booth was surrounded by tall, thin buildings, the purpose of which Clair couldn't imagine—old atmosphere processors, maybe, from the Water Wars. Between them in the near distance she saw trees, and the sight of all that green made her want to run and disappear into it, never to return. Her body and mind had endured so many shocks in recent days that they barely seemed to fit together anymore. She needed to rest, but instead she was jumping headlong into the mouth of the whale. The mouth of WHOLE, more literally.

Her lenses were bugging her with messages from the real world. Oz, Tash, and Ronnie were prominent, but Clair didn't want to read any more accusations or interrogations or reminders of her failure. Oz had sent her several messages conveying his love and hope that she was looking after herself. Clair doubted this plan would qualify.

She reduced everything except for notifications from the people around her to a single icon and let it sit in her infield, not daring to believe that this simplified anything but knowing that, for the moment, it was as much as she could cope with. One problem at a time. The rest could wait.

The booth boomed shut behind them, then a moment later opened again, revealing a squat vehicle with a fat black skirt and two elegant fans positioned vertically at the rear.

"A hovercraft?" said Jesse. "Can I drive?"

"Be my guest," said Devin.

"Do you have a license?" asked Forest.

"Are you going to arrest me if I don't?" Jesse said. "'Cause that'd make a *great* impression."

The peacekeeper inclined his head.

They climbed aboard. There were seats for four passengers, plus one for the pilot. Clair sat behind Jesse, feeling like she was making the exact opposite of progress. Here they were, the five of them at a disadvantage again. And here she and Jesse were, fleeing dupes in some weird vehicle created from an archaic pattern dredged out of the dark corners of the Air. Somewhere out there, she bet, Nobody was laughing Dylan Linwood's head off.

Engines whirred into life. Fans roared. The hovercraft rocked beneath them, then settled. Accelerating smoothly, they drove—sailed? flew?—into the ruins of New Petersburg.

Everyone knew the story. Coastal cities had faced difficult decisions during the Water Wars. Some stayed and worked with the rising seas, like New York, with its flooded streets and canal culture. Others, like Washington and London, built massive barrages to keep the oceans at bay.

The third strategy was to abandon the city and rebuild nearby, which is what Saint Petersburg had attempted. The original city was re-created in stages on the southern isthmus of the strait that ultimately connected the former Lake Ladoga to the Baltic Sea. But the development took longer than planned, and the seas rose faster than expected, so the population of the original city, some million people facing complete inundation, fled farther north. New Petersburg ended up a ghost town of skeletal skyscrapers and empty freeways.

Through this urban wasteland Jesse drove with a steady hand, the hovercraft smoothly gliding over pitted roads that hadn't seen a car for decades. The sun hung low on the horizon, a bloated red ball casting very little heat. Clair wished she hadn't ditched her armor so soon, bloody though it was, and hugged herself for warmth. The cold air kept her in a state of desperate alertness. When she closed her eyes, all she saw was Nobody's stolen face, over and over, pressing in on every side.

She shuddered. Sargent put an arm around her.

"We should have fabbed you a jacket," she said, which only reminded Clair of her mother.

Fortunately, their destination was already in sight. Ahead hung several lighter-than-air craft of various sizes and shapes, some fat like plums, others long and thin like cigars; one had the likeness of a celebrity whose fame had peaked ten years ago. Small airplanes and gyrocopters circled them like gnats, flashing navigation and warning lights. Several plumes of white smoke trailed up from the area below, which Clair couldn't see thanks to the intervening buildings.

"There are barricades ahead," said Trevin. "I suggest we take to the water."

Jesse angled the hovercraft to the left, following the

next road downhill. The straits were gray and uninviting. Clair braced herself as they swept over an embankment, but there was no perceptible difference to their forward motion when they hit the water. Spray whipped up around them, making her face feel colder than ever.

The coastline receded until it was some fifty yards away, then Jesse began following it around to the east, the shadowy bulk of the abandoned city on their right, forested slopes to their distant left. There were birds flying overhead, perhaps ordinary seagulls, but Clair couldn't hear their cries over the fans and the chattering of her teeth.

More lights appeared as the muster itself hove into view. It looked like a small town, with piers and roads and lots of low buildings, lit by yellow electric lights.

"We're being hailed," Jesse shouted over his shoulder.

Two other craft were speeding toward them, spotlights getting brighter by the second.

"Decelerate," Forest bumped back rather than yelling over the fans. "Do not provoke them."

"Surely they know who we are," said Devin.

"It will not hurt to allow them the appearance of superiority."

"I didn't come here to be taken prisoner."

Clair couldn't stand their bickering.

"Stop the boat," she shouted to Jesse, "or hovercraft, whatever you call it. Kill the engines. We'll wait here and let them come to us. Be ready to run if I tell you to."

The pitch of the fans took on a deeper, descending note and the hovercraft began to sway on the choppy water as its forward motion eased. Over the ebbing of the engines, Clair heard a twin nasal whine that had to be the two boats approaching. She stood up and, ignoring the cold, went to stand next to Jesse, where she would be most visible.

Jesse looked up at her.

"They're trying to call you," he said.

She opened her hide-the-world icon long enough to find a patch marked AA. She accepted the chat request.

"So you've come crawling back to us," said a woman in a challenging voice, high-pitched and accented. Agnessa Adaksin, Clair thought. It had to be.

"I should have come sooner," Clair admitted, "but I'm not crawling. If you don't want me here, I'll go."

"Why *are* you here?"

"I need somewhere safe to think things through without people trying to kill me all the time. You can offer me that."

"Why would we?"

"Because you owe me," Clair said, aware that she was taking a huge gamble. "I'm the girl who killed d-mat."

"If so," Agnessa said, "you didn't do a very good job."

There was a long pause. Clair had nothing else to say.

"You can come in . . . but that's not why. We'll talk about

what I owe you when you get here."

The chat closed. Clair glanced up at the approaching boats. They changed course, angling around in two broad circles that would take them back to the landing.

"Follow them in," said Clair. "We're okay for now."

The hovercraft moved beneath her, and she went back to her seat.

"There are mines ahead," Devin bumped her. "You can see them in satellite views."

"We'd better follow those boats closely, then," she bumped back.

"What I mean is: she could have let us sail right into them, but she didn't. That's a positive sign."

She nodded, accepting that this might be true but not letting herself relax. They were surrounded by explosives that could detonate at the slightest wrong move. If that wasn't a metaphor for her life, she didn't know what was.

"So that's why you wanted us to come by sea," she bumped Devin. "When were you going to tell us?"

"If she had let us keep coming unguided," he bumped back. "Or if you hadn't stopped. We're all in the same boat, Clair."

"Hovercraft."

"As long as it keeps us afloat, I don't care what it is."

[44]

THE LANDING WAS crowded with boats and ships as varied as the blimps above. They were led to a pier where a delegation of men and women in plain clothes awaited them, all carrying weapons. None were actually pointed at them, but Clair was conscious of being watched from all sides. There were no drones overhead, just people peering at them from every vantage point.

With a final whirr, the hovercraft skated to a halt next to the pier. Jesse threw out a rope, which one of the burlier men caught and tied around a mushroom-shaped metal protrusion. When it was secure, Clair stood up and let herself be helped to shore by a woman with high cheekbones and short, curly hair. And, Clair noticed, just four fingers on each hand. Clair remembered Dancer and the members of WHOLE she had met before. She told herself to expect more such injuries. People who claimed to be injured by d-mat were a key source of recruits.

When they were all on the pier, the woman said simply, "Follow." Not Agnessa Adaksin, judging by her voice. She led them uphill, away from the water, and Clair felt exposed every step of the way. None of them belonged in WHOLE territory, except for Jesse.

He stayed by Clair's side, taking her hand when he was able to and waving her ahead of him when he wasn't. His deference was calculated, she was sure, to send a message to those watching. *If you accept me, then you'll have to accept her, too.*

She hoped that was what it meant. It could equally be read as, *Don't mess with me, or my kick-ass girlfriend will have words.* Clair didn't feel terribly kick-ass. She felt filthy and desperate, pushed so far beyond her comfort zone that she could barely remember what it was like back there, let alone how to return to it. Here she was taking comfort from an Abstainer, after all. Clair 1.0 would never have imagined that.

Clair 1.0 had had no idea, she thought, about so many things.

Their escorts stopped at a locked double door in the side of a low L-shaped building. Still saying nothing, the escorts opened the doors and waved them inside. The doors shut off the frigid world behind them, the Air with it. Their escorts stayed outside.

A long, white corridor stretched ahead of them, up the long arm of the L. The air stank faintly of antiseptic.

"Up the hallway, door on the right," called a voice that belonged, unmistakably, to Agnessa Adaksin. "Don't make me come get you."

Clair took a deep breath. "What is this place?"

"It's my prison," she said.

Clair hesitated. This was too weird. Her courage finally failed her—her knees were literally shaking. Someone else was going to have to guide them the rest of the way.

Fortunately Sargent stepped forward to take the lead. Noises from the room at the end of the corridor reached them as they filed toward it. Some kind of heavy, wheezing breath. A constant mechanical hum. The light spilling out of the room was electric white, almost painfully bright. As Clair stepped into it, she blinked and made out two figures, not one.

The first was a hefty woman with hair in dreadlocks and a long, patterned smock. She was bending over the second figure, a tiny woman curled up like a child on a high-tech hospital bed. All Clair could see of the second woman's face was a narrow, pointed chin under a plastic hood that fitted almost entirely over her head.

The big woman's expression was guarded to the point of being hostile.

"Agnessa?" Clair said.

The woman lifted her eyes as though they were idiots.

"That's Nelly," said a voice from a speaker set into the side of the hood, the same voice that had spoken to them by the door. "She's my nurse. This body is my prison. Watching people's reactions is one of the few pleasures it brings me."

They were all standing around the bed now, glowered at by the nurse, who didn't seem to be armed, but Clair bet the leader of WHOLE had defenses she wasn't revealing.

"Where do I look?" Clair asked, wondering what the

expression on her face revealed.

"Anywhere you like. I'm currently viewing you through a camera at the end of the bed, but I could just as easily be in the corner behind you, or the hallway outside. I talk to you through the Air, through speakers like these, or through more secure means if I need to. I am anywhere I choose to be, virtually."

"But your body is here thanks to . . . ?" prompted Devin.

"Stroke," she said. "One damaged cell in one thin vein wall, and I am as you see me. It could have been worse, I'm very aware of that: I could be dead or a vegetable. But even so, locked-in syndrome is no fun. Without telepresence I'd have gone insane years ago."

"Was fault ever acknowledged?" asked Forest.

"By VIA? How easily you jump to that conclusion." She laughed, and the sound was as rich and full as though it came from a human throat. The body on the bed didn't move at all. "This had nothing to do with d-mat, unlike your face, PK Forest. . . . Yes, I know about that. The things you discover when you have all the time in the world to look. The great Inspector, upholding the regime that made him a cripple: there'd be something truly poignant about that if it weren't just . . . sad."

Clair stared at Forest, searching his features for any sign that what Agnessa said was true. But of course there was none.

"Blame is overrated," he said.

"A man with nothing to live for would say something like that," she said. "At least I still have my soul. I can atone for what I've done. You . . . all of you . . . are beyond hope."

"We're not here to discuss philosophy," said Devin.

"Indeed. You want somewhere safe . . . to think, you said."

There was no way to tell, but Clair knew that Agnessa was looking at her.

"Yes," she said, because that was the simple truth. "We've learned a lot about the dupes . . . at least I think we have . . . but I need access to the Air to work out what it is, and we can't have that and hide at the same time. This might be the safest place on Earth right now, because you don't have any booths or fabbers. If we can just stay here for a day or two, until we work it out—"

"What's to stop the dupes from dropping a missile from orbit on us, like they did in Antarctica?" interrupted Agnessa. "There's nowhere on Earth truly safe from these people."

"They appear to be divided into at least two factions," said Jesse. "One of them doesn't want to kill Clair. The other . . . We're not sure about him, but we think he'll hold off for a while. We should be safe."

"'Should be'? That's hardly a ringing endorsement. And to what end?"

"That's . . . complicated." Clair rubbed at her forehead.

She flinched when flakes of brown rained down in front of her eyes. Dylan Linwood's dried blood clung to her like a grotesque kind of camouflage. "One of them told me that I've known something all along, without knowing it, something important . . . if that makes sense."

"Not really. Why would a dupe tell you anything that you could use against them? That doesn't make sense."

"This is why I need time to think. And I have to try. Running hasn't worked. Fighting hasn't worked. What else is there? Give up and let Ant Wallace win?" Frustration had her hand shaking. She dropped it back down to her side. "Never."

Agnessa said nothing for a minute that seemed to last an hour.

"Leave us, all of you except Clair," she said. "I want to talk to her alone. Then I'll talk to Jesse. Nelly, show our guests to the waiting room."

The big nurse made ushering motions with her hand, and after a moment's hesitation the others obeyed. Clair watched anxiously as they left, nervous about being alone with the leader of WHOLE. She was so different from what Clair had imagined. Instead of a revolutionary leader in combat fatigues at the head of a ragtag army amassed in the grim north, she was a crippled old lady who looked like she would die in minutes if unplugged from her machines.

Nelly pulled the door closed behind her with a solid

clunk and Agnessa said, "Pull up a chair. Sit next to me. You're looming."

Clair looked around and saw a stack of plastic chairs in the windowless corner of the room. She lifted one off and put it by the bed, so Agnessa would have been looking at her if her eyes weren't covered by the hood.

"You're nothing but trouble, Clair Hill," the old woman said. "Everywhere you go, you sow discord and strife. Do you mean to, or does it just follow you around like a bad smell?"

Clair opened her mouth to protest that it wasn't intentional—all she wanted was a quiet life—but Agnessa's throaty laugh stopped her before she could say anything.

"When you get to know me better, you'll understand that I mean that as a compliment."

[45]

"I'VE BEEN FOLLOWING you, Clair," Agnessa said, as LM Kingdon had, and at first Clair feared that the conversation was going to go the same way. "Your journey has not been an easy one, and I feel that I know what brought you here. The safety we offer is more than physical. WHOLE has never lied to you. I'm sure others have told you that, but this time it's true. You may not agree with everything we tell you, but we have earned your trust. The question for us is whether you have earned our trust in return."

Clair stared at the old woman's mouth, wishing she had some visual clue to what Agnessa was thinking. She was as inscrutable as PK Forest, in her own way. At least this conversation, she was sure, was private.

"Killing d-mat isn't enough?" Clair said.

"You and I both know that was an accident."

She acknowledged that with a guilty nod. And with that acknowledgment, she felt, went the best argument she had for WHOLE to be her ally. If she confessed that she wanted nothing more than for d-mat to work again, they would throw her out on her ear in a second, at the mercy of the dupes.

"It was worth a try, though," Agnessa said, with a hint of chuckle in her voice. "You remind me of me when I was young. You see through the bullshit the way others don't. That gives you an edge—but sometimes you wish you could just see things normally and live a contented, shallow life. From the moment we learn to speak, we're destined to cause trouble, for ourselves and for those around us. We either speak up or burn up from the inside, consumed by our own vision."

Clair wondered where this was going.

"Some people here would regard you as a hero," Agnessa said, "but your alignment with RADICAL and the PKs confuses them: neither organization wants the same things as us, not even remotely. We allow them here only under extreme sufferance. Others would shoot you on sight, if not for Jesse Linwood. I offer you a middle ground, something to remember no matter what you might hear me say in public. You're neither hero nor villain. You're the girl who gave Turner Goldsmith the ending he needed—and for that I will always be grateful. *That's* why I let you in."

There was an edge to Agnessa's voice that Clair couldn't interpret.

"I didn't want him to die," Clair said. "Really, I didn't."

"Neither did I, but it's a blessing he has. Turner Goldsmith was a dreamer, and now he's a martyr. That's the only immortality he craved."

"So you knew his secret."

"About his genes? Yes, I knew. I was his deputy for so long, it was impossible *not* to know. I thought I'd go long before he did. But the way it's worked out is best for everyone. WHOLE has a new purpose now, a tangible enemy. Our worst fears walk the streets. With every hour, our numbers grow. The world is turning, and we turn with it. And you . . . you are here with us once more. Where will you turn, Clair? Or more important, what will you turn into?"

"I don't know what you mean."

"Yes, you do. Remember: I see through the bullshit too."

Clair hung her head. She did know what Agnessa meant. For days she had been wondering what kind of person she was: bad friend, Mean Girl, terrorist, peacekeeper . . .

Everything life threw at her came with another option, another choice for her. And she couldn't be all of them. She had to pick one and stick to it. But which one? How was she supposed to decide when she could barely remember who she was and how this had all started? Was it really because of a crush on Zep that had undermined her friendship with Libby? Was that *all*? Or was there something she had never seen before, something about her that made all this conflict and confusion inevitable, as Agnessa said? Was everything she did just making it worse?

She was astonished to find herself crying, but she was, and there was nothing she could do about it. The emotion was coming from somewhere locked deep away, and now that that deep place was open it wasn't going to close in a hurry. It wasn't just about her mother, or Libby, or Zep, or even herself. It was *everything*. Tears dripped from her eyes onto Agnessa's hospital coverlet, red from dried blood at first, but then becoming clear. She didn't move, except to shake and breathe, and to crush her eyelids together until the worst of it was over.

It seemed to take forever, and when it was finished she felt drained of everything except doubt.

"I could see that coming a mile off," Agnessa said, not unsympathetically. "Now that it's out of the way, let's talk properly. Tell me what it is you're trying to figure out."

It felt good to focus on specifics: "Where Q is hiding, where Ant Wallace is hiding, where the dupes come from, if that's three separate places or one and the same. Who kidnapped my mother and how to rescue her. Whether I can trust the PKs. A particular dupe's real name . . ."

She trailed off, although there were even more suspicions that needed resolving, and soon. What did the Cashiles mean when they told her that Wallace was a pawn, just like them? Could Q really be working with the dupes? What had Clair seen that made her such a threat to the dupes? If the dupes really hadn't blown the barrage in Washington or attacked Valkyrie Station from orbit, who had? How many factions of the dupes were there?

"That's quite a list," Agnessa said. "How long are you expecting to stay here? A year?"

"A few days. If you can give us that, I'm sure I can work things out."

Agnessa laughed a third time. "Listen to you! I'd say you were mad if I didn't know better. Two days . . . That's probably the most I can give you. Beyond that, I can't guarantee we'll even be here. The muster has served its purpose by bringing people together and reaffirming my new role, but if we sit around waiting too long, we'll break up into factions and be useless again. We were a target before you turned up, and now we're even more so. And I'm not the kind of leader who likes to go softly-softly, like Turner did. Perhaps it's the way I am. Other people have the power, but I have the ideas. Out there, it's all action. In here, I make decisions and others do as I say. I'm their leader. Does that sound familiar?"

Agnessa was talking about her, although that struck Clair as crazy to an extreme.

"I'm not a leader."

"My bullshit-o-meter is twitching again."

Clair didn't argue. She didn't want to be a leader, but if people were offering to listen to her decisions, wasn't that kind of the same thing? As long as she could resign when it was all over, and people left her alone to think.

"So we can stay?" she asked.

"For now," said Agnessa. "On probation. Don't give me reason to regret this."

"I won't, I promise." Clair wanted to ask what WHOLE was getting out of it, but she didn't have the energy to look this gift horse in the mouth. "Thank you."

"Thank me by taking a shower and getting changed. People are leery enough without you looking like you crawled here from the depths of hell."

Clair felt as though she had. "I will."

"Nelly'll tell you where to go. Send Jesse in on the way out."

"I will," Clair said again, and she caught herself doing it. *I make decisions and others do as I say.* Agnessa made it look easy, but maybe it *was* easy when people were scared and out of options. Being a good leader might be more about timing than the decisions themselves. Timing, and a loud voice.

[46]

THE OTHERS WERE waiting for her in a chamber bare of any furniture apart from chairs and a tatty yellow rug on the linoleum floor. They looked up when she entered.

"We can stay," she said. "Not everyone wants us here, though, so we have to be on our best behavior."

"That I can do," said Devin. "Eating real food might be the impossible ask."

"You'll eat what you're given and be glad of it." Nelly narrowed her eyes. "Is it Jesse's turn now?"

Clair nodded. "Agnessa said you'd show us where to go."

"I will. In you go, boy. She won't bite you."

Jesse looked nervous, and Clair tried to smile encouragingly. "We'll meet up later."

"Most likely," said Nelly, not helping much. "I'll bring him over when she's finished with him."

Nelly shooed Jesse up the corridor, then returned to unlock the double door leading outside. The night hadn't changed, for all that it felt as though she had been with Agnessa for hours. Maybe it had been hours, Clair thought. It was late in the year, and they were a long way north. The only visual way to tell that time had passed was by looking at the fleet of airships in the sky above them: they appeared to have gained a few new members.

Her lenses told her that it was early Wednesday evening

in New York. The Air had returned, but she was reluctant to look at it, for fear of what new rumors people might be spreading about her. From RADICAL to WHOLE: what would people make of *that*?

Nelly took them along a series of narrow makeshift paths between demountable structures that looked as though they had seen better days. Clair had forgotten what it was like being around Abstainers. In the Farmhouse, where only d-mat had been verboten, fabbers had been allowed for things like clothes and cutlery, but here everything had to be made by hand or machined and regularly maintained and cleaned to keep it as new.

She planned to scrub her undersuit until it was practically transparent, first chance she got.

They came to a wide clearing that was partly farmed, partly communal. A dozen or so young men and women were playing soccer in one corner, cheered on by a clutch of children. Flagpoles displaying a variety of different banners stood in for goals. Clair recognized the colors of several defunct nations flapping listlessly in the chill breeze. There was no sign of OneEarth's navy-blue circle on white flag, which made her wonder if some members of WHOLE were separatists as well as hard-line paranoids.

They came to a row of dormitory buildings. Theirs was third along, and had been empty for a long time, judging by the dust and the closeness of the air. Clair was glad no one had been displaced to make room for them. Within were six narrow single bedrooms, about the same size as the berths on the seastead. No fabber, of course, but no kitchen, either.

"Mess hall's across the way," said Nelly, pointing to the other side of the soccer field. "Laundry and bathroom two dorms up. Agnessa's arranging a change of clothes. Someone will come to you."

"If we need anything," said Forest, "who do we ask for?"

"You ask for me," she said. "Don't be shy, but don't be wasting my time, either."

"Wouldn't dream of it," said Devin.

"Will you bring Jesse here when he's done?" Clair asked.

"Me or someone else."

And with that she was gone, heading back the way she had come with a heavy stride and even heavier brows.

An abrupt young man came shortly with changes of clothes for all of them. They weren't new, but Clair didn't care. Devin and Forest retired to their randomly allocated rooms to change. Sargent insisted on coming with Clair to the shower and laundry block. They found it empty, and Sargent volunteered to clean the undersuit while Clair sluiced what felt like layers of blood and grime from her skin, hair, and fingernails. When she emerged from the shower, she felt somewhat renewed but far from her usual self—as though Dylan Linwood's blood had sunk into her, tainting her. She had to concentrate to stop her hands from shaking again, and if she wasn't careful her head soon filled with images of the dupes that had attacked her.

At least she could bear to look in the mirror now. Her first glimpse had shown her a face she barely recognized, caked with blood except for around her eyes, which had been smeared in rough circles when she cried. She couldn't guess how much weight she had lost, but she knew she had, because her stomach was flatter than it had ever been and her ribs were showing. That wasn't the kind of Improvement she was looking for. She looked like a photo taken of her grandmother during the Water Wars, one her mother kept in her private profile to remind herself, she always told Clair, of how bad things had once been. That they might one day be that bad again was something Clair had never seriously considered. She was sure her mother was taking little comfort from being right, wherever she was.

The undersuit was wet but wearable. Clair thanked Sargent and slipped behind a curtain to get changed. When she tried on the clothes she had been supplied with, she found them to be loose around the hips but tight across the chest. Luckily there was a belt. She did what she could with the top and hoped she wasn't bulging in any embarrassing places.

Sargent looked slightly ridiculous in clothes obviously intended for a man draped over her PK armor, but she didn't seem to mind.

"I think the Inspector and I should sleep in shifts," Sargent said as they walked back to the dormitory. "Someone needs to be alert in case our situation alters unexpectedly."

Clair could think of a thousand ways that could happen—dupes could attack, Agnessa could change her mind, the PKs could grow tired of babysitting her—but she wasn't volunteering to stay up any later than she absolutely had to.

"I'm hitting the sack," she said, heading straight into her tiny room. Jesse hadn't returned, so there was no point even pretending to be awake. "Wake me if there's any drama."

"Sleep well," said Devin. "If you're lucky, I might even make you breakfast."

"I thought you said you weren't going to eat real food."

"That was for the audience. I'm actually a pretty good cook, if a little out of practice."

"Seriously?"

He winked. "Contingencies."

She was over being surprised by anything he said. She closed the door on him, stripped out of the secondhand clothes, and collapsed onto the bed. Sleep overtook her before she could cover herself, wrapping her in blackness thicker than any blanket.

THE DREAM STARTED exactly the same way as it had before. She was lost in a giant multicolored maze that spread out all around her, a vast and impossibly complex tapestry. Something tugged at her, some thread of familiarity on an unconscious level, but she didn't know how to follow it. Promising routes took her nowhere; dead ends suddenly flowered into new possibilities; routes that had led her in a circle the first time unexpectedly sent her in new directions the next.

"This is a test," said Q in a reproachful voice. "You're failing."

She sounded like she had at the end, right before Clair had sacrificed herself.

"Give me a hint," she begged. "Just one. I won't let you down."

"You already have."

"But I didn't know it would lead to this. I didn't understand the rules."

"There are no rules," said Q. "When are you ever going to learn?"

What kind of world didn't have any rules? Clair was about to say that when the nagging sense of familiarity suddenly became stronger than ever. She had been inside this maze before, and if she could only remember when, she was sure her destination would become clear. But who would be waiting for her there: Q? Her mother? Someone else entirely . . . ?

She jerked awake, her heart pounding at the sound of a person creeping into her room.

"Who's there?" she called out blindly in the darkness.

"Shhhhh. It's me . . . Jesse."

The familiarity of his voice cut through her sudden panic, but it still took her a second to work out where she was. Her lenses were as dark as the room. The icon containing all the bumps and grabs from the outside world was the only detail glowing in her infield.

"You're back," she said, trying to shake the heaviness of sleep from her mind. Half a dream lingered . . . something about a pattern that had seemed important . . . but it was fading as she reached for it. "How long have I been out?"

"I don't know," he said, sitting on the bed next to her. She could barely see him, but she could smell him. He hadn't showered or changed his clothes. It wasn't all bad, though. She liked the muskiness of him. He smelled different from any guy she had ever known. More real, in a way that was hard to define. Maybe it was because the soaps and colognes he used were real, not fabbed.

"I talked to Agnessa for an hour," he said, "and then I went for a walk around the muster. There are thousands of people here, with more coming every day. They've spread out for miles. There are farms, factories, recycling plants . . ."

Since she couldn't see him, she reached out to touch him instead. His back was tense under her fingertips, a long, lean wall of muscle and bone.

"Why didn't you come straight back?"

He exhaled sharply.

"She knew everything about me," he said. "My family, what happened to my mother—she said she'd talked to my father a couple of times. She knew I was an Abstainer but wasn't a member of WHOLE. . . . Do you know what she believes?"

Clair sensed that he had been about to say something else, but had changed his mind at the last second.

"It's not the usual thing?" she said.

"Similar," he said. "Everyone who's gone through d-mat . . . none of them have any souls. They died the first time they went through. But that doesn't mean they're robots or zombies or anything like that. They're still people. They just can't do anything about the afterlife. Their souls have already gone to heaven or hell or wherever they were supposed to go, when they 'died' that first time. Their fates are decided."

"So why's she helping us?"

"Because people without souls can still do good. And helping them do good can be good for *her*. She's lost her health, she said, but she still has her soul—and it sounds like she has heavy stuff to atone for before she dies. WHOLE's done some things over the years . . . There were accidents. . . ."

He stopped talking, and Clair reached up and put an arm around his shoulders, pulled him close.

"Is this about your mother?"

She felt him shake his head. He leaned into her, so their temples touched.

"It's about me."

"What about you?"

"Me and all the jumping I've been doing."

A germ of disquiet began to grow inside her. This was what he had been avoiding, she was sure. For a moment she thought about letting it go unsaid, but she had the feeling that he had come to her wanting to talk. Either that or his seduction skills needed a lot of work.

"I know that hasn't been easy for you," she said, taking a middle ground between encouraging him and discouraging him, and more than a little wishing he would just get to the point. She was tired, and that dream was still nagging at her. . . .

What he said next woke her up as effectively as a bucket of cold water.

"I can stay an Abstainer if I turn my back on d-mat forever, Agnessa said—but only if I do it publicly, so everyone can see."

She straightened and pulled away from him.

"Is that what you want?"

He took a deep breath.

"I've been an Abstainer as long as I can remember," he said. "I don't know any other way to live. If I turn my back on that, what am I? But if I don't . . . I don't see how you and I could ever work out. I heard you tell Nobody that you want everything to go back the way it was. I don't want that. We'll never agree on that. And people . . . the people who look up to us . . . won't want us to be together because of our differences. So maybe we just . . . shouldn't."

Clair didn't say anything. Here they were again, arguing about their beliefs. Her heart and head were torn between sympathy and annoyance—which was nothing, she guessed, compared to how he felt. He was the one who had been interested in her for years, whereas she had barely noticed him until a week ago. With the normal rules of the world suspended, it had been easy to imagine that they could just continue on like this forever, but what he said was right. She could see it as clearly as he could. When things went back to normal—as they surely had to, soon; she had to believe that—their very different lives would tear them apart.

But there was still *right now*. Didn't that count for something?

Her chest filled with a new feeling: anger. *This* was what WHOLE was getting in return for helping her. Jesse Linwood was a much more straightforward hero for the

Abstainer movement than Clair Hill. A victim of the dupes of his own father . . . tricked by Ant Wallace into using the reviled d-mat . . . steadfastly sticking to his principles, *if* he publicly renounced d-mat . . . he was a tragic but hopeful figure that might inspire a movement already strengthened by the crash.

But what about her? What did Clair want? Did that factor in anywhere?

Did she even know what she wanted? She had been struggling so long to save other people that she had hardly thought about what *she* needed.

A stab of sadness went through her at the thought of losing Jesse. They had barely gotten together, and this was the third time he had tried to talk himself out of it. She wasn't going to let him. It felt so *right* right now, and she needed him too much to let him go.

"Don't decide immediately," she said, coming back close to him. "There's no hurry. You're here. There's no d-mat to worry about. No one's going to ask you to use it again."

"Agnessa wants my decision by tomorrow. The day after at the latest."

Clair bit her lip on what she wanted to say.

"Tomorrow's tomorrow," she said instead. "That's what my mom always tells me. Today is today. Everything ends up yesterday, anyway."

"That's a song," he said. "An old one."

"Is it?" She hadn't known that.

"Yeah, my dad used to sing it to me when I was a kid."

"Your dad . . . *sing*?"

"Hard to imagine, isn't it?"

He laughed, just once, but it was enough to break the tension. She laughed too, and then they both had their hands over their mouths, trying hard not to make too much noise. She put her arms around him and buried her face in his neck, reveling in the smell of him, and then they were kissing, and falling back onto the bed, and for a while all anxious thoughts were forgotten.

Later, still dressed in the undersuit but with her nerves singing too loudly to sleep, Clair lay awake feeling the steady rise and fall of Jesse's rib cage at her side. Her right arm was completely numb, trapped under his shoulder, but she didn't want to disturb him. He wasn't used to constantly changing time zones like ordinary people, so he was always dropping off at odd times and needing to catch up on his sleep. She didn't want to think about the choice he had to make and what it might mean for her, so her mind drifted back to the dream. It was still nagging, which annoyed her: why couldn't it leave her alone so she could ponder something important, like whether Q and the dupes were hiding in the same place and what she could do about it if they were?

She should be grateful, she told herself. At least she wasn't dreaming about the Linwoods doing something horrible to her mother. Or the Cashiles. Or the thousands of other dupes out there, all trying to get to her for reasons she no longer understood. When the situation had been about Q, she could live with it, in the sense that it didn't drive her insane trying to work it out. Now it just seemed so random. If they didn't want to kill her or interrogate her or blackmail her, what did they want? Why would they lie about her mother? Who did have her if they really didn't?

When she closed her eyes she saw lines, lines, lines.

When she opened them, her subconscious started nagging her again.

If it was trying to tell her something, why didn't it just tell her?

That was why it was called the *sub*conscious, she supposed. It was up to the rest of her mind to figure out what it was trying to say.

All right. Since she obviously wasn't going to get any sleep, she might as well try to solve the puzzle. It was better than worrying about her mother and feeling impotent.

The dream wasn't only about lines. It was also about Q. Q was in a maze, talking to her, goading her on. Could it be a clue as to where Q was hiding—like a map, or a message in writing she couldn't understand?

Unlikely. She didn't think her mind was playing that kind of trick on her—besides, how could one part of her mind drop a clue the rest of her mind knew nothing about? It had to be something she as a whole actually knew.

Or had seen . . .

The lines seemed familiar to her in the dream. Could she really have seen something like that before and forgotten it? In the Air or somewhere like that? Was it something Q had shown her?

Could this be the information the dupes were alluding to?

What did you see, Clair, in the stars . . . what did you see?

Stars made her think of the night sky, but there was nothing special about that. Anyone could look up.

Clair sighed in frustration, and Jesse stirred. She held her breath until he went back to sleep, not ready to derail this train of thought just yet. There was something at the end of it, she was sure. She trusted herself. It was just a matter of getting there.

Q . . . lines . . . stars . . .

The other place that had lots of stars was outer space. Maybe that was what "in the stars" meant. *In* them, not looking *at* them.

With that thought, details began clicking together like sections of a three-dimensional jigsaw.

Click.

The only time she had been in space was in Wallace's station.

Click.

That was where she had betrayed Q.

Click.

Before then, Q had hacked into the station map to find the patterns of Jesse, Turner, and the others.

Click.

The sheer complexity of Wallace's secret dataverse had been as blinding as the sun.

Lines in a maze, spreading out in all directions.

[48]

SHE WANTED TO leap out of bed and wake everyone up. This was it, she was sure of it. This was what the dream was telling her.

The thing she had seen, the thing the dupes were worried about, was the architecture of Wallace's secret world. The world that he had built to enable Improvement and the dupes, and that she had blown up along with the space station.

Or had she?

Clair had searched it at the time, seeking the patterns of Libby, Dylan Linwood, and Zep, but had been unable to find anything. Maybe she had been looking for the wrong thing, or looking in the wrong place, or looking the wrong *way*. . . .

It was hard to understand what she could do about that now. The station didn't exist anymore. But there had to be something in there of importance, or else why would everyone be chasing her? If she could only remember what it looked like in detail. . . .

Clair almost cried out in triumph then, but still she stayed in bed, every muscle locked, heart hammering with a different kind of excitement now.

She didn't need to remember. Q had streamed the vision of Wallace's lair through her lenses. The data might still be in there. She had occasionally lost homework assignments sent to her by her friends, so she knew there was a folder where such data was held for a while before permanent deletion—a bit like the hangover in the Farmhouse that had given her hope of finding Libby, an age ago. If she could remember where that folder was, and if the vision Q had given her hadn't been cleared from it . . .

She fumbled her way through several menus, wishing she had paid more attention to Ronnie the last time this had happened. She couldn't call her friend now because it might tip her hand, if someone was listening. Besides, Ronnie might not be willing to help her again, after what had happened the last time.

There was no point waking Jesse either, because his augs were old and no doubt his software was, too. Clair's were the latest available.

Under the most accessible layer, the one responsible for her wallpapers, infield, and personal data, she found a line that looked promising. There was a whole directory dedicated to data received and transmitted. Somewhere in there might be the file or files she was looking for: the files containing the map of Wallace's network. But without knowing what it was called, she could only look for files with the right time and date stamp, and there were a lot of them. Her dupe had been active then, and he had had access to her public profile at that time too. . . .

That thought almost sent her reeling. Her dupe. Was that why Nobody had attacked her in New York? Had he hoped that by blowing up he could damage her lenses and maybe get rid of this data? Clair remembered the sliver of bone sticking out of Sargent's tear duct. If the peacekeeper hadn't come between her and the second blast, as she had on Ons Island, that could easily have been her.

Clair copied the entire directory to another location, where it couldn't be erased by some automatic update or cleanup, and began checking files at random.

An hour later, she had found the files but was forced to admit she couldn't search through them on her own. Her dreams of mazes and lines hadn't begun to capture the complexity of what Wallace had constructed in his orbital hideout, which Q had allowed her access to. There were countless views of structure she had barely glanced at in the moment. Those people she had rescued, like Jesse, had been searchable, but others hadn't been, and admiring the scenery had been a low priority.

Now she could begin to guess where some of those lines

on the map went, but there was still so much she didn't know. A large number of the threads led from the space station to VIA, of course, since the Virtual-transport Infrastructure Authority was intimately connected with Improvement and duping. Other threads may have led to other branches of OneEarth, but having only the map and lacking the actual connections it was impossible to tell for sure. She needed someone who understood networked systems and VIA in particular better than she did.

What she really needed, she thought, was a private investigator working solely for her, so she could be sure the information wouldn't get into the hands of anyone compromised by the dupes. But there was no way she could afford to pay for someone's time like that.

She would have to be her own investigator, with the assistance of the people around her . . . in the hope that she could find and erase the dupes before they got to her, or killed her mother, or did any number of horrible things that she didn't want to begin to imagine.

"Is anyone awake?" She bumped the others, knowing Jesse wasn't but ready to physically nudge him if no one else responded.

"I'm on lookout duty," said Sargent. "What's up?"

Clair was about to open a chat and tell her what she had found, but thought better of it. The PKs had had access to her public profile; they would know what data was in there, even if they didn't know what it meant. If she told them, they could pursue the solution on their own and—if Forest had his way—erase Libby and Zep and all the others without consulting anyone, along with the dupes.

She couldn't allow that to happen. Hopefully the RADI-CAL firewalls now on her lenses would prove too much for the PKs. With luck—and she felt bad for thinking this, but for once something horrible might actually work in her favor—dupes elsewhere would keep the PKs too busy to poke their noses into her affairs. According to the PK patch that still tracked them, the world was crawling with them.

"Can I have access to everything you've got on Wallace and VIA?" she bumped back.

"Of course," Sargent said. "It's public record."

"All of it?"

"Everything verifiable."

Clair did open a chat then, and chose her words care-fully. "I want the unverified stuff too. Whatever it is the dupes think I know, Wallace's PA might know too. Or the Improved. Their statements could be full of clues."

"There's a lot of material."

"We have time."

"All right. Are you open to being deputized? It's the eas-iest way for me to give you access."

Clair thought this over for a second. "Does that mean I'm committed to being a PK?"

"No. Just promising to use the information responsibly."

"Of course," she said. "You trust me, don't you?"

"I'm happy to vouch for you," Sargent said after a short pause. That didn't really answer the question, but it would do.

"Thanks." Clair closed the chat, satisfied that this would supply some of her needs, and knowing there was still some way to go.

"Wake up," she bumped Devin. "Wake up. Wake up. Wake up. Wake up!"

"Gah. Stop it. What do you want?"

She opened a new chat. "I'm going to dig around in the information the PKs found when they were hunting for the source of the dupes. Will you help with the technical stuff? I have no idea how networks like these fit together."

"Sure." He sounded sleepy. "Send it on through. Trevin can look at the data if I'm zonked. He sees everything I see, and he hasn't given up on us yet."

"Great, thanks. Glad your big brother's good for something."

"Again," said Trevin over the chat, "right here—"

She closed the chat, satisfied that RADICAL could help her on that particular front. It still wasn't enough, though. There was one more piece of the puzzle she needed help with.

She used her lenses to find a link to the WHOLE muster and followed the trail from there to Agnessa.

"I need something from you," Clair said.

A chat request came instantly. She accepted it.

"And what might that be now?" the leader of WHOLE asked.

Her voice sounded rich and full in Clair's ears. Clair imagined her drifting invisibly from camera to camera. Even if Agnessa hadn't been a hard-line Abstainer, the Improvement meme might not have tempted her with full health. What she had now was something like being a ghost, or a god.

"I don't think the source of the dupes is going to be in the Air, since no one's found it yet. It has to be something real, something that can be disconnected from everything else when it needs to be. It's likely to be hidden, perhaps a long way from civilization. Would you be willing to help me find it?"

"Lots of room for secrets in a desert," Agnessa said, "or on the ocean floor. Sure, we'll help. We're good at exploring the spaces between. That's where we live."

"Thanks. I'll be in touch again soon."

"Have you spoken to Jesse?"

"Yes," she said, and ended the chat, wondering if Agnessa had a camera on her. Her lenses didn't indicate any kind of physical surveillance, but they were in WHOLE territory now, where a different kind of law was in operation. She would have to remember that, moving forward, and not just for fooling around: here, the watcher could stay hidden from the watched. Here, an unknown god ruled.

—————————————————————— [49]

SLOWLY, A GRAY washed-out light crept under the door and Clair decided it was time to get up. Slipping her arm out from under Jesse without disturbing him and shaking out fiery pins and needles, she pulled on her baggy pants and buttoned up her too-tight shirt over her undersuit. Easing from the room with her breath held, she headed across the common area to the toilet block, where she cleaned her teeth and washed her face and tried to get her hair under control. Maybe it *was* time to cut it, she thought. A new do for the new Clair: Clair 5.0, who had survived the nightmare and was fighting back.

She smiled sadly, thinking of Libby. It was easy to imagine that worrying about her hair while the world fell apart was something her best friend might have done—but who knew how Libby would have changed had their roles been reversed? Libby wasn't a pushover; she was resourceful and strong in her own way, just like Clair had flaws and weaknesses that were entirely her own. Libby wouldn't be holding her former world at arm's length while she sorted out the situation with the dupes in private. She would find a way to do it so everyone could see and marvel at her brilliance. Clair had tried doing that, and had only made things worse. Maybe Libby 2.0 would have already saved the world.

But Clair wasn't going to give up, and that meant facing certain realities. She couldn't hide under a rock forever— not least because she had to be prepared if someone lifted the rock and exposed her to the truth. She had to know what it was she was trying to save.

Sitting on the steps outside their demountable, breathing in the crisp, wintry air and watching the airships bob and sway above her, she opened the icon containing the real world and peered inside.

The first thing that struck her was that it wasn't as bad as she had feared. People weren't starving; most of the fires were out; ways had been found to get people in dire need of medical care to doctors and hospitals, or vice versa. Long-outdated vehicles had been fabbed back into existence, including cars, helicopters, catamarans, and other forms of personal transport. What had once been employed for recreation or out of curiosity was now finding genuine use in a world deprived of the mobility everyone had been accustomed to.

Tash had attained the edge of the forest and was rehydrating. Ronnie had finally gone out her front door, and was talking to emergency workers in her local town hall. Clair glanced at the first of the messages piled up in her infield. They were as angry as she had feared, but at least her friends were safe. Better alive and angry than the alternative.

The crashlanders in the cave were all dead, even Xandra Nantakarn, suffocated by a cloud of carbon monoxide that had risen up over them while they slept. There was still no quick and reliable way to travel long distances, as several serious accidents had demonstrated beyond any doubt. Dupe attacks were still occurring, just as randomly as before. The Consensus Court was full of petitions for emergency measures, some of them shockingly extreme in their nature, from locking up people on the slightest evidence they might be dupes to executing anyone who broke the d-mat embargo. LM Kingdon was speechifying again.

"We must be both calm and resolute in the face of this creeping menace," she proclaimed. "We must not panic. We must not give in. We must stand together against every abomination, and never shy from what must be done. We must do everything to preserve the human race from those who would destroy us from within."

Oz was watching the speech, just like she was, from the town hall in Windham with the other deputies. His angry but silent approval spoke volumes. The dupes had stolen his wife. He wasn't going to take that lying down.

This time Kingdon didn't send Clair a message, maybe because of Clair's new association with WHOLE. Clair felt uncomfortable watching the latest speech. It wasn't that she disagreed in principle with the plan to exterminate the dupes, but there was something disturbing about the logic behind the call to arms. In Clair's mind it wasn't the human race versus the dupes: it was right versus wrong. There was a difference. Once the lawmakers and peacekeepers started dividing people up into different types, regardless of what they had done, couldn't people then get away with anything just as long as they belonged to the right type? She hoped that was just rabble-rousing rhetoric, not a return to the ways of the past.

The disastrous end to the fight on the seastead had probably contributed to Kingdon's case. The entire vessel had been destroyed by missiles dropped from orbit, thankfully long after the last survivor had escaped. Clair wondered if that was the Cashiles firing on the Linwoods, as someone might insecticide-bomb a nest of ants. Either way, it demonstrated a capacity for extreme violence that some feared might be unleashed elsewhere at any moment. That potential for violence only encouraged violence in return.

"Not really Wallace's style, is it?" Devin bumped her.

"What do you mean?" she bumped back, unsurprised that he was watching what she was watching.

"Taking out the seastead. Too big, too showy. He was a lurking-in-the-shadows kind of guy, because that's how you get things done. This is more leaping-into-the-spotlight-and-throwing-a-punch after the fight is over. Posturing, you know?"

She did know.

"So we're safe here for now," she said over a chat. "From him, anyway."

"That, and at least one of the factions among the dupes still has access to some serious orbital hardware. I didn't connect the dots before because I had other things to worry about, but look at what we've seen so far. There was Wallace's space station hideaway to start with, and now the missiles and the powersat Nobody used for his attack on the seastead. Someone's either got incredible hacking skills . . . or I don't know what's going on. An invasion from OneMoon, maybe."

The only conclusion Clair could come to was that breakfast was long overdue. And possibly dinner and lunch from the previous day as well.

"Does it worry RADICAL, losing the seastead?" she asked him. "Do you wish you hadn't become involved?"

"Matter we can replace. People we can't. I have to admit that I'm not regarded as the golden boy I was a couple of days ago, but you know how it is. You've got to go with what you believe is right. And more survived than you might think. Our soldiers were testing suits that act as mobile booths when they're sealed. Take a hit and the armor will . . . uh . . . do what's needed to keep you alive. The results were encouraging."

His hesitation puzzled her until she realized what he was talking about: the d-mat suits weren't just for moving people around from place to place in the middle of battle—which in itself was pretty amazing—but they could also heal people who had been injured. RADICAL wasn't ready to make that capacity known just yet.

Her stomach rumbled.

"You mentioned breakfast," she said.

"I did. Are you game?"

"Game? I'm so hungry I'd eat anything."

"Wait until you try my legendary beetroot and porridge omelet."

"Uh . . . maybe not *that* hungry. I'll ask Jesse instead."

"Just a joke, Joyce. Meet you in the kitchen in sixty. Prepare to be amazed."

Half an hour later she was amazingly full of scrambled eggs, fried mushrooms, and two thick slabs of whole-grain toast, dripping with butter and generously dusted with salt. She had wolfed it down, having been made even hungrier by the smells produced during the cooking process—and by the delay. Cooking was almost unbearably slow. She suspected her digestive tract of eating a large part of itself by the time the plate arrived in front of her.

"You clean up," said Devin from the seat opposite her. "That's the deal."

His plate had contained less than half of hers, and he did little more than pick at that, obviously not suffering from the same gastronomic crisis she had been. They were the only people in the kitchen, maybe because they were being avoided, or maybe because the members of WHOLE were busy doing whatever it was they did to keep the muster fed, clothed, and safe.

Clair leaned back in her chair and sipped at a mug of steaming black tea, skimming over a list of untraceable links she had found in the station map. The only coffee available smelled like burnt toast. She felt pleasantly overfull, but wasn't going to begrudge herself the indulgence. She wasn't sure how long it would be before she ate again. Only the thought that her mother might not be eating, wherever she was, cast a pall over her momentary contentment.

"You know what you've done?" Devin asked out of nowhere.

"What?"

"You've assembled Clair's Bears for real, the complete set: WHOLE, RADICAL, the peacekeepers . . . They're all jumping at your beck and call. If I was one of the bad guys, I'd be feeling more than a little nervous right now."

She couldn't tell if he was serious or subtly mocking her.

"I told you not to call us that."

"But that's what we are. We're all sitting around waiting for you to tell us what to do."

She understood then that he was fishing for information. And perhaps sending a message to the dupes at the same time, since the two of them were in a public space. If she was a leader, then Devin had proactively taken on the role of media advisor, and perhaps grand vizier as well.

"You'll have to be patient," she said. "I've got a lot to think about."

He nodded. "And dishes to do."

"Can't I plead ignorance on that score as well as the actual cooking?"

"It's never too late to learn. Come on, I'll dry."

Her mind wandered while she washed the mismatched plates and cups, settling on the question of whether her mother's kidnappers were watching her right now. She wished she could search the list of people following her, but there were simply too many names now for one person to trawl through. That was something she considered asking for help with, but she decided she was already asking a lot. And if she did isolate someone suspicious among her observers, there was nothing she could do about it, short of locking herself in a Faraday shield, which would make communicating with her partners difficult, not to mention rule out any possibility of finding or—dare she continue to hope?—talking to Q.

Besides, if Devin was right and the dupes were worried, that was fine with her.

As they left the kitchen, a trio of young men stepped out of a laneway and put themselves right in her path. One held a broad, powerful-looking dog on a short leash.

Its deep-set eyes glared at her as though sizing her up for breakfast. Clair stopped and backed up, alarmed.

"Where do you think you're going, zombie?" asked the young man in the middle, a redhead with streaks of black in his hair and odd, dark patches scattered across his skin. "Taking your pet freak for a walk?"

"Let us through," said Devin. "We don't want any trouble."

"Funny way to show it," said the thug to the redhead's right. He had long, skinny fingers like the legs of an enormous spider. "You didn't think to ask what *we* wanted before you barged in here."

"I'm only trying to help," Clair said. Her heart was hammering, but her voice was steady.

"You're only nothing," said the thug holding the dog. His ears were two lumpy extrusions on the side of his head that his thin hair didn't quite cover. "Those sounds you're making, that twitching you're doing with your mouth . . . You're dead, and you just don't know it."

"You want to be careful," said the redhead, "walking around here like you own the place. People might take offense. Anything could happen. Eh, Shiv?"

The dog growled, low and dangerous. Clair backed up another step.

"I think you should back off," said Devin, putting himself between Clair and the trio in a move that only made the situation worse.

"And I think you should get out of my face, ladyboy," said the redhead, pushing Devin to the ground. "I'm talking to the zombie."

Clair felt her muscles tense in readiness as the trio surrounded her. Her fists came up in front of her. She had no idea what she would do if they did attack her, but she wasn't going to go down without a fight. If only she hadn't lost her pistol on the seastead. . . .

"Don't do this," she said as one of the thugs shoved her shoulder, pushing her closer to the dog. It barked once, a horrible, violent sound. She pushed back and raised her hands to retaliate the next time one of them touched her.

"We haven't done anything . . . yet," said the redhead with a leer.

"That's enough, Sandler Jones," said a voice from behind them. "Leave the girl alone."

Heads turned to where Nelly stood on the common area, her broad face radiating authority. Behind her, Forest and Sargent were running from the dormitory, probably called by Devin, who stood nearby, face flushed and furious, shoulder muddy from where he had been thrown down. Jesse brought up the rear, his expression horrified.

"She's no girl," said the thug with the dog. "She's a thing. Walking meat."

"Well, you, meathead, have just earned a week in the sewage treatment plant. Want to make it two weeks?"

He glared at Nelly, the muscles around his mouth

working viciously. The dog growled again.

"These people are guests of Agnessa," Nelly said. "Screw with them and you screw with her. I hope that's understood, Sandler."

The redhead opened his mouth as if to argue. Then he glanced at Sargent and Forest, two armed and armored peacekeepers at Devin's side. Forest's expression was furious—a masterwork of intimidation that made even Clair worried, even though she knew it was a fake. Or maybe he really was furious. A fake that stood in for something real was no different from the real thing, was it?

"Agnessa doesn't speak for all of us," Sandler said, but he backed away, taking the other two with him. The dog strained at the leash, unwilling to be dragged away too. "Watch your step, zombies. You're not welcome here."

Nelly said nothing as the trio retreated, and when they turned a corner and disappeared from sight Clair allowed herself to breathe again. Her hands dropped back down to her sides. Her palms were sweating. The big breakfast sat like a stone in her stomach.

"Thank you," Clair told Nelly sincerely.

"Thank me by doing what you have to do and going somewhere else," Nelly said. "And don't go wandering on your own. Next time I might not be around."

She turned and walked away, big hips swaying and hands clenching and unclenching at her sides. Clair understood, now, that Nelly was much more than Agnessa's nurse. She was probably her second-in-command, and perhaps an enforcer as well, when circumstances demanded.

"Are you all right?" said Jesse, coming up behind Clair and touching her shoulder.

"Yes," she said, pulling away. "No. Let's just get back to the dorm. Nelly is right. The sooner we get out of here, the better."

She folded her arms across her chest and hugged herself as she walked across the common area, trying to tamp down the fear and anger still coursing through her. The confrontation rattled her. *This is what happens when I start to feel safe.* She should have learned that lesson in Crystal City, or in Antarctica, or definitely on the seastead. What might have happened if no one had been there to help her? Sandler Jones and his thugs weren't just letting off steam. They wanted to fight, or worse, and neither she nor Devin would have stood a chance against them. Running away might have been an option if Devin could run more than ten yards without gasping like a beached fish. She would never have left him behind.

Then there was her automatic reaction to wish for her pistol. Sandler and friends weren't dupes. They weren't even her enemies. They were people. Horrible people who hated her, but people nonetheless. Since when did she consider threatening someone *real* with lethal force a reasonable response? That wasn't what she thought. It wasn't what Allison Hill's daughter should think.

She rubbed her hands where traces of Nobody's dried blood remained, stuck deep in the lines of her palms and under her fingernails. She imagined it staining her, poisoning her in some horrible alchemical way. He had become her, briefly. Was she now in danger of becoming a dead-eyed killer like him?

Not now, she told herself firmly, and not ever.

––––––––––––––––––––––––––– [50]

BACK IN THE dorm, she went straight to work, effectively locking herself in her room and ignoring all distractions. Jesse kept asking if she was all right, but what could she say? She was as right as anyone would be under the circumstances. The sooner she found the source of the dupes, saved her friends, and stopped Wallace, the better. From there, it was just a matter of the PKs bringing d-mat online—and with Q's loyalties as uncertain as her location, that was going to be entirely their problem.

Into the station map she dove again, tracing promising threads to their endpoints, the details of which she sent to Devin for cross-checking if they were virtual and to Agnessa if they were physical. Many of the virtual endpoints turned out to be dead ends, parts of the station's infrastructure that no longer existed. Slowly, tentatively, she began to think of it as an outline of a forest, with a dense tangle of overlapping roots leading up through a dozen or so much thicker trunks to the canopy above. The canopy was the real world. If she could trace the trunks to where they connected at either end, in the roots or the branches, she hoped to find out where the dupes came from and where they emerged. Somewhere along that route could be Nobody's name.

It felt like homework, but as it was homework that might save the world, she did her best.

Jesse wouldn't leave her alone, so she set him to work browsing through the information Sargent had given her on the investigation into Wallace's illegal activities. There was a lot of it, including the testimonies they had given in New York and those of dozens of other people who worked at VIA. There were interviews with Xia Somerset and the other Improved. There were autopsies of Mallory's victims. There was a lineup of known dupes, including the ones involved in the kidnapping of Clair's mother, who hadn't been seen since. Last, there was a highly technical analysis of the circumstances that had led to the creation of Q and the breakdown of Quiddity.

Jesse went straight to that section.

"Does this make me a deputy too?" he bumped from the room next door.

"*He* is an Abstainer who can't see through his hair," she bumped back in her best voice-over voice. "*She* is a crash-lander with the ugliest nose in the world. Together, they fight crime."

"Heh. I see your nose perfectly well and won't hear a bad word about it."

She smiled and went back to work. Coming out of the station map, she turned her attention to the answers coming in from Devin. Some of the endpoints were easily identifiable, such as pattern archives relating to technical components likely used in the building of Wallace's station. Others were more mysterious—virtual addresses that didn't match up with the traces Sargent had made of Nobody's and the other dupes' appearances during the attack on the seastead. Clair searched meticulously through them, looking for the slightest hint of a connection, but saw nothing.

Some of the endpoints were physical locations that clustered in several densely populated areas, such as Ahmedabad, Lima, and Paris. Clair could see nothing about those places to explain what was so special about them. A scan of the PKs' dupe data showed no unexpected increase in appearances there.

Maybe Agnessa could help. Clair sent that data on, with a note expressing her gratitude to Nelly for helping her with the thugs earlier.

The reply was brisk and to the point: "Common courtesy."

"I'm looking through the VIA employee records," Jesse bumped not long after, "to see if anyone's gone missing in the last few years. My thought was that they could be dupes. One of them might even have been Nobody."

"Good idea," she said, only partially paying attention. Her head was full of links and trunks and the patterns they made.

"That's what I thought, until it occurred to me that it wouldn't work that way. If someone volunteers to be a dupe, they don't have to disappear. They can leave their original behind and just work from their pattern."

She pressed her hands to her face. "Derp."

"Exactly. This is entirely crazy-making. Took me ages to think of it."

"So we'll never find Nobody that way. Damn."

"There's still hope. Nobody was one of the first dupes— is that what the Cashiles told you?"

"Yes."

"That means that if he was employed by VIA, he started some years back. And given his general screwed-upness about death, his original might not be around anymore."

"You think he killed himself?"

"I'd say there's a chance," Jesse said. "But there are a *lot* of VIA employees to check through. . . ."

They went back to work, separately wading through their respective mountains of information.

Then it was back into the map for another round of searching, punctuated by occasional bouts of pacing from one end of the room to the other, her limbs and eyelids heavy. Sargent brought her a cheese sandwich for lunch—just like Clair's mother did when she was studying for exams, which made her feel a bit teary for a moment. Sargent explained that Forest was keeping watch, in case there were any other disturbances. Clair thanked her for the sandwich and the update, hustled her out the door, and kept working.

Jesse bumped her again as the afternoon crept on toward evening.

"Sorry to bother you. Got a second?"

She opened a chat. "Absolutely. My eyes are crossing."

"Mine too. And I'm confused about something."

"Is this about Agnessa?"

"No. I haven't decided yet."

"Okay. Good." Clair let out a breath she hadn't been aware of holding. She didn't want to argue about their philosophical differences, but living in anxious anticipation of his decision was adding an extra layer of acid to that already churning inside her.

"Shoot," she said as the silence between them stretched on a little too long.

"Right. Turns out Catherine Lupoi, Wallace's PA, was quite obliging when the PKs brought her in. She guessed the password to Wallace's profile and they've been snooping through it ever since. Most of it's fairly bland, just in case anyone hacked in, I guess. There are some small encrypted files that the PKs think might be red herrings—in the hope we'll waste our time on them, only to find a picture of Wallace's butt crack or whatever."

"Thanks. I didn't want that picture in my mind."

"Sorry. Anyway, there's one particular file . . . I'll send it to you so you can take a look."

The file appeared in her infield, and Clair opened it, revealing nothing but a list of names in two columns. She scanned down them. A couple rang very faint bells.

"Who are they?" she asked.

"Dead lawmakers on the left," Jesse said. "Living lawmakers on the right."

Clair looked closer. One was Sara Kingdon.

"You don't think . . ."

"I don't know what I think. I'm just saying. If Wallace was using Improvement to put old geniuses in the bodies of young people, couldn't he do the same thing to anyone? Wouldn't it be one way of making sure you weren't investigated too carefully—if the people who supported you never ever went away?"

It was like Jesse to be suspicious of anyone in authority, but that didn't mean he was wrong. Clair looked up some of the other names in the Air. One had supported Kingdon's proposal of a shoot-to-kill order for all suspected dupes. Another was actually leading a vigilante band in Texas, in defiance of calls for calm from the peacekeepers.

"These lawmakers aren't pro-dupes, though. And they're

not young people either, like all the other Improved."

"Maybe he did this batch years ago, before he made Nobody. Or maybe he worked out how to do it with older people, later. I don't know about the rest. Could it be a cover?"

"What about the notes next to the names, the asterisks and question marks? Some of them don't have any notes at all."

"I don't know," he said again. "Maybe Wallace was recording favors he hadn't called in yet."

"Or maybe it was just an invite list to his birthday party," she said. "I don't want to defend the guy, but a list of names isn't proof that half the lawmakers on Earth aren't who they say they are. It's not evidence of anything, really."

He sighed. "I'll keep looking."

"Thanks, Jesse."

"No problemo."

She caught him before he could end the chat.

"Hey, when it's time to eat later, do you want to join me?"

"Sounds suspiciously like a date."

"Sure is. Also, I need someone to cook."

He laughed. "I'll cook, you do the dishes."

There was that rule again. How anyone got anything done in the old days, she didn't know.

[51]

OUTSIDE, THE SKY was steel gray and heavy with clouds. Lights had come on across the muster. The air was sharp with the promise of snow.

This time the mess hall was busy. They went as one group, led by Sargent, with Clair and Devin at the center. The redhead, Sandler Jones, was there, with his two side-kicks but minus the dog. He noted their entry, glared at them, but said nothing. Conversation and cutlery ceased for an instant, then resumed.

That settled one flock of butterflies in Clair's stomach. Maybe the word from Agnessa had filtered through: the zombies were off-limits. Or maybe the thugs were biding their time waiting for a moment when there weren't so many people around.

Jesse and Devin squabbled over who was going to cook what. Luckily, the kitchen was big enough for a dozen chefs, and there seemed to be no shortage of supplies. Clair sat between Forest and Sargent, feeling like a cross between a prisoner and a celebrity, wanting to be neither.

"Have you made any progress?" asked Forest.

Clair explained what she had been doing, and then Jesse did the same, from the kitchen. It was hard to define what counted as progress and what didn't. It certainly didn't seem like they were getting much closer to an answer, and time was ticking.

"Pay attention, Stainer boy," said Devin. "These sausages aren't going to cook themselves."

"I have some data for you," said Agnessa over Clair's augs.

"Oh, good," she said. "What did you find?"

"Something disturbing. Those links to real-world locations you asked me to look into? They are almost entirely where Abstainer artisans live and work."

"Artisans? They make things?"

"Exactly. Things that can't be traced, because they're made by hand rather than in a fabber. Things that are completely unique."

"What kind of things, exactly?"

"Tech stuff. Bespoke hardware, control systems, autonomous algorithms . . . along those lines. Jesse's father had a lot to do with them in his art practice. They're smart cookies and it wouldn't be easy to fool them, but Wallace must have. They were working for him without knowing."

Clair was nodding. To subvert VIA and its AIs Wallace must have needed all sorts of gear not readily available in pattern banks, and he wouldn't have wanted it to be traced even if it were. So piece by piece, he had commissioned designs for the individual parts he needed to put his plan into effect, each seemingly innocent on its own, and farmed them out to be assembled by makers who would have been appalled if they knew what the machines were really for.

Abstainers had helped Wallace kill teenagers and wage war on the world. Everybody shared the terrible responsibility for his crimes.

"Will you give me the data?" Clair asked.

"We're not proud of it, but we're not keeping it a secret, either."

A file came containing the map data, with names attached.

"They will be interviewed," said Forest. "We should have seen this sooner."

"I agree," said Devin. "I might have an explanation for why you didn't."

"Go on," said Clair.

"On the virtual side of that endpoint data, it was more complicated than I thought. There are a lot of masks and blinds, even some traps for anyone who doesn't have the right authorization. I almost got caught a couple of times. Almost."

"So what did you find?"

"Those high-bandwidth pathways—you call them 'trunks'—they're for two-way traffic."

"Which is significant because . . . ?"

"Because if they were only for dupes going out, then the data would be going in that direction. You know, if you want a dupe in the Farmhouse, you pull one out of cold storage on the space station and beam the pattern where it needs to be. One-way. The fact that it's going both ways suggests . . . well, it could mean a few things. That someone was using dupes to infiltrate Wallace's operation, for instance. But that doesn't seem likely, since he's the one controlling the means of duplication. The more likely explanation is that someone from outside the operation was supplying the patterns for the dupes, rather than just using Wallace's lackeys."

"Why?" asked Clair.

"To have dupes of their own, I guess, with different experiences, different skills, maybe different loyalties, too."

Clair remembered the Cashile on Ons Island talking about soldiers with identical blind spots. "Who could be doing that?"

"That's the question. Those trunks are heavily guarded. I can only make inferences—I haven't been able to get right into one of them and see exactly where it leads—"

"Just tell me," she said.

"My best guess at the moment is that around thirty percent of the trunks connect to the PKs."

Clair put her fists on her knees and leaned back slightly, acutely conscious of Forest and Sargent sitting on either side of her. "What does that mean?"

"It could mean that the PKs were working with Wallace all along. Or it means that someone inside the PKs was working with Wallace. Either way," he said, raising a potato masher for emphasis, "it's interesting."

"I know nothing of this," said Forest. "And I cannot imagine why it would be the case. We do not need secret squads to keep the peace."

"That you know of, or that you're admitting to," said Devin. "I've had my suspicions for a while, as Clair knows. Someone has been leaking our movements to the dupes, just like someone gave the dupes access to the seastead."

"Why the peacekeepers?" asked Sargent. "It could have been any number of people. RADICAL isn't leakproof, as much as you like to think you are."

"Wallace got into a lot of systems," said Jesse in a calming voice. "Why not the PKs as well?"

"Haven't you got enough enemies already?" asked Agnessa.

"Oh god," said Clair, thinking of something for the first time. "*Charlie.* Do you remember in the booth in New York, my dupe mentioning him? On the seastead Nobody knew about that, even though we were disconnected from the Air and my dupe had exploded. *Someone in the New York booth must have told him.*"

"One of us," said Forest, looking around the table.

[52]

SOMBER SILENCE FELL as that thought sank in. It wasn't as bad as Forest made it sound, Clair told herself. There had been other people in that booth too, including several Improved who might have found a way to get information back to the dupes later, before they were poisoned. It was just so compelling, given what they now knew about Wallace's activities, past and present. He had used Abstainers to make his dream possible, so why not the PKs as well? Perhaps their indifference when she had been running to New York to meet him, or their diplomatic stance regarding the dupes before the seastead, hadn't been so innocent after all. Perhaps their inability to find her mother was part of it too. Could those supposedly unknown dupes actually be part of the third faction?

She wasn't sure where that left her now. In a camp of semihostile Abstainers guarded by PKs she couldn't entirely trust. There was nowhere else to go, so she could only press on in the hope that, with the world watching, there would be no further surprises. As hopes went, it was a very faint one, given her life's track record recently.

Jesse and Devin served up. The table ate in silence. Dinner might have been delicious under other circumstances, particularly the mashed potatoes, which were comfortably lumpy and fragrant with real butter, but the mood had turned sour. Clair forced down as much of the meal as she was able to and tried not to think about who at the table might have betrayed them.

Thankfully, everyone else continued to leave them

alone. Apart from an obligatory sneer from Sandler Jones as he left, there were no incidents. When she was done, Clair got up to take the plates to the sink, where Sargent helped her wash and dry.

Midway through, Sargent slipped and dropped a plate, which shattered into several large fragments on the floor. Clair wondered how hard it would be to replace, given the lack of fabbers.

"Sorry," said Sargent as they paused to sweep up the mess. "I don't know why I'm so clumsy."

"We're all tired," Clair said.

"Out of sorts, my mother would say. And then Dad would say, 'Out of sorts and out of the blue,' and then he'd insist on telling the story of how they met for the thousandth time. It drives . . . it *drove* Billie mad."

The pieces went in the garbage. Sargent's missing girlfriend was one data point *against* Sargent being a dupe or a traitor, Clair thought. If Billie had been killed by d-mat, wasn't it more likely that Sargent would be working to *stop* d-mat, not help those abusing it? Forest, too, since his face had been damaged in transit . . . ?

Clair shook her head. She was getting tangled up in her own paranoid theories now. It made sense to play her cards close to her chest, but that didn't mean she had to drive herself insane, looking for jokers.

"Does your mother have stories like that?" Sargent asked Clair as they returned to their chores.

"I'm trying not to think about her," Clair said, although she knew she wasn't doing a very good job of it. "Not until I can do something to help her. I want to know that she's okay, but . . . not if she's *not* okay. Not yet. Does that make sense? I've had enough bad news for one week."

Prompted by the question, Zep and Libby came to mind, and Clair realized only then that she had stopped thinking about her missing friends as people. She didn't clearly remember their faces, or their voices, or anything they had done together. They had become holes in her life where real people had once been. Absences rather than presences. She didn't know when she had started concentrating on Tash and Ronnie and her mother—real people who she could still save—but it depressed her that she had. She couldn't give up on saving her loved ones, not yet. There always had to be hope.

"What about Q?" Sargent asked. "Are you trying not to think about her, too?"

"No. Things would be so much easier if she was here, but what can I do? If RADICAL and the PKs can't find her, I don't even know where to start."

Except for with the source of the dupes, she thought. That was something she had mentioned to no one but Agnessa, because it promised an unhappy outcome either way. Q either wasn't with the dupes and therefore remained lost, or she was, which meant she was never going to come around.

"Is that all she was to you," Sargent asked, "someone to help you?"

"No. She was a good person, like Billie. She didn't deserve what happened to her. I wish I could say how sorry I am about that."

"Q was six days old when her only friend in the whole world betrayed her. When you think about it that way, 'sorry' might not cover it."

Clair wondered if Sargent was trying to make her feel bad.

"What do you want me to do about it?"

"Perhaps you need to convince her, Clair. Prove to her that you're worthy."

"How am I supposed to do that when she won't talk to me? How do we even know she's still out there?"

"She has to be. Otherwise how are we ever going to fix d-mat?"

Clair didn't know how to answer that question. Sargent's anxiety was very real and understandable, but that didn't change anything for anyone, particularly Clair. Why was it always up to her to fix things? Couldn't someone else do it for a change?

But she was the finisher. That was what Zep had called her. Or was she just Libby's finisher? It was all a blur now. And Libby was gone, and so was Q, and Billie, and thousands of others, and *doing the dishes was taking forever*.

The last was her own fault, though. Clair insisted on

doing any dishes that came her way, including some they hadn't created in the course of their meal, and certain Abstainers were fully willing to take advantage of her offer. When she was finally done, her hands were pink and wrinkled. She wished she could fab some hand cream and a manicure kit, and then she chided herself again for being superficial.

"Back to waiting for the mob to come and put the monsters to the flame," said Sargent, wiping her hands on a towel and stepping into the night.

———————————————————— [53]

THE OTHERS WERE outside. Jesse fell in beside Clair and she took his hand, pleasantly warm against the chilly air, as they walked back to the dormitory.

"Want to join me?" he asked. "I'm tired of sitting on my own."

"Sure," she said, glad that he had asked.

"Just don't let me sleep through again. I don't feel like I'm pulling my weight."

"You're working as hard as me."

"Maybe. Do you think that'll be enough? The two of us against the world?"

She didn't want to think about the possibility that it wouldn't be. What else did they have to work with? She couldn't afford to trust the PKs. WHOLE and RADICAL had their own agendas. It was up to her to put everything together as best she could, because she was in the right place at the right time—or the wrong place at the wrong time, depending on how she looked at it.

Slow and steady wins the race, she told herself, imagining her mother's voice. *Trust your instincts. Never give up. Use the Force, Luke.*

In Jesse's room, she closed her eyes and lay down next to him as he wrestled with his augs, together but in their separate mental worlds. She told herself to enjoy their physical closeness while it lasted, but there was so much data to sort through that she found it hard to concentrate on anything else. Information pressed in on her, even as she tried to focus on his body beside her and the sound of his breathing in her ear.

Facts and names stubbornly refused to gel, and her thoughts kept drifting back to Sargent's questions about Q. It surprised her that anyone other than her was still holding out hope of finding Q. The worst-case scenario remained that Q had switched herself completely off to erase the slightest trace of her existence. Was that the same thing as committing suicide? Clair wondered. Or was it a kind of dreamless sleep? If Q had arranged a timer to switch herself back on, was that reactivation or just waking up?

Clair's thoughts drifted further. She wondered what it

was like to be a dupe, jumping from body to body, losing chunks of her life as versions of her died unupdated. Did dupes ever get holidays as their original selves? Did they ever find that their minds didn't fit when they tried to go back? Maybe that was what had happened to Nobody. It would drive her crazy, being locked out of her own body.

Nobody. No-body . . .

An image came to her in a flash, horrific in its intensity: of being trapped under a mound of dead and dying dupes, just as she had been on the seastead, only this time they were her own dupes, smothering her in her own flesh, drowning her in her own blood.

Her heart hammered, and any chance of sleep vanished. The idea of duping and Improvement, of taking out someone's mind and putting another in, felt just as horrific as it had the first time she had seen it in effect, in Copperopolis, when Q had temporarily taken over Libby's body. It shocked her to the core, as she was sure it shocked most people. Anyone who signed up to be a dupe for a living didn't deserve her sympathy.

There was something about that fear, though, something important. . . .

A sharp crack in the still night brought her out of her thoughts.

Her first thought was that the dorm was under attack.

"What's going on?" she bumped Sargent.

"Sounded like a sniper rifle, from inside the muster."

"Perhaps you should get under cover."

"Stay where you are and I'll see what's going on."

Before Clair could call Agnessa, a video patch from the WHOLE leader appeared in her infield with a note: "You'll want to see this." Clair opened it.

The short video showed one of the roadblocks protecting the muster from the world beyond. A woman stood on the outside, dressed in a heavy overcoat and thermal leggings. Her head was covered but her face exposed. A thin wind whining through the empty suburbs very nearly whipped her words away.

"I come in peace to parley with Agnessa Adaksin," she said.

Jesse surged upright next to Clair, nearly throwing her into the wall.

"Mom?"

Clair gaped at him, then back at the footage of the woman at the barricade. There was just enough of her face visible to guess that there might be a resemblance—but how was that possible? Jesse's mom had died years ago—hadn't she? She couldn't be here. It had to be a trick.

"Who are you?" asked a guard offscreen.

"I represent the hollow men."

"What do you want?"

"To talk."

"About what?"

"About a trade. We offer amnesty in exchange for the girl, Clair Hill."

"They can't be serious," Clair said. Jesse said nothing, but he was breathing hard.

"We don't negotiate with murderers," said the guard. "Or zombies."

There was a gunshot, the same gunshot they had heard earlier.

"No!"

The woman fell to the ground, limbs splayed out and lifeless. The recording ended there.

Clair gripped Jesse's arm before he could rage out into the night.

"Don't," she said, pressing both hands against his chest. She could feel his muscles straining. "You can't."

"They shot her. They killed her."

"But it wasn't her. You know that."

"How can we be sure?"

"Because she said was one of the hollow people. And she hadn't aged, had she? She was copied from an old pattern, from the last time she used d-mat. The first time she died. This couldn't have been her, Jesse. The dupes are trying to trick us, just like Wallace tricked your father. Don't you see?"

His face was contorted with grief. Tears poured down his cheeks. He looked ten years younger.

"How did Wallace trick Dad?"

That had distracted him, as she had hoped. "He didn't, really, but he tried. Do you remember when we saw your dad in the station? He said something about letting 'them' bring your mother back. Who else could 'they' have been but the dupes? They must've had her pattern all this time. They tried to use her against your dad, perhaps as a kind of bribe, but he wouldn't bite." Clair held Jesse tightly by both shoulders, trying to keep him looking at her. "What happened just then . . . It doesn't change anything. She was dead and she's still dead now. Do you understand?"

She forced herself to add, "Like Zep."

He nodded and folded into her, pressing his face into her neck. "I'm sorry."

"It's not your fault."

She felt wretched for Jesse and emotionally exhausted on her own account. Somehow the dupes always found new ways to ratchet up their attack.

"I'm going to kill him," Jesse said. "I'm going to *kill* him."

She could feel him shaking. "Easier said than done. I tried, remember? But we're going to do it. Once and for all."

He sagged. She held him tightly, even as her mind worked. The PK patch in her lenses didn't show any dupes walking boldly up to the barricades, but that could have been because there weren't any drones in the area to see them. How long until they were swarming through?

How long until Nobody returned in force? She dreaded the thought of going on the run again, but she had to be ready, just in case they had no choice.

Jesse pulled away so he was sitting on the bed, not quite facing away from her, looking down at his hands. They hung limply on his knees like empty gloves.

"I can't do it."

---

[54]

THINKING HE WAS talking about Wallace, she said, "Then I will, or someone else will. Either way—"

"That's not what I mean. Everything is wrong. Mom, Dad, your dupe—*all* the dupes, Improvement, resurrection . . . even *you*."

"I'm not wrong," she said defensively. "How am I wrong?"

"The station," he said, and her heart lurched. They had never talked about this, not once, and she had thought he either didn't know or didn't care. "What happened to you up there . . . It's hard not to think about it. You *died*, Clair. You shouldn't be here. But I want you to be here. And I know you're really you. Everything about you tells me you're you, but still . . ." His head hung down even further, until it was practically touching his knees. "It's just all so *broken*."

Clair felt like she might throw up. Every moment they had been together, every time they had kissed, had he been wondering if she was real? When he looked at her, did he see the girl he had known from school or the girl who had died with Turner Goldsmith? Was he thinking of the dead Clair even now, wishing he could be with her instead?

She desperately tried to think of something to say that would undo the damage she was doing simply by existing.

"We're going to fix it. We just have to keep trying."

"When you say 'fix it,' you mean d-mat."

She couldn't lie. "Yes."

"But d-mat did all this. Don't you *see* that?"

She reached out a hand to touch his shoulder, but he shrugged away. Now all she could see was his back.

"Are lenses wrong?" she asked. "Is the Air?"

"I know what you're trying to do," he said. "You're trying to tell me that d-mat isn't the problem—it's the people who abuse it. Maybe that's true, but without it, there couldn't be any abuse at all. I want to live in a world like that."

"Never going to happen."

"It might. We're most of the way there now. If people really think about what's happened, they can be convinced that it'd be a mistake to bring it back. I'm sure of it."

"And the fabbers? Are you going to switch *them* off too?"

"I don't know. Maybe."

"How does making people starve solve anything?"

"How does d-mat? It *takes people apart*, Clair. It'll always be abused. There's no way around it. It's evil. It has to be stopped."

Clair gathered herself together, sitting with her back in the corner and pulling her legs up so her thighs pressed against her chest.

"I don't think it's evil."

"I know," he said. "That's the problem."

"Do you think *I'm* evil?"

"What I think and what I feel aren't the same. They're the exact opposite, in fact, and I don't know how to bring them into line. Part of me says that everything is wrong. The rest knows it's right. *So* right. How do I reconcile them, Clair? How can I love you and hate everything you stand for at the same time? Can you tell me that?"

Love.

Hate.

Clair put her chin on her knees and blinked away the full feeling in her eyes. She didn't know what to say in response. I love you too? I hate what you stand for too? She didn't know if he was breaking up with her or telling her . . . what?

"Your parents were the same as us," she said. Her voice sounded like it was coming from a thousand miles away.

She was amazed it worked at all. "They disagreed about d-mat."

"And look what happened to them." He turned to face her then, and she was shocked to see that he was crying. "Dad's a monster. Mom died in a d-mat accident and turned up here ten years later with someone else inside her, and then I had to watch her die. Do you know how many times I've dreamed that she'd come back? That someone would find her pattern in a server somewhere, just as she used to be, and return her to us? Turns out that wasn't such a stupid dream after all . . . but I was stupid for thinking it would be a happy ending. She's dead and gone, and she's never coming back."

Clair remembered getting angry at him in Valkyrie Station for insisting that the people they had lost were dead. Maybe he had been weakening himself, she thought, on more than just the d-mat front. Who wouldn't want their father or mother back? Clair certainly did.

"I don't want to argue about this," she said, feeling utterly miserable. She couldn't help the way she was. But maybe he couldn't help the way he felt either.

"Neither do I. But we always will."

She thought he was about to leave, but instead, confusingly, he came closer and took her face in his hands. He had stopped crying, but his cheeks were still wet.

She pulled herself to him, and they kissed, and then *she* was crying, and she really didn't know what to feel.

"Don't decide yet," she said.

"I have decided. I'm an Abstainer and I always will be."

"Don't go, then. Stay here with me."

"What's the point? We both know how it's going to end."

"I need you. I can't do this on my own."

"Yes, you can. This is what you're good at. I'm just trailing along behind you, pretending to be someone I'm not."

"Don't say that."

"Why not? It's true."

"It doesn't have to be like this."

"How, Clair? *How?*"

She didn't know, so she kissed him again. He kissed her back, so she knew she wasn't the only one finding it impossible to let go. Just because he wanted to be an Abstainer didn't mean they couldn't be together, did it? But what if he decided to join WHOLE and actually attacked d-mat? Could she sit by and let him do that? Did she have the right to stop him?

Improvement had brought them together, but it might just as easily tear them apart. She could see how it would play out, just like he could. Jesse would become an anti-d-mat celebrity while she remained Clair Hill, the girl who broke the world. And when d-mat started working again, Abstainers would turn on her for disagreeing with Jesse, while her friends would doubt her even more for wanting to be with him. They would never agree and it would never work out, and maybe it would be better for everyone to give up now and be done with it.

Except she didn't want to.

But what alternative did she have?

"You bitch," she bumped to Agnessa. "Why did you have to do this now?"

"Me? I didn't do anything. Be glad I spared you the others."

"What others?" Clair bumped back.

"She wasn't the only emissary."

An image came with that reply. Clair hesitated, then opened it.

Three bodies lay on the icy ground. Zep, Libby, and her own mother.

Clair's heart leapt into her throat. Her first thought was that it was really her mother, and she had been killed, but then the word "emissaries" kicked in. Her mother would never have come to Russia offering to trade her own daughter for any kind of deal.

It isn't real, she told herself. *Dupes, all of them.* But it was hard to keep from reacting exactly as Jesse had. Without d-mat, none of this would have existed.

She forced herself to breathe evenly and think calmly, even as an insane thought occurred to her, one she never would have entertained before under any circumstances.

She *did* have an alternative. And it was right there in front of her.

Maybe Jesse was right.

SUCH A SIMPLE thought, but so devastating in effect, dropping into her mind with all the force of a depth charge and leaving nothing the same in its wake. What if she gave up d-mat and joined Jesse as an Abstainer? That way they could be together as long as they wanted. And why not? He had compromised his beliefs over and over; perhaps it was time she did the same in return. And it wasn't like she'd be giving up anything she hadn't already lost. Her friends, her family, her home . . . All she had to do was accept that the old way of life wasn't coming back for *her*. She could still fight for justice for anyone hurt by Wallace and the dupes. She could still try to find Q. She could still have a life of her choosing.

It wouldn't have d-mat in it. And it would have Jesse.

After days of being chased by monsters that shouldn't exist, monsters that broke all rules of reality, it seemed almost reasonable to want to try another way.

She confronted the prospect with a calmness that would have amazed her just hours earlier. This one decision made everything simpler. No longer would she agonize over being the girl who killed d-mat. No more would she struggle with the idea of reactivation. The arguments with Jesse would stop. They would have a future.

"Let's go talk to Agnessa," she said, taking both his

hands and gripping them tightly in hers. "Together."

"Why? You're not going to change my mind."

"I know. Incredibly, you might have changed mine."

He brushed his bangs aside so she could see his eyes.

"Are you serious?"

"I think so. We should go before I change it again."

"All right." He stood up and looked around him, as though he had lost something. "All right," he said again, looking at her. "Let's do this."

She opened the door, and there was Devin. Somehow she wasn't surprised.

"You can't be serious," he said.

"I am."

She pushed past him, and he followed closely, too closely, putting himself physically between her and Jesse as she left the dormitory and stepped out into the night.

Forest and Sargent were waiting for her there.

"This can't be happening," Devin told them. "Tell her to go back inside."

"It is her decision," said Forest, stepping out of her way. "She can go anywhere she wishes."

"Can't you at least talk to her, then? She doesn't know what she's doing."

"I know perfectly well," said Clair, rounding on him. "Do you think I'm stupid or something?"

He raised his hands between them. "No, no, I swear. It's just . . . Look, I know why you're doing this. I saw what

Agnessa sent you. You're upset. Things are crazy—I get that. But that's no reason to do something drastic."

"You have no idea what my reasons are."

"I think I do. You feel trapped. This looks like an escape. It's not. It's not a trap, either—I'm not saying people shouldn't become Abstainers, as long as it's for the right reasons. But you're kidding yourself if you think this will solve anything. My mother was exactly the same. She thought RADICAL was going to change the world, but all she did was change herself into an ostracized freak. Don't be like her, Clair. You're better than this."

She glared at him, not trusting herself to speak. His words had a terrible ring of truth, more than she was willing to concede. But just because he understood her didn't mean that he was right to stand in her way. His mother had nothing to do with this—and neither did hers. She doubted any mother would want her child to be an Abstainer; they were the laughingstock of the world, regarded with suspicion by everyone, whether they were involved with WHOLE or not. But if it was right for Clair, that was the way it had to be. The only opinion that mattered was her own.

"I'm going with Jesse to talk to Agnessa," she said, her angry hiss a response to his patronizing tone. "Are you going to try to stop me?"

"No, no. Please continue."

He stepped aside and fell in behind her as she resumed

her journey. She was pretty sure she remembered the way. Forest and Sargent accompanied them, scanning the shadows.

People peered out of doorways and windows as they passed. Had *everyone* been watching?

Sargent privately bumped her. "Are you all right?"

"Yes."

"Jesse's not forcing you to do this, is he?"

"Of course not."

"I'm surprised at your decision."

Clair didn't care what Sargent thought, and she didn't want to talk about it with anyone other than Jesse and Agnessa.

They rounded a corner and there was Sandler Jones. He was minus his two buddies this time, but he took Clair by surprise and she came to a sudden halt. He grinned and let her pass with a satirical bow. She felt his gaze on her, burning like a brand, but she didn't look back.

New doubts assailed her.

Was that the kind of person she'd be surrounded by from now on? Would people like him call her a zombie for the rest of her life even if she did become an Abstainer? Was she *really* doing this for herself and not for Jesse? *How long is this bloody walk anyway?*

"Listen, Clair," said Devin somewhat breathlessly. "I just got a message from a girl called Ronnie Defrain. She says she's a friend of yours and you're ignoring her."

Clair slowed. None of that was true. Her former friends weren't her friends anymore—and Clair wasn't ignoring anyone specifically. She just didn't want to know what people were saying about her.

"What does she want?"

"Here, I'll show you."

Ronnie's message appeared in a bump.

Tell Clair she can run off with Jesse if she really wants to. He can't be that bad if she's willing to give up everything for him. Besides, we're all Abstainers now, I guess. Just let her know that while she's been gallivanting around the globe the real 'Clair's Bears' have been busy, and we've got something we think will help.

Help? Clair's Bears? Calling up her courage, Clair sent a chat request.

"OMG, the girl lives!" Ronnie answered instantly. She was back home from her visit to the local town hall, and the chocolate wrappers were cleaned up and recycled. "I was beginning to feel like you were in one of Tash's old soap operas, the kind where you can't vote on the endings."

Clair felt a rush of emotion at the sound of her friend's familiar banter. It was a glimpse of her former life, from what felt like an eternity ago.

"What are you doing?" she said. "Why are you calling me now?"

"It's simple, really. Everyone following you can see what you're going through: there's *all* this work to do, you're *all* on your own, blah blah."

"I *am* busy—"

"Yes, yes—too busy to read all your messages. We know. You should've kept reading. We *were* angry with you, and we had a right to be. The Air was full of crazy shit and you weren't telling us what was real and what wasn't. It wasn't until later, when Tash got back on safe ground, that we began to put it all together. We can see what you've been trying to do now. That's why you should've kept reading the messages. We didn't stop being your friends just because we were angry with you. That's not what friends do, right? We're here. We want to help you. And since you didn't change our privileges, that's exactly what we've gone ahead and done."

There was a serious lump in Clair's throat. She almost didn't dare speak, in case this turned out to be some kind of cruel trick.

"How?" she managed to force out.

"Well, I'm a database geek and Tash is the queen of lat-jumping and geocaching. We're your invisible sidekicks, beavering away where the dupes can't see us. Those files you sent to the others? We pulled them out of your infield and took a look at them for ourselves. We found some crazy things, let me tell you. But how can we tell you what they are if you ignore us? We're invisible to you as well! I bumped you nine times before I nagged your weird little buddy here to get through. Some people might take that personally."

Clair was touched and embarrassed at the same time. She had told herself it didn't matter if Ronnie and Tash were her friends anymore. The way she felt now indicated that it did matter, very much.

"Thank you," she said.

"It's okay. Worrying about your mom, getting it on with the Lurker, stopping that Ant Wallace guy from becoming king of the world . . . It's fair to say you've had a lot going on. That's why we wanted to help. To wit, the file I'm about to send you. I've whittled the VIA employees down to something I'm sure you'll find more manageable. It took me a while, but I've been a bit more focused than Jesse—again, understandably! It's not as though I've got anything else to do. Ditto Tash, who went through the physical endpoints you gave that Agnessa lady. What else is there to do in a jungle, once you've killed all the things trying to eat you? You owe us a proper conversation when this is all over, if any of it helps."

A file arrived in Clair's infield.

"Remember that song we danced to at the crashlander ball?" Ronnie asked.

"Yes." She would never forget a single detail of the night she had kissed Zep, and Libby had used Improvement. "Why?"

"Password. Can't be too careful."

Clair saved the file in her most private cache.

"Thank you," she said again, knowing that those two syllables were grossly inadequate for what she wanted to say. It didn't matter if the file was useful at all. Her friends didn't hate her. They'd just needed time to realize that she hadn't changed *that* much. Actions, as she had said in her speech to the world, really did speak louder than words.

Ahead lay the L-shaped building that was Agnessa's resting place, and Clair 5.0's destination. Or was she Clair 6.0 now? *Schoolgirl, soldier, investigator, Stainer . . .*

"Gotta go," Clair said, feeling revitalized by this unexpected reconnection. It was as though someone had draped a rug over her without her knowing, then suddenly swept it away, letting the light back in. "We'll catch up later, yes?"

"One hundred percent yes. Just try and stop me."

The chat ended. The double door opened, revealing Nelly.

"Those two stay outside," she said, pointing to Forest and Sargent.

"Guard duty again?" Sargent grumbled.

"But you're so good at it," Nelly said, waving Clair and Jesse through. Devin went to follow and wasn't turned away.

The doors shut behind them, cutting off the night and the Air, along with Clair's view of Sargent's annoyed expression.

"And they were never seen again . . . ," Devin intoned.

Nelly shot him a sharp look. "The PKs are perfectly safe."

"I meant us. Clair, you're going to have to turn in your sense of humor when you join this lot. Have you really thought this through?"

————————[56]

NOTHING HAD CHANGED in Agnessa's room. The machines still hummed and breathed. The machines still beeped. The woman on the bed still lay on her side, giving no sign at all that she had ever been alive.

"So, Jesse," her voice intoned from all around them, "you've decided to rejoin our ranks."

"As an Abstainer, yes." He looked anxious but at the same time relieved that he had reached a decision. "Clair says she'd like to join too."

"I gather. I don't remember inviting her."

"Uh . . . but it's okay, isn't it? You let her in here. You're not going to kick her out, are you?"

"That depends. Clair, tell me why you're here. Is it because of Jesse or because of you?"

"Me," she said, mostly sure that was true. It was such a new thing; she was still working it out. "Every problem we're facing goes away if we stop using d-mat."

"You know it's not that simple," said Devin from the

other side of the bed. "Solving one set of problems by creating a thousand more isn't a solution. It's *surrender*."

"I'm not giving in to anyone," she said, beginning to feel angry again. "It's the right thing to do."

"*Now* it might be," he said, "but what if you change your mind later? Be careful which bridges you burn, Clair."

"I'm not burning any bridges. We can still work together. Or are you saying you won't work with me just because I want to be an Abstainer?"

"No," he said, running his fingers through his thin red hair. "It's just . . . you're a figurehead. That's why I joined the investigation; that's why we rescued you from the dupes. You represent something—call it the future. Or persistence, like Nobody said. If you do this . . . what does it tell the people following you?"

"It tells them that there's another way," said Agnessa. "They need an advocate who's like them, who understands their confusion. That person could be Clair. Instead of running around helplessly, chased by an endless stream of monsters, she can turn and take a stand. She can make a *difference*, if she really wants to."

Clair stared at the supine woman on the bed. Was that the deal she was being offered—the same as Jesse's? Just giving up wouldn't be enough. She could only join if she became a champion of the cause . . . ?

"When people are afraid," said Devin, "they'll agree to anything."

"That doesn't make it wrong," said Jesse.

"D-mat saved the world, for heaven's sake! Do you really want more Water Wars? Because that's what we'll have on our hands if you clowns are ever in charge."

Clair could feel the temperature rising fast and she raised her hands for calm. "There's no need to be melo-dramatic—"

"*Melodramatic?* I'm playing it down, if anything. What's happening right now is a fight for the future of the human race—and it's all Wallace's fault. If he hadn't created that damned entity, we wouldn't be here, seriously considering turning off d-mat—because people *will* vote for Abstainer lawmakers if they're driven to it. That may look like a solution to you, but it's utterly wrong. It can't be allowed. We won't stand for it. You think you've got problems with dupes right now? Wait until they team up with my lot to stop you turning back the clock. Then you'll really have a war on your hands."

Clair gaped at him. Was he serious? Would RADICAL really side with Wallace against WHOLE? That would be a bloodbath.

"No one's fighting anyone," said Agnessa in a calming voice. "That's what Wallace wants. Divide and conquer. The trick is to stop him *first* and worry about d-mat later. And there's something very important you need to know about me, Devin, that you obviously haven't realized yet: I'm not Turner Goldsmith. I don't expect to change the world. It is the way it is, and I can be content with my small corner of it—just so long as I have a voice and my people are left in peace."

Devin was flushed. "On your word?"

"On my word. There's been enough fighting already."

"Then . . . I apologize. Please forget everything I just said." Devin leaned against the bed. "And Clair, I apologize to you, too. You have the right to decide how to live your life. It's a free planet. We can agree to disagree, I'm sure."

Clair nodded, although that wasn't what worried her now. A new fear was rising up inside her, so large it was drawing others to it and casting a shadow across all her hopes for the future.

"When people are afraid, they'll agree to anything," she said, quoting Devin's words from just moments ago. The thing taking shape in her mind drew its power from many people's words. *A new age is coming. Divide and conquer. King of the world.*

"Jesse, what was it Turner said about creating a dictatorship? Something about two steps?"

"Uh . . . robbing people of their individuality was the first one," he said, looking puzzled.

"And putting people under constant observation was the second," said Agnessa. "I told you. Turner was a dreamer. If he'd been right, we'd have been living under an iron boot years ago."

"I think Turner was half-right," said Clair. "And Wallace knew it. Anyone can be copied now, so who's real and who's not? That's the first part. The second . . . Think about what the dupes are doing. They don't seem to have much of a plan beyond attacking us whenever we get in their way. They're just deadly and dangerous, which is making people scared. And the lawmakers are responding. Shoot-to-kill orders. Deputies. Vigilantes. That's the second part of the plan."

"To make people *afraid*?" said Devin, looking skeptical.

"Wait, I get it," said Jesse. "I can totally see how Wallace meant it to go. First he'd fake some kind of emergency—maybe a problem with d-mat—which he or one of his plants would fix. Sound familiar?"

"He steps in and saves the day," said Agnessa, "and people are so grateful they vote in laws that make the Earth his playground?"

"Yes—and then there's that list," said Jesse, snapping his fingers. "His pet lawmakers! They're the ones putting all the new measures forward."

"But you can't rule the world if you're dead," said Devin.

"Is he, though?"

"Actually," said Clair, at last seeing the full extent of the thing she had been reaching for, "I think he really might be dead, and we've been too stupid to see it."

——————————— [57]

ALL EYES TURNED to her.

"People don't often call me stupid," said Devin. "You'd better explain."

"All right." She looked down at her hands, trying to put her thoughts in the right order. "Our working theory has gone back to being that Wallace is still alive because of the dupes. He's looking for revenge, taking over the world, whatever. But as you said, it's not in his character to do all this in public. Also, if he was around, you'd think he'd have made a new version of Mallory by now . . . and she would've come after us for sure."

"Right," said Jesse. "You killed her, after all."

Clair shied away from those memories.

"That's not to say, though, that Wallace wasn't part of the plan at some point," she went on. "An integral part. He had his own operation—Improvement. I figure he was approached by someone who heard about it somehow, someone who wanted to create a secret army of dupes for themselves. Wallace made that possible, but it wasn't his idea, and he wasn't in control of them. Not absolutely. Maybe he had some dupes of his own—probably the prototypes, the earliest versions, Nobody—but the rest didn't work for him. They were independent, a dupe squad that couldn't be traced back to their masters. The people who have really been pulling the strings all this time."

"Wallace was a pawn, just like the Cashiles said?" Devin asked. "Who for?"

What do the other dupes want? she had asked Nobody on the seastead.

The same thing they've always wanted.

"The people who really want to take over OneEarth,"

she said. "Someone public, someone seen to be doing good, someone in a position to influence the Consensus Court . . ."

"The lawmakers on that list," said Agnessa. "Is that what you're suggesting?"

"Maybe some of them," said Clair. "Maybe all of them. I don't think even Wallace knew. That's what the question marks and asterisks were for. He was trying to work it out for himself."

"LM Kingdon is on the list," said Jesse. "With an asterisk."

"I know," she said, remembering the woman's easy but determined charm. "It fits, doesn't it? She's pushing for harsh measures against anyone suspected of being a dupe. How long until she starts accusing the people who disagree with her? How long until you don't even have to be a dupe to get in trouble?"

"You think she's really her?"

"I don't know. And I don't know how to find out. That's the trouble with dupes. Unless they slip up or confess, there's no test to see who's who and who isn't. That's why this is so clever. People are suspicious of dupes, which means they're suspicious of everyone. You can see exactly how it'll happen, how paranoid everyone is going to get. How desperately in need of a bad guy. It's almost like the real bad guys *wanted* Wallace to be discovered. . . ."

"Maybe they did," said Devin, looking like he was

starting to come around. "He takes the fall and they get everything they need to stage their coup. It's all very convenient."

"And maybe that's why he wanted Q so badly," Clair said. "He could see what was coming for him and was trying to avoid it."

"But he failed and he's dead now, leaving Nobody flailing about at a loose end." Devin was ticking points off on his fingers. "The rest of the dupe squad don't know what to do with Nobody. Maybe they don't want to admit what's going on to their masters. So they come to you, Clair, in the hope that you'll do something about it. First they try to recruit you, then they warn you so you'll warn us. There are at least two factions among the dupes, but only one of them is dangerous—not Nobody, although that's what they'd like you to think. The Cashiles, who are helping the lawmakers take over the world. And *that's* why there's all this orbital hardware in play: they have friends in high places."

"Hold it," said Agnessa. "This is all very well as a theory, but I don't buy it. You've let Turner's wild ideas go to your heads. Forget the crazy dupes for a moment. The rest is never going to happen the way you say it will. People aren't stupid. Random acts of terror don't lead automatically to a totalitarian government."

"Maybe not overnight," said Jesse, "but if you can use Improvement to steal new bodies every generation or so, you can afford to play the long game."

"Or," said Clair, only then thinking of another plausible take, "the lawmakers could dupe voters to vote the right way for them."

Devin's eyebrows went up. "Whoa. You don't think small, do you?"

"Is that possible?" asked Jesse. "I mean, could they really do something like that with no one noticing?"

Clair didn't know. "Maybe if they duped whole families and friendship circles . . ."

"Whole towns," said Devin. "Whole regions. Why not the whole world?"

"They can't do anything while d-mat isn't working," said Agnessa, again playing devil's advocate.

"That's Q again," said Clair. "Things weren't supposed to go that way. Wallace died. The Nobody dupe freaked out. The lawmakers have done their best to take advantage of it, but really Q's the monkey wrench in their works as well. That's why everyone wants and fears her at the same time. She changes everything around her without even realizing she's doing it."

"I told you she was dangerous," Devin said.

"But she saved us," said Jesse. "Without her, where would we have been in fifty years? Kingdon and her buddies might have won and our kids would all be slaves. Now that we know, we can put a stop to it."

"How?" asked Agnessa.

For a full minute, there was silence.

58

CLAIR'S MIND WAS crowded with sudden, new thoughts. She had come to Agnessa expecting to turn her back on d-mat, and here she was uncovering a plan to take over OneEarth from the inside. If that was what it really was. Just because it felt right to her didn't mean that some lawmakers were really intending to *mind-rape* the world. They needed evidence. And they needed some kind of leverage before they could possibly take something this incendiary public. Her mother was still vulnerable. *She* was still vulnerable. What did she have on her side apart from a band of argumentative misfits hiding out in an abandoned city?

She had Clair's Bears, she reminded herself, and there was a chance they might already have provided the information she needed. Calling up the file Ronnie had been trying to send her, she opened it up in a window of its own. It asked for a password, so she entered "Elevate," the name of the song she and her friends had danced to at the crashlander ball. That didn't work, so she tried "Silent P," the artist who had sung it.

The file opened, revealing that Ronnie and Tash had whittled a mountain of data down to just three personnel profiles and two locations. The three profiles were of men. One of the locations was some kind of scientific installation in the Middle East, the other a borehole on the other side of Russia.

"We need access to the Air," she said. "Is there any way to get that from in here?"

"If I drop the Faraday shield, we'll be exposed," said Agnessa. "But I have a landline, of course, to maintain my telepresence outside. You can ask me and I'll find you anything you need to know."

Clair nodded. That would have to do.

"Here are two places you didn't follow up on the end-point data." She sent the information. "I want to know what they are, who uses them, and what they use them for. And here are three names to search for, as well. They're our potential Nobodies. Anything you can pull on them will be good."

"So the plan is still the same," said Devin. "Find the source of the dupes and shut it down. With or without Nobody's help."

"If we take out the dupes, the lawmakers will be toothless," she said.

"There are still the PKs," said Jesse.

"Until the law is changed, they can't move against us," she said.

"Unless we become a threat," said Agnessa.

"That's right."

"The definition of 'threat' is very slippery these days."

"I know," said Clair.

"We have to handle this carefully," said Devin. "If whoever's behind this gets the slightest idea that we know what they're doing, they'll come down on us hard. And we know they have the means. The only thing keeping us alive right now, most likely, is that we keep banging on about Wallace, diverting attention from what's really going on."

Data flooded from Agnessa into Clair's infield. The pit was in fact the Baikal Superdeep Borehole, the deepest artificial hole in the world, drilled twenty years ago at the bottom of a massive freshwater lake, then flooded and sealed to stop urban spelunkers from killing themselves when they reached the superheated bottom. It now served as a geothermal power supply for the national park responsible for its surrounds. No one had been inside for years, according to park rangers, although lat-jumpers like Tash did regularly drop in to see the lake.

The other location was a high-gain antenna on the tiny island of Mesaieed, just off the coast of Qatar. The island sported enormous sand dunes that drew tourists in droves, plus competitors in a popular endurance contest. Few people visited the antenna itself, but it was a major telemetry hub for the network of VIA satellites responsible for coordinating global d-mat traffic.

"Another connection to satellites," said Devin. "I think we're on to something here."

"Can we hack in and see what the uplink is talking to?"

Clair asked, telling herself not to get too excited too fast. It was hard, though: this looked very plausible. "I mean, d-mat has crashed, right? If that uplink is talking to anything, it has to be where the dupes come from."

"I'll ask Trevin to look into it," Devin said.

"You're linked to him even in here?" Jesse asked.

"I'm linked to him anywhere." Devin lifted his left eyebrow. "Maybe it *is* telepathy."

While Clair waited, she called up the personnel profiles of the three VIA employees Ronnie had flagged. Two were in their fifties, technicians who had worked on relay stations like the one in Mesaieed. The other was in his midtwenties, a security guard named Cameron Lee. Born in Manchester, schooled in Boston. In his photo he looked cocky and cheerful, with a shock of blond hair and lively blue eyes.

He was the one.

Cameron Lee was a young man who had his entire life ahead of him. Clair didn't know how or why he had been recruited into the dupe program, but in this optimistic beginning she recognized the devastation of Nobody's fall. A middle-aged man might endure it with more grace. Someone vibrant and full of hope had so much more to be bitter and twisted about.

Agnessa came through with extra information regarding the three candidates. The first of the older men had been gunned down in a bar fight a year ago. The second had died in a fall while hiking in the Rockies. Cameron Lee had contracted a form of motor neuron disease that was treatable but had led to him taking a desk job, five years after he was first employed by VIA. The disease wasn't what had killed him, though. He had been beaten to death by an unknown assailant shortly after the crash of d-mat, beaten so badly, genetic records had been needed to identify his body.

"That's him," she said. "It has to be."

"Are you sure?" asked Jesse.

"He was born in England," said Devin. "That would explain the accent."

"I'm sure of it," she said. "Cameron Lee is Nobody. He was copied before he got sick, when Wallace first started experimenting."

"So, are you going to call him on his promise? He said he'd give up if you told him his real name."

"I know," said Clair.

"But he's the crazy dupe who has nothing to do with the others," said Jesse. "How does that even help us?"

"And how are you going to contact him without letting anyone else know?" asked Devin.

Clair worried at the top of her nose with the thumb and forefinger of her right hand. Then she looked up.

"Jesse, you said there are people coming here every day?" He nodded. "I bet he's already here. Agnessa, can you put the word out among your people to ask around?"

"Using the name?"

"No. Just 'Nobody.' If you can do it without the PKs hearing, all the better. We don't want them freaking out and calling in the cavalry."

"I will do so. But I'm certain you're wrong. All our members are carefully vetted."

"I bet they are, but Nobody is crazy enough to try something like this and experienced enough to get away with it. Short of all-out invading, it's the only way he'd get close to me."

"All right. I've got people asking."

"That uplink," interrupted Devin. "It's quiet at the moment, but the traffic has been heavy recently. Freakishly heavy, in both directions. There's some serious hardware in there."

"Could it be where the dupes patterns are being kept?" Clair asked, not wanting to mention Q just yet. One possibility at a time.

"Unlikely. Somewhere on the ground is too easy to take out: a guy with a grenade could do it. Here's a list of all the satellites it's communicated with in the last week."

A stream of meaningless names bumped into Clair's infield, an apparently random combination of letters and numbers. As she scrolled down them, one stood out.

"V468," she said. "That one comes up a lot. What's it for?"

"Unspecified," said Devin. "Same as Wallace's little

hideaway, except this one isn't equipped with life support."

"Who owns it?"

"It's a OneEarth asset, loaned to VIA for reasons unspecified."

Clair felt goose bumps rising on her arms.

"That has to be it, doesn't it?" she said.

A knock resounded up the hallway from the external door of the L-shaped building, followed immediately by the sound of Nelly talking to someone. Clair thought she heard Sargent's voice. The door closed. Footsteps came up the hall, two sets.

"Maria Gaudio to see you," said Nelly. "Signed up with the contingent from Brussels this morning. Said you asked for her."

She led a tiny brunette into the room. The woman was in her midthirties, dressed in drab khakis and high leather boots. There was a pink-dotted bandage under her right ear. Her eyes were so deep a brown they were almost black. Her gaze swept the room and locked on to Clair.

"Hello," the woman said.

"Hello, Cameron Lee," Clair said.

The woman smiled. There was no humor in that smile, just a thousand lives' worth of self-loathing and pain.

Nobody.

59

"SO YOU FOUND him," said the woman who was no longer herself. "You found *me*."

"Not before you did," said Jesse. "Why did you kill him—your original, the real Cameron Lee?"

"Because he condemned me to this life. It was his decision, and he deserved to suffer as I have suffered. I regret that he had just one life to give."

"But he was sick," said Clair, "and you're still him. Why not stop punishing yourself?"

"Perhaps I would, if I could find an alternative," said Nobody. It was hard to think of him as *him* in the body of a woman. It was even harder to think of him as someone with a name. "Nobody" fit much better, so Clair decided to run with it, even if he wanted her to think of him the way he was.

"Death stops everything," he said, "in the end."

Just as it had stopped Maria Gaudio, Clair thought.

"You said you'd give up if I found out who you were," she said. "Do you remember that?"

"I know that I intended to tell you that," he said, "and that you took one of me captive on the seastead. I have acted on the assumption that you and he reached that arrangement. I speak for all of me."

"Will you do what you said you'd do?" asked Devin.

Nobody nodded. "If that's what you want."

"Of course it's what we want," said Jesse. "I want you out of my father's body—out of everyone's bodies—"

"Not yet," said Clair. "We've been trying to find the source of the dupes, and we think we finally have. If you really want to die, you'll tell us if we're right, because Cameron Lee's pattern must be in there too. If we don't erase him, he—you—will be brought back all over again."

"This is true." Nobody inclined the woman's head, as though acknowledging a point well made—or perhaps a test successfully passed. "Tell me what you've found."

Clair outlined what they knew about the satellite, V468, and the uplink in Qatar.

"Yes," he said, nodding. "That would fit, wouldn't it?"

"You're not sure?" said Devin, still looking skeptical.

"I wasn't privy to every detail of Wallace's operation," Nobody said. "I was just a hired thug, infinitely expendable."

"So what *do* you know?" asked Agnessa. "What can you tell us that we haven't already figured out?"

"Wallace's repository is vaster than anyone realizes," he said. "Not just the hollow men, but the Improved, too, and anyone connected to the Improved, and anyone connected to *them* in turn. The patterns number in the millions, perhaps tens of millions. Anyone who used d-mat could in theory be copied by Wallace and put in cold storage."

"Just in case he needed them?" asked Jesse, a look of bitterness on his face.

"Like your father, yes. Wallace's definition of 'need' constantly changed. He became a collector of frozen souls, the curator of his own private mausoleum. I heard him talk about it that way once. He called it the Yard. Graveyard or prison yard—I don't know which. Perhaps a bit of both."

"And that's where your original pattern is stored," asked Devin. "Destroy the Yard and we destroy you."

"Yes," said Nobody as though Devin had asked a child's question. "Of course."

Clair felt a sudden surge of hope, on two fronts. This was how they would destroy the dupes. When they did that, the world would be out of danger, and so would her mother. But Libby would be in the Yard, and Zep, and maybe Q, too, for better or for worse. How long had she dreamed of a breakthrough like this? "Tell us how to get in there."

"I don't know."

"We have the map of his other station," Clair said. "They must have been linked."

"Undoubtedly. Sadly, that other station no longer exists."

"We could hack the uplink," said Devin.

"Too obvious. It will be protected."

"So . . . what?" asked Jesse. "We go up there in person

and throw a grenade at it?"

"That *would* solve the problem rather neatly," said Nobody.

"And it's not as crazy as it sounds," Devin said. "The satellite's in L4—one of the stable Lagrange points in the Earth-Moon system. It's crowded up there, but there are very few people. V468 itself is completely empty. We could get very close without ringing any alarm bells."

"Are you volunteering?" asked Agnessa.

"Yes."

Devin caught Clair's eye. She could tell just by looking at him that he was thinking the same thing as her. If they could get close enough without raising an alarm, they might be able to access the Yard and the data it contained before destroying the satellite.

But would Nobody agree to anything that didn't mean the immediate destruction of his pattern?

Should *she*?

Of course, she decided without hesitation. Libby and Zep were where it had all started. If she had the chance to bring them back and didn't take it, could she live with herself? Giving up d-mat would be infinitely easier after that. And so would deciding what to do about Q, once she knew either way. . . .

"I'll go too," she said, and when Agnessa immediately started to object, she said, "I know, I know—I'm sup-posed to be an Abstainer. But another jump or two isn't going to change anything, and I want to be sure it's done properly."

"Then I'm going too," said Jesse.

"You don't have to," she said.

"Are you kidding? We're talking *space*. This will be my only chance."

"We're not going by rocket," said Devin. "You do understand that, don't you? I'm not riding up there on the top of a bomb."

"No," said Jesse, "I know. It has to be d-mat."

He reached out and took Clair's hand. "And afterward, we won't do it again."

"All right," she said, meaning that with all her heart but knowing she was deceiving him by not mentioning her hopes for Zep and Libby. She would tell him everything, once she had done what she had to do.

"So we have a plan," she said. "It means leaving here, of course, and we'll need a d-mat booth. Maybe we can use that freighter we came in on—perhaps relaying through the Maze to make us harder to trace."

"Wait, wait, wait," said Devin, pointing at Nobody. "We're trusting him now?"

"All he told us was what the Yard was like," said Jesse, "not where it is."

"He's right," said Clair. "We worked that out on our own."

"Turns out you didn't need me after all," said the dupe.

"I expect you to keep your end of the bargain all the same."

"If everything goes as planned," said Clair, "you won't have to worry about that."

"What are we going to do about Forest and Sargent?" asked Jesse.

Clair remembered Sargent shadowing her through the seastead, then standing guard all night long in the muster. No way was the PK going to let her go off on her own.

"They can't know," she said. "They can't even suspect."

"I can distract them, if you like," said Nobody.

"No," said Clair. She was afraid of what he meant by "distract." "If they find out you're in here, they'll be even more edgy. We need to get them out of the way somehow."

"It has to look completely convincing," said Devin. "The slightest suspicion and the lawmakers will be all over us."

The figure on the bed didn't move the smallest amount, but her voice was all smile.

"I think I have just the person for the job. . . ."

[60]

THE DETAILS FELL into place with surprising ease, and in moments they were ready to go. The plan was simple in conception, complex in execution. There were a lot of moving parts, every one of which needed to work as planned for the entire thing to come off. Clair couldn't oversee all of them. She had to trust that the people around her wanted this to work as badly as she did.

She felt a renewed fluttering in her belly. She was doing everything in her power to save the world. If the plan worked, great. If it didn't, if any one of the pieces failed, then the chances of her surviving the night were very small. The powerful enemies she had thought she had were nothing compared to those she would gain.

Nobody, one of those former enemies, volunteered to go with them to the station, probably to make certain they kept their end of the bargain. There seemed no reason to deny him that. Someone would keep a close eye on him at all times.

Space, she thought. The last time she went there was the worst experience of her life. But this time it was her choice, like Jesse and d-mat, and she was making it with her eyes wide open. There would be no lies, no tricks, no need for sacrifice. When she returned, the threat of the dupes would be removed and the lawmakers attempting to take over the world would have suffered a major setback—sufficient perhaps that they might abandon their plans. Realizing they'd been beaten, they might even release Allison Hill without being asked. Clair didn't want to contemplate the alternative.

"Ready?" she asked.

"Ready," said Devin and Jesse.

"What about you?" she asked Nobody.

"You are certain this is what you want?"

Clair nodded.

"Then I am ready too," he said.

"We're in position," said Agnessa.

Clair took a deep breath.

"Let's do it."

She led them down the hallway to where Nelly was waiting by the exit. The big woman swung the doors open. Forest and Sargent were waiting outside.

"This is bullshit," said Jesse in a loud voice, pushing past Clair and out into the night.

"Well, what did you expect from a pack of ignorant dinosaurs?" said Devin, playing his part with equal commitment. "Let's get out of here while we can."

"What happened?" asked Sargent of Clair as she followed Jesse and Devin through the door. "What did she say to you?"

Clair did her best to look disappointed and frustrated.

"I don't want to talk about it," she said, heading down the slope, toward the water. "Is the hovercraft still where we left it?"

"Yes." Sargent's lenses sparked. "It hasn't been interfered with."

"Good. We have to think of somewhere else to go. It's too dangerous for us here."

"I will make arrangements for a safe house," said Forest.

"That'll have to do," said Clair.

"Why?" asked Sargent. "What went wrong?"

"Everything," said Jesse. "We'll tell you when we get there."

Nobody hung back, unnoticed.

Barely had Clair and the others traveled twenty yards when five sinister figures stepped out of an alleyway.

"Where do you think you're going, meatsack?" said Sandler Jones.

The violence in his voice shocked Clair. She backed up a step.

"Out of the way," said Sargent, using her height to its full advantage. "We don't want any trouble."

"You shouldn't have come here, then."

Suddenly all five had pistols in their hands. Clair's heart raced.

"Don't," said the redhead as Forest reached for his side-arm. "Weapon on the ground, Peeker. You and your spies have got some explaining to do."

"We are peacekeepers, not spies," said Forest, putting his pistol in front of him.

"Same thing. You too, blondie."

Sargent hesitated, then did as she was told.

"Lenses off," barked the redhead.

"You're making a terrible mistake," said Sargent.

"I said, lenses off, or I'll reach into those eyeballs of yours and switch them off for you."

Clair, Devin, and Jesse switched off their augs, and after a moment the PKs obeyed.

"Right," said Sandler Jones. "Now we're getting somewhere."

Out of the shadows behind the PKs stepped two brutal-looking men, followed by Nobody. The first brute raised a meaty fist and brought it down hard on the base of Sargent's skull. She bent forward and spun around with a return blow that sent her assailant back a step. The second man hit Forest just above the ear. The peacekeeper's eyes rolled up into the back of his head and he dropped to the ground, unconscious.

"Inspector!"

Distracted, Sargent took a blow to the chin. She swung wildly in return but missed, and staggered in Clair's direction. Nobody extended a leg and tripped her. The redhead clubbed her once, twice with the butt of his pistol. She stayed down.

Clair's breath was coming in ragged gulps as though she had been doing the fighting. It had all happened so quickly. But it was done, and they were fully committed now. Forest and Sargent were safely out of the equation, as they had to be for her plan to work. She hoped they would be okay, and that they would accept her apology when they woke up and it was all over. Nothing appeared to be broken, but the necessity for deception and violence—Agnessa's idea—still appalled her.

"Good work," said Devin to the thugs and brutes, seemingly unfazed. "Much obliged."

"We didn't do it for you," said spider-fingers.

"Are they going to be all right?" asked Jesse, looking as shocked as Clair felt.

"They'll wake up eventually," said the man who had taken down Sargent, rubbing the knuckles of his right hand. "What do you care, anyway? They're dupes."

"We should just kill them right here," said Sandler, hefting his pistol. "You included," he added for Nobody's benefit.

"No!" said Clair, placing herself between him and the PKs. "We have no proof that either of them are dupes."

"But they might be," leered the redhead, coming entirely too close. "It's not murder if they're already dead."

"Give it a rest, will you?" said Devin. "We're going to have an army of PKs raining down on us if we don't get on with it."

Clair blew out a ragged gust of air as Sandler Jones turned away.

"Bring them on, I say. . . ." But he obeyed Clair's plan as Agnessa had told him to, gesturing for two of the younger thugs to lift Forest by the armpits and the older men to do the same with Sargent, with considerably more effort. As a group, they all began moving back down to the pier, Clair hanging back so she could see the men from WHOLE at all times.

They reached the hovercraft in good time. The thugs put the two unconscious PKs on the rear bench seat so they were leaning against each other. Clair sat in the next row forward, between Nobody and Devin. Jesse took the front seat, ready at the controls.

Clair forced herself to say thank you to the thugs with good grace as they retreated back into the shadows. The plan couldn't have worked without them, but that didn't mean she had to like it.

The feeling was mutual.

"We're done," said Sandler Jones, spitting into the boat. "Don't even *think* about coming back."

That was the last thing on Clair's mind. It was time for the next stage of the plan.

She reactivated her lenses and called PK Drader on an open chat.

"Clair!" His voice burst into her ears with unfiltered urgency. "What happened? Are you all right?"

"We're fine," she said, trying to inject a note of desperate relief into her voice. "Those idiots we met before took us by surprise. There was an argument. It's all sorted out now, but I knew someone would be watching, so I called you. You're the only other PK I really know."

"We're trying to get hold of Forest and Sargent. Where are they?"

"Right here." Clair glanced over her shoulder to where the PKs slumped on the backseat so her lenses would catch the view. "They'll be all right. We just need to get out of here. Is that safe house ready?"

"Yes. I'll send rapid response via Net One to escort you. I might even be able to come myself—"

"No need, PK Drader," chipped in Devin. "Things are messy but under control. We'll relay your peacekeepers back to you once we make the freight booth."

"You're using the same one you came in on? Sensible. Take care. Call if anything else goes wrong."

Clair closed the chat and turned off her lenses again. Hopefully PK Drader would take that as part of the *messiness* Devin hinted at without giving any specifics. It wouldn't do to have the PKs watch too closely, since they had no intention of going to any safe house. Once they were in space their plan would be harder to conceal. The less time the PKs had to mobilize against them the better.

She gave Jesse the thumbs-up. He started the fans and pushed the throttle forward, raising a powerful roar from the rear of the hovercraft. The surface under them shifted as it lifted into the air and moved out on the water.

Something touched Clair's shoulder. She spun around. Sargent had fallen forward into the back of her seat. Clair reached out to right her, assuming it was the motion of the craft that had disturbed her. It took her a second to realize—

Forest was gone.

"Wait!"

Jesse pulled back on the throttle, looking around to see what was going on.

Clair climbed on the seat and looked around. There was no sign of the peacekeeper, on the hovercraft or off it.

"Forest—he's fallen overboard!"

Devin got up on his knees next to her, whipping his head back and forth. "He'll drown—he's out cold."

Jesse brought the hovercraft about, moving in slow arcs. They searched the dark waters for any sign of him, but saw nothing. Clair grew increasingly desperate. She didn't want to delay too long, but she didn't want the death of a potentially innocent man on her conscience either.

Then she remembered the way Forest had fallen when Agnessa's thug had hit him. He had turned, and his eyes had rolled back into his head.

There's something wrong with his nerves, Sargent had told her. *He has to consciously make every twitch and glance. . . .*

"He didn't fall," she said. "He jumped. He was awake the whole time!"

[61]

"SHIT," SAID DEVIN. "That means he heard everything we said back there. He knows we arranged the attack—"

"But he didn't tell anyone," said Jesse. "PK Drader didn't know."

"Maybe Drader was pretending he didn't know in order to surprise us at the freighter." Clair ground her fists into her forehead, trying to think through this sudden new development. What did it mean? If Forest was nothing but a dutiful PK, he should have immediately called in their deception—but he could have done that just as easily from the shore, or from his slumped position on the seat, without abandoning Sargent. He could have called PK Drader without jumping overboard and Clair would never have known. She and the others would have walked right into a trap.

The same applied if he was a dupe. Taking the opportunity to escape would only have alerted Clair to the fact that he knew what was going on.

There had to be another reason why he had escaped. But what was it?

Nobody lightly slapped Sargent's face while Devin held an oar upraised, just in case. There was no response. Behind them the lights of the landing and its cloud of airships reflected in the cold water as Jesse brought the hovercraft back around.

There was only one other place Forest could go.

The muster, she thought. Forest was going *back*.

"This is all messed up," she said. "We didn't say anything about where we were going, did we?"

"I don't think so," said Jesse. "And our lenses are off now, right?"

She nodded. "So he doesn't know everything. That's good. But I think he's trying to find out. We have to stop him."

"That'll take time," said Devin.

The decision wasn't an easy one. There could be PKs or dupes on the way already, intending to stop them going anywhere, forever. "We have to split into two groups: one to take out the station, the other to sort out Forest. Maybe we can bring him around somehow. . . ."

"You're the best one to do that," said Jesse. "It'll mean more coming from you. So I'll go to the station while you stay here. Everyone would pounce on you anyway, if they saw you leaving. No one cares about me."

"That's not true," Clair said. The thought of being separated from him dismayed her, but his ready acceptance of what she had been about to suggest moved her more than a little. "Are you sure? I'm happy to do it the other way around, to save you the jumps."

"I'm not as charming as you," he said with a wry grin. "I think Forest likes you."

"Not anymore, I bet." She felt the situation slipping out of her control, and her anxiety rising with it, but the plan did make sense. Jesse was a lone Abstainer, not a threat. Even if Forest got word out quickly enough, Jesse might slip through unhindered by taking a different route back to the freighter.

"Devin, you'll go too?" she said.

"No," he said. "I'm staying here."

"But—"

"Let me explain. If we're going to split up, we'll need to communicate by some means other than the Air, some way that can't be monitored. There's only one secure way I can think of that we can put in place quickly."

"Trevin," Jesse said.

"Exactly."

"But isn't he the one who stays at home while you get your feet dirty?" asked Clair.

"I'll work on him. Age before beauty, right?" Angry whisperings fluttered at the edge of Clair's hearing. "Okay. T will meet Jesse at the freighter and they'll go to L4 together from there. I can set up closed networks so you can piggyback on our link. That way we can chat without anyone overhearing."

"Great idea," said Jesse, swinging the hovercraft back to the shore.

"But no mushy stuff, okay? It's bad enough being around you two as it is."

"I'll go with him," said Nobody.

"No way," Clair immediately said. Maybe the dupe just wanted to stay in the loop, but Clair wasn't going to take a chance on him using Jesse against her somehow. "You stick with me."

He didn't argue.

The hovercraft sped back to shore, where the three of them wrestled Sargent's unconscious form off the hovercraft and stretched her out on the wooden surface of the pier. Their return had been noted; Sandler Jones and his crew were already converging on the scene. Clair grimaced at the thought of being around him a second longer, but there was no choice. This was the way it had to go.

She hugged Jesse before he could leave.

"Be careful," he said into her ear. His breath was warm.

"You too. Enjoy space."

"I will." He grinned. "I'll get to see the stars this time."

She remembered only then that he had been in Wallace's station with her, briefly. Stars were a much better vision to cling to than Zep's body and his father's tortured face.

"One last jump," she said, and they kissed hard.

He leaped aboard with a wave, gunned the fans, and sped off alone across the Neva Straits.

[62]

WHEN THE LIGHTS of the hovercraft had faded to a twinkle, Clair turned to face the music.

"What the hell?" Sandler came to a breathless halt in front of her. His cheeks were as red as his hair, emphasizing the odd blotches on his temple and neck. He looked down at Sargent's unconscious form. "I thought I told you—"

"Yes, yes," said Devin. "One of our friends here got away. You didn't hit him hard enough."

"That's not my fault."

"Well, it's not ours. We have to do something with this one before she wakes up."

"Take her to Agnessa's rooms," said Clair. "Unless there's somewhere more secure . . . ?"

"We have a cellblock," Sandler said, showing his teeth. "You should've been in there from the beginning, if you ask me."

"Thankfully, no one is asking you," said Devin. "But that's not a bad idea in Sarge's case. Come on. Let's not stand out here freezing our butts off."

He took one of Sargent's legs, and Nobody took the other. Perhaps out of a sense of obligation, the redhead took the PK's right arm and waved for one of his thugs to help. Together they moved Sargent off the pier and onto solid ground. There, they were met by the same two burly men as before, and Nelly, her breath puffing in rapid clouds of steam.

"Trouble," she said, handing Devin and Clair an earpiece each. "Put these on so we can talk securely."

Clair squished the cold, clammy aug into her right ear, where it provoked a piercing but thankfully brief squeak from her ear-ring. "What's happening?"

"I was about to ask you the same question," said Agnessa. "There's a regular zombie apocalypse outside our walls."

"What do you mean?"

"You should see in person. Leave the PK with the boy. I guarantee they'll both be safe. Bring the dupe with you. Nelly will take you where you need to be."

Clair glanced at Devin, who nodded nervously. "It's all right. We coppertops will get on just fine."

Sandler Jones looked unhappy about the prospect, which Clair took as a sign that he would do as Agnessa told him.

Nelly gestured impatiently for Clair to follow her. Clair hesitated, then did so, not seeing any alternative, even if it did mean being alone in the muster, far away from Jesse and heading into a crisis she knew nothing about. With Nobody at her side and Nelly's breathing becoming more labored with every step, they hurried up the hill.

She checked the PK patch. Still no multicolored dots at the muster's gates, thanks to the absence of drones, and just two clumps of green dots converging from far away.

Static burred in Clair's ear.

"Be cool," whispered Devin's voice. "I'm just reassuring you that we're not out of touch. This ancient tech is easier to hack into than my tutor's pattern bank. You'll see a patch in a moment. Accept and we'll able to communicate the usual ways. Be careful, though. It's only as secure as WHOLE's Wi-Fi."

Clair could barely hide her relief at hearing his familiar voice in her ear. This way, she would know if Agnessa betrayed her. She would also feel much less alone.

Her relief didn't last long, however. As they reached the common area and kept going, past the dorms, the sound of regular gunshots became audible, punctuating the stillness of the night in bursts of two or three.

"In here," said Nelly.

She waved Clair and Nobody into a garage, where two utility vehicles with thick black wheels rested. Clair climbed into the passenger seat of the nearest while Nelly took the wheel. Nobody slipped in the back. The engine started with a click and a whirr.

"Seat belts," said Nelly.

"What?"

"Do this, like me."

Clair found a thin black strap by her left shoulder that clipped into a slot at her right hip. She was instantly glad of it when Nelly shot out of the garage with a loud roar.

"Where are we going?"

"Main gate." The utility skidded down narrow lanes and across other common areas little different from the one she was familiar with. There were very few people out. The ones they saw were watchful and wary, stepping quickly out of the way as Nelly rushed by. Clair was thrown from side to side.

A patch appeared in Clair's lenses, in the shape of Devin's face. She selected it and a limited number of the usual options appeared.

"Uh, they've put me in the cell with Sargent," said Devin over a chat. "They say it's so I can look after her. Shall I run with it?"

Instead of speaking aloud in return, she bumped back.

"Have they hurt you?"

"No. They're pretty insistent, though. I'll resist if you want me to, but I don't think it'll achieve much. You might think it necessary to dent my self-esteem a little, but I'd rather not give them an excuse to break anything more valuable than that."

"No, don't fight them," Clair sent back. "Sorry you drew the short straw."

"That depends on where you're going, doesn't it? Keep your fingers crossed the big lug here doesn't wake up anytime soon. She's bound to be both sore and ticked off."

Clair turned to Nelly.

"Where are you taking me?"

"To the main gate."

"Why? Are you kicking me out?"

"No." The big woman glanced at her, then back at the narrow ways ahead of them. "Don't try your luck, though. *Coming back* wasn't part of the plan you sold us."

"I know, and I'm sorry. It's my fault. Any fallout's on my head."

"Mighty big of you," Nelly said. "Doesn't help us if we're all dead."

They skidded to a halt on a major road leading to a tangle of barbed wire atop a high stone wall stretching left and right to the limits of Clair's vision. There was a guard post looming over the gate. Two giant trucks were parked in front of it.

"Out." Nelly walked her and Nobody around the trucks, to the ladder leading up to the guard post. "After you."

The gun cracked twice above her, startlingly loud. Clair hesitated on the first rung, then climbed as fast as she could. Whatever awaited her, there was no point in delaying.

At the top she found two members of WHOLE. One, a man in his fifties with close-cropped silver hair, held a pair of binoculars that he swept back and forth across the darkened streets. The other, a woman not much older than Clair, trained an automatic weapon on the far side of the fence. Clair's eyes tracked down to see what she was aiming at.

"Hollow men," said Nobody.

There was a crowd of people milling in a circle outside the gates. *Zombies,* Clair thought, as Agnessa had said, because that was exactly what they looked like. They were all sizes and all shapes, and all silent, staring forward as though waiting for a signal.

A floodlight clicked on, splashing the scene with white. Clair inhaled sharply. The area in front of the gate was covered in bodies. The faces she saw, on the bodies and in the milling crowd, were all familiar ones, belonging to Libby and Zep . . . members of WHOLE such as Cashile and Theo . . . people like Tash, Ronnie, and Oz, who had nothing to do with any of this . . . the potato-headed man from Ons Island . . .

Most shocking were dupes of her mother and—

"Jesse!"

Her heart seemed to stop in her chest. He had been caught already! Had the dupes brought him here as a hostage to ensure she did what they wanted?

He looked up at her but said nothing in return, and she realized then that she wasn't looking at Jesse at all, just his body. There was no gun to his head, no expression of fear on his face. And his clothes were wrong. She remembered that T-shirt. . . . He had been wearing it in Wallace's office, when everything had gone wrong.

She understood then. His pattern had been recorded in Wallace's private network and was available for duping too. They had dusted it off now for a final showdown. But how had they known she was there?

Forest, she thought. It had to be.

The dupes shielded their eyes when the light clicked on them. They were looking up at her but not saying anything, just waiting expectantly for her to do something. More were coming, winding between the empty, rotting buildings. Her eyes tracked them, estimating their size in groups of ten. She quickly reached two hundred.

"PKs are on their way," Agnessa whispered through the aug in her ear.

Clair knew. Green dots were converging quickly on her location.

"That's good, isn't it?" She hoped it had nothing to do with Sargent's disappearance.

"Depends on where you're sitting. That wall isn't going to hold back a substantial push from one army, let alone two. And as for a full-on fight between the two groups, we're bound to sustain some collateral damage."

"Why am I here?"

"They're still asking for you."

Please don't make me go out there, she thought with a flash of terror.

"Talk to them," Agnessa said. "Find out what they want. Send them home, if you can."

"And if I can't?"

We offer amnesty in exchange for the girl, Clair Hill.

"We'll pull you back in and see what happens."

Relieved that Agnessa wasn't going to hand her over in the hope of getting the dupes off her back, Clair bellied up to the railing next to the sniper and leaned out so she was sure they could all see her. None of them seemed to be armed, which only made the slaughter at the gate more horrible. That deliberate defenselessness was a kind of weapon, she supposed, attacking people's social mores rather than the people themselves, in the hope that they'd cave. Luckily, Agnessa was made of stern stuff. The dupes weren't going to walk past her just because they pretended to be harmless.

"What do you want?" Clair called down. "Why do you want to talk to me?"

The dupe in Jesse's body stepped forward.

"There might not be any point anymore," he said. "What's *he* doing here?"

Not all the dupes were staring at her, she realized then. Some of them were staring at Nobody, as though they could see right through the face to the person that lay beneath. Maybe they could, Clair thought. Who knew what new skills the dupes had learned to tell one another apart?

From the body of Maria Gaudio, he said, "Nothing has changed. I still want the same thing."

"That makes you our enemy."

"I know."

"Let me make it absolutely clear that *I* haven't taken sides," Clair said, which was true. "I want all of you gone."

"You shouldn't be anywhere near him," dupe-Jesse said. "He's dangerous."

"And you aren't?"

"Only to those who stand in our way."

"What about—?"

She stopped herself in time. *What about the innocent people you've been slaughtering just to scare the survivors into giving up their rights?* Accusing the dupes of working for the lawmakers would be dangerous. If the lawmakers knew what she had figured out, their reaction would be swift and deadly. She had to wait until the source of the dupes was destroyed before she could go public.

"What about WHOLE?" she asked instead. "They're just sitting here, doing no one any harm."

"They're dangerous in their own fashion. They belong to the past, not the future. The future is ours."

It was so weird to see Jesse's mouth move and hear dupe-Jesse's words, the opposite of anything the real Jesse would actually say.

She hid her dismay and responded, "The future belongs to everyone." That was the closest she dared go. "People, I mean. WHOLE are people. You're not."

"Harsh," said a dupe-Tash nearby. "Are you trying to hurt our feelings?"

"More than your feelings are going to be hurt if you stick around here," Agnessa said, her voice booming loudly over a public address system Clair couldn't see.

Headlights flashed in the streets behind the growing crowd of dupes. Clair could hear engines growling, coming closer. The cavalry, she hoped, summoned by PK Drader. She imagined him riding at the head with a gun as big as a cannon, cocked and ready on his hip—he would enjoy that, no doubt. It wasn't an entirely unwelcome thought.

"I know you believe that right makes might, Clair," said a dupe of Clair's mother. Clair hated that it was speaking in a parody of one of her mother's favorite quotes. "Do your duty as you understand it and we'll do ours."

"Just remember," said dupe-Jesse. "Nobody's dangerous. Don't trust him."

The dupes turned to face the oncoming vehicles, squat things with many wheels and turrets that Clair hoped were water cannons protruding from the top.

"Come back down," said Nelly. "You're too exposed up here, and I have a feeling it's going to get nasty quite soon."

Clair let herself be led down, followed by Nobody. The lookout and the young sniper stayed behind. Neither had said a word through the entire exchange, to Clair or to anyone. Only as Clair descended the ladder did she detect a resemblance between them, in the precise line of their noses. Father and daughter, out shooting dupes together on a dark fall night. Was this the future she had to look forward to if Jesse didn't destroy that satellite soon?

NELLY DROVE THE utility with wild haste through New Petersburg to the cellblock where Sargent and Devin had been imprisoned. Along the way something flickered in Clair's inactive infield—another patch, this time in the steel gray of RADICAL. She accepted it and a window opened, showing her the view through Jesse's lenses. The interior of an empty freighter booth, much like the other one but slightly smaller. In her ears, his breathing.

"Hello?" she said. "Can you hear me?"

"Oh, it's working." He sounded fantastically close, practically inside her head. "It wasn't a minute ago. You must be in range of Devin now."

"What's happening at your end?"

"Trevin's here." Trevin appeared in Jesse's field of view, waving nonchalantly as he went by—the gesture faintly forced, as though a cover for nervousness. "We're going in a moment. Just wanted to check in first. Is everything okay there?"

"Tense," she said, not wanting to lie, except by omission. "I'll let you know if anything too sketchy goes down."

"Thanks. Not that I can do anything about it if it does." She couldn't see him, which irked her. She could only access Jesse's lenses, not Trevin's. "We're getting outfitted and checking our air supplies and stuff. Space suits,

Clair. I'm trying to put on a *space suit*. Can you believe this is happening?"

"I'm glad for you," she said, holding on tightly to that thought—and to the door handle as the utility skidded around a corner in a shower of mud and gravel. She had forgotten to put on her seat belt. "Just do what you have to do, and do it quickly, all right?"

"Roger," he said. He held a clear plastic helmet up to his face, preparing to put it on. There, at last, reflected in the translucent bubble, was a glimpse of him, albeit a dark and distorted one. "Is Nobody behaving?"

She glanced behind her. The figure on the backseat was staring at her, unmoving.

"Talking about me?" Nobody said through his stolen body.

Clair faced forward again.

"He's creeping me out," she bumped back to Jesse. "But that's all."

"Do you think he's telling us the truth?"

"He says he wants to die, and destroying the source will give him that. I can't see why he'd lie."

"Except that he's crazy."

Clair could feel the dupe's hot gaze burning into the back of her head.

"Except that."

Nelly wrenched the wheel one final time and jerked them to a halt outside a concrete building with high, barred windows and a single, heavy-looking steel door at the front. Everything about it said *prison*.

Nelly banged a fist on the front door and it opened of its own accord. The interior of the cellblock was just as stark and forbidding as its exterior, with scuffed security doors and locks, and bars everywhere. There was no desk or barricade, just a secure double gate leading to rows of cells deeper in the building. Several of the cells were occupied, mostly by men. A background hubbub of muttering and catcalls echoed around the hard-walled chamber.

Clair caught sight of Devin's red hair through the forest of bars.

"Over here." He waved.

Nelly opened the double gates with a key and walked them along the cells. Devin waited anxiously, both hands gripping the bars. Beside him, Sargent lay on her side on the cold stone floor, eyes shut and unmoving, a huge figure even when felled. Clair felt a flicker of concern. Sargent looked so limp and still. The plan had been to knock her out temporarily, not put her in a coma.

"Is she all right?"

"Wait."

Instead of taking them straight to the cell, Nelly had stopped one down and opened the door.

"You, in here," she said to Nobody.

"Why?" he asked.

"I don't trust you, either."

He shrugged Maria Gaudio's shoulders and did as he was told.

"It won't make any difference, but if it makes you feel better . . ."

"It does." The door clanged shut on him. "Now, you," Nelly said to Devin, still not opening his cell door. "Tell me why Agnessa shouldn't leave you in here."

"Because that's not the deal," he said. "We're allies."

"Clair and Agnessa were allies. She left, and then you came back. I don't like it when plans change."

"If Forest hadn't escaped, we wouldn't have needed to come back. He's out there somewhere—"

Nelly dismissed his objection with a sharp wave of one hand. "Now we have armies of dupes and PKs massing outside our gates. Perhaps you should've kept going."

"Perhaps," said Clair.

Nelly regarded her with resentful eyes. "Don't think I'm not considering locking you up too."

Clair understood, and didn't protest, although the thought of being imprisoned made her hands ball up in a fight-or-flight reflex. Neither was an option at that moment. It was up to Nelly to decide.

"At least put me in a different cell," said Devin. "When Sarge wakes up, she's going to be pissed."

"That I can do." Nelly swung open the door and Devin hastily slipped through it. The door clanged shut behind him.

"Shouldn't someone check on her?" said Clair.

Before Nelly could answer, the front door of the prison boomed open, admitting Sandler Jones and his earless thug. Between them they dragged a small figure in a PK undersuit.

"Guess who we found creeping round the back," the redhead crowed. "Looking for a way to rescue his friend, no doubt."

It was Forest. He hung limp between them, dripping blood from his nose and water from his undersuit. He must have slipped out of his secondhand clothes and armor in the water before being dragged to the bottom of the Strait.

"Good work, boys," said Nelly, unlocking the double doors with her key and waving them through. "Now we're all here. Let's get him inside before he does any more damage."

Sandler and friend turned sideways to bring Forest past her. When the trio was all bunched together, a tight concentration of four people with the prisoner in the middle, Forest suddenly moved. Clair didn't see exactly what happened, but first Sandler's friend fell away, then he went down too. Then Nelly staggered into the bars with her head lolling back and slid heavily to the floor with a sigh.

Forest flexed his right hand. His left held the keys. He wiped a fleck of blood from his nose with the back of that hand and then looked over at Clair and Devin.

Devin backed away, tugging at Clair's elbow to bring her with him.

"If you have killed her," Forest said in a stern voice, "you will regret it."

[64]

"WHO, THE BIG lug?" said Devin, voice betraying a slight quaver. "She's only out cold."

"Good. Where?"

"In the cell back there."

Forest took a step toward them, and Clair pointed behind her, to where Sargent lay. The lack of expression on Forest's face was somehow much more threatening than if he had been glaring.

"Tell us who you really are," she said as he walked past.

"I am exactly who I say I am," he said.

"Who you work for, then."

"I have never lied to you, Clair." He stared in at Sargent, but made no move to open the door.

"So why did you call the dupes?"

"I did not. I have called no one."

"It must have been you. No one else knows we're still here."

"That cannot be the case." He turned to look at her. "Who did you tell?"

She didn't know that she had backed away again until her right elbow caught on one of the metal bars, reminding her of that old injury. What was Agnessa doing about Forest? Surely she had seen and was calling for backup.

"Hey, man?" called one of the other prisoners. "You, with the keys. Let us out!"

The call was taken up by the others. Within seconds, the prison was a riot of banging and cries, impossible to talk over.

Forest looked around him, considering. Then he turned and opened the nearest empty cell.

"Step in here," he told Clair and Devin. "I will release you afterward. You have my word."

"Why should I believe you?"

"Because you have no choice."

Clair considered trying to run past him, but she had seen how fast he could move when he wanted to, and she didn't want him to hit her.

She went in first, brows knotted in frustration, and Devin followed, looking resigned to being locked up again. Nobody watched from his cell with something that might have been amusement.

"This cage is as good as any other," he said.

Once Clair and Devin were secure, Forest walked to the cage of the first prisoner who had called out to him. They exchanged hurried, low words, and then Forest unlocked the cell. Together, they dragged the unconscious Nelly and the two thugs into another cell, disarmed them, then set about releasing the rest of the prisoners.

"Remember the deal!" Forest yelled after them as the escapees ran through the double gates and out the main doors. When they were gone, he locked the gates again, lightly holding the pistol he had taken from Nelly in one hand.

"What was the deal?" asked Clair, unable to keep an edge of bitterness from her voice. How come a prison full of criminals got to go free but she stayed locked up?

"They will keep Agnessa busy," Forest said. "I estimate that we have approximately five minutes before a spare key arrives."

Agnessa's voice boomed out of a speaker in the ceiling. "Already on its way. You're only delaying the inevitable."

Forest nodded. "I just need long enough to fix the mistakes we have made."

"What mistakes?" asked Devin.

"You told someone," said Forest. "They sent the dupes. Who was it?"

"It really wasn't you?" asked Clair.

Forest shook his head.

Devin frowned. "But it couldn't have been PK Sargent, unless she did it before we knocked her out . . .?"

A dreadful certainty settled into Clair as she weeded out all the possible sources of the leak.

"Oh my god. It was me," she said. "I called PK Drader."

"So? But . . ." Devin trailed off.

Clair felt like she might weep. "He was on the seastead, and in the New York booth too. He poisoned Tilly Kozlova and the other Improved so they couldn't reveal anything else about Wallace's operation. He was the one who told the dupes where we were, every step of the way."

Forest came to their cell and unlocked it.

"Yes," he said, not unsympathetically. "It must be so."

She remembered Drader's rough bluster and eagerness to fight. All an act—but the act of a dupe or a traitor? She wondered if she would ever know.

"So these two have been themselves all along?" said Devin, nodding toward Forest and Sargent.

"Maybe they have," said Clair, not making any immediate move to signal her acceptance of Forest's innocence, such as leaving the cell, "but that doesn't mean they aren't still working for the people trying to take over the world. PK Forest is a peacekeeper, after all."

"And some peacekeepers knowingly or unknowingly undermine the peace," Forest said, nodding. The pistol was still in his hand. "The irony is not lost on me. Some might say that the definition of peace has ever been a movable one, but that excuses nothing. OneEarth is a perfect system of governance that people have tried and failed to subvert since its inception. For each faction trying to take over the world, there is another trying to stop them. I am in one of the latter factions."

"So you say," said Clair.

In reply, Forest offered her the pistol. She stared at it for a moment, then shook her head.

"You keep it. I'm sick of guns."

"What about the big lug?" Devin looked from Forest to Clair and back again. "Is she one of the bad guys too, like Drader?"

"No," said Forest. "She is her own agent."

Jesse's voice rang out in Clair's ear.

"Clair? Can you hear me? We're going now."

Clair's attention shifted to the interface linking her to Jesse, via Devin's twin-link.

"Bit busy here right now," she bumped back.

"Is that Forest with you? Is everything okay?"

"Yes. Don't worry about me. Just go. Let me know when you get there."

"Uh . . . all right. That was the deal, I guess. Don't forget what I said earlier: he *likes* you."

Trevin loomed in-frame and raised a stagey thumbs-up. Light flashed and the signal died. The d-mat booth was working. In a moment, Jesse and Trevin would be in transit. A couple of minutes later, they would be in space.

"Was that Jesse you were talking to?" asked Forest. She hadn't realized she was speaking aloud. "Where is he? What is he doing?"

"Finishing what we started," she said, not wanting to go into any specifics in case someone else was listening. She might already have said too much. "If you hadn't escaped, it would've been done already."

"I escaped because that was the only way I could think of to force you to return to the muster," he said. "It is too dangerous for you out there without our protection. Sending Jesse was a wise strategy. Does this mean a target has been confirmed?"

"Yes," said Devin. "No thanks to you."

"Excuse me, I have a question," said Nobody unexpectedly. He pressed against the bars with one hand upraised. "What did PK Forest mean when he said that PK Sargent was her own agent?"

Forest glanced at the only remaining person in the cell-block, apart from Clair, Devin, Sargent, and himself, as though surprised to see anyone there at all.

"You did not escape with the others," Forest said, "but I do not know you. Unless you are not the person you appear to be . . . ?"

"At your service," said Nobody.

"Real name Cameron Lee," said Devin. "Our very own domesticated dupe."

"He's helping us, on behalf of all of him," said Clair. "Or at least not getting in our way anymore."

"I asked you about Sargent," Nobody prodded.

Forest looked uncertain. He glanced at Nelly and the two thugs, still out cold in their cell, then up at the ceiling. Checking who was listening, Clair thought. Coming to a decision whether to proceed or not.

"You suggested earlier, Devin, that PK Sargent and I have been who we say we are all along," Forest said, letting the gun hang down at his side. "That is not true. My friend PK Sargent has not been herself for a long time. She was taken during our jump through Net One in New York. I have seen flashes of her at odd times, but never for long. I fear very little of her remains now."

Clair thought of all the times she had seen Sargent watching or stalking her, and all the odd questions she had asked.

"If she is a dupe," said Devin, "why on earth didn't you do something about it?"

Flick. Forest glanced at Clair, and suddenly she understood. She put her hands over her mouth, hardly daring it to be true but *knowing* it was true, in her heart and in her mind. Only one explanation covered so many odd moments and discrepancies. It was the only possible explanation.

"Because she's not a dupe," Clair said. "She's Q."

[65]

"Q?"

"Yes," said Forest.

Devin gaped at them both in amazement.

"How?" he asked.

"When she was in Wallace's station," Clair said, seeing it all so clearly now. "She had access to all that information."

Forest nodded. "Maybe it was not her immediate intention to transfer to permanent human form, but the experimental data Wallace had collected was available to her when she did decide. The opportunity was hard to find, after the crash. When Net One presented her with both a means and a suitable subject, she took it."

"*This* is why we couldn't find her," said Devin, clapping both palms to his forehead. "She had left the Air entirely. She was in Sargent all the time."

"Yes. I believe she has an inert backup off the Air somewhere, but that is accessed only in direst need—such as when she was reactivated on Ons Island."

Clair had guessed that too. Sargent's apparent return from the dead wasn't a matter of the PKs breaking the law, but of Q bringing herself back when her stolen body was inconveniently killed.

"That's not the way duping works," said Devin. "Sargent would have been wiped completely if it was. But it's not Improvement, either, because that takes days to kick in. You think this is something new?"

"Yes," said Forest. "She is smarter than us. She always has been. What keeps her at our level is her inexperience. I am unsurprised that she came up with something more suited to her needs in such a short time."

"Why Sargent?" asked Clair, remembering with dismay the worried peacekeeper who had babbled about three meals and grilled her regarding Zep because she didn't want her girlfriend to be dead. She didn't deserve to be written over like Libby had been. "What did she have that Tilly Kozlova's body didn't?"

"She had access to you," said Forest.

"Why? To spy on me?"

"Exactly. Q has been watching you closely ever since she broke parity and brought you back. Not just watching you: interacting with you, and placing you in situations that put you under extreme pressure."

"Washington," said Devin, his expression very grim as he turned to look at Clair. This time he was ahead of her. "The barrages. And Antarctica."

Forest nodded. "No evidence was ever recovered to indicate that dupes were responsible for either crisis. The same still holds for the kidnapping of your mother. I believe that Q has been behind these incidents, and perhaps others, too."

"Why?" asked Clair. Dismay blossomed into alarm. "No, wait. I know this, too. *Friendship has to be earned.* That was the last thing she said to me. She's been testing me. She's been trying to decide if I'm worthy."

"If she's been testing you," said Devin, worrying at his right ear, "she's been testing all of us. You're a proxy for the human race, Clair—in which case knocking her out was a pretty bad idea."

"But I didn't *know*." Clair rushed past Forest and out the open cell door. Sargent's inert body was three cells along. Clair peered in at her, appalled by the thought that this hidden truth could have ramifications far beyond her relationship with Q. "She asked me about herself when we were cleaning up. I can't remember what I said. *I can't remember.*"

"How long have *you* known?" Devin asked Forest.

"My suspicions were raised on the seastead. She threatened to turn off the powersats, which is not something a peacekeeper would say. It is beyond our capabilities—but not beyond hers."

"You kept it quiet."

"It seemed prudent to do so. Encouraging Q to trust Clair again has always been one of our objectives."

She whirled on him. "So you could use her to put everything back together?"

"It was my hope that she would volunteer."

"And if she didn't?" asked Devin. "A bullet in the back of the head before she broke out again?"

Forest looked horrified. "I am not a monster."

"Maybe," said Clair, "but your face is too good at lying."

His expression relaxed into its usual blankness. "Why do you think that I *could* have killed her? You saw what happened when the dupes tried: she just came right back.

I chose to keep her identity to myself in the hope that she would do the right thing, knowing that anything else I did might make the situation much worse."

"Yeah, well, I guess we'll never know." Devin shrugged. "Told you they wanted the same thing as us, Clair."

"Everyone knows," said Nobody.

It took Clair a moment to realize what he meant. Nobody wasn't talking about Forest's intentions being revealed. He was talking about Q.

She raised her right index finger and poked Devin in the chest. "Who have you told? Who has Trevin told?"

"T's still in transit, so he can't tell anyone. But I did notify RADICAL that the entity has been found."

"*Why?*"

"Agnessa is watching this live," he said with a wounded expression. "If WHOLE knows, I want my people to know. It's too important. And I bet Forest here has told the rest of the PKs too, now that he has no choice. While he kept the secret to himself, the situation could be contained. Now, it's anyone's guess what will happen."

Clair checked her popularity stats. The number of people observing her, and therefore the Q situation, was growing so fast the numbers were a blur.

"The bullet option is off the table," Clair said, putting herself protectively in front of Q's cell. "I won't let you harm her."

"It's a shame she's not awake right now," Devin said.

"Your spirited defense would surely win her over."

The sound of fighting came from outside the prison. Clair assumed it was one of Agnessa's minions with the key until the WHOLE leader said, "PKs are on the move. So are the dupes. Our gates are under attack."

"We are receiving reports of suborbital launches," said Forest.

"Some of them are ours," said Devin. "The rest are probably dupes."

"PKs too," said Agnessa. "LM Kingdon has just pushed through an emergency order authorizing deadly force against anyone resisting the rapid response teams she's sending. She says the muster is the source of the dupes. Needless to say, we're not going to take that lying down."

"Why did you say anything?" Clair asked Forest. "Why couldn't you keep it secret a little longer?"

"To keep the peace," he said.

"By starting a war over Q?"

"Conflict here was inevitable. That was what PK Drader wanted—to bring the peacekeepers and the dupes together until another flashpoint was reached, another flashpoint that would justify harsher crackdowns of civil liberties. Now the eyes of the world are on us for a very different reason. People can see what this conflict is really about. The pursuit of Q is the pursuit of power. Those hungriest for it have just revealed themselves. It is not too late for lovers of peace to stand against them."

His lenses were active. Clair was certain every word was being broadcast all over the world.

LM Kingdon had just been name-checked in the context of a conspiracy to take over the world. Kingdon's profile was already broadcasting a denial, promising an official statement within minutes, but there was no taking PK Forest's suggestion back from the public record.

His expression didn't change, but he looked satisfied.

"You know," said Devin, "you're a little short to be a revolutionary."

"I assure you that I am quite the opposite."

"Maybe, but on which count?"

Clair, at ground zero, felt less than amused.

"The dupes are still out there, remember?" she said. "Let's not throw any parties until they're dealt with."

At that moment, her lenses stirred.

[66]

"WE'RE HERE," SAID Jesse. Clair saw a black backdrop in his corner of her infield. There were no visible stars. Angular shapes moved in ways that defied terrestrial gravity. "It's going to take us a moment to put the gear together."

"Just let me clarify something," said Trevin, leaning into shot. "Are we destroying this thing or hacking into it? Because I can see advantages in doing the latter."

"That wasn't the plan," said Jesse. "This is where the dupes' original patterns are stored. Destroying it is the only way to stop them forever. They'll be like cockroaches, otherwise. They'll keep coming back. Do this now, or we might as well surrender."

"There's no need to be a drama queen. I'm just suggesting—"

"I know what you're suggesting, and I say it's already been decided. Clair?"

She closed her eyes, thinking of Zep and Libby. For so long, it seemed, she had dreamed of saving them. This was her last chance to do it. When the satellite was destroyed, the last copy of their patterns would be erased and they would be gone forever.

But did she have the right to put the world at risk simply to save her best friend? Q had done just that, and everything had ended up worse as a result.

Libby and Zep and both of Jesse's parents . . . and who knew how many other lost teenagers like Tilly Kozlova . . . versus the fate of OneEarth and civilization as she knew it?

There was only one possible decision.

She wished she had squeezed Libby's hand just a little tighter at the crashlander ball, the last time the two of them had been together.

Good-bye, she thought. *For real this time.*

She opened her eyes and imagined the whole world watching her. No one outside the muster knew where

Jesse and Trevin were, so there was no harm in telling everyone what she had in mind. Nothing could stop the plan now. No *one.*

"Rest assured," LM Kingdon was saying in her latest, desperate speech, "that any rogue elements acting in concert with illegal duplicates will be dealt with swiftly and forcefully. None shall remain when our task is complete. The good name of OneEarth will not be stained, except by the blood of our enemies."

"Do it," Clair said. "Blow the dupes to hell."

"Roger," said Trevin. "Give us a minute."

"Thank you," said Jesse.

If only she could see him. She wanted to say that she didn't deserve anyone's thanks—if anything, *she* should have been thanking *him.* He seemed to be the only person she knew committed to a philosophy that didn't make things better for him. The example he set gave her the strength to do what was best for everyone.

His hands were moving, assembling something that looked like a giant rocket launcher. Distracting him seemed like a bad idea.

"Clair?" Devin pulled her out of the feed from outer space. "When you can spare a moment from sounding off like an action hero . . . ?"

Devin was in Q's cell with Forest, and together they had raised Sargent to a sitting position.

Clair hurried to join them.

"Is she awake?"

"Just coming around." Forest was leaning into the unconscious woman's face. There was a medicinal blister stuck to her neck, something from her own suit, Clair presumed, since Forest had lost his.

Clair squatted down next to him. Sargent's eyes were moving behind her eyelids, as though she was dreaming. Her hands shook at her sides. Seeing that made Clair anxious: she had witnessed such tremors before. What if Agnessa's goons had punched her too hard and damaged something permanently?

Sargent's hands settled. Her eyes opened, revealing the same jade green Clair remembered from their first meeting.

"What happened?" Sargent tried to sit up and winced. "Why does my head hurt?"

"Tell me who you are," Clair said.

Sargent sank back onto her elbows. "What do you mean?"

"You're not PK Sargent. I want to hear you say your real name."

A shudder rolled through Sargent's body, as though Q had momentarily lost control of it. Her gaze focused on Clair, then twisted away.

"I was attacked. From behind."

"Only because we thought you might be a dupe," Clair said.

"But I'm not a dupe. I'm . . . I'm . . ."

"Kari," said Forest. "Stay with us."

"I'm Kari Sargent," she said, her wandering gaze settling for a second. "And at the same time I'm not. I'm . . . new. I'm . . . a secret. I'm . . . still here. I'm . . . *deciding*."

Clair recognized that uncertain, childlike tone. With a lump in her throat, she reached out and took Q's shivering hands, as she had in the Farmhouse. This time those hands didn't grip her back. They just hung limp in hers, slowly growing still.

"Whatever you're deciding," said Devin, "hurry up and do it, will you? We haven't got all day."

Clair shushed him.

"I want to say I'm sorry," said Clair, "but I want to be sure of who I'm talking to, first."

Sargent slumped back onto the floor and her eyes closed.

Before Clair could try to rouse her again, Jesse's voice came over the twin-link.

"Okay," he said. "We're ready. Fire on three. Clair, are you seeing this?"

"Yes," she said, squatting back on her heels. This was a moment she didn't want to miss. "I'm here."

"One," said Trevin. "Two. Three."

The image of the rocket launcher jerked. A flash of thin blue light filled the view for an instant, then it went to black.

Two cells along, Nobody closed his eyes and tilted his head back, as though bathing in distant fire.

"It's done," he said.

CLAIR WAITED A second for the visual to return. Until Jesse confirmed the destruction of the station, she wouldn't believe it was real. When the patch stayed dark, she folded Sargent's hands carefully on her midriff and glanced at Devin.

"Interference," he said. "But we've detected the detonation. There's a debris field."

"That's good."

"Yes."

"So why are you frowning?"

"Interference," he said, eyes shifting, "is not acceptable."

She directed her attention to her own lenses, which were still empty.

"Can you hear me, Jesse?"

No answer. If the blast had disconnected the twin-link between Devin and Trevin, that would be much weirder for Devin than it was for her, Clair thought, since the twins were used to being intimately connected to each other at all times. That didn't mean there was a serious problem, though.

The important thing was that the satellite was dealt with. The source of the dupes was destroyed. Whatever happened with LM Kingdon and the rest of the lawmakers, that threat was finally gone.

"The dupes have seen it," said Agnessa. "They're pulling back. If they die now, they stay dead."

"It worked," Clair said. "It worked!"

"Are the PKs going to withdraw too?" Agnessa asked Forest. "Even the ones loyal to Kingdon?"

He nodded. "That is the most likely outcome. Kingdon's secret war was lost the moment it became a public war. People won't support her now they know she's been using dupes. She's being arrested as we speak. The world is best served by talking, not fighting, at this juncture."

"Good."

That single word couldn't convey her immense relief. The war against the dupes and their masters was effectively over. Whatever happened next would depend on the Consensus Court, not LM Kingdon. With the flood of dupes dammed, the future belonged to people like her and Jesse. Their choices would be their own. When the temporary communications glitch between her and Jesse was fixed, she would celebrate. They had saved the world!

"Whoa," said Devin. "That's weird."

She came out of her thoughts. "What?"

"I'm receiving reports of an energy burst."

"We're seeing it too," said Agnessa. "Is this related to something you did up there?"

"No, it's way beyond the specs of the missile Trevin was using."

"*What* is?" asked Clair, trying not to feel prematurely alarmed.

A video feed came from Devin. It showed a grainy, shaking image of an expanding blue sphere.

"This is what we're seeing," he said. "Several orbital assets have been affected."

"How?"

"We don't know, exactly, except that we're losing signals all over L4."

As Clair watched, a second bubble appeared at the attenuating edge of the first, as though spawning a new one.

"It's spreading," she said.

Everyone was staring into their lenses. Another new bubble appeared, closer to the source of the video than the previous one. Then another, closer still. Blue filled the screen, and the image winked out.

"It's a chain reaction," said Devin. "What the hell is going on up there?"

A hand gripped Clair's shoulder. Sargent had struggled back to consciousness.

"L4," she said weakly. Now she sounded like Sargent rather than Q. "Did Devin just say L4?"

"Yes," said Clair. "Wallace had a station there."

"*Had?*"

A new image appeared in Clair's lens. This showed what looked like a cluster of blue bubbles spreading like fireworks against a black sky.

Sargent pulled herself upright, almost yanking Clair down in the process.

"Tell me what you've done."

"We took out the source of the dupes," she said.

"The Yard."

Clair nodded. "Yes. That's what Nobody called it."

"In the Baikal borehole, yes?"

"No, in space," Clair said. "That's what we're looking at right now."

"No." Sargent's eyes grew wide. "No. No. *No!*"

Her voice changed. In new, panicked tones Clair heard again the Q she had known.

"What's wrong?" she asked. "What are you trying to tell us?"

"That station is not the source of the dupes at all," Q said. "It was designed to look like it is, but it's not."

"Seriously?" said Devin, tsk-ing in annoyance. "Still, it's not the end of the world. We'll just attack the real thing now."

"Too late. L4 wasn't just a decoy. It was also a trap, and you've triggered it."

"What kind of trap?" asked Clair. "What does it do?"

"It solves the problem," said Nobody, and Clair turned to look at him.

Don't trust him.

Nobody's dangerous.

"What have you done?" she asked him, coming to her

feet and leaving her heart behind. "Jesse was right on top of that thing."

"It was his decision to be there," Nobody said, "and your decision to send him there. Don't blame me."

Behind her, Devin helped Q stand.

"V468 contained a charge of unstable matter," Q said, "rigged to catastrophically decay if anything attacked it."

"What does that mean?" asked Forest. *"Exactly."*

"Unstable matter releases a quantum cascade when it disintegrates, a wave spreading outward that affects other pockets of unstable matter. Decay triggers decay, forming a chain reaction. If there's enough unstable matter, the reaction becomes explosive."

"Just how much of this stuff is up there?" asked Clair.

"Well, all of it is unstable," Q said in a trembling voice. "Anything that's been through a d-mat booth comes out that way."

Jesse had called anything that came out of a fabber "fake stuff." Like Charlie and every other impermanent thing. Like her. Like him.

Jesse, Clair thought, the true situation only slowly becoming real to her.

"We've lost contact with all the satellites inside those bubbles," Devin said.

"Ashes to ashes," said Nobody. "Dust to dust."

Clair's thoughts vanished into a white noise of grief and fury. Without thinking, she ran to Nobody's cage and lunged at him.

His stolen body leaned just out of reach of her grasping hand and grinned.

"Give me the keys," she yelled at Forest. "Give me the keys!"

"It's too late," said Nobody. "He's gone."

[68]

JESSE.

The boy who had walked her home to meet his father had started off a complete stranger. Somehow, against all odds, that boy had become the most important person in the world. She felt closer to him than she ever had to Zep. And now . . .

"Jesse can't be dead," she said, pulling back from the cage on legs that barely had the strength to hold her upright. She felt like she might throw up. *"He can't be."*

"It's just the beginning," Nobody gloated. "Soon everyone else will be gone too. The end has come at last, in devastating blue."

Clair shook her head violently, the image of expanding bubbles taking on new significance.

"No," she said. "It's not true."

"He's right," said Q from behind her. Devin and Forest were helping her walk. Devin's face was a waxy gray, blank with shock. "Each quantum cascade spreads until it meets more unstable matter, where it triggers another cascade, which triggers another. The cascades overlap, forming an expanding front."

Clair struggled to get her head around what Q was telling her. She was still unable to accept what Nobody said had happened to Jesse.

"It's the light?"

"No, that's just a side effect. The cascade follows more slowly, triggering the light."

"And you're saying that everything that's been through a d-mat booth is potentially unstable?"

"Yes, when exposed to the cascade. Early d-mat engineers knew about the effect, but they thought it was only a theoretical quirk, nothing to worry about. There has to be a trigger event, one that is highly unlikely to occur naturally."

"They used one too many shortcuts," said Devin bitterly. "The idiots!"

"Wallace's engineers found a way to weaponize the effect," Q went on, "using the decoy satellite as a lure. He thought the only people who could find the source would be those in OneEarth who knew his secret, turning on him, and if he was going down he was taking everyone with him. He thought he was going to live forever, remember? He didn't count on you and me, Clair."

"What happens when the front reaches the Earth?" Clair asked.

Q didn't say anything. She didn't need to. She had said enough already.

Clair backed away from the triumph in Nobody's eyes. He had tricked her. No—he had *let her believe* what she wanted to believe. He hadn't actually said that the satellite was the source of the dupes, just that it plausibly might be, and that attacking it would be a good solution.

The solution to *his* problem, which was dying. Taking everyone else with him was a bonus. Giving them what he desired most of all.

He's gone.

It's not the end of the world.

Wasn't it? Clair could barely think for grief. But if everyone else was about to follow Jesse and Trevin, that was what she needed to think about. She had to force herself to think.

"We need to get people to safety," said Forest. She heard him distantly, as though through a heavy fog. "There might yet be time. . . ."

"Where are you going to send them?" asked Devin. "The safest place on Earth is right here."

"The walls are unlikely to hold," said Agnessa. "Reclaimed gravel. I can't guarantee the original material wasn't fabbed."

"Great. The one time you really need Abstainers they let you down."

I let him *down,* Clair thought. *I should have found another way. If he hadn't gone to L4 . . . if I had only realized that Nobody was letting them reach the wrong conclusion . . .*

"How long do we have?" asked Forest.

"Five minutes. Maybe longer. It depends how that front moves, what it feeds on along the way."

"Ordinary matter will stop it," said Q.

"Well, that's a start. Tell people to start digging."

Clair snapped out of her useless thoughts. Her cheeks were wet. She hadn't even known that she was crying.

"Why didn't you tell us?" she asked Q, her voice so close to a shriek it was painful even to her ears.

"I didn't tell you because I thought I didn't need to," Q said. "Everything was under control. I didn't anticipate . . . *unconsciousness.*"

"We wouldn't have knocked you out if we'd known who you were." Clair resisted the urge to wail wordlessly in frustration. "You didn't give us a hint. You did everything but help us. You took over PK Sargent and you killed people. You bombed Antarctica and you flooded Washington. You took my mother!"

"Only so you could understand how I felt!" Suddenly they were yelling at each other. "I lost a parent, so you needed to lose one too. And even then it's only temporary: I put Allison in the Yard so I can bring her back at any time. But you made me choose. I could have you or I could have my parents: I couldn't have both. You had it so much easier than I did! That was why I made the flood in Washington."

"What does that have to do with anything?"

"I needed to know how *you* would choose. I engineered that to make sure that you would bump into Tilly Kozlova. You had the choice of saving her or leaving her behind. You chose to save her, and I should have trusted you then, I know that now. But I didn't want to take sides until I was sure. Look what happened last time!"

They were standing toe to toe, and somehow eye to eye as well, despite the difference in their heights. Clair was the one shaking now, in pure distress. Jesse was gone, the world was going to burn, and somehow this was her fault too. It all came back to the decision she had made in Wallace's hideout. If she had thought harder and found another solution, things might have turned out utterly different.

Q's plan to test Clair felt very much like *punishing* her, and Clair didn't have the surety in herself to protest that she didn't deserve it.

He's gone.

He didn't deserve it, she wanted to say. But neither did Billie. Neither did anyone hurt in the crash.

"I'm sorry," said Clair.

"No, *I'm* sorry," said Q. "It wasn't supposed to go like this."

Clair had gone from wanting to strangle Q to feeling a powerful urge to hug her in less than a minute. She wondered if this was what it was like having a younger sister.

"You two can argue about who's most to blame later,"

said Devin. "If there *is* a later. We need to do something to save ourselves, and fast."

In Clair's lenses, L4 was a bright star shining over the Western hemisphere with a halo of blue spreading around it. The halo was caused by powersats and other satellites burning in the terrible quantum cascade. Nothing operational was spared, since everything in orbit apart from old space junk had been sent there by d-mat. Already cities were going dark as their powersat beams were cut off, and that was just the beginning. When the cascade touched the surface of the Earth, cities themselves would begin to crumble, and all the people inside them, as well.

"What can we do?" she asked. "Is there any way to stop it?"

"No," said Q. "There is not."

"Well, I'm not going to stand here and wait to see what it feels like," said Devin. "There has to be somewhere to hide. Underground, perhaps?"

"Our cellars will be full of my people," Agnessa said. "I'm not risking their lives on the off chance Q is wrong."

Clair understood, even though fear was starting to cut through the grief and self-blame. If anyone deserved to survive, it was the Abstainers and WHOLE. Forest obviously agreed; he had already opened Nelly's cage and was doing his best to wake her and the two thugs. They would need to get to safety.

But where were Clair and the others going to go? They

could commandeer one of the airships, she supposed, if they were quick enough, but what would be the point of that? They couldn't possibly outrun the coming storm. Perhaps a submarine hiding deep in the straits would be an option, but there had been no sign of one down at the pier. And simply swimming underwater wouldn't work. The straits were freezing—and how could they possibly hold their breath long enough? They would drown long before the front passed over them.

Underground, she thought again, internally echoing Devin's suggestion.

Underground *where*?

"Prison," she said, although that didn't feel like the answer she was reaching for. "An underground penitentiary. That's where we'll go."

"You want to ride out the apocalypse in a tin can full of murderers and rapists?" asked Devin.

"What choice do we have?"

"I'm not sure we even have that one. There's no booth in here, remember?"

"If we're quick," she said, "maybe we'll make it to the freighter we came in on."

"Not without the hovercraft, we won't."

"My god," said Forest. He was standing stock-still in the center of the prison, staring into grim infinity. "It has begun."

Clair didn't want to look, but she had to. The front had

touched the Eastern Seaboard of North America and the effects were being perfectly captured by drones. New York was exploding into a thousand hurricanes of gray dust. Washington wasn't far behind. On the other side of the Atlantic, London was a swirling storm of ashes, and Paris was already half-gone. Each glimpse came and went in a strobing catalogue of disaster as one by one the drones recording them succumbed in turn, leaving nothing but dust.

[69]

HE'S GONE.

The pain in her chest was undiminished, but the terrible gyres sweeping up from the remains of civilization were all she could allow herself to think about. Jesse had died trying to save her. She wasn't going to let that count for nothing.

"There *is* a booth," said Q, in her grown-up voice.

"Where?"

"I don't see how it changes anything," said Devin. His eyes were red and the skin around them looked papery and white. How did it feel to lose an identical twin? "There's still nowhere safe to go."

Clair ignored his fatalism. She wasn't giving up. "Where, Q?"

"Shall I tell them, Agnessa?"

"No need," said Nelly. The big woman was standing in her cell holding the two thugs by the scruffs of their necks. Sandler Jones was groaning and shaking his head. "I'll take you. But let's be quick about it. I can see what's coming as well as you can."

Clair looked to Q for an explanation, but she was already moving for the door, ushering Clair, Devin, and Forest ahead of her. Nelly left the thugs to fend for themselves.

"Don't leave me here," Nobody called after them.

"You'll be all right," said Devin. "I'm sure the walls won't actually fall in."

"Exactly!"

Forest hesitated, then threw him the pistol.

"Good-bye, Cameron Lee."

As they went through the door, a single gunshot sounded behind them.

Nelly hurried to the utility. They climbed in after her, seeing no trace of the defense of the prison that had played out earlier between the escapees and Agnessa's enforcers. Everyone had fled for shelter. There were bigger things to worry about now than who was locked in where.

Wheels spun and the utility sped through New Petersburg. The front was spreading across Russia at a frightening rate, along with the rest of the world. Tokyo was gone. Hong Kong was gone. New Delhi was under threat. Tehran would be next. There was confusion and panic in the streets. No one knew what was going on.

Was it better to know or not to know?

Clair had one last chance to speak to the world, and she had only moments to make it count, before the world *really* ended, this time.

"Hide," she broadcast. "Get underground or underwater if you can. Don't rely on anything or anyone that's been d-matted or fabbed. Stay covered until it's passed over you—and even then, don't move until you're completely sure. Do it quickly. Do it now. There's no time to ask why or to argue about it. Just know that this is happening, and that there will be time to lay blame later."

I hope, she added silently to herself.

The usual babble of replies from the Clairwatch crowd was muted. That sobered her more than the sight of whole cities turning to dust. Half the people on Earth were already dead. The only person she knew who had any chance of surviving was Tash, who as Clair spoke was already running for the jungle's edge. There was no reply from Ronnie. Miami was gone. Clair choked on the thought that they would never have that conversation now.

A wind was rising through the muster's empty lanes.

"How much farther?" she asked.

"Nearly there."

They were in familiar territory. There were the dorms they had occupied so briefly, and there was the common area. It all reminded her of Jesse, awakening the shock of his death anew. Nowhere had Clair seen anything that looked remotely like a booth, but she presumed it was safely hidden. A demonstration unit, she guessed, to teach terrorists how best to sabotage one in the wild. Or contraband seized from one of the muster's many recent arrivals. As long as it was connected to power and the rest of the world, Clair didn't care where it had come from.

Blue dawn flared on the western horizon.

"Shit," said Devin, ducking down. "It's here already!"

"The light's just a side effect, remember?" said Q.

"Yes, but the cascade can't be far behind. Get a move on, will you?"

Nelly ignored him and kept driving just as recklessly as ever.

Clair guessed where they were going twenty seconds before they skidded to a halt in front of Agnessa's L-shaped building.

"This is it?" Devin said.

"Yes." Nelly opened the utility door and bundled herself outside. Ordinary dust whipped in after her, stinging Clair's eyes and making Forest sneeze.

"You're saying there's a booth in *here*?" Devin was dragging his heels, and Clair didn't understand why.

"Yes."

"Why?"

"She's using it to keep herself alive, of course," Q said,

[461]

holding up a hand to keep the wind out of her face. "You know, like you did on the seastead? She won't fix herself completely, but she'll do just enough to keep on living. Who could blame her?"

Devin muttered something about principles that Clair didn't catch.

There was a sizzling noise and a flash of blue light. Devin fell back against the utility, fountaining gray dust from where his right arm used to be. He screamed in pain and shock, and his wide eyes twisted to meet Clair's. She automatically reached for him but something heavy hit her in the right shoulder and suddenly she was facedown in the dirt.

Q was pushing her flat with all of Sargent's weight and muscle. Dust was flying everywhere, blinding her and filling her nose with the stink of electricity. The sizzling noise grew louder and closer. Next to her, Devin's feet exploded into dust. Clair kicked out against the earth, rolling both her and Q under the utility, where the shadow was deepest. The blue light receded, then flared again. Over the sound of it she thought she heard Forest cry out.

"Inspector!" Q called. This time her voice was all Sargent. There was no answer.

He's gone too.

They clutched each other until the wind receded and the dust began to settle. Clair was crying and so was Q. Their tears left muddy tracks down the ash on their faces. Some of that ash had come from their friends. Maybe, she thought, the ash that had once been Jesse would rain down on the destroyed world and mingle with hers. That was cold comfort.

"Come on," said Nelly, holding down a hand. "I think it's clear now, but you'd better be quick. There's no predicting how it moves."

Clair checked her lenses. What Nelly said was true. The front rippled and wriggled across the surface of the Earth, missing small pockets that it occasionally twisted back to snare later.

She took Nelly's hand and let herself be hauled out into the light. The sky was wracked by a flickering, electric-blue aurora. Everywhere she looked she saw scars left in the cascade's wake, from wide slashes across buildings and roofs to craters that had opened up in the Earth—a shocking demonstration of how far fabbed material had penetrated the world, even in areas where it was supposedly forbidden.

Sizzling from nearby. The cascade wasn't done with the muster yet. Clair grabbed Q under one armpit and, feeling like a child between two such enormous women, allowed herself to be dragged into Agnessa's sanctuary.

[70]

IT WAS DIM and quiet inside. Behind a Faraday shield it was easy to pretend that they would be safe, when there was no safe anymore, for either of them. The deadliest girls in the world, she thought with a slightly hysterical edge. Everything they touched, they destroyed.

"Where's the booth?" she asked.

"In the ward," said Q. "Behind a false wall."

"Is it going to work?"

"There are subterranean power networks. They can carry a signal if the Air is too degraded."

"Where *are* you going to go?" asked Nelly.

That was the question, a question that was hard to contemplate in the wake of so much grief and shock. How could she be alive when Jesse, Forest, and Devin were not?

She was too stubborn to give up, though. If their patterns could only travel via cable, that meant space wasn't even an option now. . . .

Underground, she thought again. Was prison really the only possibility? Maybe RADICAL's Antarctica contingency would be safe, along with Hassannah and Akili—but how would she get there? She didn't think Devin's friends were going to let her or the *entity* barge on in.

The ward was empty apart from Agnessa's curled body, silent apart from the hissing and beeping of machines.

"Why isn't she talking to us?" Clair asked. "Is she all right?"

"She's angry at me for giving away her secret," said Nelly. "But it would be wrong to deny you the chance.

You won't tell anyone, will you?"

That the new leader of WHOLE was a secret user of d-mat?

"No," said Clair. She doubted she would have the opportunity anyway. Or that anyone would care, in the face of Wallace's revenge.

Wallace, she thought as Nelly shifted the stack of chairs and unlocked the panel behind it, and Q did whatever she needed to do to get the booth ready. Wallace had done nothing at all since she had killed him. The dupes, with the recent exception of Nobody, had been controlled by LM Kingdon and her allies. But once again his actions had profoundly changed the world, thanks to Nobody and his deadly trap. Was anyone immune to the effects of the cascade? Was anywhere safe on Earth now?

Baikal, she thought.

Tash had found two odd locations in the data. One was the satellite uplink that had led to V468. The other was the lake on the other side of Russia.

The Baikal borehole, Q had said.

The Baikal *Superdeep* Borehole.

Where better to hide than the deepest artificial pit in the world? One that had its own geothermal power supply, to boot?

"The Yard," she said, gripping Q by the arm. "That's where we're going to go."

Q came out of her focused state. "What?"

"You know where it is, don't you? You've known ever since you took over Wallace's space station. You know where the dupes come from, and you know where everyone's patterns have been stored."

"Yes."

Q's matter-of-fact tone was excruciating. How long had Clair been hunting for that information? If only Q had *told* someone . . .

Another thought hit her with near-physical force: Jesse was in there. She had seen him duped earlier that very day. He wasn't dead yet.

But would he let her bring him back?

Clair forced her own tone to remain level, even in the face of near-crippling confusion.

"So what's in there, exactly? Is it just a big data cache or is there more to it?"

"Just data, right at the bottom of the pit," Q said. "The cascade won't touch it."

"If you could get down there," said Nelly, "you'd be safe, but it's on the other side of Russia."

"The only way we'd get in there is as data," Clair said, seeing the flaws in her idea now. It was too crazy. "Anyone could erase us and we'd never know. We might as well go to prison and take our chances."

"Hang on," said Q. "There are processors there as well. Big ones. I could try kick-starting a virtual shell. You know, like the Maze and its shortcuts? This would be the same—constantly in the act of transmission except we'd never arrive anywhere. We'd be nothing but what Devin called a shortcut. Entirely virtual, until we decided to come out."

That was a giddying thought.

"Would it be safe?"

"I don't know," said Q. "I guess it would be no different from being in the Air."

"Is that supposed to reassure me?"

"It's not that bad. I was *born* in the Air, Clair."

"Still, I don't know. . . ."

What was the phrase Devin had used long ago—"data ghosts"?

Q smiled without humor. "'He ne'er is crowned with immortality,'" she said, "'who fears to follow where airy voices lead.'"

Clair couldn't place the source, but she knew who Q was quoting. Keats again, just like when they'd started. And the message was plain.

She would almost certainly die if she didn't do what Q said. The cascade would get her, or angry survivors, or starvation, or disease. By escaping into the Yard she would probably have to forget about ever being an Abstainer, but at least she would *be*. There would be hope.

Her mother was in there, Q had said. And Jesse. Maybe Devin, Trevin, and Forest too—and who knew how many people wiped off the face of the Earth in the last few minutes? If they had used d-mat, anything was possible.

The terrible irony was not lost on her that this place, the last place on Earth that could possibly give her shelter, was the very same place she had been trying to destroy a short time ago.

"All right," she told Q, unashamed of the faint tremor she couldn't disguise. "Do your best and let's see what happens."

"Okay. We will." Q grinned, and Clair wondered if Sargent was grinning with her. It certainly seemed so.

The booth opened. It was big and wide enough to hold Agnessa's bed. Clair saw her image reflected in the back wall mirror and barely recognized herself. She was so thin and fierce-eyed. What had happened to the girl she remembered?

She had *survived*, she guessed. She had gone from Clair 1.0 to Clair 2.0 and so on through the numbers to end up here, about to be scanned into data and fed into a server at the bottom of the deepest pit on Earth, where her worst enemy maintained a secret stash of stolen patterns, including all manner of dangerous dupes. What could possibly go wrong with that plan?

Q's grin fell away. She stepped inside and turned to face back into the room. Clair did the same next to her.

"Thank you for helping us," Clair told Nelly, who remained stoically outside.

Nelly nodded. "Common courtesy."

The door closed.

sssssss—

A familiar sound and a familiar ache in her ears. As the booth worked around her, Clair wished she was about to step out into a familiar world, restored exactly as it had been. But everything familiar was gone now, literally. When the blue dawn had finished its work, everything that had been d-matted or fabbed would be left as dust. What lay ahead no one could guess—except maybe Q. She was the smartest mind on the planet, and growing, but had a long way to go before she stopped making stupid mistakes. She stood silently beside Clair, as immobile as a statue, as expressionless as Forest. Clair wondered if that meant she was worried.

"I'm glad you're back," Clair told her.

Q said, "Me too."

[71]

—pop

The booth doors opened. All Clair saw outside was Nelly and Agnessa. They were in the private ward exactly as they had been before, except that Nelly looked startled.

"Did something go wrong?"

"We didn't go anywhere," Q explained. "It was a null jump, simply to take our current patterns."

Clair leaned against the back of the booth. "What does that mean?"

"Our patterns are going to the Yard exactly as you wanted, Clair." Q looked pleased with herself, but not in a way that offered Clair any reassurance. "They'll be safe there."

"But what about us?"

"You and I are going to stay here and face the consequences of our actions."

Clair's knees felt watery. "I don't know what you mean."

"I think you do." Q held out her hand. "Come with me."

A primitive part of Clair instinctively recoiled. There was nowhere else to go except outside, and Clair didn't want to go there—to do *that* again—not after everything she had done to avoid it. Couldn't she stay right where she was, in case the other Clair didn't survive the Yard? Didn't it make sense to keep a backup of her, just in case?

But that was cowardice speaking, and she had never been ruled by cowardice before. Not in Wallace's station, and she wouldn't be ruled by it now, particularly when she was supposed to be an Abstainer. For Jesse, if nothing else.

Besides, who wanted to be a *backup*?

Clair straightened, took Q's hand, and nodded. Nelly didn't intervene. She probably approved, Clair thought.

This time it wasn't sacrifice. It was justice, and a way of publicly making amends.

They stopped at the double doors. A faint sizzling came from the other side.

"Ready?" asked Q in her most grown-up voice of all.

Clair nodded. Her throat was too full to allow her to speak.

Good-bye, Jesse. Good-bye, Mom. Good-bye . . . me.

Together they stepped out to greet the blue dawn.

[71 redux]————————

—pop

Sargent stumbled and steadied herself against the mirrored doors with both hands.

"Where'd she go?" she said.

"Who? Nelly?"

"No, the girl . . . in my head."

Clair looked at Sargent closely. The green eyes were the same, but someone else was staring back at her. One person only, triggering a sharp spike of panic.

"Q? Where are you? Can you hear me?"

Had Q tricked her and escaped again?

"I'm right here," Q bumped them both, coming through on the crest of a wave of new information that filled their lenses with colors and movement, like a fairground in fast motion. "We made it . . . even if we did get a little split up along the way. The shell I created seems to be interfering with something else in here. Everyone's pattern has defaulted to the original—including mine."

The details didn't matter. They were inside the Yard, alive, and Karin Sargent was free. Something had gone right for a change.

But what was the Yard *like*? Why were the doors to the booth still closed? Was there anything out there at all, or just a terrible, empty void?

The information flooding through her lenses suggested otherwise. There were maps of a world that looked just like the one she knew. There were pictures of places and people plucked from myriad profiles. Bumps poured in—but not like the torrent of panicked communications she had left behind. These were cheerful, excited, *normal*.

It was as though everything that had happened in the previous week had rewound and everyone had gone back the way they were. The way they should but couldn't possibly be.

"Xandra Nantakarn is *so* jazzy," said Tash over an open chat.

"Did you hear she has a private booth big enough for thirty people?" Ronnie replied.

"I'll believe it when I see it," said Zep.

"This is going to be the best crashlander ball ever!"

Clair felt a hitch in her throat. That last had come from Libby. Was this live or another recording? Were the dupes enacting another cruel play for her, with some new twist?

"What's going on?" asked Sargent.

"There have been some unintended complications," said Q. "The patterns stored in the Yard have been activated. I'm still trying to work out what that means."

"Clair's missing," said Libby. "Tash, Ronnie—has anyone seen her?"

Clair opened her mouth to say *I'm here* when another voice came over the chat.

"Keep your hair on. I'm coming as fast as I can."

Sargent turned to look at her, her expression one of utter puzzlement.

"That was you," Sargent said.

"Impossible," said Clair. "She must be a dupe."

"There are no dupes here," said Q. "It appears that even they have defaulted to their originals."

Clair stared in shock at her reflection in the booth's interior doors.

"But that means . . ."

"Yes, Clair," said Q as, with a hiss, the door of the booth slid open. "Both of you are real."

————————[Author's Note]

This book is dedicated to my wife, Amanda, who doesn't like me to be too gushy.

Huge thanks to Kristin Rens and everyone at Balzer + Bray for a thousand and one reasons. To Jill Grinberg, Cheryl Pientka, Katelyn Detweiler, Kirsten Wolf, and Ant Harwood. To Jo Hardacre, Eva Mills, Stella Paskins, Hilary Reynolds, Sophie Splatt, Lara Wallace, and everyone at Egmont UK and Allen & Unwin. To Sarah Shumway. To Garth Nix. To James Bradley, Alison Goodman, Alaya Dawn Johnson, and Scott Westerfeld. To Anne Hoppe. To John Joseph Adams, Jason Fischer, David Levithan, and Steven Gould. To Sputnik and Morgan Martin-Skerm. To Linda Shaw and Jon Reding. To Nick Linke and Robin Potanin. To Kate Eltham and Judy Downs. To Val and Lee for all the names. To Rachel Yeaman for the sandwich. To Patrick Allington, Brian Castro, Jan Harrow, Sue Hosking, Nicholas Jose, and Ros Prosser. To the real Catherine Lupoi and the Cora Barclay Center ("Teaching Deaf Kids to Speak"). To the real Devin and Trevin for being so patient. To everyone on the SF Novelists list for their support and advice. To Sean E. Williams and Deb Biancotti also for being so patient. To the quoted, misquoted, and paraphrased: T. S. Eliot, Nathan Hale, John Keats, Graham Kennedy, Abraham Lincoln, Frank Loesser, Michael Wilson, and the anonymous author of "I Saw a Peacock with a Fiery Tail." Finally, to Caroline Grose for taking me on one of those extraordinary journeys that would be entirely ruined by leaping straight to the destination. Getting there is at least half the fun.